BO**N**~~ED~~

to the

WIND

BONES
to the
WIND

Book I

A FORGING OF AGE

Duology

TATIANA OBEY

Wanderlore Publishing LLC

www.tatianaobey.com

Cover illustration by Asur Misoa

Wanderlore Publishing LLC
325 North St Paul Street, Ste 3100
Dallas, TX 75201

v 1.01

ISBN: 979-8-9856649-1-1 (trade pbk.)
ISBN: 979-8-9856649-0-4 (e-book)
ISBN: 979-8-9856649-2-8 (hardcover)

For Agueda "Agatha" Lopez
sometimes you miss each other the first time around
then one day your paths crisscross again
some friends, like you, are woven

"The native language of the infamous Rasia the Barbarian, whose origins hail from the uncharted wilds of the southern continent, most notably uses two pronouns based on age: one for children, and one for adults. Below follows samples of the language. For the sake of comprehension, all pronouns have been translated to reflect one's comparable Alohverian gender identity."

—Vincent Alcantara, "The Becoming of Pronouns: A Study of Language and Identity," a thesis

First Name is Rasia
Pronounced Ra-ja
You'll remember it

CHAPTER ONE

O

Most kids took their palm sweet time with the bones. They rattled them in cupped hands, rubbed together sweaty hopes and dreams, blew on them four . . . five . . . forever times for luck, before *finally* tossing all that childish fat up to the air.

Rasia snatched up that same assortment of vertebrae from dead folks she didn't care about. She lifted her leg for balance, wound back her arm, and aimed for the horizon.

Rasia pitched her bones to the wind.

The sun devoured her throw. With a satisfactory nod, Rasia brushed the crust of black charcoal off her hands and turned to the crowd's stunned silence.

The Mythkeeper ground her teeth on the two syllables of Rasia's First Name. "*Ra—sia*. You were supposed to toss them up. They're bones, not a spear."

Rasia grinned. "No one said I couldn't, though."

Years of reprimands, lectures, and strained patience weighed the Mythkeeper's heavy sigh. The Mythkeeper reluctantly announced to the crowd, "In all of settled history, no one has outright *thrown* their bones before, but it does not mean it can't be done. The Grankull accepts the odds, but"—The Mythkeeper's scowl pierced every generation to come after—"this is the last time."

The Mythkeeper eyed the attendant scribe expectantly.

"She threw her bones beyond the Tail! How am I supposed to find them?" the scribe, first-named Jilah, complained.

"Fix. Your. Face," the Mythkeeper reprimanded.

Jilah mended her expression with much effort. Over the Mythkeeper's shoulder, Rasia and Jilah's eyes met. With a smug waggle of Rasia's brows, Jilah cracked like overheated pottery. Saving face, Jilah sprinted off in the direction Rasia had thrown her bones and disappeared from view over the Great Elder's Tail.

The crowd murmured in the pause, and exasperation punctuated Rasia's name. Rasia's tah shook her head, always disapprovingly, and left. After several vibrations, more scribes were sent after the first.

Rasia locked hands and stretched toward the Mythkeeper. "So . . . you must have been bored till I came along?"

Another one of those sighs. "You certainly never disappoint."

Triumph chimed beyond the Tail. Jilah returned, careful to hold the bones in the same position as they landed. She then dipped the bones into a charcoal mixture and pressed them to a blank scroll for the impression to be analyzed for later, which would determine this year's Forging teams.

The Mythkeeper spoke the name of the next child, and Rasia moved back into the crowd toward the towering spire of Ysai, her elder sibling. To see over the crowd, many kids watched the bone-throw ceremony from atop the Elder's Tail. Ysai, meanwhile, was using the vertebrae as an armrest.

The Great Elder, a colossal skeleton of a long-deceased dragon, spanned from one end of the Grankull to the other. The size of its head yawned so huge that the crater of its jaw formed a lake. On the opposite end, the tail curved around the arena they used for celebrations and ceremonies.

There were all kinds of wacky reasons why the Grankull existed under the shadow of a dead dragon, but more than likely, someone had stumbled upon its skeleton and decided it was a good enough place to live. Though, if you were to say that to the scribes, they were more likely to stab you with their quills.

"Really, Rasia?" Ysai asked. "You had to throw your bones halfway across the Desert? You couldn't give Jilah a break?"

"She's your kulani, not mine." Rasia climbed atop the vertebra where Ysai rested his elbow. She knocked off his arm, and Ysai had the nerve to act affronted, as if he hadn't been saving the seat for her anyway. "I see tah decided not to stay."

"She asked you not to embarrass her."

"Why does she think everything is always about her?"

"Because you are obviously not taking this seriously."

"I *am* taking this seriously. The bones can place whomever they want on my team. What does it matter? I can hunt a gonda all on my own. And come on, Ysai-ji, did you see the Mythkeeper's face when I threw those bones? It was funny."

Ysai slumped over in surrender. "It *was* kind of funny."

Rasia crowed in victory, then yelped when Ysai shoved her off the bone plate. She landed face first into the sandhills gathered at the base of the Tail. Dust blew up into a cloud, burning her vision and sticking to her skin.

"Now *that's* funny," Ysai said. That jerk watched her flounder a bit before reaching down to help her to her feet.

Rasia coughed and spit sand from her mouth. She shook out her dirty shroud and reached under the caftan to adjust her undergarments. Everything was starting to itch. "Ugh. Now I have to take a bath."

"Good. You haven't had one in days."

"*Lies.*"

Suddenly, the crowd pushed back. They would've knocked Rasia off her feet again if Ysai hadn't been so quick to pull her out the way. She couldn't see anything peeking through shoulders or squinting through legs and quickly climbed atop the vertebrae to find out what was going on.

The crowd had completely shifted, broken, and formed two separate sides, all to avoid touching the kid ambling toward the Mythkeeper to take his turn at the bones.

"Oh, the runt."

"Don't call him that," Ysai said. "You don't like it when people call you 'Rabid Rasia.' He's still the Ohan's child. He deserves respect."

"You *earn* respect."

Since children were required to cover their faces until they came of age, few knew what the runt looked like. The rumors were ridiculous—he obviously didn't have a tail. He didn't have scales or a twisted, deformed limb, either. Rasia would know since she had once snatched his shroud right off his face in the middle of the belly market. She had been sorely disappointed to discover he wasn't the twisted, deformed creature everyone thought he was. He was just . . . sick, pitifully so.

The only monster Rasia had found was the illness eating away at him. It clawed gaunt lines of exhaustion across the kid's face, squeezed air from his lungs, and buckled his shoulders under its weight. But that was four years ago. In morbid fascination, Rasia often wondered if that parasitic disease had the runt almost devoured, if now he were nothing but brittle bones and leather. He should have been culled a long time ago.

The runt dragged his feet through the crowd, eyes aimed at the ground as he walked. Children weren't allowed to be bare faced outside of the home, they weren't allowed jewelry, and they weren't allowed color in their clothes or anything of distinction. And yet, everyone could identify the runt. His caftan was three sizes too big for him. It was dirty, and the color of it was worn and faded to grey. His shroud had been wrapped around his face double its natural length and knotted over one shoulder, as if to deter curious hands from "accidentally" pulling it off. And his eyes, something he could not cover or hide, were gold. His irises were sharp and bright and ever-shifting, like many of the Ohan's bloodline. Gold eyes typically signified magic and power, but on the runt, they were cruel irony and bad luck.

"I bet everyone's wishing he's not placed on their team. Hasn't he already failed a year?" Rasia asked.

Those who failed the Forging must try again next year, costing them shame for every year it took to come of age.

"At least he survived," Ysai said. "Many do not."

As the runt stepped up to the Mythkeeper, a group of kids sitting above Rasia placed bets to see how high the runt could throw his bones. The crowd leaned forward in anticipation when the Mythkeeper placed the lacquered bones into the runt's skeletal hands. Even though the entire Grankull knew that the runt had failed to inherit the Ohan's magic, they all waited with bated breath as if he were about to do some great magic trick. It was ridiculous. What did they expect him to do but to throw his bones like everyone else?

The runt flipped his hand over. The bones landed with a plod. No toss. No throw. Nothing.

It was anti-climactic and sort of awesome, and Rasia wished she had thought of it first. With a flick of the wrist, the runt had thrown everyone's expectations back in their faces. Amid everyone else's disbelieving silence, Rasia broke out in gleeful laughter.

"Kailjnn," the Mythkeeper said gently, "do you want to try again?"

The crowd joined in on Rasia's laughter, transforming the tone into something cruel and mocking. Rasia broke off, uncomfortable, as the kids above her cackled. One said, "He's so dumb, he didn't even know what to do."

Instead of a second attempt, the runt walked away. Like before, the crowd parted. Some still laughed, and others placed bets on whether he would survive the Forging again or if this would be the one that would kill him.

"Well, that was stupid," Rasia said. She slapped her hands on the vertebra and vaulted off the seat. "I'm out. Besides, I should probably take that bath sooner rather than later, no thanks to you."

"You're welcome," Ysai said with a chuckle before his expression morphed into a warning. "Wait, Rasia—watch out!"

Rasia turned in time to see the runt, eyes on his feet, dragging straight toward her. She could have moved out of his way like everyone else, but she stood her ground. He walked straight into her, then he flinched back from the shock of the collision.

"Watch where you're going, runt," Rasia demanded.

"*What's your problem?*"

Nicolai came through the crowd charging at Rasia. Of course. Nico to the rescue. She was the runt's younger jih and the uncontested Ohan-heir to lead the Grankull when she came of age. Most wouldn't pick a fight with her; but Rasia budged for no one.

"*He* bumped into *me.*"

"Rasia . . ." Ysai placed a hand on her shoulder. "Just apologize."

"Apologize?! He's the one not looking where he was going."

"You were standing there on purpose," Nico argued. Unlike her older sibling, Nico's eyes were a conventional brown, but while the runt did not possess magic, she did. Rasia could feel the moisture gathering in the air and sliding across her skin. "You are despicable. First you laugh at him, and now you embarrass him in front of everyone."

"Trust me," Rasia scoffed. "He doesn't need me to embarrass him."

"Says the person who snatched off his shroud!"

"That was four years ago!"

Rasia hadn't noticed the crowd go silent. She hadn't noticed anything was amiss until she swatted at Ysai's hand yanking on her shoulder. Everyone's eyes were on them. Rasia paused, and Nico stiffened at the sight of the Mythkeeper's impatient glare.

"This isn't over," Nico swore to Rasia before leaving to take her turn at the bones.

"Boneless," Rasia cursed, stomping away from the proceedings. Ysai followed, and Rasia whirled on her jih the moment they were away from the crowd. "What was that? Apologize?! I didn't do nothing and you know it."

"What will tah say if she heard you got into a fight again?" Ysai argued.

"I'm going to have a face soon, and it won't matter what she says. I'm not singing Nico's name when she has the whole Grankull to do it for her. Why don't you go back and wait for Ji-*lah.*"

"I'm here for *you*, Rasia. To support *you*."

"You never cared before."

"Raj, you can't be angry at me forever. Let me help you prepare for the Forging. We can take out the windship. It'll be like old times."

"Old times are over. You made that quite clear a year ago."

"That's not fair, Rasia. Life isn't some grand adventure. It isn't songs and legends and glory. Eventually, we grow up. I'm an adult now. I can't live your fantasies anymore."

It strained Rasia's neck to look at him, his height further extending the distance that had grown between them over the years.

They used to be best friends.

"I don't need you. I don't need anyone. I'm going to beat tah's Forging record and reach a time no one will be able to match. They'll sing name-songs of me. They'll recite my story. They'll know my face. I'll show you glory and honor and triumph. Keep your dull existence, jih. I'll live my fantasies. You and tah and this capsized Grankull all think you can control my fate. Only *I* determine how my bones fall."

CHAPTER TWO

I

Nicolai walked the bowels of the Great Elder, where livelihoods pumped through the back-alley veins, rooftops, and side streets of mud-brick buildings. Vegetation flourished and thrived in the shadows. Incense breathed around every corner, and the water pumps gurgled when it rained. Sometimes, on a clear night, Nico could hear the marrow sing.

Most professions were defined by their location in the Grankull. The hunting kulls lived in the Claws because of their easy access to the shipyards. Merchants and artisans lived near the belly market. The sentries lived in the stacked buildings that poked through the ribcage, giving them easy access to scouting positions on the Spine. The farmers lived in the shoulders of the Wings, where ancestors long ago had stretched leather across the wingspan to collect rainwater for carefully tended fields and groves.

Nico trekked uphill, hiking the vertebrae steps to reach the warehouse at the Neck. She entered, noticed, as the white speck in a crowd of color and skin. Because of Ava-ta's death and Kenji-ta's profession in the hunting kulls, Nico was one of a few children granted permission to carry a family seal. She often found herself the lone white in rooms dominated by adults.

The day's heat drenched sweat through all the assorted styles of linen and silk waiting to be serviced in the winding lines. Clothes ranged from patterned to dyed, from stitched to woven, from twisted to clasped. Feathers, leather, and dragonglass hung off earlobes and decorated wrists, ankles, and bare stomachs. A few wore little but the beautiful shades of their own skin. Nico longed to shed the white and join the tones of amber and rust, the copper and bronze, the gold and the dust. She longed for the right to display jewels on her wrists, to wrap rainbows about her shoulders, and join the sea of color.

Nico chose the longest waiting line, but it was no time at all before she arrived at the counter and greeted her elder cousin's bored face. Despite his demeanor, he was sharply dressed, wearing an off-the-shoulder top that left one pec uncovered to display the tattooed art around his nip-piercing. Typically, he worked in windship construction, but he also part-timed in the warehouse calculating rations. He was one of the rare few with two jobs.

Nico reached into the concealed pocket of her caftan for the family seal to affirm her identity. Ajen had already begun running the numbers through the abacus, skipping over the formalities.

"How was the bone throw?" her cousin asked as the abacus clacked between his fingers. In comparison, the other two warehouse attendants counted their numbers out loud, their abacuses clack-clacking in slower rhythms.

Nico's bone toss had been uneventful, but she couldn't say the same for Rasia's mad throw across the arena. "I'm surprised you haven't heard yet. Rasia gave Jilah-shi quite the sprint."

"Ugh, jih complains about her enough already," Nico's cousin, and Jilah's twin, grumbled. He finished his equations, then disappeared into the warehouse to return with a bundle of food and a list of its contents. Nico looked at the small bundle with dismay.

No matter your status, whether you were a hunter or a tanner, as long as you contributed to the Grankull, every person earned food rations depending on the hunt and harvest each season. When the Grankull flourished, everyone flourished. But when it struggled, everyone grew thin. The Ohan's family was no exception. Nico received the same rations as the poorest child in the Hindlegs.

Food had been scarce ever since Aurum began ravaging their hunting grounds, but this past year had been especially tough since Kai had failed last year's Forging. He wasn't an adult, but he was no longer a child, either. Because of this in-between status, Kai had no rations to his name. When you were given a set amount for a certain number of mouths, many families had no choice but to force out those who couldn't contribute. Failing a Forging was as much a death sentence as being swallowed by a gonda, but Nico refused to abandon her jih.

Her cousin added a bag of petrified bone chips onto the counter. Although everyone received the same rations, the bone salary differed. Among the hunting kulls, one's salary depended on the amount of their haul. It paid extremely well during good seasons, but during bad . . .

"Join us for dinner," her cousin suggested. "You should eat well before the Forging."

"I can't. Tah's kull is pulling in today."

Her cousin nodded, understanding.

Nico carefully stored the rations and currency into her inner caftan pocket. She escaped to the cooler night air, where the warehouse lines had grown to snake outside the door and down the steps.

Nico knew the rations weren't enough; she needed more food to supplement dinner, but acquiring some wouldn't be an easy task. Food was strictly controlled by the Grankull, and one's salary was expected to be spent on everyday items and services. Food, unfortunately, wasn't openly available for sale.

Kibari Oshield, Rasia's tah, for whatever reason, always had extra food. Unfortunately, she was shrewd and particular about when and to whom she sold it. There had been rumors that she planned to hoard her supply during the Forging.

A person could also get food from the illegal market, an underground scam selling anything and everything at exorbitant prices out of the shipyard. Nico didn't know where the food came from, but she suspected the source was a mixture of people selling excess rations, stolen rations, and food smuggled in by tent gangs and scavengers.

For Nico, there was only one certain option, but it wasn't necessarily the safest.

She traversed the body of the Great Elder all the way to the Tents, a literal slum of tents bordering the Hindlegs, home to those the Grankull had banished from its protective shadow. Some who'd been banished had retreated to the sands to become scavengers, but a long time ago, one outcast had refused to take their chances in the Desert and pitched their tent right at the feet of the Grankull. The community had grown larger and larger over the generations, much to the Grankull's chagrin.

The sentries at the checkpoint allowed Nico to cross the border unbothered, although she would have to show her family seal and recite the full names of triarchs three generations back to be allowed back in. Through the Great Elder's feet, Nico viewed the massive expanse of tents.

Children weren't supposed to carry weapons, but Nico would be a fool to walk the Tents without one. She retrieved the sword strapped underneath her caftan and displayed it more prominently about her waist. She tightened her shroud.

In the Tents, even the adults wore shrouds. Some hid their faces, so ashamed of their dishonor and fall from grace, while others used the coverings to their advantage for more unsavory purposes. For Nico, her shroud allowed her to blend in with all those the Grankull had defecated out.

Barefoot children kicked up mud as they raced through teetering shelters of patchwork linen and leather. A roar of laughter, then shouting erupted from a gambling circle gathered around a bonfire. A flock of tent whores, distinguished by their feathered veils, entreated customers. The smell of grubworm mash overpowered all else, even that of unwashed bodies and haphazard latrines. The smell hit you in the throat, and it took Nico a long while to learn how not to gag on it.

"She's nothing but a burden."

Nico chose a shortcut through a cluster of lean-tos and found three shadowed figures around the corner. The impending new moon, marking the start of tomorrow's Forging, cloaked them all in darkness. One of the figures shoved another, smaller one forward.

A child.

The child was tall enough to have blossomed, but you could never be certain of age or sex due to the shrouds and formless white caftans. Nico should mind her business, but she tightened her grip around the hilt of her sword.

"There are no refunds," the third figure sneered. Nico frowned at that accent. It didn't belong in the Tents, nor the Grankull. Most likely a scavenger skulking about. Scavengers took their chances eking out a living in the Desert, stealing and raiding kull ships to survive, but sometimes you could find them blending into the cesspool like everyone else.

"My child has no skills. She's terrible at everything. There is no way she is going to survive the Forging. I'd rather get something out of her while I can," the child's parent said with the accent of one who had never left the Grankull but for their Forging.

The scavenger clawed into the quivering child's shroud and flayed the linen right off their face.

Nico unsheathed her sword.

No one should ever have their shroud taken without their consent. She remembered the time Rasia had yanked off jih's shroud in the middle of the market. Everyone had laughed and stared and mistaken the hollow angles of his sickness for those of a monster. She remembered the way he'd trembled and covered his face with his hands—in embarrassment, in shame, in fear. The female child covered her face in much the same way, violated.

Nico stepped forward to interrupt the clandestine meeting. "Scavenger, the Heron won't appreciate you doing business in her territory."

Even the Tents, for all its lawlessness, had rules.

The scavenger snatched a snaking blade from his belt, then paused to laugh at Nico's bright white caftan, an exact match for that of the child adjacent. The color glowed among the sepia tones like two eerie moons.

"You're not one of the Flock. Why don't you stay out of other folks' business?"

The scavenger spun his sword flippantly. Nico timed the spin of his blade, and with a quick maneuver, slapped the back of his hand with the flat end of her sword and knocked the scavenger's weapon to the ground. Nico evaded a hidden dagger and cut across the scavenger's thigh. He tripped over her planted ankle and fell.

Nico pinned him at sword point, and the white dragonsteel dripped red with the scavenger's blood. Giving it back to him. Nico warned, "I will allow you the chance to leave if—... *oomph.*"

Nico stumbled forward, almost stepping atop the scavenger as she was knocked off-balance. She adjusted her stance and froze when she found the child shoving at her back.

"What are you doing? I'm saving you."

"No." The child sobbed under a crop of blond curls. "If I . . . If I do this, my family has enough to eat."

"There are other ways." Nico thought of her family's rations in her cloak. She could offer the meager amount she had, but what would *her* family eat? "You're giving up before you even try. You can survive the Forging."

"And if I don't? At least this way I'm worth something."

"You know," the scavenger said, having slithered back onto his feet, "that sword you have is worth far more than that boneless little child, *Ohan.*" The scavenger slid his tongue over the title with venom.

"I am not Ohan yet," Nico said. Not until she completed the bloodrites. Nico glanced at the terrified child once more. The child's parent watched the exchange anxiously behind their donned shroud.

Nico faced the smug scavenger. "Throw the money over, and I'll give you the sword."

"How do I know you're not counting bones?"

"Because I keep my word," Nico snapped. Even so, she wasn't

fool enough to give her sword over first. The scavenger reached into his pockets for a clatter of bone chips. When he threw them over, they landed spilling out at Nico's feet. The child's parent lunged forward and pecked the chips from the dirt.

As promised, Nico held out her sword. She watched with thinly veiled disgust as the scavenger curled a callous hand around the carved dragon-hilt. The scavenger smiled, his missing teeth an infinite darkness in the night, and melted into the shadows.

"Thank you," the parent said, still on their knees from clawing the money from the ground. "Thank you so much, Ohan."

The child wouldn't look at her.

Nico forced her feet a step forward at a time, all too aware of the weight missing at her hip. She had promised herself that she wouldn't sell the sword unless circumstances became dire, and here she was, giving it away so some kid could live free another day. Her heart pained her, tightening in her chest and thudding louder with every beat.

She felt both relieved and tired when she finally reached her destination, the largest dwelling in all the Tents. The tent flaps were pinned open, which was usually an indicator that guests were welcome, but you'd be foolish to believe you could walk in uninvited. Nico spun the bell of gold windchimes. The chimes danced, and the reflected stars glittered across the shimmering, translucent fabric of the entrance.

The dogs barked.

Zephyr peeked out from behind the curtain leading into the main body of the tent. The bare-faced male smiled at the sight of her, and the hint of his dimples sparked warm embers in her stomach. The reaction was ridiculous. He was still the same kid Nico had known all her life.

Yet something seemed to have changed during Zephyr's year-long expedition with his father. She hadn't had the time to see him since he'd returned, and she regretted stumbling upon him without the proper chance to truly catch up. The slopes of his bare face flamed in the shadowed starlight, and Nico felt as if she were on the edge of some great height, her stomach churning with nerves at a bottom she couldn't see.

"Hey," Zephyr said softly, knowing who she was without introduction despite the shroud.

"Hey," Nico said in turn, dumbly, and then apologetically explained, "I'm here for Zara-shi."

"Right, right." He stumbled over his feet to step aside, and, for a brief moment, his hand brushed her arm. The touch ignited sparks and fogged their surroundings with magic. The sudden humidity made it harder to breathe.

As children-not-yet-adults, they had not earned their place in the Grankull. They hadn't earned their names, the right to their face, the right to color, or the right to touch. When one donned the shroud, all that mattered was counting down the years to their Forging.

But this was the Tents, and no one around them cared. Nico wrapped Zephyr into the hug she should have delivered the moment she'd heard he was back home. Zephyr returned the embrace, and Nico couldn't get her hands all the way around him, considering how broad he had grown.

"I'm sorry. I should have come to see you sooner."

"We're all busy getting ready for the Forging. Go talk to tah. I'll walk you to the border when you're done."

Nico nodded, and they broke apart. The air had become so thick with water, the coils of Zephyr's hair began to frizz. Nico felt embarrassed by her lack of control. Maybe she missed him more than she was willing to admit.

Zephyr led her deeper into his family's tent, where his dogs greeted her, and his family sat eating a veritable feast for dinner. The food was as colorful as the patterns and fabrics that adorned the serving room. Zephyr's father welcomed her with two kisses on her shrouded cheek.

Zara lifted from her seat at the table. She was one of the few in all the Tents who refused to wear a shroud both inside and outside her home. When Zara's parents had discovered her affair with the foreigner, Zara's tah ousted her from the family and carved a hot knife through Zara's face, forever scarring the word "whore" upon her cheek. Out of respect, Nico promised herself to never flinch away from it.

Zara had a reputation for taking care of people in need, and an even greater reputation for killing anyone who dared to cross her, her kulani, or her children. Out here in the Tents, Zara had become a Han in her own right. Her kulani, the one everyone had said would leave her on the first gust of wind, had become one of the most important sources of wealth and food for the Grankull as the merchant of an international trading company. The richest family in the entire Grankull lived in its poorest part.

All the wealth in the world couldn't buy you a face, but Zara made do with her scarred one.

"I hadn't meant to intrude," Nico said, regretting the fact that she had interrupted their dinner. Zara had paused in her meal nevertheless and motioned Nico to follow.

Zara led Nico to her office. Every time Nico stepped inside, she remembered the nervousness and guilt that had plagued her the first time she broke down and came to Zara for help. Nico had irrationally feared her judgment, feared the knowledge that Nico couldn't take care of her family would elicit disappointment. Nico had long ago lost all shame, but she remained vigilant, careful of the consequences if the Grankull ever caught her in possession of illegal food portions.

Nico folded down onto the handwoven carpet, plush and forgiving to the knees. A brass scale leaned crooked on the low-sitting desk. She counted out her bone chips, glanced at the scale, continued counting, and then, with a defeated twitch, reached out and balanced the scales.

"Not today," Zara said as she exited a storage room and handed over a bundled pack of dried fruit and vegetables. "It's on me. You kids have a big day ahead of you. You need all your strength."

Nico's throat swelled. Others would go begging to Rasia's tah, rack up debts at the market, or sell a family heirloom at the shipyard, but Nico had always had the favor of Zara's kindness. It reminded her of everything at stake.

"Thank you. You have always been kind to me. Your family has always felt like an extension of mine, and there is something you ought to know. I have come to you tonight for another reason. Yesterday, the Council of Representatives voted to purge the Tents."

Zara lowered to the floor. She closed her eyes, and her head tilted toward the laughter and unaware voices in the other room. "How long do we have?"

"The vote was a tie. I only learned of it this morning from tajih."

Zara visibly inhaled. It had been years, since Nico's grantah, that the Grankull had ordered a purging of the Tents. The Grankull saw the Tents as a parasite, but for all its admitted roughness, there were good people here. There were children who had never done a thing wrong but be born on the wrong side of the Tail.

"When I pass my Forging, I'll succeed the bloodrites and automatically join the Council. I'll be that tiebreaker vote and make sure the purge never happens. I just thought . . . you ought to know . . ."

Ought to know how close they had come to losing it all.

Zara gave an empty laugh. She poured herself a drink of Alohverian grape wine and offered a cup to Nico. Nico politely declined.

"It won't matter," Zara said. "More seasons of little food, and the votes will be against us eventually. The Tents need to prepare."

"Prepare for what? War?" Nico asked. "There are people in the Grankull that I care about, too. I become Ohan after the Forging. Give me a chance to save everyone."

"You cannot save everyone, ohani. Maybe someone will finally slay that dragon. Maybe there will be more food. But there will never be enough for everyone. The Grankull survives by tossing anyone who refuses to row to its beat overboard to stay afloat. The Tents are not a part of the Grankull. You are, ultimately, not my Ohan."

"You know the histories as well as I do. The Tents had

forewarning when my grantah approved the last purge. Tent Hans began slaughtering each other, making deals with the Grankull for protection that were reneged on in the end. The only people who survived were the ones who fled. To have any sort of chance, you would have to establish a truce between all the Tent Hans. Is that even possible?"

Zara sneered at the thought. "Maybe. It's possible. If we had enough time. If you bought us enough time."

"I gave you this information so you're prepared if anything happens. But the Tents have never won a fight against the Grankull. Why not flee? Why does it have to be a fight?"

Zara's gaze went sharp to almost a deadly point. It was no wonder Zara had earned the title of "Scorpion" within the Tents. "My kulani's land is his own, but this territory is mine. How dare the Grankull determine that our lives are worthless, that our children's lives are worthless? The people here have no one on their kull but me. I can't abandon them. I can't forsake them."

Nico thought about that curly-haired child she'd met moments ago in the shrouded darkness. She understood the impulse to fight for people who couldn't defend themselves.

"I won't forsake you, either," Nico promised, determined.

Zara huffed and smiled to herself. "It's at times like these you remind me of Avalai Ohan. Back then, during our Forging together, Avalai's biggest concern was her tah's disappointment. We grew up in a time when the kull was prosperous. She never knew struggle or hardship until the day your jih was born. On that day, she was the strongest I had ever seen her."

That's not how the Grankull told the story. They said Ava-ta's refusal to cull her sickly newborn had been her weakest moment, whispered that she hadn't been strong enough to do what needed to be done. In turn, they questioned her leadership and her ability to lead the Grankull. Death-touched children, like Kai, often brought misfortune. It was both a mercy and a responsibility of the Grankull to give them back to Death. Zephyr, the result of Zara's unapproved pregnancy, was also considered Death-touched, a child not meant to be alive.

"I have no doubt that same strength is in you," Zara said.

Nico feared disappointing her; she had never felt very strong. She didn't feel strong every time Rae, her younger jih, complained of hunger. She felt helpless watching the entire Grankull laugh at Kai like the butt end of a joke. She was tired of children sacrificing themselves for their family. She was tired of watching people starve.

"All I want to do is save everyone."

"Everyone can't be saved."

"Then we build a bigger boat!" Nico snapped, frustrated. "We dig better irrigation systems. We re-allot the land. We make smarter choices. We put in the work. But we sacrifice no one. We abandon no one. I fight for every life no matter where they are born or who they are. That, Zara-shi, is the Ohan I want to be."

"*No*," Nico immediately corrected herself, "that is the Ohan I *will* be."

CHAPTER THREE

O

At its heart, the Forging is a hunt, and Rasia had spent her entire life preparing for it. Her last birthday felt like a forever ago. All are born at fifteen years till, and every year counted down to the Forging.

She ran her hand along the smooth carapace that formed the hull of her windship. She remembered the time when she, Shamai-ta, and Ysai-ji had stripped the behemoth scorpion of its exoskeleton. They had beaten and shaped the carapace for days into the perfect shape for the hull. They had braided rope, measured the dimensions, and chopped the best date palm for the mast. The sail had been stitched from the wings of a dragon her tah had once slain.

Rasia looked back at the Grankull, with its neighborhoods choked by ribs bent around the city. From inside the gut, cramped homes obstructed the view like bars blocking sunlight. Even the fields that generations had toiled fertile were denied to the general populace. A child couldn't brush their hands along the fuzzy tails of grown millet or play hide-and-seek in the flax stalks without getting fined half a year of rations (Kiba-ta was not amused). Rasia barely breathed between the restricted zones, the narrow alleys, and brick walls she couldn't sail over or knock down. For all the Great Elder's immensity, there was no space to run.

Rasia tore off her shroud. She stripped off the stupid ankle-biting, neck-itching white linen caftan. She hopped into a pair of pants, buckled her sword-belt round her waist, but fuck a shirt. Her undergarment bandeau was tight enough. She loosened the ropes and unfurled the sail. The dragon-wing stretched taut, the wheels creaked, and the windship rolled onward.

Sparse shrubbery and hard dirt gave way to shifting sand dunes that tossed and turned with grubworms crawling underneath. The sky swelled open. The speed-draft combed through Rasia's hair and encouraged her faster toward the horizon. One day, Rasia promised herself, she'd catch that too.

But for now, she'd been tracking a kull of gran-scorpions. She followed the dawnward wind toward the ocean, then turned headward, navigating by the stars. She found her quarry in a wadi valley. From the scout's nest of her windship, Rasia watched scorpions ferret out the grubworms that lived underground.

The behemoth scorpions, much larger than their smaller counterparts, always traveled in groups. They were nocturnal animals, and their black red-gleaming shells camouflaged easily in the moonless night. The lucky few that lived to their prime could grow to a size rivalling the largest sand dunes. The kulls liked to hunt the gran-scorpions for their hard carapaces, which were used to make everything from ship hulls to armor to soup bowls. Rasia had killed her fair share of them, but tonight, she hunted what hunted them.

"Here's the plan. We need enough alive to act as bait tomorrow . . ." Rasia trailed off, turning to the ghostly whispers of wind beside her. She remembered abruptly she had declined Ysai's help. Whatever. She didn't need him.

She didn't need anyone to debate strategies with. She didn't need the stories they told each other to pass the time during long stakeouts. She didn't need his stupid teasing or campfire laughter, nor did she need that one smile shared after escaping danger by the knot of their shroud. She didn't need him at all.

Why did he have to go and become an adult?

Rasia promised herself that no matter what, no matter how

21

much her coming-of-age attempted to forge her into someone she's not, she would come out the other side nothing but herself.

A vibration jolted her limbs. It always began with five vibrations, each stronger and more ground-shattering than the last. Rasia grinned.

Finally.

Tentacles burst from the ground.

The colossal limbs lacked the suckers that decorated storied sea krakens, and were instead patterned with smooth gradient scales. They struck like eight springing cobras. Each limb snatched up its prey and coiled around the scorpions with such power that the carapaces splintered and cracked apart.

These octopedal titans of the Desert were gonda, the very creature a team of five youths had to hunt and kill for their Forging.

Eight tentacles turned into sixteen.

Fuck, there were two.

If the gonda ate all the scorpions now, they wouldn't be where Rasia needed them for the Forging tomorrow. She slid down the mast and pulled up the weighted anchor. The wind propelled the ship toward the valley. To avoid an incoming rock spire, Rasia leaned her weight onto the outrigger, so low her hair swept sand.

Rasia wrapped a foot around the length of rope holding the steer in place as she nocked an arrow and drew back her bow. She guided the ship with her foot, hung almost sideways as she aimed. The muscles of her arms burned. Wind whipped through her hair and lashed her face with a sweet sting. How could Ysai ever forsake this feeling for boring bones and dead jobs? This adrenaline rush, pounding thud-thud in her ears, was the best song in the world.

The arrow hit true, right at one tentacle's center.

Eight tentacles retreated underground. Rasia yanked at more ropes to turn sail, catching the wind. Rasia rode the speed up and out of the valley.

One gonda gave chase.

Rasia popped open the compartment containing her store of

weapons. She lifted a long spear over her shoulder and balanced atop the forward-moving deck.

She pitched the spear straight at the lurching tentacle. It grazed the flailing limb. The limb drew back, but a second tentacle swept incoming.

Rasia yanked at the rope she had tied to her ankle. The windship lurched to the side and narrowly missed the tentacle sweeping overhead. The nearby rock spire exploded, leveled. The ship slanted off-balance.

Rasia grabbed her two faithful khopesh blades, dragonsteel white, and cut through the ankle-rope. She charged across the deck, leaped off the railing, and flew into the air. The curved blades caught the tenacle flesh. She dangled while the windship crashed beneath her.

The eyeless gonda lifted itself, full-bodied, out of the sand in anger. Rasia wrapped her legs around the flailing limb, and the tentacle she clung to curled, lowering.

The gonda opened its rending-sharp beak, the chitin the dirt-yellow color of petrified bone. This was the moment most pissed their pants, but time it just right, and . . .

Rasia hurled her dagger at the siphon, the venom gland that produced the poisonous gas often used to cover the gonda's retreat. The siphon burst, splattering liquid venom. The green toxin leaked around the wound, audibly hissing, to corrode the sensitive under-flesh. It burned a hungry void down to the gonda's three hearts.

A roar, like rolling thunderclaps, boomed in the sky.

Shit.

Rasia abandoned her dagger, rushed down the tentacle, and landed at a sprint. She was almost at her overturned windship when a massive dragon crashed through the clouds and swooped toward the gonda with such a speed that Rasia was physically launched off her feet from the current. Upside down, she watched as the gold dragon clawed talons into the dying gonda. Rasia covered her head as sand rained down, pouring a waterfall as the dragon lifted the gonda into the air and flew off with Rasia's kill.

Rude.

That dragon has been a pain in everyone's hull. They stole hard-won hunts off windships, ruined grubworm traps, interrupted supply lines, and snacked on prized camels. The kulls had named them "Aurum."

Aurum might not rival the massive size of their ancestors like the Great Elder, but Aurum was still a dragon and as large as the greatest warships of the Grankull's armada. Only the most experienced and skilled kulls dared to hunt to Aurum. Even Shamai-ta, for all his feats, had only killed two dragons in his lifetime.

One day when Rasia becomes Han of her own hunting kull, she would take that dragon down.

Rasia heaved her windship upright and looked across the valley. The second gonda had left four scorpions still alive, which meant it would be back tomorrow for the first day of her Forging. It was enough.

Rasia glided her hand along the hull of her battered and bruised windship and patted it with fondness.

"Tah, I'll make you proud of me."

CHAPTER FOUR

I

Nico's home was the largest and oldest residential dwelling in the Grankull, located in the Elder's Heart, tucked behind the gardens of the temple. From vibrations away, Nico could spot the wind-catcher tower crowning the roof. Old paint licked at the faded cracks and chipped mosaics webbed through the outside adobe walls.

Nico nodded to the sentry guard and entered through the front archway of the veranda. The glass windchimes twinkled above pottery of succulents and sage. Vines wove through the pergola. The night air swayed, deepening the smell of lavender growing on the outside shelves. The deck had recently been swept of dust and dirt, and Nico straightened the tower of woven sitting mats as she passed.

The veranda was the area of a dwelling where a household welcomed and entertained visitors. Typically, children donned their shrouds before stepping outside. The space acted as a transition between the inside and the outside worlds.

Nico opened the front door and slipped her sandals into the cubby holes of the small shroud room. One of the alley cats, who constantly wandered in and out the house, blinked bright eyes at her from one of the cubbies. She unraveled her shroud and hung it on the wall hooks, then stepped up through the paneled archway into the serving room.

The sound of racing footsteps, and then the sight of Kai running out the hallway after their younger jih greeted her. They didn't have the money to pay for a caretaker, but since Kai couldn't get a job, he'd elected to take care of their youngest sibling instead.

When Rae ran by, Nico scooped up the naked rascal and knocked the budchild chidingly on the forehead. Kai collapsed against the serving table and clutched Rae's thin night robe as he sucked in air.

"What took you so long?" Kai wheezed.

"I visited Zara-shi, then got caught up talking to Zephyr on the way back," Nico answered.

Kai pulled at Rae's foot, then dragged Rae into his lap and shoved on their clothes. Nico brought the rations into the kitchen—goat's milk, raisins, lentils, onions, salt, emmer grain, a brick of farmed canine meat, the green-yellow fruit and vegetables Zara had given her, and a glossy heron egg.

Nico prepared the brick stove. Kai joined her while Rae occupied their time with clay toys. Together, Nico and Kai boiled the water, cut the vegetables, and kneaded dough for the flatbread.

When it was the three of them like this, Nico felt as if they could do anything. They'd survived two years without Ava-ta. Certainly, they would survive whatever the Forging threw their way.

The front door burst open, sucking out the heated kitchen air. "TAH!"

Nico leaned her head into the serving room as Rae tossed their toy windship in a flail of limbs. The eleven year-till budchild scrambled to their feet and rushed the figure coming through the door.

"Grubworm!" Tah exclaimed. He caught Rae in the air and spun them into a hug.

The sudden stiffness of Kai's shoulders tempered Nico's excitement at seeing Kenji-ta for the first time in a season. She felt both nervous and joyful, anxious and relieved. These conflicting

how Kenji-ta spoiled and coddled her, of how Nico needed to learn how to face her fears. But Kenji-ta would snuggle her close and teach her that anything could be overcome with a song.

Tah didn't sing anymore.

It was that thought that broke her, that had her shoulders folding inward and sobs bursting from her chest. Nico slapped at her tears in frustration as she grieved for a parent that wasn't even dead. She shouldn't be crying over a person who threw jih into walls and ignored him for most of his existence. He was a horrible, horrible person, and Nico missed him so much.

"I'm sorry," Nico cried. "I'm so sorry."

She fought to pull herself together. She wasn't the one who had been physically hurt. She unwrapped the shroud from Kai's head and winced at the blood.

Nico focused her magic. She could shift any liquid, but water was always easiest. Blood was the hardest. She flicked the blood into Kai's makeshift kitchen shroud and wiped the wound clean.

"He's not wrong," Kai said in a whisper she almost didn't catch.

"What?"

"I am a burden. He is right to hate me. I am the reason our food is stretched thin. I am the reason you go to the Tents. I am the reason *she's* dead."

"Enough, Kai."

Nico slumped down and leaned her shoulder against his back. She couldn't look at him with how angry his words made her. "It's going to be fine. I am going to find you tomorrow, we are going to hunt a gonda, and we are going to survive the Forging together."

Kai shrugged, and Nico hated his indifference. He didn't use to be like this. Yes, he was a cynic and a pessimist at the best of times, but last year, he had been hopeful. This year, he hadn't even bothered to throw his bones.

"Kai, we are going to survive, then I'll apply for triarch. If I'm head of the house, he can't throw you out."

"You know the Council doesn't like either of us. If he disputes your application, he'll win."

"I'll fight it," Nico promised. "I swear, when I become the Ohan, no one will ever hurt you again."

Kai tapped his fingers against Rae's back. She knew that tic; he was trying to figure out how to say something she wouldn't want to hear. Then, after all that thought, he said one word: "No."

"No what, Kai?"

"I don't want you wasting your Forging on me. You're important. The Grankull needs you. The Tents need you. You need to pass the Forging, and I'll only weigh you down. Let me go."

Kai sounded so much like that child back in the Tents who had given up. Nico turned to his front where Rae had fallen asleep curled in his lap. Kai refused to look at her. She gripped him by the back of his neck and forced him to face her. She glared at the gold of his eyes that had raged with storms all his years.

Sometimes Nico envied jih in that way, the way he carried their parents in his face. He had Ava-ta's eyes, and no matter the fact Kenji-ta had disowned Kai when he was a babe, neither could escape the physical similarities of their cheekbones or the stubborn set of their jaw. The tragedy was that Nico didn't think tah had ever seen Kai's face except for the day he was born.

"Kai, we either survive the Forging together or not at all. I am not giving up on you, so don't you dare give up on me. Promise."

"Nico, I don't—"

"*Promise me, Kai.*"

His jaw clenched shut. His shoulders drooped. He mumbled. Defeated. "I promise."

THE FORGING

Rasia's Map

CHAPTER FIVE

O

"From this day forward, you are your choices and decisions. You earn your name, you earn your face, and you would do well to heed my warning: Cowards don't survive the Forging. Sometimes, not even the brave. The weak perish and only those who endure remain," the Mythkeeper, crowned by the sunrise, recited the words at the center of the Great Elder's tail. "The Forging ends at sunset of the second Hunter's moon. Now, like a snake shedding old skin, abandon your shrouds and begin anew."

Rasia didn't hesitate to rip the shroud off her face. Everyone else took their palm sweet time, pulling at their shrouds all shy and self-conscious, stealing glances at one another, as if anyone cared about their appearance. What did it matter what Rasia looked like? They would know her for her feats.

Thankfully, the Mythkeeper didn't allow much time for everyone to stand around gawking at each other. She immediately called names and assigned teams. At least twenty windships were located around the Grankull, facing outward like sunrays toward the Desert. Rasia could save time if she were assigned a ship dusk of the head.

Rasia bounced on her toes and waited for her name. She waited. And waited. Until almost everyone had been called before her. The sun was almost over the horizon! Once first drum rolled, the

Forging would begin.

Rasia was done waiting. Rasia stomped over and cut in front of the child currently receiving his assignment.

"This isn't fair," Rasia complained. "You're saving me for last."

The Mythkeeper had the audacity to give her an amused smile. "You want to know a secret? Your assignment number is determined by the distance your bones are thrown."

Rasia blinked at the implications of her reckless throw. The runt had been given first assignment because he hadn't thrown at all. "Are you kidding me? *Come on.*"

"Wait your turn, Rasia. It will come soon enough." The Mythkeeper addressed the next child and gave out their assigned windship number. Rasia circled the Mythkeeper, round and round, waiting for her chance to swoop in.

When the second-to-last child stepped forward, Rasia clawed her face in frustration. The team numbers were uneven, which meant she still didn't know her windship assignment even after the second-to-last ran off in the direction of their ship.

Not bothering to wait for her name to be called, Rasia pounced before the Mythkeeper. With a knowing smile, the Mythkeeper looked toward the sky. "Looks like you don't have much time."

"Are you doing this 'cause of all the grief I've given you over the years?"

"While I am rather amused that fate has you standing here with me at the end, I did not plan this. But I am relieved it is you. Any of the others would not have made it on time, but you . . . windship number 7, headward, *need to run.*"

"Shit."

"Language!"

Rasia sprinted off to make the lap around the Grankull. Despite their contentious relationship, the Mythkeeper had always displayed faith in Rasia's abilities. Let her go last, it didn't matter. Rasia would still finish first.

The Elder roared with the sound of first drum, which vibrated through Rasia's legs. Rasia raced the sun and counted windships as she passed. Those on board cheered her on. When the seventh finally came into view, she pushed herself harder and faster and accelerated through the burn of her thighs.

Rasia slapped her hands against the hull of the seventh ship and crowed in victory. The sun broke free of the horizon. A new day. The beat of first drum faded. She looked up at the unfamiliar faces of her teammates who were leaning over the railing.

Just in case they didn't recognize her awesomeness, she proclaimed, "I'm Rasia, in case you didn't know."

"*It would be you.*"

Rasia didn't recognize the face, but she knew that haughty voice from anywhere. With a groan, she dropped her forehead against the hull.

Nico.

Fate could go fuck itself.

It was high noon, and Rasia was still stuck at the starting line.

"That doesn't make any sense," Rasia argued for the granth time. "I know where a gonda is going to be *to-night*. We slay it, and we're back in the Grankull by morning. Easy."

"Killing a gonda isn't easy," Nico said in that tone of voice that grated Rasia's nerves. Rasia isn't some child batting wooden swords at the wind. "I have an actual plan. We should team-up with one of the other teams. Most are headed toward the oasis. With more numbers, we all have a better chance of survival."

"But the rules are a maximum of five people per kill, which means we will have to kill *two* gonda. That will take twice as long!"

"Why are you in such a rush? We have the entire Forging. It is better to be cautious and safe than reckless and stupid."

"Your plan is stupid."

"Your plan is going to get someone killed!"

Rasia rolled her eyes so hard the world turned around. She had worked too hard for Nico to mess this up for her. Rasia glared at her other teammates and hoped she could convince them over to her side.

The blond round-faced reed with a ponytail didn't look like much, but Rasia had learned to judge a person by their hands. Those calluses suggested she knew how to use that longbow strung across her shoulder.

The only male on the team carried a large dragonsteel fan-axe strapped to his back, the sort perfect for cutting gonda. Rasia recognized the work of the Grankull's most esteemed family of blacksmiths. Only a member of the family was allowed to carry their seal on the hilt.

The last team member carried a collection of knives in every pocket of her clothes. Judging by her bandage-wrapped hands, she either had a lot of practice or she sucked at it. No one smart brought knives to a gonda hunt. At least the kid had enough sense to also bring a spear.

The team didn't seem all that bad. Everything would be perfect if they could just get going.

"Suri," Nico addressed the blond, followed by the other two brunets: "Azan and Neema, what do you think? My plan is sound and reasonable. I will make sure we are safe and that we survive this."

Fuck. Soon, Nico would have them singing her name-songs. Rasia had to think of something. She might not know everyone's First Names but Rasia knew what anyone with a spine wanted most of all: a name worth remembering.

"No one has ever achieved anything worthwhile being safe," Rasia countered. "Think about it. What if you could take down a gonda within a day? Can you imagine the weight of that feat? Sure, you can play it safe, but I'm offering you more. I'm offering you glory. I'm offering you a name a rare few possess."

"Rabid Rasia has a point," the knife-kid said, unsure. Ugh. Rasia had already forgotten their names. "Safe is easy. What if we can do it? We have an opportunity here to change our lives."

"Wait," Nico interrupted, no doubt sensing the shifting sand dunes. "Are we really going to listen to Rasia?"

"Of course, *you* don't understand," Rasia sneered. "People listen to you, and they respect your opinion. You were born with a name, *Ohan*."

"A name that must still be earned. I'm not Ohan yet."

"Fine. Ohani. Same difference."

"I starve, Rasia, the same as you."

"Except when you starve, people care. They pity you, treat you with kindness, and coddle you because they hope to earn your favor."

"*You know nothing!*" Nico shouted, and, for the first time in their argument, encroached on Rasia's space. Rasia met her challenge grain for grain. "And you're such a hypocrite, Rasia. Your family has always had enough food to eat. Your tah is Han of the sentries. She has money and a good job. Have *you* ever known hunger?"

Rasia narrowed her eyes knowing she had argued herself into a corner, but she stubbornly dug in her heels. "I hunt my own food," she said, slow and unflinching.

"You don't give it to the Grankull?" Fan-axe asked. "Isn't that illegal? People are starving."

The way Nico looked at Rasia, as if Rasia was some goat turd stuck to the bottom of her sandal, which wasn't anything new, but now they *all* were looking at her that way.

"Nico's right. You're no better than a scavenger," Fan-axe said.

"Shut up. You've never even met a scavenger. I track, I hunt, and I kill with my own two hands. No one is stopping you from doing the same."

"Some of us don't have the luxury of owning our own windship," Knives said.

"Tah and I hunted down the materials for that windship ourselves. You want one, make one."

"Not all our tahs are hunters."

"Not all our tahs are dead. Fuck you."

Rasia stomped away before she did something . . . she wouldn't regret it, per se, but it sure wouldn't help her get any closer to convincing these idiots to go along with her plan. With a sigh, she glided her hand along the glittering red hull of the Grankull-issued windship. Rasia considered stealing the thing and striking out on her own. They were close enough to the Grankull that Rasia didn't worry about these idiots dying but taking their only form of transportation would certainly sentence them to failure, and Rasia didn't know if she wanted to be the reason the Ohan failed her Forging. Despite what tah often claimed, Rasia *did* consider the consequences . . . sometimes.

Rasia studied the artistry of the ship while the others continued to argue. Sounded like they were putting it to a vote. Rasia didn't have to guess whose side they'd choose. She wished she had stashed her windship somewhere closer, but to be fair, Rasia hadn't anticipated getting stuck at the rutting starting line. Maybe if she set out now, she might be able to make it.

"You win, Rasia."

Rasia turned, startled. "What?"

"Your plan won the vote," Nico bit out.

Rasia crossed her arms, unable to stop the grin stretching across her face as she turned to the others. "I thought I was a no-good scavenger?"

"But you know what you're doing," Knives retorted.

"I'm just ready to go," Fan-axe said, following Knives up the steps of the windship. Longbow, who had watched the entire argument in silence, wasn't far behind.

Rasia looked at Nico toothily, still grinning. Nico's nostrils flared, and Rasia swore Nico was fighting back tears. In all the years their tahs had tried unsuccessfully to push them together as friends, Rasia had never seen Nico so upset over something so nonsensical. Rasia didn't get why it was such a big deal anyway. Her plan sucked.

"I hate you," Nico spat.

"I know."

It felt good to win.

Rasia threw her a wink, kicked up the hull, and flipped onto the deck. She skipped over to the steer and admired its smooth polish.

"Wait, Rasia," Nico said, climbing up the stairs. "We need to take an inventory of our supplies first."

Rasia spun her head to look back over her shoulder. "We've been stuck here for long enough. Someone, release the ropes so we can get moving."

"You mean the lines?" Knives asked.

"They're fucking ropes!" Rasia threw her hands up in exasperation. "Yes, release them from the black hook thingy."

"The wench?" Nico asked slowly, and all of a sudden, everyone was looking at Rasia with second thoughts. "How about *I* helm the tiller?"

"Helm the tiller," Rasia mocked in a high-pitched voice. "My ass I'm letting you steer."

Rasia spat on her palm, then rubbed her hand over the steer while all her teammates watched on in disgust and dismay. "You might know all the fancy words, but have you actually steered a windship before? No? That's what I thought. Now, someone go release the fucking ropes."

"We are so going to die," Fan-axe muttered. He reached for the ropes and frowned when he couldn't get the knot to loosen from the hook. Reed-bow moved over to help him, then Nico came over, then Knives, while Rasia waited impatiently for one of them to figure it out.

"It goes like this. We learned this in class, remember?"

"We pull it inside out," Longbow, the rightest one out of the whole bunch, spoke too softly to be heard over the other discordant voices. Rasia couldn't believe it took this many people.

Finally, the rope snapped loose. The sail unfurled. Rasia lifted the anchor.

The poor fools went sliding across the deck, tumbling over each other.

Knives lost a few knives, one flying backward and embedding itself right below Rasia's elbow into the deck. Fan-axe hadn't braced at all and tripped, stomach-punched by the railing before barely catching himself from falling overboard. Longbow looked ill. Nico screamed something at Rasia, but too bad Nico's words

41

were lost to the wind.
Rasia laughed and sailed on.

CHAPTER SIX

—

Kai's team sailed off without him.

He felt a little windblown by how fast they tossed him overboard and hustled to get away. Clouds of dust billowed in their wake and showered him with disappointment. He'd failed his jih, again, and he had done nothing but exist.

Last year, Kai found one of the oases to hunker down in until the Forging was over. He didn't know if he could find one again. Kai looked around: at the bone dragon hunched over the city behind him and the dunes of gold and copper cliffs ahead. He walked the only choice he had.

With every step forward, Kai wondered why he had even bothered. He didn't want Nico risking her life to look for him. Nico often asked what happened to him last year, assuming Kai had endured some traumatic experience that left him even more wretched and hollow than before. But it had been nothing so dramatic. Instead, he had *hoped.*

Kai wouldn't make that mistake again.

A hawk screeched while flying overhead. Kai watched the bird of prey soar, weightless, above it all. Then, he looked down and discovered a green speck breaking the overwhelming colors of gold, brown, and more brown of the Desert. Last year, Kai thought he had found the oasis through a lucky boon of circumstance. Once again, after only a few drums of walking, an oasis welcomed him to its shade.

Sprawling ferns and lush palms clung to the edges of resilient blue. Wild millet stalks and cottonwoods bowed to the wind, and the purple tamarisks bloomed despite their dry and cracked limbs. Ripening dates clustered high in the palm leaves and carried a note of sweetness in the air. Kai weaved through a flock of ibises and herons to reach the water. Far on the other side, a group of wild camels lounged in the shade under a hill of broken foliage.

His assigned windship last year had pointed in the opposite direction. This oasis was larger than the last one, and less isolated. From what he understood, this was the only oasis headward of the Elder.

Kai scooped water into his hands and dampened the shroud fastened around his face. Nico had washed his shroud last night, but all her efforts of scrubbing for the white had been irredeemably ruined by the dirt and dust after Kai's team had thrown him overboard. His stupid eyes, gold and clear like palm oil, shone bright and undeniable in the pond's reflection. He had an itching compulsion to disturb the water.

The birds squawked, fluttering off into the sky. The tall grass bent behind him. Kai hoped it wasn't a pack of hyenas like last year. The grass parted, and several kids splashed into the shallow bank with brazen noise that sent every animal scurrying.

Worse than hyenas.

There were five of them, no doubt a team with a windship nearby. Two of them served as pack camels, carrying multiples of everything—five canteens, several swords and spears, and large satchels strapped across their backs. Kai had been warned that some teams ambushed and stole supplies from others but had never experienced it himself.

"Look who it is." A kid stepped forward and scrutinized Kai with eyes hunting for opportunity. He carried himself tall, sharp, and alert like a jackal. A talon dagger, by the size and curve of the sheath, sat comfortably on his hips.

The kid's eyes lingered on Kai's own weapon, a dragonsteel

dagger tah gifted him to protect himself. Fear ached through Kai's bones—a fear that had solidified after tah's death. He knew how this was going to go, and he didn't stand a chance. Kai pulled his sole weapon from his belted sash and tossed the sheathed dagger at the bully's feet.

"You're not as stupid as they say, runt." The kid scooped up the dagger. Kai exhaled a trembling breath to watch the kid leave.

"Wait, Kelin, that's it?" One of the others cried out in alarm.

"He doesn't got anything else."

"I thought you were supposed to be this badass from the Tents. You went easier on him than the others!"

"Because he didn't fucking argue and complain like the others. He gave us the dagger."

"What if he's still hiding something? Look! He's still wearing his shroud. Come on, Loryn. We'll take care of this ourselves."

"You're right, Tarick. This is kull business anyway."

Tarick charged forward and snatched for Kai's shroud, clutching at both fabric and hair, and pulled. Kai fell with the momentum, splashing into the muddy bank as Tarick and Loryn attempted to wrench it off. Gasping, Kai hugged a cluster of reeds and tried to straighten the damp linen, which trailed from his neck to snake through the muddy bank. Tarick yanked at the end, so hard the shroud tightened around Kai's throat and pulled him like a dog through the mud.

The second tug, thankfully, snapped the shroud free. Kai grabbed at anything for purchase, found a floating leafstalk, and used it to pull himself out of the water. Kai collapsed over it, nose and throat burning.

"Looks like all he was hiding was his ugly face!" Tarick laughed. Kai bowed against their laughter as mud sludged down his forehead. The more pathetic and defeated he looked, the more likely they were to leave him alone and move on.

Loryn slammed through the water toward Kai. He braced himself. She kicked the stalk out from under him, and it popped from his grip toward deeper water.

"This is a waste of my time," Kelin said. One of the pack

mules shouted encouragement. The other looked ill but did nothing to help.

"Jih died last year in his Forging, but you survived? *You* survived. Not this year." Loryn pinned Kai down into the shallow water, which flooded his nose. Dirt burned his eyes. She anchored him to the soft sediment bottom and blocked all Kai's attempts to flail for air.

Kai used to fight back when he was younger. Then tah died. After an incident almost left him for dead in the Ribs, he had been too afraid to leave his house. He didn't use to be so scared, but now he'd been infected with this fear that dried out and deadened everything inside of him.

In that moment, he wanted it all to end.

He went slack and gave in.

Just Kai's luck . . . that's what saved him. They jerked him back and twisted his neck crooked, all the while asking, "Is he dead?"

A cough racked Kai's throat. He spat up and expelled water down his chin.

"Guess not." Loryn tightened her fingers in Kai's hair and forced him to face her, but all he saw was the sun, shining so brightly it washed out everything else. "I bet you've been eating good, huh? Watching the rest of us starve while the Grankull pampers you."

Everyone seemed to think Kai was somehow hoarding all the food in the Grankull. Tah might have coddled him to some extent, but she never gave him extra rations. Still, Kai didn't bother correcting the assumption because, in his experience, they would just find another excuse to attack him with.

Tarick cocked back his fist.

"Let him go."

Kai lolled his head to the side and watched as a newcomer stepped through the ferns. Immediately, the newcomer's sword drew the most attention. It was forged of the same white dragonsteel metal as Kai's dagger, and it was huge, like a large cleaver that spanned Kai's entire body. No doubt the sword's intimidating size was partly the reason Loryn finally let go of

Kai. Only one kid had a sword like that.

Zephyr.

Zephyr was one of Nico's best friends. Kai has heard stories of him all Kai's life, and yet, because Zephyr was a Tent kid forbidden from entering the Grankull, they had never met until now.

What an introduction.

"Think you can take us all on at once, mutt?" Tarik asked, inflating his chest.

Zephyr raised a brow and turned his gaze to Kelin. Kelin pushed Tarick back by the shoulder and said, "It's time to go."

"But the mutt is alone. We should take his things too," Loryn said.

Zephyr hadn't spared anyone his attention but Kelin, and he demanded in a low voice, "His dagger too."

Kelin handed Kai's dagger over to Zephyr.

"What are you doing? You're just going to listen to the mutt bastard?"

"To be fair, the bones stuck me with these parasites," Kelin said, ignoring his team members and solely talking to Zephyr. "We got no problem, right?"

"No problem," Zephyr said.

Kelin nodded, rubbed at the heron feather pierced through his ear, then turned and walked away. His teammates gawked. When Zephyr lifted his sword, they broke into a run after their de facto leader. Once their footsteps had faded, Zephyr crouched over Kai and offered his hand.

"I'm Zephyr."

"I know who you are. I didn't ask you to save me."

"You'd be dead if I hadn't gotten here in time."

"Not dying seems to be the only thing I'm good at." Kai ignored Zephyr's offered hand. He crawled on all fours until he had dragged himself away from the damp and sopping ground. He used a palm to hike himself onto his feet then almost toppled over when a large frog hopped between his legs.

Zephyr caught him by the arm and staked the frog all in one

motion. "Clean up. Then we'll talk."

Kai forced himself to take a breath, knowing he was angrier at himself than he was at Zephyr. Kai looked back at the oasis and mumbled, embarrassed: "Can you not look?"

The large kid studied him, and for a moment, Kai had the feeling that Zephyr would deny him the request to clean up in private, as if Kai couldn't be trusted to even do that correctly.

"I won't be too far. Shout if you need me."

Kai's shoulders dropped in relief when Zephyr left to stand guard with the ferns. Finally, the adrenaline began to seep out his bones. It left him empty and cold and numb. He pulled his shroud from the muddy bank, washed it, and hung it to dry across the shrubbery. Cracked, sandy mud peeled from his skin where he stripped off his linen robe and went through the same mechanical motions.

Without his shroud and robe, Kai felt vulnerable, exposed. He'd always been a fascination people tried to peek at. Kai quickly stepped into the water and submerged himself to his chin. The setting sun melted red over the oasis. Overhead, a vulture circled.

Kai looked over his shoulder to make sure Zephyr was nowhere nearby. Then he dipped his head under the water. Unlike the chaotic thrashing and flailing of before, this time the water drowned out all sound and cocooned him in a world of stillness.

He closed his eyes, let go his breath, and circled his arms to keep him underwater—but no matter what he did, his body kept floating back up. His arms burned in exhaustion, and Kai eventually gave up trying. He popped up back to the surface.

Kai didn't understand how he failed so hard at everything, even dying.

"You're here because of Nico."

Zephyr bit into the frog leg he'd finished cooking over the fire.

He attacked and sucked the meat as most people did, chewing and pulling the fat and ligaments until there was nothing left but smooth bone. As he ate, he didn't bother to deny Kai's accusation.

Kai reached for his portion of the frog. His stomach roiled at the smell of it, disinterested, and yet his stomach happily preferred to gnaw at Kai from the inside out instead. Logically, Kai knew he needed to eat, but it was easier said than done, especially since often his body acted as if it no longer knew what to do with food. Sometimes Kai was so hungry that he wasn't.

Kai picked a tiny piece of meat from the bone, which he forced into his mouth, bit into it laboriously, chewed mechanically, and swallowed down hard. It tasted like ash. Most things often did.

"Is there a plan?" Kai asked, setting the frog aside hoping eventually to gather the energy for another bite.

"Nico hoped your kull wouldn't abandon you, but I think she knew that wouldn't be the case," Zephyr said. "She asked me to find you. I figured you'd go to the closest oasis from your starting line. She plans to meet us. We'll team up with her kull and hunt a gonda together."

"I don't need a caretaker."

Zephyr had these expressions about him that were so immovable, so insusceptible to change or argument once set in their ways. It took many kids time to become comfortable with their faces once the shrouds were off, but Zephyr was undeniably a boulder in his intensity. And right now, Zephyr's entire face arched with disbelief, from heavy eyebrows to skewed lips to the darkening depths of his colored eyes.

Point made without ever saying a word, Zephyr moved the conversation. "What took you so long to get here?"

Kai could have continued to argue, but what was the point? This is how it always was with Nico too: He gave up the argument before it got too far. He swallowed his words. He listened to opinions and arguments without ever getting the chance to articulate his point of view. It was an obstacle he'd never managed to maneuver around. It blocked his path, this stone of well-meaning concern.

With a sigh, Kai answered, "I came straight here."

Implacable, Zephyr said: "It's been two days."

An itch of panic scratched at Kai's throat. Two days? That couldn't be possible.

"I came straight here," Kai insisted.

"Two days," Zephyr stated with such force that he beat the words into facts. Was Zephyr always like this? Nico had never mentioned. "Maybe you're finally coming into your magic?"

It was well-known that the Ohan's bloodline came into their magic at five-till. Kai's magic never came. Without the promise of magic, the Council reasoned, what was the point of Kai's existence?

"If I haven't already, I'm never going too."

"Then how do you explain losing two days?"

Kai squeezed his eyes shut and tapped a chord out on his knees. None of it made sense.

"I'm wrong," Kai said, convincing himself. Everyone knew the dry season heat did funny things to people. He pressed his shroud to his eyes and asked, exhausted, "If it's been two days, where is Nico?"

"That's what I'm worried about," Zephyr said. "But you know your jih. There is nothing that can stop her from getting to you. She'll be here."

Zephyr stoked the fire higher to ward off surrounding animals but not the least bit concerned about the human ones who would also be attracted to the light. Kai envied the fact that Zephyr could exist with his differences—his coiled hair, darker skin, and green eyes—and not be afraid.

Zephyr tilted his head to question the whisper of grass-shift. Kai pressed his hands to his face to assure himself that his shroud was still there. It wasn't the best defense, but at least it was something against the rest of the world.

Kelin stepped into the light of their fire. "I seek shelter," he said to Zephyr.

It was an odd request, and immediately Kai knew there was something more to the statement. Zephyr responded by filling the space without ever having to physically make himself bigger. His sizeable presence weighed heavy and hushed.

Kelin glanced at Kai, and suddenly Kai felt conscious of his barely touched stick of food. Kelin looked back at Zephyr. "I did not know he was of your territory. I apologize. I meant him no harm."

"You're welcome to my fire," Zephyr said after some consideration.

Kelin's sharp shoulders fell in relief as he came and sat across from Zephyr. Automatically, Zephyr handed over his water gourd but never offered any food. Kelin took a sip of it.

"I'm glad we crossed paths," Kelin said, chattering away and electrifying the camp with his energy. While he talked with Zephyr, Kelin's accent thickened. Kai had to focus to understand. "Granted, stealing from parasites never gets boring. Either they learn to survive now, or they learn to survive later. They should be thanking me."

"What do you want?" Zephyr asked.

"Maybe I'm looking for a stimulating conversation?"

Zephyr pressed with a flat stare, and the pressure broke Kelin into an awkward laughter. "Ever heard of foreplay? You're so straight to the hole."

Kelin leaned forward over his knee, and the heron feather in his ear danced with the shadows of the fire. He wore a flood of bone necklaces, rings on each finger, and beads in his hair, but they were just ornaments—distractions from the earring, the one thing that identified who he was to the rare few in the know. Kelin wasn't just a kid from the Tents; he was of the Flock, a child of the tight-knit community of those who organized the selling of pleasure in the Tents.

The Flock chose their children. As a group, they chose which child to invest in and to value. A child to one was a child to all. They raised talented orphans as their own with the sole purpose of positioning them to earn good jobs in the Grankull when they came of age. In turn, these children owed a part of their income to the Flock, to support them when demand was low and food was scarce. There were feather earrings in all professions of the Grankull. It was an entire system that sailed under the Council's awareness and fascinated Kai when Nico first told him of it—how a group that others had entirely dismissed had become powerful in their anonymity.

Would anyone else know, by watching these two, that it was more than a meeting between a halfling and a whores' child? Would they know it was a meeting of heirs, hani of their own spaces and in their own right?

Kelin's eyes sharpened, narrow like a dagger's edge. "I want in on the deal. That's why you saved him, right? His jih is coming for him. So what? You're keeping an eye on him to earn some sort of favor from the Ohan? It's ingenious, and I wish I thought of it first."

Zephyr didn't respond.

"I get that you might want the rewards all to yourself, but we Tent kids got to stick together . . . regardless of our respective allegiances. We're all we've got out here. I could help protect him."

"Instead of trying to drown him?"

Kelin showed his bare hands. "That wasn't me. I told those parasites to leave him alone, nor am I here empty-handed. I offer two things: supplies and information." He dragged out a large leaf-full of supplies from the tall grass where he had first appeared. "First, I offer you a thieves' bounty."

Zephyr immediately investigated the supplies, full of stolen weapons, food, and various tools like pots, twine, fletching, whetstones, and flint. Zephyr lifted a pair of pants.

"Hey, a good pair of pants always fetches a nice price back home," Kelin said, chuckling.

Kelin swiped Kai's practically untouched frog leg from the ground and ate it with relish. Zephyr glared at Kelin in response, but he only shrugged. "He wasn't eating it."

"You also said you had information?"

"I was assigned the windship next to the Ohan. Her ship didn't pull off with the others. You've heard of Rasia the Undefeated?

The one they call Rabid Rasia across the bones? Apparently, they were assigned the same kull. There was some sort of argument between them, and it delayed their start."

The way Kelin spoke, it was obvious that he was not aware of the infamous rivalry between Nico and Rasia or all the implications of it.

Because it meant this wasn't going to be as easy as Nico had hoped. Nico had accounted for the possibility that Kai's team might leave him behind. She'd considered that Kai would most likely seek the closest oasis for refuge. Nico had recruited Zephyr for backup. But Kai was certain Nico hadn't planned whatsoever for Rasia. Probably didn't think she'd need to. Probably didn't think in the whole grand span on the Desert, their paths would barely have any reason to cross.

Zephyr's face, that solid steadfast boulder of directness and weight, crumbled pebble by pebble into horror. Both Zephyr and Kai knew enough to know that no one could get under Nico's shroud quite like Rasia. Nico was supposed to have met them *two days ago*.

Laughter howled from a distant end of the oasis.

CHAPTER SEVEN

1

The windship came to an abrupt stop, and Nico banged her chin on the railing. Azan tripped into a pair of lines. Neema's gourd-curves caught Suri's reed-limbs as the two of them went sliding into the mast, rattling the clay lamp and dripping oil.

"This is it," Rasia announced, both hands on her hips. She hadn't so much as flinched.

Through the tousled strands of her hair, Nico squinted at the valley crawling with black shapes that gleamed red in the sun. Not a gonda in sight.

"Those are scorpions," Neema said flatly.

"Congratulations. You can see." Rasia stomped toward the bow and stopped as a gust of wind greeted her head-on, slapping her dry, tangled, wild mane of hair straight into Nico's face. Nico coughed on the sudden onslaught and batted her way through the storm of hair.

"The gonda we are looking for has been hunting this band of gran-scorpions for a while now," Rasia said. "All we need to do is wait, and it'll come to us."

"How are you so certain?" Neema asked. "It goes against everything we learned in school. Gonda don't hunt in hard terrain."

Rasia rolled her eyes so hard that her neck rolled too, sending hair flying full force back into Nico's face, *again*. So. Much. Hair. "We aren't the only ones starving. A gonda hunts in any terrain if it's hungry enough."

Nico finally fought herself free of the tangles and flung herself to the other side of the windship. To her right, Azan grasped his knees and his shoulders shuddered in barely contained laughter.

Nico gathered herself. She shook the sand from her pants, bright white and used to belong to Ava-ta. She straightened her top, combed back the strands of her hair that had escaped in Rasia's mad dash across the Desert, and tightened them all into a clean, no-nonsense ponytail.

Then, all Nico's effort was for naught when Rasia grabbed the corded end of the sail and jumped over the railing, taking the entire windship with her.

The deck lurched to the side.

Nico hit her elbow, slid down, and rolled into the rough, sandy ground. The interspersed rocks scraped and tore at her pants. Her hair popped loose, and every crevice crunched with sand. Nico spit grains from her mouth as she jumped to her feet, furious. She's lucky she didn't land wrong on the glaive strapped to her back.

It was common for kulls to make camp out of the windship sail by turning the ship on its side. The sail often doubled as shelter and shade from the sun, but who in their right mind staked the ship while their kull was still on board?

Enough of this!

Nico stomped over to Rasia who slammed her heel atop the stake and knotted the line in one efficient loop.

"What is wrong with you?" Nico asked. "Someone could have gotten hurt!"

Rasia leaned over the knee of the foot pressed onto the stake. Because their tahs were best friends, Nico had fuzzy recollections of what Rasia looked like as a budchild, specifically, because a toddler Rasia could never keep her shroud on. That wild and energetic bud had bloomed wilder and more maniacal with age. Her brows sprouted bushy, her hair was barely combed, and she wore sand like a second, sunburnt skin. Rasia's lips curled into a hyena grin. "You really need to lighten up and have a little fun."

"That was dangerous! It was selfish! You continually display a complete lack of regard for your kull!" Nico pointed to the others to further her point. Azan crawled, emerging out of a hill of sand. The ground flashed and glinted with all the knives that had fallen from Neema's clothes. Suri inspected her crushed satchel of herbs.

Rasia shrugged. "They're not dead, though."

Dealing with Rasia made Nico want to wring her shroud, except Nico wasn't wearing her shroud anymore. She had tied it around her waist as a makeshift belt. In substitute, Nico pulled at her face and water smudged her fingertips. Why did the bones have to choose Rasia?

"Relax. You all hang out here, out of my way, and I'll handle the rest."

"What are you talking about? You can't kill a gonda by yourself."

"Yes. I can."

"That's nonsense. How are you going to steer a windship and attack a gonda at the same time?"

"*Multitasking.*"

"That's insane! No one can do everything!"

"*I* can," Rasia declared, then spun on her heel. This time, Nico ducked under the hair.

Rasia rummaged through the inventory compartment of the windship. She grabbed a whetstone, an unstrung bow, and a spear to add to the curved khopesh swords strapped to her back. She threw a two-fingered wave behind her (a gesture equivalent to, "get sand in your cooch"), then walked toward a ledge off the rise to become a lone speck in the distance.

Nico had no words to describe the sheer vastness of Rasia's audacity and ego. She hoped Rasia didn't get them all killed.

Nico's head hurt. She didn't know if it was the stress, the heat, Rasia, or a combination of all three. She pressed the heel of her palm to her forehead and cooled the gathered sweat. Nico turned to find Azan climbing out from the underbelly of the windship with a large supply of rations in his arms.

"What are you doing?" Nico hastened over and entered under the cool shade of the wing-sail. "We need to save the food until we absolutely need it. We don't know if Rasia's plan is going to work. We might be out here for days."

"But I'm hungry *now*," Azan complained.

"We need to be smart about this. Azan, start sharpening the weapons that Rasia didn't take with her. Neema, help him. Suri and I will look for kindling to start a fire. The sun is setting quick."

"I thought Rasia was doing this all by herself," Neema said, sharp and biting. Several of Neema's braids had unraveled, with many of the beads lost in the overturn of the windship. Seemed that she had found most of her knives, though.

"We are a kull. Get those weapons sharpened. We might need them sooner rather than later."

Azan and Neema grumbled but eventually collected the weapons Rasia had left behind. Apparently, the Grankull had provided only one whetstone, which Rasia had taken, but luckily, Azan had brought one of his own.

There was so much to do in so little time. They needed to build a fire to ward against predators and the cold of the Desert night. They needed to establish a schedule for watch and turns at tending the fire. They needed to take an inventory of every item the Grankull supplied them with so they knew what they had on hand, something they should have done before they set sail, but Rasia hadn't given anyone the time to do so! Regardless of whether Rasia's gonda showed up, Nico wanted to be prepared for everything.

"Are you okay?" Suri, her best friend, asked as they hunted for kindling. Plenty of dried and cracked shrubbery littered the shadows and crevices of grand sandstone formations. They trekked through a small rainwater channel. Sand rolled into mud and pulled at their feet.

They were pretty far from the others, giving Nico the space to vent. "Rasia is just so, so, so . . . *Ra-sia*! She never does anything easy, everything always has to be her way, and she's so inconsiderate of everyone around her. Rasia lives in her own world, and there is no room for anyone but herself!"

"Maybe you should tell them about Kai. Maybe they'll be sympathetic."

Nico could imagine how much of a shipwreck that conversation would be. She turned dawnward where she sensed Kai, oddly, walking in circles.

"They are not going to risk their Forging to help Kai. Especially not Rasia. Especially not Neema. You know Neema's family history." Nico broke the branches off a parched shrub. "What if he's in danger? What if Zephyr never finds him?"

Suri placed a hand on Nico's arm, and Nico flinched at the contact. Suri withdrew, and Nico immediately felt embarrassed by her childish reaction.

They'd been best friends their entire lives, ever since Suri's tah was entrusted with Kai's healing and care. It was ridiculous that every touch felt so new and unfamiliar.

Nico turned to Suri's face; to her drapery of wheat hair; her soft, round expression; and unblemished bronze skin. Suri soothed, "Kai survived the Forging last year. He will be fine."

"This isn't how I expected the Forging to go. I thought we would have met up with Kai and Zephyr by now. Then here comes Rasia ruining all my plans. Now I'm stuck here, hunting her stupid gonda."

"Have you thought about what we're going to do if Rasia is right? What if we do kill a gonda tonight?"

Nico took a moment to pause. In all her mental preparations, she'd never considered what would happen if Rasia's scheme did come to fruition. "Then you and the others can return to the Grankull, but . . . I can't abandon jih. Perhaps I'll convince the team to drop me off at the oasis on the way back. Then, I'll continue. I'll do it on my own if I must."

Suri pressed branches and twigs and dry brush to her chest with one arm, then reached out with her free hand. Her fingers smelled of the herbs she had touched earlier. The fragrant scent wafted over Nico's senses like a hit of incense when Suri caressed Nico's cheek. Nico didn't think anyone had ever touched her face as intimately as this.

"You don't have to do it on your own."

Suddenly, Suri's lips were on Nico's. Nico melted into the soft resistance and sucked in cloying air. Then, just as quickly, the kiss ended.

Nico felt unprepared for anything.

"Suri . . ." Nico felt herself tilting, off-balance. "I can't."

Suri scurried away.

Nico clutched the tinder to her chest and quickened her pace to catch up. Immediately, once Nico fell into step, Suri bowed her head and mumbled, "I'm sorry. I know you're dealing with a lot. I didn't mean to put that on you. But I've wanted to kiss you the moment we were freed of our shrouds."

"I . . . it was nice." It was Nico's first, and she couldn't have asked for anything sweeter. Perhaps it should be more of a shocking revelation that her childhood friend had a flame for her. If Nico were honest, she'd always known. But she had always been too busy treading water after tah's death to pay it much attention.

"You shouldn't let your feelings for me lead you down a path you'll regret," Nico said. "You are third-named, and the last-named of your siblings. You can't afford to fail your Forging. If you choose to return to the Grankull with Rasia's gonda, I won't hold that against you. You need to make a name for yourself."

Nico had never seen Suri angry. Nico had *heard* her anger, but she had never seen the flustered line on her brow, or the taut pull of her bowed lips.

"You're the ohani, Nico. I care about Kai too, but you are far more important. I know you, Nico. You'd waste this entire Forging searching for Kai if forced to do so. You'd sacrifice everything for him. Despite how much you hate to hear it, you matter more. You are more important, and if this thing comes crashing down, I'm dragging you back home."

Nico set her face to the wind, angry, frustrated, and conflicted by Suri's promise of betrayal. Then Nico beseeched those steady brown eyes she'd known all her life. "If I make it out of this alive, and Kai doesn't . . . I don't know if I could keep pushing forward."

Suri—soft-spoken, shy Suri, who had always been too afraid to raise her voice in class even when she had all the right answers—now spoke unwaveringly. "You will."

Suri turned on her heel and walked briskly toward camp.

Nico hung back a few paces behind her. Nico could count on one hand the times she and Suri had disagreed. She understood Suri's perspective, but if faced with the choice to abandon jih . . . Nico couldn't do it. As Nico walked a half-step behind Suri, she promised herself that it would never come to that.

It wouldn't. She'd save everyone. Nico promised.

They returned to the camp, and despite the lack of communication, Suri and Nico worked in a familiar tandem. Suri prepared the kindling, and Nico used the whetstone to spark the fire. Oddly, Azan watched all their actions with intense scrutiny, so close Nico felt Azan breathing over her shoulder.

The moment the first spark caught fire, Azan immediately asked, "Do you want to play rattle-bones?"

"Really?" Neema sneered. She studied a chip in one of her knives. "Out of all the things we're able to bring, you brought a game?"

"You brought knives. What gonda are those going to kill?"

"There are things out here as dangerous as any gonda that my knives can kill just fine."

"Whatever. My jihs agreed the most important item to bring for the Forging is something to pass the time." Azan rattled a bag of colored black and white bones.

Rattle-bones was undeniably one of the most popular games in the gambling dens, the school yards, and the decks of windships. The pieces were created from animal bones, filed down and shaped into small pinky-sized squares. Each side was painted with a different combination of white, black, and one sole red face.

Azan looked at them all with round, shiny eyes and a practiced pout, an expression no doubt perfected as the last-named of four. It reminded Nico of Rae, her youngest jih, and she couldn't help but to give in.

"Fine," Nico relented. It was all worth it when Azan smiled. At rest, Azan had a plain face, but when he smiled, he was dazzling. Nico imagined he'd quickly learn how to use it to his advantage.

"I'll play too," Suri offered.

Not wanting to be the one left out, Neema eventually huffed over. Azan shuffled the bag of bones. He threw them into the redware clay skillet that came with the windship. They clanked and clattered. Quickly and efficiently, Azan pulled five from the fifty at the center, a standard practice to maintain the element of chance to keep the players from knowing which bones were in the game. You guessed the black faces.

"Twenty-five," Nico called, choosing a number close to the bone average. Players could not guess the same number in the same round.

"Ten," Suri said, cautiously.

"Forty-five," Azan said, going extremely high even though he didn't know if that number of black faces were available in the game.

"One," Neema snorted out.

Azan threw the hand. Twenty black faces. Nico won. Nico swiped up the difference, grabbing five, and added the bones to her pile. Right of Azan, Suri threw the next hand, with each person either calling out random guesses or calculating the odds based on the number of bones Nico had pulled from the previous round.

Suri won the second round. Since she won the hand she threw, she collected double the bones. On Nico's throw, Neema guessed the exact number of black faces and picked that exact number from the pile, then lost it all when Neema threw red. She tossed all her bones back to the middle.

They went around and around like that, collecting bones and often throwing them back.

Sometimes the game lasted several rounds. Sometimes it lasted forever, until either fewer bones were in the skillet per player or the red-faced bone was the sole piece left. The person with the most bones at the end of the game won.

"This game is stupid."

Everyone jolted at the interjection. Suri scattered her throw, with several bones bouncing off the skillet's edge. Azan scrambled after the pieces, and Nico turned to Rasia's abrupt presence. Nico had been so focused on refining her strategy that she hadn't noticed when Rasia came to loom over them.

"It's nothing but luck. It's too easy," Rasia said.

Azan reached for a piece that had rolled under Rasia's foot, and even when Rasia noticed him grabbing for it, she didn't move at all. She just stood there, watching his futility with indifference. Why couldn't she just *move*?

Eventually, Azan dug the bone from under Rasia's boot. Azan blew sand and dirt off the bone piece and argued, "It only seems easy if you don't know how to count faces."

"Do *you* know how to count faces?" Rasia asked.

Azan pouted.

"If you don't care for the game, why don't you leave?" Neema asked. Ironic, since she hadn't initially been invested in the game herself. But as they played, and began laughing, and competed against one another, a sense of camaraderie had strengthened between them. It was admittedly jarring for Rasia to come stampeding through it.

Rasia rolled her eyes, then stomped away, not away toward the distant ledge she'd claimed as her territory, but toward the windship underbelly. Rasia disappeared through the hatch door and climbed back out with the food rations.

"Wait, hey," Azan sputtered. "We're not supposed to eat those yet."

"What?" Rasia looked at all the faces around the clay skillet. "Wait, are you telling me you haven't eaten yet? Why the fuck not?"

Those faces turned to Nico. Nico lifted her chin and owned

her decision. "In case this plan capsizes, I thought it best to save the food."

"It won't. And besides"—Rasia flung her hand toward the valley of lounging scorpions—"There's plenty food right there. These rations won't last but for a few days. The Grankull expects us to hunt for our food. That's part of the fucking test."

That . . . actually made sense.

But rather than admit her error, Nico doubled down. "We don't know if your plan might fail; we should be cautious in our approach—"

Rasia popped a strip of dried apricot into her mouth, then chewed, slowly, mouth open to show the mushed pieces in the firelight.

Neema and Suri stilled, strengthened by the solidarity formed over a good game of bones, but Azan looked at Nico, back at Rasia, then Nico again. Azan scrambled forward to snatch the bag of food from Rasia's hands. He blubbered and apologized as he ate. "I'm so sorry. I'm hungry. I'm *so* hungry."

"I can't believe my family paid money for this horseshit," Neema grumbled.

"What money?" Both Rasia and Nico asked in unison. They also cringed in unison.

"The money our parents paid to put us on a team with you, the *Ohan*."

Of course, the Council would be selling kull spots. Nico wished she could be more surprised, but as was often the case in the Grankull, the corruption dripped from the top.

Neema glanced around at all the confused faces. "Come on, you didn't know? You thought this team was the bones' doing? Rasia is the child of the Rib Councilor. Azan might be fourth-named, but his family is loaded. Suri is the child of the Neck Councilor and the most respected healer of the Grankull. Clean your faces. We're the dream team. Or at least, supposed to be."

"I knew it," Rasia spat. She glared at Nico as if this were all her fault.

"I didn't have anything to do with this," Nico defended. She

63

understood the desperation to have your child do well in the Forging, but it wasn't fair to those families who couldn't afford such advantages.

Besides, there were always consequences for cheating the bones.

Azan offered Nico a piece of jerky, completely interrupting her train of thought. With a sigh, and internally admitting that her stomach did feel a little hollow, she took the offered piece. Azan smiled and distributed the rest of the food to the others. They all gave up on the game to eat. (Nico had been winning.)

Now that she had Rasia here, they needed some sort of plan. Nico rubbed at the incoming headache. "Can we just . . . we need a plan for this gonda. We need some sort of strategy in case it does appear. I can use my magic to . . ."

"No magic."

"What?"

"That's cheating."

Nico blinked at Rasia. "This isn't some game of rattle-bones. This is our lives."

"*I'm* not the one out here playing games."

Nico bruised at the pointed judgment in Rasia's voice. "Magic isn't cheating."

"Look, apparent-fucking-ly, this entire team is already an unfair advantage. My tah didn't need magic to set the best record of the Forging. Neither do I."

Azan, Neema, Suri, and Nico all looked at one another. At least with this, they were on the same ship.

"Yeah . . ." Azan said, tossing it out there for the team. "I vote for magic."

"Same," Neema agreed.

"We should use everything we have at our disposal," Nico argued, but as was so often the case, reason never worked with Rasia.

"How can you take *her* side?" Rasia demanded. "Our parents hunted their gonda and came of age and earned their faces on the strength of their own skill. In fact, the magic-born are the only ones in the entire Grankull who aren't required to live by the strength of their feats. She gets to be the Ohan, the person who leads us, because she was born with magic. How fair is that?" Rasia turned to sneer at Nico. "You're the *chosen one*. What have you ever fucking worked for?"

Rasia's words flayed at Nico's skin, cutting to the heart of all Nico's doubts. Because Rasia wasn't wrong. Who was Nico? What had she done? Was it fair that Nico was born as heir to the Elder's magic? Was magic wrong if others weren't afforded the same advantage?

Was Rasia . . . *right?*

"You're wrong," Nico insisted. "I can't become Ohan if I don't complete the bloodrites. It's not a title I automatically inherit. It's a title I too have to earn."

"Right. A ceremony no one knows anything about. How *scary*."

"Heirs have died during it, Rasia."

"How pathetic were they?"

Nico choked on Rasia's cruelty. So many ancestors had died in the bloodrites. That fate could be hers. Then, where would her family be without her? Where would the Grankull or the Tents be without her? Nico couldn't afford not to be chosen.

Suri came to Nico's defense. "I thought you were hunting this gonda all by yourself, Rasia? What do our opinions matter anyway? Go hunt your gonda. We'll be here playing our bones."

Rasia threw up her hands, then twirled on her heels. She dug into her shirt and adjusted her wrap as she stalked away.

"She's such a fucking kulo," Neema said.

"We're not supposed to use profanity," Nico chided automatically.

Neema shrugged. "I'm just calling it like it is. Besides, it's not as if there are any adults around to censor our language."

"Regardless, no matter how we feel about her, we *do* need a plan in case the gonda comes tonight," Nico said.

"After all that, you *still* want to help her?"

"Yes," Nico said. "We're stronger together. She's still our kull."

"Except she doesn't consider us *her* kull," Neema argued.

"She doesn't even know our names. It is no wonder no one likes her. We shouldn't have chosen her plan in the first place. There's nothing out here. There's no gonda. This is nothing but an empty fucking hunt made up by the delusions of Rasia's rabid mind. Fuck. Her."

A vibration shook the ground.

They all froze, in a moment of disbelief, as the realization swept over them. The next vibration came stronger. All in that frozen warp of time, Rasia sprinted through the camp, leaped the fire, stabbed her sword against the sail stake like a shovel, and popped it free with ease.

It was that audible pop of reality that finally scrambled everyone into motion.

Azan scooped all the bone pieces into his draw-pouch. Neema scrambled for the weapons. Nico and Suri collected the supplies loitering around the campfire. They worked in panicked chaos while Rasia single-handedly righted the windship and reconnected the sail with practiced, calm efficiency.

"Last chance to jump ship," Rasia warned as she grabbed the tiller. Everyone had managed to throw themselves on board and, despite being in way over their heads, no one moved.

"Then you might as well be of use. We're going against the wind. Double-up on the oars and zag the ship," Rasia commanded. She pushed down on the tiller and, traumatized too many times, everyone leaped to grab for the railing.

The ship lurched, stuttering slow in the opposing wind.

"The oars."

Nico and Suri grabbed one set of the clawed bone oars, while Neema and Azan grabbed the other. They tacked the ship forward. Once they reached the lip of the valley, with just one strong stroke, the ship was off on its own, plummeting at an indescribable speed toward the bottom.

The ground cracked and crumbled, then powerful tentacles rose forth and constricted the giant scorpions in their clutches. The hard-shelled scorpions bent, folded, and burst.

Nico had harvested a gonda before and thought she understood the breadth of their size. She'd prepared its meat, oiled its skin for leather, extracted its venom, and processed the sharp beak at its frightening center. But nothing could have prepared her for the power of a gonda's limbs in motion or the heft of its weight bearing down to crush her.

Nico nocked an arrow to her bow, fighting the wind to stay on her feet. "Steer us around."

Rasia steered straight toward the carnage.

"Grab the steer!" Rasia yelled.

So many sounds at once. Nico barely heard Rasia over the roaring wind, the cracking carapaces, and the gonda's whistling hiss.

"What?!" Nico turned to ask, then a blur raced across the deck.

With a spear in hand, Rasia caught the metal tip between the railing, then pole-vaulted her way into the sky. The spear clattered backward. Rasia caught her double swords in the tough hide of a swinging tentacle.

Nico stared, shocked.

They all stood there, slack-jawed, as Rasia jumped from one tentacle to another, rending entire limbs apart as she went. It occurred to Nico at that moment that nothing Rasia claimed had been an exaggeration. She was going to take this thing down, by herself, if she had to.

The windship tilted to its side. Nico shook out her shock and ordered Azan, since he was closest. "Grab the tiller!"

Azan lunged for it and whined, "I don't know what I'm doing!"

He did enough to keep them from crashing over the shattered remains of a dead scorpion. The ground shifted, creating an unexpected hill. Rasia had angered the gonda enough for it to break ground and show its mouth.

This was the moment that had been drilled into all of them by various instructors—when you saw the mouth, the gonda was most vulnerable but also at its fiercest. Nico lifted her bow but didn't trust herself not to accidentally hit the tentacle Rasia was currently bucking and riding.

"Suri," Nico commanded. "Can you make the shot?"

"I think so." Suri drew back the string of her longbow. She stumbled when the ship dipped and squished over a grubworm.

"Azan, keep the ship steady!"

"I'm trying!"

Again, Suri pulled the string taut to her lip. She released. The arrow struck true, flying through the tangle of tentacles to land a piercing shot to the gonda's soft inner flesh. It released a sharp whine. Nico covered her ears at the piercing sound.

Everyone except Rasia.

Rasia jumped at the opportunity. With swords curved like fangs in each hand, she lunged toward the gonda's mouth.

A tentacle flailed right in front of the ship. Azan lost control. The windship careened to its side.

Nico instinctively caught her fall with a wave that discolored the ground. She grabbed her glaive, which had landed in reach, and took stock of the situation. The bulk of the stern had landed on top of Azan, pinning him underneath. Both Neema and Suri picked themselves up from where they had rolled against hard gravel and sediment.

Rasia flew out of the sky, feet flopping as she landed with an *oomph*. She looked at Nico with a wicked smile. "Think I made it mad."

A tentacle swung toward the ship. Nico feared for Azan and worried if they lost the windship beyond repair, their Forging could be over. Nico ran to meet the swinging limb head-on. She planted her feet and thrust out the sharp point of her polearm. The force almost snapped the glaive out of Nico's hand, but the glaive sliced through the tentacle, clean, severing it.

The gonda lifted out of the sand with a hissing roar. No eyes. Along its body were two deep, bloody wounds. No doubt with one more hit, it'd be dead.

It launched toward them.

"Don't move!" Rasia shouted.

Nico's limbs locked painfully in place, holding position. The gonda carved waves of sand as it rammed closer and closer. Neema, staring wide-eyed, broke. She turned and ran.

A tentacle swung, cleaving the air, and snatched Neema off the ground. The gonda opened its chitin mouth to rend Neema whole.

"Neema!" Nico yelled.

"Throw me the glaive," Rasia shouted at Nico.

Nico froze with Rasia's prior words ringing in her ears. If Rasia slayed this gonda on her own, then what had Nico earned?

This was Nico's chance to prove to herself, to Rasia, and to the others that she knew what she was doing. Nico tightened her grip on the glaive and ran forward to put an end to the gonda. She aimed for the hearts.

And never saw the tentacle coming.

Nico should have counted the tentacles before her attack. She hardly had time to brace before it slammed into her. Nico fell head over feet, landing hard on rough ground and dashed hopes.

The tentacle that was wrapped around Neema moved to throw her to the gonda's beak . . .

—and jerked to a stop.

Neema hung precariously, her life hanging in the balance, with a sole arrow punctured into the tentacle. A piece of rope had been tied around the arrow's shaft, holding the tentacle at bay, with Rasia pulling at the rope's other end.

Rasia braced herself against the tentacle Nico had severed earlier and pulled hard. Suri rushed forward to join Rasia. Nico picked herself up from the ground and limped over to help. But even with all three of them pulling at the rope, the tentacle still moved forward.

"This isn't working," Suri said, worried.

"I'm going to use magic."

"*No. Fucking. Magic,*" Rasia gritted out. Before Nico could take a breath, Rasia had stepped onto Nico's shoulder and began shimmying up the rope. Once Rasia reached the gonda's tentacle, she gripped it halfway around with her legs, then stabbed it with her knife, again and again.

The tentacle dropped Neema.

Nico heard herself gasp as Rasia swung upside down and

caught Neema before she fell to the sharp beak. Neema openly sobbed as she reached up to get a solid grip on Rasia's arms.

"I've got her!" Suri shouted.

Suri raced forward, and Rasia swung Neema in her direction. Suri managed to catch Neema, not with her arms as she intended, but a little with her face and chest, and they both crashed to the sand. Neema wept and clamped her legs together to hide the dampness of her pants.

The tentacle where Rasia still hung upside down careened through the air, and she couldn't get herself upright in time. She was helpless to do anything as the limb slammed her to the ground. The sound hit like a gut punch.

Rasia didn't get back up.

No. Rasia was too stubborn to die. Nico rushed over and never felt more relieved to hear blood pumping through Rasia's chest like drumbeats.

The gonda loomed and hissed above them.

Rasia was out of the fight. Neema was a mess, and she might have landed wrong on Suri's shoulder. Azan was still stuck under the windship. Their weapons were scattered. They needed to regroup. Nico had to make a decision.

One gonda wasn't worth dying for.

Nico breathed magic out of her veins. It moved with the power of a torrential downpour, drizzled through her bones, and dripped down the core of her. Storm clouds formed.

Gonda didn't like rain, it confused their ability to sense prey. At the first drizzle of water, the gonda hissed, and the siphon swelled. Nico shouted to the others in warning and pulled her shroud over her nose. She crouched to cover Rasia's unconscious face.

A thick, noxious cloud covered the gonda's retreat. Nico's eyes burned, and tears fought against the sting. The gaseous form wasn't often fatal, but those pregnant sometimes lost babies to it. Nico thickened the rain to disperse the poison.

Underfoot, every vibration came weaker than before. The gonda fled farther and farther away.

The magic taxed what little energy Nico had left. Her legs turned numb and stiff. Shivering, Nico dropped to her butt and took a vibration to catch her breath. She couldn't help but to replay all her mistakes in vivid detail. She knew she would be churning over them for days to come.

Maybe Nico should have given Rasia the glaive. Maybe Nico should have continued the fight instead of forcing the gonda to retreat. Maybe they would have won. Maybe Nico wasn't as ready for this as she had hoped.

Maybe when Rasia woke up, she wouldn't be *too* angry.

Nico winced. Maybe.

CHAPTER EIGHT

O

The sun shimmered when reflected through the translucent dragon-wing sail. It casted shadows and flakes of gold across Rasia's skin. She smelled cooked gran-scorpion meat and a fire burning. Heard it crackling outside the pitched sail.

Then Rasia remembered the gonda, Nico refusing to hand over the glaive, and the crunch of Rasia's own body when she had hit the ground. The latter memory brought with it pain, specifically around her ribs. Rasia shifted experimentally and yep, something was broken. Or fractured, maybe. She groaned at the effort to sit up, fought for every grain against the bandages keeping her ribs together. Someone had also bandaged the rope burns on her palms.

But this was nothing. She'd been hurt worse than this. There wasn't a pain she couldn't fight her way through.

Rasia wobbled into the bright sun of high noon, where she found Nico, loser-who-got-stuck-under-a-windship, and pretty-good-with-bow-Rasia-didn't-actually-have-a-problem-with smoking the dead scorpions. Braids-who-pissed-herself sulked under the ship's front. Rasia looked around, searching.

"Where is it?" Rasia rasped. "You got the gonda, right?"

They all turned toward her. Good-with-a-bow placed down a bucket of salt beside strips of uncooked meat ready for the smoke. She wiped salt on her pants and rushed over.

"Careful," Good-with-a-bow said. "You fractured a rib. It's going to hurt for a while."

"*Where. Is. The. Gonda?*" Rasia demanded. Nico and good-with-a-bow looked at each other. Their nervous glances were answer enough. "It got away? How? We had it!"

"You were unconscious, Rasia," Nico said. "No one had any idea the extent of your injuries. Azan was trapped under the windship, and Neema was almost eaten."

You know what that sounded like? *Excuses.*

"*You let it go.*" Rasia snarled. "Boneless!" She kicked at the sail stake so hard it leaned crooked. "Whatever. It's fine. If we hurry, we can still make the two-day record. We just need to . . ."

"Rasia," Nico interrupted gently. "You've been unconscious for an entire day."

Rasia ran the calculations in her head. She had to find a gonda and get back to the Grankull by sundown to beat her tah's record. It was already high noon. Foregoing the time it took to hunt down a gonda, she was so far out that even if she pushed the windship as fast as it could go, she wouldn't make it back in time.

Rasia failed.

The realization settled in the pit of Rasia's stomach hot and sticky like palm sap. It stuck her joints together, tightening nerve endings and tendons until her entire being coiled into a boiled ball of fury. She exploded.

Rasia propelled her fist across Nico's stupid face.

"This is all *your* fault! If you had thrown the rutting glaive, we'd be halfway home by now! I could have taken care of that gonda! If all of you had stayed out of my fucking way, I could have done it! Why didn't you wake me up?! I could have gone after it! It was half-dead already!"

"You have a fractured rib," Good-with-a-bow answered, as if that was a logical reason for allowing Rasia to sleep an entire day away. Good-with-a-bow wisely stayed out of Rasia's range of fire, or Rasia would have punched her, too.

Nico remained bowed where she'd landed, and her right eye

was beginning to bruise. The look of it was oddly satisfying, and Rasia hoped it hurt as much as this broken rib she got for saving all their asses.

"I hate you!" Rasia pointed at Nico, and then pointed toward the rest of her incompetent teammates, who were rushing over to try and help. "I hate all of you!"

It wasn't fair. It wasn't fair a bunch of bumbling idiots had kept her from fulfilling her promise to Shamai-ta. It was the last promise she ever made to him. She missed him. She missed every time he told her how proud he was. She missed his smile and his laughter and the way he'd lift her on his shoulders to reach her dreams. And it wasn't fucking fair that a too-hard hit to the head had taken him away from her.

The world blurred, and Rasia slapped at the tears burning her eyes. She turned her back on Nico and the others, determined not to let these fools see her cry. Every breath burned her throat, each intake harder than the next as she swallowed down the grief.

"Rasia, I'm sorry," Nico said from behind her. "But we still have to finish our Forging. We need to hunt for another gonda, and we'll do better next time. We'll learn from our mistakes."

Nico had that part right. Rasia would learn from her mistakes.

Rasia shoved past Nico and limped toward the windship. Now that the adrenaline had faded, her ribs flared with pain. Rasia gathered her water-gourd and her pair of khopesh and stuffed supplies into her satchel. Rasia looked toward the horizon that had never questioned or failed her.

"Rasia." Nico stepped in her way, again. "Where are you going? I can't let you go out there by yourself. You're injured. You're not thinking straight. You'll die out there."

"I'm not your responsibility."

"Look, Rasia, you're right. I messed up. This is on me. You got hurt because of my actions and decisions, but you're wounded, and you have no windship. You're not invincible."

Rasia ta-fucking was.

And yet, Nico held fast in her way. Rasia looked to the sky in frustration. How could someone who hated her so much justify blocking her path? Rasia dropped her supplies and plucked the two curved khopesh from her back. "If I defeat you, I'm obviously well enough to go my own way."

"This doesn't have to be a fight, Rasia."

"Then let me go."

"Fine," Nico said, determined, and planted her feet. Nico twirled that rutting glaive over her shoulder into a fighting position.

Rasia studied Nico's balance and stance. Avalai Ohan had also been skilled with polearms; the magic-born were infamous at inventing fighting styles that complemented their magic. The previous Ohan would trip an opponent off their feet, then smack a tree in their face. Rasia wondered what sort of tricks Nico had in store for her.

"Feel free to use your magic," Rasia goaded.

"You're injured," Nico said, aghast. "You didn't want me to use it against a gonda, but now you want me to use it against *you*?"

"'Cause you need it."

Rasia lurched forward.

Just as quickly, Rasia skipped back to evade the long reach of Nico's weapon. At the very least, Nico knew what to do with it, but her all wasn't in it. She wasn't taking Rasia seriously and hadn't that *always* been the problem?

Rasia stepped into Nico's half-hearted thrust and Rasia caught her leg around the pole. Rasia dropped, rolling across the ground, and yanked the glaive right out of Nico's hands. She dropped the polearm from between her thigh and calf as she stood, and all in the same sweeping motion, threw one of her khopesh at Nico's face.

It splashed and bounced off a wall of water. The blade rebounded, whistling past, as Rasia lunged through the chaotic spray. The sharp tip of Rasia's second blade nipped Nico's neck.

Head up, Nico glared down at Rasia. "That throw would have killed me if I hadn't used my magic."

"Good thing you blocked."

Rasia moved to collect her fallen blade. She had to bend

awkwardly over her bandages to reach for it, and she hissed when Nico handed her the hilt. Rasia grabbed what food she could carry, slung her supplies over the shoulder on her good side, and turned toward the sun. Fuck 'em.

She didn't turn back around again.

Rasia found a rotted scorpion carcass, dried out and picked at by carrions. She'd walked far enough away that the Desert had swallowed the sight of her former teammates like specks of sand.

Rasia allowed herself to collapse and exhale over the pain aching in her ribs. Clouds of flies took flight at the motion, sweeping up from the hollowed, decomposed gran-scorpion. Grubworms retreated underground, but after a moment of stillness, they peeked back up. One brushed smooth and slimy against Rasia's arm. She patted the squishy thing as it shimmied past. She took a swig of water and wondered, *what now?*

The shadow swept over her first, then the sky broke with the rolling thunder of a roar. Rasia looked up and watched that gold bastard of a dragon fly overhead, probably off to make a meal of the gonda Rasia had cut into easy pickings.

The grin of an idea stretched across her face.

Technically, a team could hunt any creature of the Desert and bring it back to the Grankull to come of age. But anything less than a gonda didn't earn you respect. Anything more was certain death. But Rasia was crazy enough to try.

She'd failed to overwrite her tah's record. She had wanted to honor his memory, to make him proud of her one last time. If he were here, he'd tell her to get back up, and run faster, and reach higher. He'd tell her that at the end of the day, the only person who mattered, the only person she needed to make proud—was herself.

Rasia was going dragon hunting.

CHAPTER NINE

-O

Rasia couldn't hunt a dragon by herself. Despite what others might claim, she knew her limitations. Even Rasia, in all her skill and experience, admitted a dragon was too big for her to handle alone. But she sure as fuck wasn't going back to Nico.

The night before the Forging, Rasia had stashed her windship at the nearby oasis. It was supposed to have been a "just-in-case" contingency. According to Rasia's jih, quite a few stragglers tended to congregate around the oasis, sometimes forming impromptu teams.

Rasia had a ship. All she needed was a few volunteers.

Rasia spotted the kull ship on the horizon, following her.

Either Nico was dumb enough to follow Rasia because Nico didn't trust her to take care of herself or smart enough to realize that she had no idea what she was doing and had followed Rasia out of self-preservation.

Definitely the former.

Rasia searched around the scorpion corpse for anything she could use and found a few carapace fragments in good condition. She shoved one of the plates underneath her bandages to help brace her ribs, then carried the second piece to the top of the sand hill formed over the scorpion's pincers. She dropped the slab of exoskeleton, and then jumped atop the makeshift sandboard to ride the momentum down.

She used to race jih all the time to see how far they could manipulate the terrain to go faster. She knew which hills her current speed could not take her over and which dunes were best to go around. Every curve and adjustment lived in her bones. It was almost all too easy.

Nothing was as fun as it used to be.

Rasia knew the Desert so well it didn't surprise her anymore. It felt good that this new hunt sparked shivers of excitement. She'd hunt a dragon that no one, not even the best hunting kulls, could slay. She'd be the first ever to bring back a dragon for her coming of age. Oh, how she enjoyed a challenge.

Rasia reached the oasis by nightfall. Many campfires weaved through the palm fronds. Rasia crept through the ferns and water lilies, out of sight, curious to know what her options were. Some kids had injuries, others looked exhausted, and others were passing through to replenish their supplies of water and food. One group cheered each another on as they climbed a date palm.

For the most part—*the losers.*

One campfire caught her attention the most, not because she spotted anyone who could be of use, but because of the sheer amount of uselessness that had been gathered together in one place: the runt, the mutt, and an orphan.

The loser's losers.

Rasia didn't have a lot of options, but she would make the best of her bones. Rasia tightened the bone brace around her ribs—never show weakness—and started at the largest fire where they had been climbing the date palms. Rasia strode out of a bush and slammed her foot atop a fallen tree, unsettling several who had been using it as a seat.

"All right, losers!" Rasia pointed her khopesh at those who'd fallen to the ground, then those eating unripe dates. "We're going to slay a dragon. Follow me. Make your name. Dare something no one has ever dared before. Heroes are written, but legends never die!"

The campfire lit their faces, burnt by confusion or disinterest.

"Isn't she that crazy kid that runs around the Desert naked or something?" someone asked.

"Yeah, she threw her bones right over the Tail, remember?"

"Rabid Rasia? She's as crazy as that Tent kid."

"You think if we ignore her, she'll go away?"

"Are you listening to me?" Rasia demanded hotly. "I'm offering you the chance to make a name for yourself. I'm offering you glory!"

They laughed at her—that same narrow, unimaginative laugh that had followed Rasia all her life.

Rasia scowled at Faris, a hunter's kid. Certainly, he would understand. "What about you?"

Faris shrugged his shoulders. "There are real things to worry about, Rasia."

Fuck 'em all.

Rasia clenched her fists and walked away. She didn't have time for these losers, these kids who'd given up or who were too afraid to try. Rasia sucked in several trembling breaths, then walked to the next fire and tried again.

Same story. Same ending. Different characters. They all thought her crazy. They all laughed. They all refused to take her seriously even though she was the only person in this rutting Desert who knew anything about what they were doing!

Rasia shrugged through the bushes to reach the last campfire. The distant laughter preceded her arrival. Nevertheless, Rasia gathered herself and faced their oncoming mockery. She glared straight at the runt, daring him, of all people, to laugh at her.

"I'm going to slay a dragon. Do any of you stupid fucks want to come with me?"

"Okay."

Rasia did a double take because she had already turned around. She stared at the runt, whose face was still oddly covered by his shroud. But you know what? Rasia didn't care about his weird at the moment. "*Really?*"

"*No,*" the mutt spat out. "Kai, what are you doing? We have a plan."

"A plan I never agreed to."

"You're going to go off with *Rasia* chasing dragons? If Rasia is here, Nico isn't far behind."

Rasia frowned and looked between the two of them, just the two because the orphan flock kid had quickly disappeared the moment Rasia had appeared out of the bushes.

It all clicked in that moment—why Nico had been so adamant about allying with another team. "That two-faced skink. She was trying to get to *you*."

"Where is Nico?" the mutt asked.

Rasia couldn't care less where Nico was right now. Rasia had shaken her drums ago.

"Probably sulking off somewhere over her failures."

"What did you do?" the mutt demanded.

"Why does everyone always assume it's *my* fault?" Rasia asked, annoyed. She looked at the runt. "Are you coming or not?"

He stepped forward only for the mutt to catch him by the arm. "Kai, no."

"Let go of me," the runt demanded. "You might be Nico's friend, but you're not mine."

"*We're trying to help you.*"

"I never asked for help!"

Rasia saw how this was going to go: It would be no different than any of the other campfires. Rasia turned and left them to argue. She had things to do and dragons to slay.

A crescent moon spilled milk and stars into the water. She walked through rivers of slim light, weaved through sleeping camels, and stopped before a mountain of fallen palms. Rasia yanked at the fronds, shook off the insects and the moonlight drizzled on the leaves, and peeled back the layers to reveal her windship underneath.

"Looks like it's just you and me," Rasia said, grabbing at the mast and dragging it out of its hiding spot. It was back-breaking work, as a suction of dung clung to the hull. When Rasia finally plucked it free, she collapsed against the beaten, bruised, and misshapen ship. It wasn't as pretty or as large as the other windships, but it had never let her down.

That was more than Rasia could say for anyone else.

One word, "Okay," fell from Kai's lips, as unexpected as the way Rasia had looked at him, not over or through him, but right at him and gave him a choice. People didn't ask his opinion. They didn't invite him anywhere or seek out his help. Even those closest to him, like Nico, didn't truly listen to him. They made choices on his behalf, to protect him, when Kai would rather they protect themselves. Rasia had asked him a question and it was the first time Kai felt heard, for Kai's words never held any weight until that one word had the power to turn Rasia around.

Just once, Kai wanted the ability to make his own choices— even stupid ones.

So, Kai waited.

He waited for Zephyr to assign watch between himself and Kelin, not once considering that maybe Kai wanted to be more than a waste of space. Kai could feed the fire, he could shout as well as anyone else, but unsurprisingly, Zephyr overlooked him for even the most menial of tasks. Kai waited for Zephyr to settle into his bedroll and for Kelin to wander toward the edge of camp, turn his back, and pass water.

Kai didn't have many things to gather. He had his dagger, his rucksack with an extra caftan, a spare shroud, and a water-gourd. Wary that Zephyr would take note of his absence too soon, Kai stacked rocks and a broken branch underneath his bedroll. It wasn't going to fool anyone come morning, but Kai doubted Kelin would notice. It was the only advantage of people constantly underestimating and overlooking him.

Kai crept quietly into the darkness of the oasis.

The oasis looked different at night. Kai jumped at every rustle and stilled at every owl hoot. Paranoia and vigilance followed him through the shadows, waiting and ready to take any shape from cruel children to hungry predators. He hadn't realized how secure he had felt until he was walking away from Zephyr's fire.

At least Kai was accustomed to this fear. It was the same fear that followed him through the streets of the Grankull and into the serving room of his own house. It was a fear he had grown tired of, exhausted by the sheer effort of pushing through it every vibration of every day. But he had a reason to fight it now. Kai carved his way through the oasis, propelling himself forward on sheer force of will to find Rasia on the other end.

Until he began to doubt. He imagined Rasia's disappointment when he stepped from the reeds and she realized it was just him, the runt. His steps slowed. All around him, the darkness threatened to consume him.

Kai heard the distinct sound of a sail snapping in the wind. He rushed forward, afraid she was leaving and he'd miss his only chance. He stumbled out of the grass.

Without her shroud, Rasia looked as Kai always imagined: black eyes full of stars and a wicked smirk that could cut anything in her path. Leaves decorated her flag of hair and every shift of her hip staked the ground like some fierce creature with the Desert at her command.

He braced himself for her disappointment.

But Rasia's lips curled at the corners, and Kai had never seen anything as beautiful as that mad moon-crescent grin. She glowed and all shadows receded before her.

"What you waiting for?" she asked. "Get in."

Kai climbed the windship's stairs. The foot grips were so worn that he almost slipped, but he managed to reach the deck without breaking himself.

"Go sit somewhere," Rasia ordered. "I'll handle everything."

Not wanting to get in her way, Kai sat down in the front corner and watched her tackle every task with a flurry of motion and speed of purpose. She used one of the oars to turn the ship away from the soft ground of the oasis. She batted dirt from the sail, clouding the air with dust and smoke that burned the eyes.

She knotted ropes, locked the hatches, and raised the anchor.

"Let's go get us a dragon!" Rasia slammed her hand on the steer.

Kai rolled.

The world turned and righted itself with a sudden oomph. Kai stared, dazed, from where he'd landed in the sand.

He had fallen off the ship.

Rasia's feet rushed tip-tap across the deck. She looked over the railing down at him, and Kai knew this is where she'd reevaluate her invitation. Instead, a quivering laugh burst out of her.

"How the fuck? I told you to sit!" Rasia yelled from the deck.

"I did," Kai said, utterly confused.

Rasia vaulted over the railing and dropped to the ground. With a laugh infecting her movements, she reached out a hand. "You are so pathetic. Here."

Kai blinked at her offered hand. She offered it to him without hesitation when others either shied away from him like he was diseased or met him with violence. The imprint of Zephyr's grip still throbbed and bruised around his arm. A voice in the back of his head cautioned the contact, but he fought through the fear and touched her.

With a tug, she set him on his feet.

"And take that stupid thing off. It's not as if you have horns under all that linen," Rasia admonished, snatching off Kai's shroud before he had a chance to grab for it. He expected her to flinch back in revulsion or mock him. Or react in disappointment like the last time she'd yanked it off in the middle of the belly market.

Instead, this time, she demanded, "Respect my face, and I'll respect yours," before shoving his shroud back into his arms.

Kai clutched at his shroud, his face feeling vulnerable in the open air. He should be afraid. He should be wary and guilty for running away from Nico. But fuck it.

It was time he threw his bones.

CHAPTER TEN

—

It had come to Kai's attention that Rasia was not joking, she was not exaggerating, nor was she boasting about slaying a dragon. He felt somewhat guilty because, inevitably, Rasia would realize how useless he was, and this short-lived adventure would come to an end. But for now, he'd revel in the wind through his hair and the sun on his skin and the touch of freedom on his face.

Rasia dangled her legs from where she balanced atop the thin, wobbly railing of her windship while she smoothed down the flapping corners of a map on her thigh. Kai couldn't help but glance from Rasia to the steer, then back to Rasia again. The windship was driving itself.

Kai had never seen or read anything like it, nor had he seen or read anything quite like this windship. Rasia had a rope rigged to the steer that reached from the carved handle at the tip of it to an arch built into the deck. Rasia often adjusted the rope, sliding or pulling it out of a knot to change the steer level and thus the ship's speed. Sometimes, Rasia bounced over to stabilize the ship when there was a divot in the terrain, but for the most part, she let it sail on its own.

"Before we go after our dragon, we'll need to stop for more supplies," Rasia said. "I don't have enough food in the windship to last the both of us the entire Forging, which means we need to go hunting."

Kai couldn't discern if Rasia was talking to herself or if she was talking to him, and if so, if he was expected to respond. If she were waiting for a response, she never gave him enough time, forging forward with the conversation either way.

"We need something big. Something that will last us a while . . . Oh, I know."

Rasia leaped from the railing—how she did that from a sitting position, Kai had no idea—and climbed the mast to the scout's nest at the top of the sail. Most masts have foot grips to help the scouts maintain balance, but Rasia's foot grips looked rigged with hidden compartments. She retrieved an eyeglass and observed the terrain. All Kai could see were oceans of sand on each side, sporadically broken apart by dry brush and rock formations curling one atop one another like fungi.

Rasia dropped down with an excited flail of her arms. "Of course, it's skinkos mating season!"

She snatched up the rope from the deck arch, wrapped it around her arm, then jumped atop the outrigger and pulled the steer a hard right all in the same motion. The ship lifted off the ground, flipping on its tail to make the sudden turn.

Kai clutched the rope he'd used to tie himself to the railing. His stomach whooshed, and for a blinding few moments, he flew. Streaks of gold swept below his dangling feet. Rasia glided beneath him, throwing her weight into the outrigger. She pulled all her strength into the ropes, teetering the ship to its edge until they had turned a whole 180 degrees.

They landed with a jolt, back upright.

Kai had never experienced anything that thrilling his entire life. He sort of wanted to vomit his guts out or cheer the same way Rasia did as she jumped back to the deck. She turned to him like a performer after her grand finale, and all good performers deserved a captive audience.

Kai clapped.

Rasia bowed so deeply her hair swept the deck. She came up with a laugh. "And that move is what's called 'The Blindside.' I'd like to see another kull turn a windship as fast as I can."

Back in the Grankull, Kai knew Rasia as Nico's nemesis. He knew the exact day Nico first met Rasia and how Nico had cried when Rasia stomped on Nico's favorite doll. He knew when Nico and Rasia got into their first argument and their first physical fight. When Nico began to focus more on her studies and responsibilities, however, Rasia disappeared from Nico's tales.

Kai had never had much interaction with Rasia. Other than that incident at the market, she was never one to seek Kai out like the other bullies. As long as Kai was careful enough not to get in her way (or walk into her), he wasn't worth her attention.

Kai had really only seen Rasia through Nico's eyes. He was ashamed to admit he'd once thought of Rasia as nothing more than a villain in Nico's story. With a different point of view, Rasia was the hero of her own.

She was laughter and movement. She was sharp skill and smug expertise. The things he couldn't imagine, she breathed like air.

It made Kai feel simple and small in his wrap of dirty grey linen.

"There they are," Rasia said as she slowed the ship. Kai peeked over the railing and went wide-eyed at the hundreds of windship-sized lizards dancing atop a mesa of sun-bleached sandstone. Dotted shrubbery crawled around the wide base of the stratified rocks.

Kai had only ever seen the name of this place, Skinkos Outcrop, marked on a map. It was dangerous due to the territorial, hyper-regenerative lizards that called it home, so much so that only the hunting kulls ever dared to approach it. The sketches in the library scrolls depicted their multitude of tails, small legs, and lack of pronounced neck rather accurately, but no amount of paper could capture the deep warble of their mating calls or the weird, sharp movements of their dance.

"See those two over there," Rasia said, appearing out of nowhere crouched next to him. Kai jumped at her sudden proximity. She pressed into his shoulder, lips lowering toward his ear as if holding a secret. Kai followed the direction her finger pointed and saw two skinkos stacked one atop the other, sort of lying there, lounging. *"They're fucking."*

"Really?" Kai found himself asking. It was nothing like walking in on his tah, which had happened so frequently he had gotten accustomed to skirting the walls. In the Grankull, once the shrouds came off, people fucked whenever and wherever.

"I know, right? It's as boring as watching rocks try to run."

Kai had always wondered where the word *skink* came from, one of the Grankull's worst insults to either accuse someone of being bad at sex or a cheating merchant at the market. The person with the bones to fling the slur should be ready for a fight every time.

"Maybe they get tired from all the dancing?" Kai suggested, thoughtfully.

Rasia sputtered out a laugh and shoved Kai's shoulder. "You'd think the females would pick the largest ones, but they don't. As far as I can tell, they choose the best dancer. How crazy is that? Their essential life skill is dancing."

The temple scrolls had never told him that. The scrolls described the skinkos' incredible territorial temper, their regeneration, how the oldest of them could grow up to six tails, and a bite that grounded rocks to dust.

"So . . ." Kai looked at her askance. In the sun, her black eyes were a deep russet. "You spend a lot of time watching skinkos mate?"

"You've got to know what you're hunting. It's a known fact that animals are more aggressive during mating season. For example . . ." Rasia pointed to a skinko much closer to their position. It seemed jerkier and more awkward than the others. All potential partners were actively avoiding him; Kai could relate.

"You can bet that one isn't getting any. He's alone. He's isolated. He's our dinner."

Rasia stood from her crouch, slammed her foot against the railing, and took stock of the terrain. "I'll set up a trap between these two rocks. Then I'll get his attention."

"Do you . . ." Kai cleared his throat. "Do you want any help?"

"So you can mess things up like your jih? No. Sit down and keep out the way."

Rasia indicated a shady spot underneath a stunted arch of rocks. Kai didn't question why she thought him safer off the windship and did as instructed. He carefully set his feet on the worn steps and wondered if their poor state was the reason why Rasia either jumped or flipped off the windship—as she did now, swinging over his head with a piece of rope. Kai made it to the ground safely. He sat down in the designated spot and enjoyed the shade.

Rasia used the windship itself to prepare the trap: She pinned it around one rock and pulled the rope of the mast to the other. Kai had never heard of anyone using a ship as a counterweight in an animal trap . . . The things he'd learned spending half a day with Rasia felt equivalent to an entire shelf in the temple library.

Kai frowned when he noticed Rasia limping. She paused to clutch at her side before throwing her weight back to tighten a rope around a spear. After tying the second spear, Kai realized her plan. She was going to skewer the skinko after the trip line.

Despite Rasia's clear order to remain out the way, Kai approached her. "Are you alright?" Kai asked, uncertain if he could offer any help if she wasn't.

"Why are you bothering me?"

"You're . . . hurt?"

Rasia rolled her eyes as she kicked sand over the recently tied spear. "Exactly, which is why I'm trapping the thing and not going in swords waving."

"I thought they were hyper-regenerative. Isn't a physical fight dangerous?"

"Not if you can cut faster than they can regenerate," Rasia said, then glared at him, eyebrows raised, as if daring him to challenge whether such a feat could be done.

Kai nodded. "Okay."

Rasia squinted at him for a moment. "I can do it, you know."

"I believe you."

"I'd do it too, if your stupid jih hadn't broken my rib."

"You broke a rib?"

"I can probably kill a skinko with my eyes closed and *two* broken ribs."

"Maybe we should just stick to the trap."

Rasia looked down at the spear thus far half-covered by sand. "Yeah . . . besides, we've got bigger hunts to chase. But I could do it, you know."

"I know."

"*Good.*"

Kai shuffled around Rasia, a little intimidated. Without anything else to do, he kicked sand onto the other end of the spear and, with a huff, Rasia did the same. She rigged two more spears into the ropes.

Kai was constantly amazed by the sheer number of weapons she pulled out of the windship, often from secret cracks and crevices. Nor did Rasia ever waste time thinking about where an item was located on her ship. She *knew.*

Rasia tossed Kai a bow. He blinked, unsure if she had thrown the bow to him so it would have somewhere soft to fall, or if she expected him to do something with it.

"Since you're so keen on helping, go get the skinko's attention and run back this way. I'll be ready to pull up the spears. He should trip on the first rope and land straight onto the second line to skewer himself dead. Easy."

Kai nodded his head, uncertain, but it was the first thing she'd asked him to do, and he didn't want to mess this up. He wanted to contribute. He tightened his grip around the bow and turned toward the lizard.

Get its attention. Run. That didn't sound so hard.

With a steely resolve, Kai slung the quiver of arrows over his back and hiked toward the rock and its owner.

The skinkos were louder as he moved closer. The mating calls vibrated a deep, pounding warble through his chest. The lone skinko didn't notice Kai when he came close enough to press himself into the shadow of the mesa. Kai climbed the banded rings of color, and when he reached the top, the rock underfoot wobbled an odd beat under the power of the skinko's jilted dance.

Kai's hands sweated around the acacia wood of the bow. He tried pulling the string around the arrow like he'd seen so many others do countless of times, but every time the arrow fell away.

How did you work these things? It was a lot more complicated than it looked.

The arrow dropped away. Again and again.

In frustration, Kai took the whole bow and threw it. It fell short, but the sound of the bow skidding and clattering across the rock caught the lizard's attention. It swiveled its head toward Kai more like a snake than a lizard, with eyes a molten copper. In its anger, the deep bass of its voice came impossibly fast, vibrating like a drill and quaking the ground. It charged.

Kai ran.

He slipped down the mesa, sliding to land on the sharp bones of his butt. The distance Kai needed to overcome to reach Rasia's trap wasn't far, but four steps in, his lungs burned on every intake of air. His breath squeezed out his throat, and Rasia's trap stretched further and further away.

He tripped, or stumbled, or collapsed onto his face. Kai wasn't sure how his body had betrayed him, but he was certain of the fact that he had been upright one moment, then curled into the painful tightening of his chest the next—as if someone had reached inside him to bend and twist his organs into one large knot.

A whoosh of air. Kai forced his eyes open as Rasia landed in front of him.

She looked so small in the face of the massive skinko stampeding toward them, but she did not run. Instead, Rasia met its furious roar with a war cry of her own. The skinko flinched, startled by this challenger in his territory.

Rasia widened her stance and held twin khopesh like a pair of talons extending from her arms. She raced forward and slashed with wild abandon. Every stroke and thrust punctuated the sound of Kai's dry wheezing.

Tails and arms and even its head grew back every time she

hacked them off. Spots swirled in Kai's vision, flashing with the movement of Rasia's swords, growing in multitude with every failed breath. It was Rasia's own sort of dance.

Kai clenched his eyes closed. His throat burned, stripped raw by trapped air. He felt like he was about to explode. If he didn't hold himself tightly enough, he'd burst and leave a mess on everything in his vicinity. Something pushed hard against his shoulder and turned him flat on his back.

Kai blinked his eyes open. Light-headed, the image of Rasia swirled over him, bloodied and triumphant. The sun spun around her, faster and faster till light turned black.

CHAPTER ELEVEN

1

"Ready? Heave!" Nico shouted. Azan and Suri pried at the sides of the windship with one of the oars. Nico pushed against the bow, but the windship refused to budge from where it had run aground a patch of rocks.

The sun beat down on their heads, and Nico slipped forward, hands sweaty, under the weight of it. Surrendering to the momentum, she fell back against the unyielding hull. The heat pulled at dry drags of breath. It wasn't even high noon yet, but soon the sand would burn so hot it would melt the soles off their sandals. They had to get the windship un-stuck or they'd be forced to wait out the worst of the heat and lose even more time.

"That was pointless," Neema said from the high rock where she watched the proceedings.

"Are you going to help or not?" Nico snapped. Admittedly the heat was shortening her temper, but she was tired of bearing the brunt of Neema's deteriorating attitude.

Neema raised a sharp brow, placed her hands on her hips as if the day had all the time to wait for her, and shrugged. "You're the one who steered us into these rocks."

Nico deflated. Neema wasn't wrong. Rasia purposefully led them through ground hard to follow. The entire area was covered in rocks puncturing the sand, but more dangerous were the rocks you couldn't see, hiding beneath the surface. It was going to take them forever to clear this stretch of the Desert. Nico should have gone around, but once again she'd had too much confidence in her own abilities.

"How is that fair?" Suri asked. "None of us have any practical experience steering a windship. Nico is doing her best. You didn't volunteer."

"She's the ohani. You'd think she wouldn't be so useless."

"So what? It's on her alone to make sure we succeed? It's her responsibility to make sure we all survive? She must steer the ship, and scout the terrain, and row the oars all by herself? Perhaps Rasia could do so, but ultimately, we're a kull. We're in this together."

Suri's anger on Nico's behalf, more than anything, pushed Nico to her feet. They couldn't afford to fight one another.

"I have an idea," Nico said. "Everyone, back on the windship."

Nico caught Azan by the shoulder when he reached for the stairs. "I might not be able to steer after this . . . do you think you can do so in my stead?"

"But I could barely keep it upright against that gonda," Azan said. He licked at the sweat on his upper lip, anxious. "I can't steer us through these rocks any better than you can."

"Despite what happened, you did good during the hunt, Azan. That was an impossible situation for anyone."

"Can't you ask Suri?"

"I'm asking you." Nico didn't want Azan to be terrified of taking the steer the rest of his life. "I mess up too. Doesn't mean we shouldn't try again."

Azan blew out a harsh breath, then nodded. He climbed the stairs, and the fabric of his shirt rose as his arms reached for the next rung. Nico spotted the large bruise, which spanned across his entire back, from where the windship hull had pinned him. Suri said it looked pretty bad, but Azan claimed it didn't bother him. Nico was so thankful they had all made it out of that last skirmish alive.

Nico stepped on the bottom rung of the stairs and, out of habit, scanned the harsh yellow of the horizon. Rasia was long gone. If someone had asked her if anyone could outrun a windship with a sandboard, Nico would have claimed it impossible, but Rasia continued to plow through all her expectations.

Nico had come to accept the fact that Rasia didn't need Nico to save her. Despite her injuries, Rasia would be fine. Nico worried more about Kai. Every detour, lost path, and vibration stuck in a ditch wasted too much time she didn't have to find him.

Nico climbed onto the deck and stood at the front corner of the bow. They pulled up the oars. She concentrated on the bass song pitched deep underground. She inhaled, then exhaled magic.

Water bubbled from the aquifers, rising, bursting forth to spurt symphonic fountains. A mini rainbow winked at them. The rocky patch flooded over and buoyed the ship free. The water expanded further, surging outward to compose the shimmering bells of a lake. Nico would take care to rock the water back to sleep once they'd crossed.

Those without magic could never grasp how massive the Desert truly was, from the sky-home of cloud-clusters to entire ecosystems living below the sand. Nico felt the landscape in all six directions—this grand, ever-shifting, ever-changing force even Death sometimes bowed to.

Nico turned to Azan, who stood beside the tiller staring at the ripples of her magic with bud-like wonder. The windship bobbed, floating higher than any obstacles in their way. Azan steered the windship smoothly across the water.

"Why didn't you do that in the first place?" Neema huffed.

"Because it's dangerous," Suri said, immediately wrapping her shroud about Nico's shoulders. Nico accepted the covering gratefully, even though this time the magic had only left behind a runny nose and a persistent chill. Magic exacted a toil, and the icy void left behind always thawed slowly. Expend too much, and it was true: Some magic-born have accidentally frozen themselves to death.

"No," Nico said softly. That's not why Nico hadn't used her

magic sooner; she hadn't wanted to become reliant on it. "I fear Rasia is right," Nico muttered. She stared at her feet, allowing the sun to wash heat down her neck. "I can't do anything without my magic."

"It's not fair to compare yourself to Rasia," Suri said. "The Forging is a blink and a half for a reason. We don't have to do it all in a day."

It's so easy to get dragged along Rasia's breathtaking pace, but that didn't change the fact Nico should have thrown Rasia the glaive, or the fact Nico could barely survive the Desert without her magic. Rasia had gotten her all mixed up in the head with doubts and insecurities, and Nico feared Rasia right—that she was a naive child unable to protect anyone.

"Kai isn't at the oasis anymore," Nico whispered between her and Suri.

"What do you mean?"

"I'm not sure what it means."

Nico could reliably find Kai's magical signature anywhere in the Grankull. While Nico would describe their tah's magic as a lake of freshwater, Kai's magic always felt murky and contaminated in some way. Although the Desert was considerably vaster than home, with a little focus and a taste of moisture on her tongue, Nico could pinpoint his location.

She sensed Kai dawnward, farther than he should be.

Nico heard the oasis before she saw it. The melodies of still water differed from water that ran and rushed and moved. The oasis swayed, slow dancing with graceful palm fronds and elegant reeds.

An oasis symbolized many things to one's Forging. It was often a place of renewal and rest, a safe haven where kulls licked their wounds and felt pressured to try again as the moon ticked down. It was a place to convene and organize and strategize. But it was also a place to give up, a temptation many never overcome. To Nico, it was supposed to be a reunion.

Azan brought the ship to several stuttering stops. He mowed over a few ferns but managed successfully to park right at the grassy rim. The oasis water was so clear and reflective, it saw them coming.

"Great job, Azan," Nico praised.

Azan beamed. He had one of those easygoing dispositions hard not to be fond of. Nico felt guilty lying to both him and Neema. They both deserved the truth. She worried about Neema's reaction the most.

"We'll camp here for high noon," Nico ordered. "Rest. Fill your gourds and the water supply. I'll go have a look around."

Suri nodded between them.

Clothes rained to the deck, and Azan streaked off into the water. All anyone had time to see was his pale ashy backside. And Neema actually smiled for once when she found the perfect palm to shade her lounge.

Nico didn't have the luxury. She didn't know why Kai left the oasis, but someone must have seen something. It wasn't Kai's nature to have left on his own.

Nico walked the water's perimeter and found several groups dug in at established camps. Since it was high noon, Nico wasn't surprised to find them engaged in low-energy activities such as napping, eating, or playing rattle-bones. A couple kids were in the water and had noticed Azan and broken off to approach him.

"Fair winds and shadowed eyes," Nico greeted the first camp.

The kids snapped up from their naps. They froze their game of bones. One particular male stood up to challenge, "Depends on which way you're blowing."

Nico recognized that voice. They went to school together. He was the child of one of Kenji-ta's regular kull members, and the grandchild of a legendary one. Nico wanted to ask about Kai, but their reactions had her reassessing the situation. None had any weapons. They slept on palm leaves. They had a small pile of unripe dates hoarded by their fire.

"Faris," Nico said. "What has happened? Where are your supplies?"

Faris squinted at her. ". . . Ohan?"

"Not yet," Nico corrected, automatically, even though she

knew it never made much difference. The moment Ava-ta's ashes were scattered to the winds, the weight of that title overshadowed her. "What is going on?"

"My kull and I stopped here to fill our water supply, and we got jumped by this other team. They stole all our stuff."

"And my pants!" Another child shouted, wearing nothing but a loincloth and on the verge of tears.

Nico empathized. The Forging was the first time a child was allowed to wear pants. In preparation for the Forging, a child would visit the tailor to fit either a pair of pants inherited from a family member, or for more affluent families, new pants entirely. Nico imagined these pants, if worth stealing, were the latter. While unfortunate the kid hadn't brought a second pair, Nico was more concerned about the theft of the weapons and the supplies.

Faris pointed behind him, down the trodden path. "Another kull is down the bank. Same thing happened to them."

"Do you know the kids who stole from you?" Nico asked. Without their supplies and weapons, these kids were practically incapable of completing their Forging. They'd never get the chance to try, or try and fail, or try and fail again. They'd never get the chance to try and succeed. Their Forging had essentially been stolen from them.

"It was some tent rat with this fighting style I've never seen before. Had me and my kull down before I knew what was going on. He was on a team with Loryn and Tarick. I'm not sure who the other two were."

Nico knew Loryn and Tarick. Loryn lost her older jih in last year's Forging. Tarick was a bully, especially around the wrong sort of crowd. The others probably weren't school kids. School cost money, and sometimes families prioritized children who had a higher chance of succeeding. Those who didn't attend often helped with the childcare and chores, like Kai. Generally, the kids who went to school all knew each other by name.

"Where are they?"

"No one has seen the tent rat, but Tarick and Loryn are on the other side of the oasis."

"Let's pay them a visit," Nico suggested.

Faris smiled. The others immediately gathered themselves and followed after. As she made her way around the oasis, more and more groups joined until their numbers swelled to at least thirty strong.

Except the supposed thieves didn't seem to have much of anything themselves. Tarick, Loryn, and the two others quaked at the sight of the angry mob. Nico quickly stepped in before someone threw down a shroud in challenge.

She raised her hand, forming the kull signal for silence, and the yelling and cursing quieted.

"It is time you gave back the things you have stolen," Nico said.

Tarick and Loryn looked at each other nervously, then Loryn cried out, "*We can't.* It's that tent rat's fault. He lied and double-crossed us. He's the one that stole all your stuff. It's gone!"

"What do you mean all our stuff is gone?!" Faris growled out, then leaped forward.

Nico swiveled to block his advance, and Faris dug in his heels to refrain from crashing into her. Nico pushed at his chest. She was neither short like Rasia or reed-thin like Suri, nor was she gourd-curves like Neema. She was built rooted, and few intimidated her physically. Faris budged when she shoved at him, and she situated herself as a formidable barrier between the two groups.

Nico couldn't allow this to get out of hand.

"*We're sorry,*" Tarick pleaded. "It was the tent rat's idea to steal from you, then he betrayed us for the other one! They were in cahoots all along!"

"That doesn't absolve your part in all this," Faris argued.

"Enough," Nico demanded. "Everything is long gone. Let it go. What's done is done. I know that is a difficult thing to hear, but not all hope is lost. My kull has plenty of scorpion jerky to share. I'll come back around and give you what food and weapons I can spare. Return to your camps and remember the strength found here together. That is what is going to get us through the Forging."

They hesitated and grumbled at first, but none were willing to go through Nico for their revenge. They eventually trudged back toward their separate camps.

Nico looked at Tarick, Loryn, and the two others over her shoulder. "You will not steal again. You dare do so, and I will not protect you the next time."

They bowed their faces and thanked her profusely.

"You said there were two kids from the Tents? Tell me about them." Not many tent kids went through the trouble of going through the Forging, a competition they oft thought, rather accurately, was rigged against them. "Did you get their names?"

"The one on our team called himself Kelin. Who knew if that was his real name or not?" Tarick insulted. "The other one was that mixed-breed bastard."

"And was my jih with them?"

"Who?"

They hadn't realized who she was.

"Kai-ji," Nico said. That word others used to describe him remained tight in her teeth. For as long as Nico lived, she would never say it. "Can't miss him. He has gold eyes."

"*Ohan?!*" Tarick, Loryn, and the others jerked to attention. Tarick and Loryn answered at the same time: "We didn't see him." "The tent kid tried to drown him."

Nico didn't have the patience for their lies. She turned to the unnamed team members and demanded, "What happened?"

One, a female, glanced between Tarick and Loryn before whispering. "We saw him alone and thought to take his stuff like the others. The tent kid took his dagger, but the other one, the mutt, stopped him. Tarick and Loryn tried to drown him."

Anger struck her at the information.

Let it go. What's done is done.

Isn't that what Nico advised Faris and the others? She had cautioned them not to give in to their feelings of hatred and revenge, and for a magic-born, the price of such emotions could be even more costly. After all, one moment of anger was *the* mistake that defined Ava-ta's reign. One moment of anger had soured the Ohan's relationship with the Council, had turned the Grankull's adoration into fear, and doomed her children to carry the weight of that one mistake long after Ava-ta was gone.

Behind her, the crowd of kids walked the tip end of the oasis. They were too far away to see. They wouldn't know if Nico drowned her jih's abusers right here, right now. But who would Nico be if she proved herself no better than the bullies?

"What became of Kai-ji?" Nico asked.

"He left with the mutt. We don't know what happened to him."

"And what is your name?"

"It's Rianis."

"And Gysen," the male offered.

Nico promised, "I'll remember them."

Nico continued her trek around the oasis. She brushed her hand through the reeds and listened to the murmuring water ballads. The oldest palms protected this area of the oasis. They were tall, resplendent, and wreathed with hefty necklaces of aged gold.

Nico licked her lips to the dewdrop taste of a sudden presence. She didn't hear any footsteps or shifts in movement to give her stalker away, but every person's body thrummed an unmistakable beat.

"I know you are there."

A face peeked from behind the thick date palm. The kid stepped out of the shade, and immediately Nico noted the heron's feather in his ear. That explained a lot. Not only was he a tent kid, but he was also of the Flock. In Nico's experience, they tended to be self-entitled, spoiled, and dangerous.

"You have made many enemies, Kelin."

"Fortunately, one only needs the right friend. The halfling left you a message. The ru—*Kai,*" the tent kid corrected quickly, "left with Rasia the other day. The halfling went after them."

Nico stared, not comprehending the words for several buzzing vibrations. What did Rasia have to do with all of this? Rasia and Kai have barely said a word to one another, aside from the times Rasia belittled him by laughing and snatching off his shroud.

"I'm sorry, what? Rasia did what?"

"Something about slaying a dragon. I don't know. But your jih went with her."

"How do I know you're telling the truth? How do I know I can trust you?"

"You don't," Kelin said with a smirk, suggesting that she shouldn't, "but I have something that might gain it."

Kelin motioned her deeper into the palm grove, and Nico was aware this could possibly be a trap. But Zephyr had vetted him, and more important to Nico, Kelin had treated Kai equitably compared to all the other Grankull kids. Based on the information she'd gathered, she decided to give this flock kid a chance and followed him into the deep shadows.

Kelin often made fun of her trust by smirking back at her with sharp, deadly amusement and shifting his grip on the curved dagger at his hip. Would he try to kill her? Would he dare try to steal from her? He seemed to be asking these questions with every glance he lobbed at her. But Nico was used to these tent tactics. If Kelin planned to steal from her or do something more unsavory, he would have done it the moment Nico stepped into these trees.

Nico walked into the small camp unafraid and unflinching. As she surveyed the surroundings, Kelin dropped a confused expression before shaking it off and fixing his face.

Kelin brushed aside a thick flooring of fronds to reveal a stash of supplies, weapons, and clothes—no doubt all the items stolen from the other kulls. Kelin studied her for her reaction or for some other indication she was pleased with his gift.

Nico grabbed a hilt sticking out prominently from the pile. She yanked free Zephyr's dagger, the one Zara had gifted for his last birthday, one he would not have left if it weren't meant to be found. Nico inspected the dagger and pulled out a folded message hidden inside the sheath, written on paper torn out of Zephyr's books. In the corner of her eye, she saw Kelin frown. He obviously hadn't known it was there.

Nico opened the message to the airy script of Zephyr's second language. She was still learning it and hadn't had to use it since before Zephyr left on his yearlong sojourn with his father. Nico read the language better than she heard it, and Zephyr wrote his message in short, simple sentences. The different noun-verb order still confused her sometimes, but she understood.

Death Kailjnn courts. Rasia together dragon hunts. Kai safe will keep. Promise.

Bitter storm clouds rolled through Nico's chest. The bruise from where Rasia had punched her began to pulse. *Why would Rasia do this?*

Nico adored Kai, but who in their right mind would ask him to hunt a dragon? He could barely run a vibration without passing out! Nico couldn't imagine any reason other than spite. Was this Rasia's revenge for their failed hunt? How *dare* Rasia drag jih into the middle of this.

Nico crumpled the paper in her hands. Kelin stared wide-eyed at her, in equal parts fear and awe, as the thunder clouds broke and a drizzle of rain slid down their faces. The wet tap of sharp cold reminded Nico that if the oasis overflowed, it could be as disastrous for the Forging kids as getting all their supplies stolen.

Control, Nico reminded herself. She focused on her breathing, inhale and exhale, and stuffed all the rain back where it had pooled. She'd deal with Rasia later. First things first: She had to deal with what was in front of her.

Nico tied Zephyr's dagger to her belt and positioned herself at the end of the cloak beneath all the items and supplies. She looked at Kelin expectantly. "We must deliver these items back to their proper owners, and you must apologize to each person for the strife you have caused them."

Kelin's cool demeanor faltered at the unexpected request.

His face smoothed out quickly, but his eyes remained sharp and calculating. He glanced at the clear sky then clicked his tongue. "Sure."

Kelin grabbed the other corners of the cloak. They tied the ends, wrapped the supplies together into one large sack they could carry between them, and hauled it back the way Nico came.

They arrived at Tarick and Loryn's camp, but it seemed they had dispersed. Nico wondered if the team had gone their separate ways and received her answer when she found Rianis and Gysen with a group on the other side of the oasis. All the kids were grateful and overjoyed to have their belongings back. Hope flared again in their eyes.

Apologizing proved difficult for the tent kid. Kelin could barely hide the disdain in his voice, but nevertheless, he spat out the apology under Nico's watchful eye. She knew Kelin only went through the motions and said what he needed to say to curry her favor, but it was important to Nico. This act was a small thing and would most likely do little to bridge the massive bone border between the Tents and the Grankull, but at least, maybe, it could be a start.

"Thank you, for everything," Faris said to Nico. "Is there anything I can do to repay you? Perhaps join your kull?"

In the distance, the campfire of Nico's kull glowed bright as night cloaked the sky. "I fear that I have priorities other than a gonda. I must find my jih first."

Faris's nose scrunched at the mention of Kai. "It does not matter. I owe you a debt. I'll go through sandstorms if you asked it of me."

Even though chasing after Nico's jih was the last thing Faris wanted to do, he still made the offer. Nico would remember that.

"No," Nico responded. Faris was a kull kid who had grown up on stories of the Desert as Nico had. He knew more intimately how to survive in ways the others didn't. Like the Grankull, everyone had their own strengths and weaknesses, and they'll survive together. "Take care of these kids, and your kull, and yourself. I'll see you on the other side."

"Same, Ohan. Good luck on your hunt, and wary the Hunter."

"Stay wary the Hunter."

Nico turned toward camp, and Kelin stood tall and lean in the waist-length grass, waiting. They had distributed all the supplies and apologies. Kelin could choose to go his own way, but Nico had suspected from the beginning he planned on joining her. He had that distinctive tent kid aura Nico could never emulate, that hungry mentality to survive at all costs.

"You've heard where my priorities lie," Nico told him. "You are free to join me if you wish."

"You deny pretty-bauble over there but willingly agree to my company?"

"You are alone. He isn't."

"I don't need your pity."

"I heard what happened between you and Kai-ji. You're pragmatic, and you are smart enough to know you can't survive out here on your own. It's why you went through all this trouble of gaining my favor, and while apologizing to these kids took a lot of humility to do, I am not impressed by basic acts of decency. And while I'm disappointed when others fail to meet my expectations, even if you refused to give back those supplies and refused to apologize, I wouldn't have denied you. It's not pity. It's the right thing to do."

"That's stupid."

"Kelin, you were *wrong*. You made a grave error in judgment. You thought stealing supplies would get you ahead, and yet now you're alone. This is exactly why many tent kids don't survive the Forging, because they don't comprehend the true purpose of the test. Think about it. There are no limitations to how many can succeed. We aren't competing with one another. The most successful kulls are often the ones that work together. The intended purpose of the Forging is to bind us closer, not pull us apart. You can either be the villain everyone expects of you, or you can survive this Forging. There are many ways of thinking, Kelin, and many ways of surviving."

Kelin stared at her. His response this time was pure emotion, like that of someone who always rolls a red finally winning a round of bones. "You're not who I thought you'd be."

"You'd be surprised to find that's true of everyone. If you wish to join me, know I expect you to treat everyone with the dignity they deserve. Jih's name is Kai. The halfling is Zephyr. These parasites are your teammates—your kull. Learn their names."

Kelin, if anything else, was a quick study. "In that case, do you prefer Ohan, ohani, or Nicolai?"

Nico smiled.

"My First Name is Nicolai. You may call me Nico."

"You said you would be gone just for high noon. It's past sunset!" Neema complained once Nico returned to camp. The kull had been playing a game of rattle-bones around the fire and had been waiting for her to eat dinner.

Suri visibly focused on the shadowed figure arriving beside Nico. "You found him."

She frowned when Kelin stepped into the light of the campfire.

"Found who? Who is he?" Neema asked.

Nico couldn't hide her intentions any longer. "Neema. Azan. I've been lying to you both, but it's time I tell you the truth. At the beginning of the Forging, I wanted us to partner with another kull, potentially Kai-ji's team. He was supposed to be here at the oasis, but it seems Rasia has taken him. I can track jih with my magic, and thus I'm going after them. This means I'm taking the windship."

"The fuck?" Neema jolted to her feet. "Are you rutting kidding me? You were willing to risk our lives for that runt? And now you're abandoning us, your *kull*, to chase after that pathetic piece of shit? My older jih is dead because of him!"

"That is not his fault, Neema. It was Ava-ta who killed your jih. It is my tah who owed your family a blood price."

"*Four innocent children,*" Neema snarled. "That is how many people died for him. A babe born of that much blood is a *monster.*"

Nico knew each and every one of those children's names. When her tah refused to cull Kai as a newborn, the Council decided to take matters into their own hands. They took Kai away while tah slept. In response, in a moment of anger and fury, Ava-ta took the Council's children and slaughtered four of the seven before the Council gave Kai back.

Most repercussions were like a stone skipped across still water, ripples disrupting the surface for a time before returning to normal. But that one moment was instead like rain. It drummed constantly atop the surface. The ripples were never-ending. The raindrops refused to cease. The water was still no longer.

That was how deep one night of duty and anger and rebellion had altered the consciousness of the Grankull.

It was never the same again.

"I understand," Nico said.

"*You understand*?! I lost my jih! She died faceless! You know, Rasia was right. You have no idea what you're doing. You're supposed to be the Ohan. You're supposed to put the needs of the Grankull above everyone else, and yet you're out here wasting your Forging and proving you're no better than your fucking ta-skink. You had me fooled. You have everyone fooled. I hope your jih dies faceless. That's the only blood price I'll ever accept."

Nico stood steady against Neema's righteous anger. "Neema, you don't have to come with me. None of you have to come with me. Plenty of kulls here at the oasis will gladly accept you. They have windships, and you're free to take as much scorpion jerky as you can carry, but a gonda is not my priority right now."

Neema turned to Azan and Suri. "This is our windship too. She can't take it from us. We can't let her do this."

Suri stood beside Nico in solidarity. Nico was thankful for Suri's support, but she had not forgotten Suri's promise to her only a few days before. Nico had no doubt Suri would try to drag her back home if this all crumbled apart.

"This is insane," Neema spat. "Who in their right mind would trek across the Desert searching for the runt? Why should we put our lives on the line for him? If he can't survive on his own, then he shouldn't. Azan, are you with me?"

Azan glanced between Nico and Neema. Nico found herself surprised when Azan took a step forward and stood beside her.

"Azan," Nico said, "you can join another kull. You don't have to follow me. She's right. It's not fair to ask for your help to save my jih. That's my responsibility. It's on me."

Azan shrugged. "I choose you."

"She's going to get you all killed," Neema warned, "like she almost did with the gonda."

"Neema, we failed," Nico said. "*All of us*. But you brush off the sand and try again."

Neema narrowed her eyes at them all, sizing them up, and eventually came to the realization she couldn't take them on alone.

"I damn your bones," Neema spat at Nico's feet before spinning toward the windship. She grabbed her knives, her belongings, and all the scorpion jerky she could carry and disappeared into the night.

"Technically, an ohani has never failed the Forging before, so our odds are still better with you," Kelin pointed out.

It was a fact that weighed heavily on Nico's shoulders. Nico glanced out at the thick blackness of the Desert. She wished she could set out immediately after jih, but Nico had learned her lesson and had a better understanding of what she was capable of. She wouldn't dare steer the windship at night over terrain she couldn't see.

"For right now, let's all get some rest and set out at first light. And thank you, to all of you, for your faith in me. Once we find Kai, I will not give up until we have all succeeded in our Forging. This I promise you, on my name."

CHAPTER TWELVE

O

The runt was a useless pile of skin and bones.

Rasia didn't know why she'd saved him. She'd been racking that moment in her head ever since. She killed the skinko but had attracted the attention of the others. With them all bearing down on her, Rasia had to make a choice. Either abandon the skinko she'd expended so much effort to kill or save the runt.

Everyone had always said he was sick, but no one had ever explained his limitations. At first, Rasia had figured it was something she could work around, but how was she going to slay a dragon with a kid who could barely run half a vibration?

She should have left him.

Rasia was no stranger to danger, but she was used to going at it alone, and before that, she'd had Ysai. He had listened to her, he had respected her, and he wasn't so easily breakable. This was the second time, first Neema and now the runt, that someone in her vicinity had almost gotten themselves killed. Maybe there was a pattern here. Maybe it was her.

Nah. Fuck that. She wasn't going to blame herself for their shortcomings.

Nevertheless, she couldn't sit here and continue drifting with the wind. Rasia took a breath and stared unflinchingly at the sun. She bit down on a piece of rope and pushed against the misaligned rib. She screamed into the palm twine as she adjusted the bone back into place and quickly wrapped her shroud tight around the injury. Her ribs were far worse now than they had been before. A fracture now broken.

Rasia lolled her head toward a nearby scurrying sound and found the runt staring at the garish wound in shock. Finally awake.

"*You*," Rasia seethed.

"*I'm sorry*. I didn't mean for this to happen." The runt quivered, like some cowering mouse. "What can I do to help?"

"What the fuck can you possibly do?! Are you capable of doing anything of actual use?! No, you aren't! Stay the fuck away!" Rasia threw her boot at him for lack of being able to get up and hit him herself. The runt flinched when the boot hit his shoulder. He should be grateful she didn't hit him in the face.

The runt curled into his arms, like a grubworm, and didn't come back up for air.

Rasia slapped her hands atop the deck, then pushed through the pain to stand. She tied off her other boot and left her bloodied shirt on the ground. Barefoot and in nothing but her bandeau and pants, she hopped toward the steer. She leaned against the bone protrusion like a cane and angled the windship headward, toward a trail that wound through mountainous sandstone. During the rainy season, a full river ran through the narrow channel, cutting through the deep gorge.

The blended sandstone narrowed, and Rasia carefully steered the windship through the precarious stone teeth gnawing up from the ground. Most kull ships wouldn't have been able to navigate the sharp twists and turns, but her ship was smaller and a damn fine steer. She guided the ship all the way inside the gorge and parked in front of a yawning, cavernous mouth. Greenery populated the cliff rocks and dry riverbed.

Rasia decided to take the steps down, figuring they were safer. She tossed a foot on the worn steps.

Then slipped.

Her head hit the hull before she crashed down to the rocky

ground. On top of it all, she bit her tongue. Rasia stared, stunned, at the bright sky. She blamed the sun for all the bad luck she seemed to be soaking in.

The runt leaned into her field of vision, wide-eyed and concerned. She shoved a hand right into his stupid face.

Rasia squeezed her eyes shut, took a breath, and forced her limbs to move. Every part of her screamed. It had been a long time since Rasia had hurt this badly, not since the shadowcats. She'd had Ysai back then, but now she didn't have anyone but herself.

"Let me help you," the runt insisted uncertainly, offering a tentative hand but never quite touching her. She hated how uncertain he was with the way he moved and the way he spoke, too scared to move about the world. It annoyed her. Besides, he barely looked as if he could hold his own weight, much less hers.

Rasia pushed him away, again.

She focused on getting her knees under her. There was a cave, so she didn't have to bother expending energy setting up the windship for camp. All she had to do was create a fire so she didn't freeze at night. Then she could pass out and sleep this off.

Rasia found her feet, then lost them. She tipped over, and that's when the runt surged forward, catching her before her face became reacquainted with the ground. How pathetic of her. She couldn't find the energy to break his hold.

"I don't need your help. If I were out here on my own, I'd have no choice but to push through and get done what needed to get done."

"But you're not alone."

"I might as well be," Rasia said, even as she clung tighter to the runt's arm to make sure she didn't fall. It took too much effort to stand, nor did she feel like falling again.

"You're right," the runt said as he adjusted her over his shoulder. "I can't do much of anything. I'm no healer. I can't fight or run very far, but at the least, you can lean on me to help you stand. You saved my life when you didn't have to, and I refuse to let anyone else die for me. You can keep pushing me away, but I'll keep coming back."

Rasia spat at the ground and watched her feet shuffle forward with every one of his steps. "I'm not dying, especially not for you."

"Good."

It felt like an eternity trying to reach that cave. They were both breathing heavily by the time the runt sat her down against the damp cave wall. He wiped sweat from his forehead and looked around the shelter in confusion. There were ash marks of past fires and the faint impressions of old footprints. A rock ramp led to a higher level where Rasia knew bedrolls and supplies were tucked away into shelves. A faded charcoal symbol of the trinity had been etched into the cave's entrance—a rod for the Elder, a horizon for the Desert, and a circle for Death.

"It's a kull camp," Rasia explained. The kulls had these camps all throughout the Desert, specifically to prepare meat they couldn't take back to the Grankull before spoiling. "They should have some herbs and fresh bandages stashed, but first we need a fire. Can your twig little arms even do that?"

"I can make a fire."

"I'll believe it when I see it." A lot of kids thought they knew how to make a fire until they were stuck with naught but their bare hands. "Good luck finding the right wood for a bow drill."

The runt gave her a hard, disbelieving look. "Where do you keep the flint? In the hatch under the mast, steer, or the nest?"

Rasia admittedly paused. She hadn't thought he had been paying any attention. For that, she'd let him call her out on her horseshit.

"The mast."

The runt nodded and immediately set himself to the task without complaint. He disappeared out of the cave into the harsh light of the sun.

At least he listened.

Rasia adjusted her bandeau to relieve that nagging back pain and closed her eyes. She took a moment to bask in the coolness of the cave. She smelled the water in the air and heard the wellspring drip deeper in the tunnels. During the rainy season, rain trickled and filtered through the sandstone cliffs to overflow the wellspring and form a river vomiting up the cave's mouth. The kulls hung herbs from the ceiling in bat bushels to avoid the rainy-season river.

Rasia slid her eyes open at the distinct crackling sound of fire. The runt had returned and was now nursing a small flame in his nest of kindling. He placed it under the tented dry sticks and twigs he'd gathered from outside and breathed his tiny flame into a campfire. Rasia watched the light tiptoe on his small, satisfied smile.

He looked at her, the smile gone as if it had been a figment of the shadows. "What's next, now that we have a fire?"

Rasia shimmied into a sitting position. "I grabbed some scorpion meat from your jih and put it in the underbelly. It needs to be cooked before it spoils."

Rasia watched judgmentally as the runt found the spit frame and dragged it over to the fire. He set it up correctly and soon had the scorpion meat dripping fat into the flames.

He cooked. That much was obvious. So . . . one not useless thing. That was sure to be helpful against a dragon.

Rasia couldn't believe she was stuck relying on the runt, of all people, for help. Every time she shifted and felt the sharp, stabbing pain of her ribs, it made her angry. She didn't make mistakes like this.

"I thought this is what I wanted," Rasia bemoaned. She hit her head back against the rough cave wall. "I was going to crush Shamai-ta's record for the Forging, then become a kull leader just like him. But being on a team *sucks*. I have to constantly worry about other people and no one listens to what I have to say . . . but they listen to Nico! Despite the fact she obviously doesn't know what she is doing. I just . . . I don't understand how tah did it. *Why is this so hard?*"

The runt looked at her, then quickly returned to rotating the meat over the fire.

"What? Do you have something to say?"

He shrugged.

"Spit it out."

The runt looked back at her, opened his mouth, closed it, scrunched his brow, and, after a slow, torturous moment of silence, he finally replied, "You don't need a kull."

"Well, yeah, no shit."

Rasia couldn't believe after all that waiting, he says the most obvious thing in the world.

"No. I mean . . . A windship is so large that everyone on the kull has their assigned tasks, right? Everyone is important and essential in operating the windship. But you've designed your windship to only need one person to operate it. Your windship no longer has space or room for other people." He paused, "I'm surprised you didn't go after the dragon alone."

"I'm not stupid," Rasia said, hotly. "I *can* defeat a dragon by myself, but I don't have the time. I would have to memorize the dragon's movements, I'd have to set traps, and I'd need to collect the supplies for those traps. It would take me blinks of planning to go at it by myself. If I am going to kill this thing by the time the Forging ends, I need help. But I . . . I've never been good with people."

"People have never been good with me," the runt said in turn, with a shrug. He handed Rasia a leaf bowl of meat and wild figs he had foraged from the gorge during her brief nap. It was annoyingly well-cooked.

She looked at the runt with a sudden thought.

"What was your plan in all this? How by the Elder were you going to help me defeat a dragon?"

The runt said, completely serious and straight-faced, "Distraction? I figured it'll take a while for a dragon to eat me."

Rasia gave a sharp laugh and groaned at the pain of it. "We are small enough for a dragon to swallow us whole. It'll only take a vibration."

"I guess I am entirely useless then."

"I don't know about that. You can cook," Rasia said. She inhaled the last of her portion. She looked over to where the runt picked at his own food, frowning at it. "Out of all the kids at the oasis, you were the only one who agreed to join me. You confronted a skinko with a bow you didn't know how to use. For all your patheticness, you are brave, and that counts for something."

The runt stared at Rasia, caught off guard by the compliment. He quickly dismissed it. "Bravery is not the same as idiocy. It was certainly the latter."

"Sometimes bravery and idiocy are the same," Rasia said, amused.

Rasia laid down on the ground, twisted to find a position that didn't hurt so much, and settled in for sleep. She yawned. "Take watch."

After a moment, she peeked an eye open and glanced at him.

"You can, at the very least, yell for help?" He looked at her grumpily. "Don't look at me like that. I didn't know you could talk until yesterday. Who's to say you won't run out of breath screaming?"

"Go to sleep, Rasia."

"I'm just saying. And don't forget to feed the fire. If that fire goes out on your watch, I'll murder you."

"I imagine it wouldn't be too hard."

Rasia snoghtered (that's a snort + a laugh) as she turned over and mumbled into sleep, "And for fuck's sake, stop making me laugh. It *huuurts*."

Rasia slept most of the day. She woke several drums into the night and found the runt dutifully minding the fire. She imagined him crouched over the flames, studying for any signs of wilt or hunger, for drums on end. Judging by the considerable lack of dusty footprints in other parts of the cave, that's probably exactly what he did. Rasia's endless curiosity would have compelled her to explore under every rock and poke her head into every crevice. Rasia studied him as if he were the strangest creature she had ever come upon in the Desert.

Rasia rolled across the rocky ground, all the way around the fire, toward him. The unexpected movement jolted the runt from his feet, then he looked down at her strangely, as if she were the strangest thing he had ever come upon in the Desert.

"Are you feeling better?" He asked.

"Better than before. Now get some sleep. Shoo. It's my turn at watch." He stared at her a moment longer, then nodded. He took her place along the cave wall and curled into the warmth she had left behind.

Rasia really did feel better. She still hurt, but at least it felt less like her insides were going to come spilling out at any moment. She watched the runt sleep for a few vibrations, took a deep breath, and rolled to her feet.

Perhaps she couldn't hunt a dragon by herself, but it didn't mean she shouldn't try.

She packed her belongings and a few extra items from the kull stash onto the windship. As she packed, she didn't understand this ugly feeling of guilt in the pit of her stomach.

It's not as if she could take the runt with her. He'd surely end up dead, nor was she leaving him behind to die either. He had water and food here, and she'd decided to leave the spare flint behind. He could survive until the end of the Forging or until his jih found him. He'd live, so why did she feel so twisted up inside?

The ugly truth was that Rasia enjoyed his company. They got along, and Rasia never got along with anyone. He listened and trusted her judgment. He was funny and aware of his lack of skill and experience. He was the one that said, "Okay."

For a brief time, Rasia had regained that easy camaraderie she once had with her big jih. A selfish, ugly part of her wanted to keep it. A more vulnerable, soft part refused to admit she didn't want to be alone anymore.

Better lonely than to get someone killed because he couldn't keep up. She wasn't her tah, and that transparent truth scraped harsh across her bones. She wasn't the leader he was. People liked Shamai-ta like they liked Ysai, but Rasia, for all the feats she could accomplish, couldn't inspire people to follow her.

The runt was right. Rasia could only be herself: a kull of one.

Rasia prepared the windship to sail. From atop the deck, she took one last look at the cave and froze at the sight of the runt standing at the entrance. She wondered how long he'd been standing there. She felt awkward and wondered if she should say goodbye. But she refused to apologize for doing what she had to do. He was dead weight. She couldn't afford to bring him along.

"I understand," he said, face without a hint of anger or betrayal. He looked resigned. "I hope you slay your dragon."

And that frustrated Rasia the most, because he understood. He didn't argue. He didn't hate her for it. He wished her all the best.

Rasia despised being stuck in a corner like this. Her tah had once told her that her true strength lay not in her sword arm, or in her foolhardy fearlessness, but in her imagination, in her ability to look not at what a thing was supposed to be, but what a thing had the potential to be. Where others saw a corner, she saw a springboard.

It hit her like thunder. First tingling in her toes, then traveling with excitement up her spine. She looked at the runt and saw him for the first time—not what he was supposed to be, but what he had the potential to be.

"*Kai.*"

Broken rib forgotten, Rasia jumped from the windship (terrible idea and she'll pay for it later). She scrambled over to him, catching him by the shoulders. "What do you know about windships?"

". . . nothing . . .?"

"Perfect," Rasia cheered. "That means you have no bad habits. I can teach you how to steer a windship. Think about it. All it requires is knowledge and skill and experience with the terrain. Even you, with your disability, should be able to do that much. With you steering the ship, it will open me up to all kinds of offensive maneuvers against the dragon. It could work. What do you say? Want to be my windeka?"

Kai responded without hesitation.

"Okay."

CHAPTER THIRTEEN

—

Rasia stayed.

In the haze of Kai's exhaustion last night, the entire scene had felt surreal. Kai didn't question the memory of Rasia boarding her ship and preparing to set sail, but in what reality does Rasia offer anyone a second chance? An unreliable sense of hope began to return in vague and formless fragments.

No. Hope had betrayed him before. It had stabbed him in the stomach and left him barely alive. If Kai ever deigned to forget those painful lessons, it would no doubt rip him apart all over again.

Thankfully, Rasia didn't give him time to dwell on the shadows of his hopes as she dragged him out of cave and shoved him toward the windship. She had dismantled most of the windship's contraptions, all the jerry-rigging Rasia used to steer the ship by herself.

"What happened?" Kai asked.

"I made space," Rasia said triumphantly. "It's no longer a one-person ship. It is now a kulani!"

Kai eyes widened as he felt the creep of a blush. "Kulani" can literally mean "a kull of two," but the word was never used to describe the size of a kull. Instead, it was colloquially used to describe two people in a deeply committed relationship, like how "kulo" can mean a kull of one but was more often than not used as a slur for someone who was extremely selfish."

Rasia rolled her eyes. "You know what I meant."

Kai nodded his head quickly. Of course, he did. That's not a word anyone would ever use to address him.

Rasia clapped her hands and paced a circle around the windship deck. "Okay, we'll start with the different parts of the ship . . . or maybe we should start with what everything does? I think that's what the teachers do. No, maybe we should . . ." Rasia spun toward Kai. "This is my first time teaching anyone anything before. I'm not sure where to start."

Kai asked, patient and curious, "How did you learn about windships?"

"Shamai-ta dropped me and jih off in the middle of the Desert and told us to figure out how to get home."

"Oh," Kai said, blinking. That probably wouldn't work for him.

"But you know, I've grown up on a windship my entire life," Rasia said. She wobbled her fingers, baby steps, across the railing. She walked the stiff wood away from him and lingered on the scruffs and scars, soothing the wounds with a thumb.

"Apparently, I was a nightmare of a baby. Can you believe that?" Rasia's back was turned to Kai, but he could tell she was laughing by the way her shoulders rose. "The way tah told it, I refused to sleep. I was a terror, until one night, tah strapped me to his back and took me out to make repairs to a kull ship. He set the ship to sail, and suddenly . . . there was silence. Ever since that night, a ship rocked me to sleep."

"That's where it started. I learned how to walk on a windship deck. I played on it while tah drilled his hunting kull. Ysai-ji and I helped with repairs, learned how to construct the wheels and strengthen the hull. During downtime between hunts, he'd take me and jih out to chase wind currents or to the oases to swim. But at night . . ." Her voice softened. Her back still turned, she whispered to the mast, "the night was our time. That never changed. We sailed a sea of stars together . . ."

Her voice cracked. ". . . and now he's gone. All because of a stupid fucking rock."

That's . . . not exactly how Kai understood what happened. Two years ago, gonda had attacked the Grankull. Shamaijen Windbreaker had been helping with the evacuations, when an entire adobe spire had collapsed on top of him. They say an injury to the head from a piece of debris was what ultimately killed him, even though he died days later. Kai certainly wasn't about to correct her version of events. Grief did weird and illogical things.

Kai had lost Ava-ta in that same incident, when she had died saving him. Even two years later, when you thought you'd climbed the mountain of grief, sometimes you slipped, and it all came rolling back on top of you. Kai didn't think Rasia was the type of person to welcome condolences or comfort, and Kai knew all too well that empty sentiments, and sometimes even sincere ones, did little to catch your fall. Still, he felt compelled to respond in some way.

Kai took a step forward, creaking the deck of the windship and the sound reminded Rasia her and her memories weren't alone. Rasia spun on her heel as if nothing had happened.

"Anyway," Rasia said, forcing the conversation forward. "Before the day tah abandoned me and jih in the Desert, I already knew what parts did what. I knew how to fix them. I knew how a kull functioned. I never really had to learn, so I'm not exactly sure where to start."

"I-I . . ." Kai stammered. "I liked Shamaijen Windbreaker. He was kind to me."

Kai didn't know why he needed to tell her this, but it was important. Kai always remembered those few who had shown him kindness. "He always acknowledged my existence. And I know that I can never miss him as much as you do, but I do . . . miss him. He was an amazing person."

Rasia smiled to herself, smug. "He was."

Kai stepped to her carefully, slowly, but finally certain of the words he needed to say. "This ship has so much of his memory, and I know teaching me about all of this can't be easy, but thank you, for sharing him with me."

"This ship is all I have of him . . . and, you know . . ." Rasia touched her forehead. "What's in here."

She moved her legs where she sat atop the railing and curled them against her chest, to make room for him. Kai occupied the space she left behind. He almost felt as if he were stepping inside of her, how close they were, and Kai made sure to treat the open wounds with care.

"Isn't it customary to write the names of lost kull members onto the mast?" Kai asked. It was a common gesture when a kull member retired or, more often than not, met the face of Death.

"We did." Rasia frowned, her face scrunching in displeasure. "I had a run-in with that skink of a dragon a year ago. Almost completely wrecked the ship, and I couldn't recover the mast. The one I have now is new, but I haven't been able to replace tah's name because Ysai-ji is always so rutting busy with *Ji-lah*. And I can't read. Or write. Whatever."

Rasia shrugged, pretending to be unfazed even though Kai could tell by her defensive posture that it bothered her immensely.

"I can teach you," Kai suggested after a moment. Rasia laughed in the next beat, and Kai hunched his shoulders. Many didn't think him capable of reading.

"And here I thought *I'm* supposed to be teaching *you*," Rasia said. Her laughter melted away the previous melancholy. "Don't bother. What do I need to know how to read for?"

"Don't kulls exchange messages from one to the other?"

From her crouch, Rasia stretched to a standing position and balanced her heels atop the railing with ease. Rasia might have been shorter than average, but she was built solid, and Kai never worried she might fall. She regarded him with a raised brow. "I thought you didn't know anything about windships."

"I've read stories," Kai said defensively. "I know some things. I know that there are five roles in a kull."

"Oh, really?" Kai whipped around when Rasia hopped from the railing. She looped her arm around the mast to circle herself around to face him again. "And what are each of these roles for?"

Kai gave the answer written in the temple library. "The five positions in a kull are the Scout, the Han, the Windeka, and the two Oars. The Oars row the ship when the wind is adverse, they use their weight to turn the outriggers, and they are the primary offensive arms in a hunt. The Scout watches for terrain obstacles and predators and is proficient with long-distance weapons. The Han is the leader and typically your most experienced kull member. The Han knows the terrain, the animals, and the Desert. The Han determines the course of the hunt. The Windeka steers the ship."

"Boring. *Boring*. And wrong."

"What?"

"I've been on a windship deck when the horseshit hits the hull, and it's the kulls that assign themselves clear-cut roles that struggle the most. When my tah trains a kull, he trains every member to do everything. Fuck the scrolls. If you think it takes five people to operate a windship, that's all you'll ever know how to do."

Rasia pointed to the slim opening of the canyon and all the sharp and treacherous rocks in between.

"When you can make it out of this canyon, you're ready. I can talk at you all you want, you can *read* about it all you want," Rasia mocked, "but you're never going to learn until you do it."

Kai eyed the terrifying distance he would have to overcome. Back at the Grankull, children went to school and learned about windships for years before anyone allowed them to steer one. Figuring out how to steer a windship by himself seemed insurmountable. He felt overwhelmed and in over his head, already resigned to failure.

"Hey, don't get your shroud in a twist. I'm going to show you how to do it . . . *once*."

"What if I can't?" Kai asked. "What if I crash the ship? What if I can't figure it out in time?"

Rasia inclined an eyebrow so sharply, repugnance hiked across her face. "You know what I hate about you? You don't believe in yourself. Nico, for all her faults, at least believes in every one

122

of her stupid decisions. You're never going to be able to steer a windship if you don't think you can. Now where is that kid from the oasis brave enough to join my kull and take on a dragon? Where is that kid that faced a skinko without hesitation? Where is your *hunger*, Kai?"

Kai stared wide-eyed at Rasia, trembling at the rawness and sharpness of her words. Rasia thought him brave, but in truth, all the actions she praised him for, he did because he had nothing to lose. But staring out at that great chasm, it felt as if he could lose everything. Because this was finally his chance to be something, to have skills that were valued, to prove to himself he was capable of more than the death and destruction that follows him. But how could he *not* fail when he had failed at so much already?

Either reading his thoughts or reading his face, Rasia declared, "You *will* fail, but then you try again. And if you can't figure it out by the time I heal? We go our separate ways, you survive this Forging, then meet me after it's all done and try again. You fight for it, and don't stop fighting till you're dead. Never give up. Or do you want to be a worthless piece of shit for the rest of your life?"

Kai shook his head.

"Words, Kai. I know you can use them."

". . . no?"

"Say. It. Like. You. Fucking. Mean. It."

Kai blinked at her, unable to force the words from his mouth because he didn't believe, and he knew Rasia was too perceptive not to hear his lack of conviction. Kai would work hard and put his all into the task, but he didn't have the courage to imagine himself capable of anything more.

He was Kai. The runt. Worthless.

"I won't give up," he said, because that, at least, he could promise. All he had in him to give was day by day, one rock at a time. Kai saw the moment Rasia's understanding of him shifted, how it wobbled from solid ground to uncertainty. He wasn't the person she thought he was, and he hated himself for disappointing her.

"Fine," Rasia yielded. "I'll hold you to that."

Rasia shoved Kai toward the stairs of the ship. "I'm hungry. Fix me breakfast."

"But what about the windship?" Even though they were barely second drum into the morning, Kai felt he needed as much time as possible to learn how to steer the ship. Kai hesitated on the edge of the stairs.

"I can push you down or you can climb down. Take your pick. But one of those options will break your neck and you can kiss this whole windship thing goodbye."

Kai chose breakfast.

Back at the Grankull, Kai cooked with dried fruit, jams, grains, and salted meat. The Grankull often reserved fresh fruit after the harvest, so Kai found himself pleased by the opportunity to pluck ripe figs from the trees sprawled along the canyon rocks. He searched through the kull supplies for other ingredients he could use and found himself surprised by the sizable stash of items ranging from soaps to oils and twine to liquor. Kai reached for one of the skillets overhead and stumbled over a bag of salt. A sharp clang struck the cave.

Kai picked up the ilhan that had fallen to the ground and paused when he saw the carved symbol under his thumb. He angled the palmwood neck of the instrument toward the firelight and stared at the swooping symbols of Kenji's name.

Kai imagined the ilhan sitting vertically between Kenji's legs. Kenji plucked at the goat strings with his forefingers while the remaining fingers curled around the two handposts drilled at the top of the resonating gourd. Kenji played the strings inward, toward his chest, and the melodious music swelled in Kai's memories.

Kai shook his head, fleeing the memories as quickly as he

scurried along the walls of his home. Kai heaved up the ilhan to tip the skillet into his hand, stuffed the instrument back where he found it, and returned to the campfire to begin cooking.

Kai liked cooking. It made him feel useful, and it settled his nerves. Kai cooked a fig porridge using water from the spring and the sacks of millet, which were definitely not part of the Grankull's initial Forging supplies, that he'd found in Rasia's windship hatch.

As Kai cooked, he went over everything he knew about windships, every story he'd read and overheard, and every lesson Nico had recounted from school. As he finished, Rasia entered the wide-mouthed entrance of the cave, sweaty from a round of early morning katas.

"I thought you broke a rib."

"I'm going slow," Rasia huffed. She took a deep swig of water.

Kai handed breakfast over in one of the calabash bowls he'd found in the kull supplies. Rasia theatrically eased down onto the ground.

"Here's the schedule," Rasia said as Kai sat across from her. "First thing in the morning, we'll put you through light exercises, nothing too extensive like the hunting kull's regimen, but for this to work, you've got to at least be able to run the length of a windship deck. We'll run through some drills, then I'll show you how to steer the windship out of the gorge. We'll break at high noon, and the rest of the day you're on your own."

Kai nodded as he aimlessly stirred the spoon in his porridge. Rasia's gaze narrowed sharply.

"You're starving."

"What?" Kai asked, confused by the non sequitur. "Everyone is starving."

"Not what I meant. When Aurum broke my mast, my ship was so wrecked it left me stranded in the deadlands. When they say that place is dead, they aren't kidding. There's nothing to eat. By the time it took me to intercept a kull ship, I had eaten, at the most, a single mouse. When I got back to the Grankull, I was hungry as fuck but could barely keep food down. Without food, your body gets accustomed to going without. That's why you're struggling to eat. That's probably why you're so rutting sick all the time."

Kai didn't feel like talking anymore. He hunched his shoulders and stared blankly. Kai thought he was over it, that it had cooled, but apparently, it had been sitting on him until it could catch flames again.

"Ava-ta didn't know what was wrong with me, nor do the healers." The words fell from his mouth, hard and heavy, like burnt and bitter charcoals. "All my life, there has never been an explanation to why I am the way I am, and you suggest the reason I'm so messed up is because *I need to eat*?"

"Well, yeah," Rasia said, doubling down. "Obviously, the healers don't know everything. How would they know what it's like to starve for a prolonged period of time? They get rations. And maybe you're right. It's not that simple. There could be a million different things wrong with you. But I know for certain whatever is wrong, it will never get fixed until you eat." Rasia slapped her hands on her knees and leaned forward to stab him with her gaze. "When is the last time you've actually had an appetite? The last time you've eaten a full meal? How many times do you shit?"

Kai leaned away from both the intensity and intimacy of her questions. To be honest, Kai couldn't remember the last time he ate a full meal, but certainly that couldn't be the answer to a medical mystery that had stumped the Grankull for years.

"I'm just sick," Kai insisted.

"*And* you're starving. I don't see why it can't be both." Rasia rolled forward from her crouched position to poke a finger into his shoulder. Kai stared at that finger, affronted, but did nothing to stop it. "Operating a windship is about more than figuring out how things work. It requires all your attention and energy. You need to feed your body. You need to take care of it. Scratch everything I said before. As your first official lesson, I demand you eat."

It was so at odds with his life in the Grankull, where no one cared if he ate little. Kai looked at the insurmountable food in his bowl, and his stomach lurched in violent protest. It was hard to commit yourself to doing something you didn't think was very important. "I don't see the point. So what if I don't eat much? That's more rations for you, and they'll last longer."

"Uh, no, Kai. You don't eat anything at all. Crumbs isn't a meal and honestly, I'm shocked you're still alive. Look, if we are going to be a kull, I need to know you've got my back. I need to not constantly be worried you're going to faint on me . . . oh, like you did yesterday."

"I'm sick!"

"*People are stupid*, Kai. They look at you and see what they want to see and automatically assume that's the problem without seeing the obvious. Take your shirt off, Kai. I bet I can count your ribs."

Kai hugged his chest defensively. She was wrong. It wasn't hunger that had hollowed out his body. It was this disease that had no name, that burned his lungs and ate him from the inside out, that had twisted him into something monstrous.

"There's no point, like you don't see a point in learning to read. It's better this way. This way, I'm less of a burden to the Grankull."

"But it makes you more a burden to *me*." Rasia jolted to her feet in her anger. Kai didn't understand why she was so frustrated and angry on his behalf. "A kull isn't a place where one person starves for everyone else. When there is food, we eat our bellies full. When there is none, we starve together. That's what it means to be a kull. If you don't eat, you're going to end up dead."

Rasia paced after her thoughts as though they were shadows on the cave wall, then walked over and sat down so close, her knees touched his. "Teach me how to read, and in exchange, promise me you'll eat. One pointless task for another."

That seemed reasonable enough.

"Deal," Kai agreed.

Rasia shoved the bowl of food into Kai's chest, like a shroud thrown down in challenge. Kai took a spoonful of the porridge and stared down at that miniscule portion. Suddenly, the chasm he needed to conquer with the windship seemed easier.

This shouldn't be so hard.

Why was this so hard?

Kai forced a huge chunk into his mouth before he could think more about it. Every swallow was a battle—an exertion of determination, sweat, and a little bit of vomit. Kai hardly thought this task worth so much effort and trouble, but Rasia sat there urging him on.

He gasped at the end, feeling wrung out and exhausted by the time he consumed the last bite. He stared down at the bowl, at this simple task of eating that most people did three times a day and felt ashamed of how arduous it had been. This shouldn't have been one of the the hardest thing he'd ever done in his entire life.

Kai curled around himself, feeling ill and taxed of all the strength he had allotted for the windship. He breathed for a while, then opened his eyes when Rasia pressed a cool gourd to his forehead. He didn't understand why she wanted to be around him after witnessing such a pathetic display.

Rasia pushed at his shoulder.

"Enough lying about. Come on, let's go. Time for those laps."

Kai groaned, took a drink of water from the gourd she gave him, and crawled after her. He followed her out into the sun, farther down the canyon path, and out onto the endless stretch of sand and red rocks.

"All right, for this first time, I want to see what you've got. Give it your all. Run as far and as fast as you can. It'll give me a good sense of where we need to start."

Kai stared down at the endless expanse of Desert and realized he had never *run* before, at least not until the skinko. Even as a child, he had always been confined to the sidelines under Avata's protective shadow. In the Grankull, there were too many alleyways and too many animals and people out on the street to break out into a headlong run. You would have to go to the training fields or the school for the space to really gather your wind, and those destinations had always been far from his home, especially if you had no purpose being there.

All these thoughts weighed on him as Rasia began to count down. Then, she shouted: "Go!"

Kai ran and immediately found himself annoyed by the inconvenience of his caftan. It restricted his movements and threatened to tangle up around his legs, and in one particular instance, a gust of wind blew it up too high. Kai caught the billowing cloth, hiking the hem above his thighs to give his legs full range of motion. Kai slid to a stop when he felt the oncoming burn in his chest. He glanced back at the distance he covered and thinks he had made it farther than when he had run away from the skinko.

Kai looked at Rasia, somewhat confident.

Rasia burst into a towering, tumbling laughter. She folded over her knees and grasped at her right side as she crumbled, and then curled over into the sand. She didn't stop laughing until she was out of breath, and even then, it slowly petered out of her in random chuckles. "That was the worst thing I have ever seen in my entire life!"

She rocked into a sitting position and looked at him. Kai tensed defensively, knowing he had messed up. This was the moment where Rasia would decide to leave him behind.

"Okay . . . where to even begin? First, the wind is working against you with all that flopping around you're doing. Form, Kai, *form*. Second, the fuck you stop for? You don't run until it hurts. You run until you've got nothing left. Third, you're thinking too much. Fourth, *go change into some pants, for fuck's sake*."

Kai blinked at her. "I didn't bring any."

"What?"

For Kai's first Forging, Nico had gone through so much effort to personally tailor an old pair of Ava-ta's pants for him just for them to be ripped and destroyed by the first kull who had abandoned him. This Forging, he hadn't even bothered.

Rasia studied his face, her eyes and nose scrunched, and clicked her tongue. "You come out here to die, Kai?"

Kai honestly didn't know the answer to that.

"A basic pair of pants isn't that expensive. The only person who comes into the Forging without at least one pair is the person who doesn't expect to come out of it."

Rasia stood up and left, leaving Kai to wallow alone in his murky emotions. He wiped at the tears drying sticky on his face, feeling more adrift than he ever had in his entire life. He rubbed at the mild burning in his chest, then flinched as an item hurtled toward him. It hit him at the heart and flopped to the ground. Kai stared at the fallen linen pants.

"*Put them on*," Rasia said, exasperated.

Kai quickly picked them up to, if anything, save them from the sandy ground. He clutched the fabric to his chest. He appreciated Rasia's thoughtfulness, but he had nothing to wear them with. "I didn't bring a shirt."

Her eye twitched. She clawed at her back, ripped her shirt over her head, and threw it at his face. He caught it this time before it reached the ground.

The shirt's absence revealed the dirty bandages wrapped around Rasia's waist and a frayed wrap, common for females of the hunting kulls, tapered around her breasts. Kai hadn't seen her shroud since they met. Even after the Forging, most people continued to carry it around, either in the event of a sandstorm or for simple tasks like wiping at sweat, but Rasia had completely discarded it. Or maybe it was that yellowed piece of cloth holding her ribs together.

Rasia flung out her hands impatiently.

He peeped out, "Can you turn around?"

"You are rutting ridiculous. I do know you don't have a tail or some such shit. I saw that pretty fucking clearly when your robe flew up," Rasia said, spinning on her heel and huffing.

Kai blushed and turned his back to her back, self-conscious. A part of him wondered what would happen if he disrobed completely in front of her. Would it be like years ago when Rasia snatched off his shroud and spat out, utterly baffled and disappointed, "Where's your horns? What the fuck?" before proceeding to throw his shroud back at him and stomping off.

Would she finally glimpse the monster she hadn't seen that day?

His hands trembled as he peeled off the dirty robe; he cringed at the sun-warmth and open air on his skin. He pulled on the shirt first, then the pants over his loincloth, and secured the pants' leather waistband. Expensive pants were often crafted with gonda leather around the waist and ankles to prevent sand from creeping into unwanted places. Kai had never worn it before, and immediately he understood why everyone claimed gonda leather was more durable, flexible, and cooler than most animal skins. It barely heated in the sun.

"Looking better already," Rasia said over her shoulder, peeking.

"I can't wear this. I've never worn anything this expensive in my entire life."

"It's fine. Kiba-ta bought them for me for the Forging, so these are pretty much new." Rasia skipped over and didn't hesitate to adjust the clothes. She tucked the loaned shirt into the pants, then tightened the leather cords of the belt waist. She grumbled under her breath, "You're so fucking tiny."

Kai jumped when she drummed her fingers up his rib bones, counting them out loud. Rasia laughed at the reaction, then skipped back and looked him over with an approving nod. "You can keep them."

"Rasia, I can't."

"I still have a good set that the favorite tah secretly gifted me for my birthday a few years ago." Rasia indicated the obviously well-tended, patched, lengthened, and restitched pants she currently wore. "Also, Ysai-ji has pants he constantly grows out of. The stuff he doesn't give to our cousins he retailors for me, so I have a lot."

"Yeah, but how many outfits did you bring for the Forging?" Most kids only brought a set of two outfits to switch out when the other pair got dirty.

"Initially two, but I have another set in my windship. I learned to always bring spares . . . especially since I bleed on everything once a blink."

Kai couldn't help but to look down at the pants.

"They're washed."

"Okay!"

"Now that we got that out of the way, let's get back to running and proper form."

"Wait, Rasia." Kai clutched the hem of the shirt, the fabric soft and lived-in. "Thank you, for everything, but . . . why? Why the food? Why the pants?"

Why me?

Rasia pursed her lips. 'Because I think you and I could form a pretty solid kull . . . once we straighten out the knots and all," she said as if it should have been obvious. "A kull is more than roles to operate a windship. It's a family. It's the people you hunt with, sometimes blinks on end, and while you *are* utterly pathetic, at least you're hilariously pathetic. So, you're tolerable. I'm willing to see what you can do, but it's impossible to gauge the possibilities if you're constantly limiting yourself. Eat like you're fucking worth something. Dress like you're fucking worth something. Run like you're fucking worth something. You'll never fly if you're clipping your own wings. Understand?"

Kai nodded.

"Words. I'm tired of fucking talking at air."

"I understand."

"Good." Rasia looped an arm around Kai's shoulder and pulled him close, unflinching and unapologetic. "You may not believe it yet, but one day soon, you and I are going to slay a dragon."

Kai was feeling that hope thing again.a

CHAPTER FOURTEEN

O

It had only been a day in the grand experiment of Rasia's teaching academy. Thus far, Rasia had performed every kata she knew, rummaged through all the kull supplies, sharpened her weapons, collected ingredients for a soup, and even took a bath in the cave springs. She was trying to give Kai space to learn things on his own, but she was extremely bored.

Teaching is so hard.

It was about time to check on his progress.

Rasia hopped over and observed Kai struggling to shove the windship back into place. It took him three times as long to get the windship back to the starting position than it took him to prepare it for sail. She climbed on board the ship as Kai prepared to make another attempt. Step by step, he followed all the actions Rasia had taken the day before, even completing knots stroke for stroke that she'd only shown him how to do once.

When he went to adjust the sail, Rasia tested, shouting at him, "Wrong!"

Kai jumped and stared at Rasia, wide-eyed. He turned back to the sail, reassessed, and readjusted in the wrong direction. Rasia made snide comments over every little action. Her presence threw him off so much so that when Kai reached for the steer, Rasia gripped her hand around the railing to brace for the inevitable disaster.

The windship remained still. Kai narrowed his eyes at her accusingly, having tested her in an evaluation meant for him. He had figured out she was fucking with him. Kai stomped over and fixed the prior things he had done wrong and rechecked all the things he had done right. Rasia was sort of impressed.

By the time Kai returned to the steer, he had the windship prepared in the exact way Rasia had shown him yesterday, down to every last detail.

Kai unanchored the ship and sailed past the first rock fine, but the second rock came so quickly that the steer did not have enough thrust alone to turn the ship in time. Normally, one would use the outrigger, but in this scenario, it was located on the impact side of the ship. When Rasia had made the pass yesterday, she had used one of the oars to push the ship out of the way of the rock.

Kai ran with the oars. Predictably, he failed to run down-length before the outrigger scraped against the second rock. The windship came to a slow stop, and Kai slid to his knees in frustration.

Rasia walked over and kicked up the oar with her foot, catching it in her hand. "You know you're not fast enough. There's no one right way to do a thing. Nor are you going to succeed always doing everything 'Rasia's way.' You've got to figure out the right way for you."

Sometimes it was the hardest thing for people to do—to step outside the rules and find yourself in the loopholes. Rasia observed the furrow in Kai's brow as he thoughtfully took in different parts of the ship. She smiled when he began experimenting and testing different configurations with the ropes and the oars.

To get out of the gorge, you had to raise the ship's speed high enough to move along the hard dirt but slow enough to maneuver around the rocks. Going fast and going slow were easy, but maintaining speed in the middle was hard. Kai understood that problem after his first attempt.

That understanding persisted in the way he looped ropes about the mast and climbed to the scout's nest to create a makeshift swing. It fascinated Rasia to watch him discover and innovate and learn.

He was far more observant and intelligent than the Grankull gave him credit for.

Kai moved to the steer and glanced at Rasia. She smirked and raised her hands, not bothering this time to grab the railing. Rasia wobbled with the ship as it moved forward. She watched him go through the same motions as before, but this time, when the second rock loomed, Kai swung from a rope, scooped up the oar, and used it to push the ship safely past the second rock.

So shocked by his own success, Kai didn't move quickly enough to prevent the ship from crashing into the third. Rasia laughed at his dumbstruck expression as the windship went down.

Rasia might have misjudged her timetable. She'd figured it would take Kai a while to get out of the gorge, enough time for her to heal and gather the supplies they would need to take on the dragon. But Kai was already at the third rock within the span of two days. She admitted she might have underestimated him and that, most of all, excited her.

She liked to collect secrets. She enjoyed finding landmarks that didn't exist on maps. She enjoyed pushing at the horizon and hunting things no one else dared. She enjoyed discovering something new. The more time Rasia spent with Kai, the more he shined and sparkled.

Rasia thought back to the words Neema accused her of, how Rasia was better equipped than other people because of her tahs. Watching Kai drove home how much of a foundation her parents had given her. Kai was pathetic not because of his physical shortcomings, but because no one had been willing to give him the time of day.

Rasia helped Kai wheel the windship back to the starting line. Before he could start again, Rasia punched his shoulder. "Come on, it's high noon. Break time."

"But I can keep going."

Rasia raised a brow, and Kai relented with a grumble.

They returned to the cave and found Rasia's soup bubbling over. She rushed to save it. It wasn't that bad. Rasia poured Kai a sizable portion of the soup.

"It's burnt," Kai complained.

"If you don't like it, eat around it." Warmth grew in her face, embarrassed. She had forgotten to take the soup off the fire before checking on Kai.

"And here I thought you were good at everything."

"Har. Har," Rasia said, kicking at his foot teasingly. Kai ladled the soup and ate one of the scorpion chunks whole, burnt parts and all. He took considerable breaks between each bite to gather his energy for the next.

"Did you practice your letters?" Kai asked.

"What?" Rasia glanced at the scrolls of parchment Kai had written for her to study. Rasia might have been bored, but she hadn't been *that* bored.

"How do you know how to read anyway? I don't remember you at school," Rasia said, mischievously changing the subject. Rasia might have agreed to learn how to read, but they never put a deadline on it.

"I went to school for fourteen days," Kai replied defensively, "which is better than your record."

Rasia cracked a grin. "Well pointed."

"Tajih taught me to read," Kai explained. "Ava-ta figured if by some miracle I passed the Forging, I could be a scribe."

"Is that what you want to do, though?" Rasia asked. "Why would you want to write down someone else's legend when you could make your own?"

"I don't have many options available to me. And being a scribe isn't that bad. They turn words into an art form. They shape history into poetry. Isn't the windeka the scribe of a kull?"

"Yeah, but they just write day-to-day reports for the real scribes to sort out later."

"It's a shame it has to be that way. I've learned more from you than any legend I've read in the library. I think the Grankull could benefit from the way you see the world. When you read about kull hunts, it's about how you kill the target, not how they dance. There's a lack of . . . intimacy. The scribes could learn from you. We need those stories."

Rasia couldn't help but smile at his apparent awe of her. It was nice to speak to someone who valued every word she had to say, appreciated her skills, and recognized her as the awesome-sauce person she knew she was. Her conversations with Kai were a breath of fresh air compared to the doubting naysayers back home.

"You can write my legend if you really want to be a scribe, but I think you'd make a better windeka instead."

Kai scoffed. "I've hardly passed the second rock."

"And many would not have passed the first. You give yourself too little credit. Most people can't get a windship to *move* in the first day. I should know. Sometimes I watch the classes when they first start practicing on actual windships. It's hilarious. You know Nico somehow managed to crash into the Lakejaw?"

"Her nerves got the best of her."

"Sure. If that's what you want to call it. You're not the worst, Kai."

Kai quieted, thoughtful. He took another large bite, as if testing if bigger bites made the process go quicker. "Have you figured out what you want to do? The other day you said you didn't want to be Han of a hunting kull anymore."

"I don't know. Honestly, I don't know how I thought I could deal with five people when I can barely deal with one. I don't . . . I just . . . but what else is out there?"

"You could be a scribe."

"Shut up," Rasia said with little bite. She smacked her lips after downing the rest of her soup. "I can't be a scribe. I can't even write my name."

"But you have to sign your name for the Naming Ceremony. How are you going to accomplish that?"

"I plan to bribe Ysai-ji to write my name on my palm beforehand and close my fist until it's time."

"Isn't that against the rules?"

"What idiot follows rules? Oh wait, probably your jih."

Kai burst into sudden laughter, getting most of his soup all over his face and some up his nose. Rasia tossed him her gourd, and he rinsed out the burn from his nostrils. After he cleaned himself up, he looked at her with wide eyes, blushing. "That's never happened before."

"That tends to happen when you're talking and eating with someone at the same time. I forgot to warn you how dangerous it could be."

"You shut up," Kai said, throwing the gourd back at her. She ducked under it with a laugh. "I am eating and holding up my end of the bargain, unlike some people. Instead of bribing your way through the Naming Ceremony, you could learn how to read."

"*I tried*," Rasia complained, bemoaning the memory as she dramatically collapsed to the ground. "I tried going back to school once. Figured I'd give it another shot. But I had no idea what the fuck they were talking about and it made me feel . . . stupid. I know more than any of those fucking assholes."

"So, the 'never give up' speech only applies to me?"

"Don't give up on the things that matter, unless it's stupid. Then by all means don't waste your time."

School had been torturous, and *boring*. None of the lectures or word drills ever stuck in Rasia's head, and she had better things to do than sit in some classroom.

Kai sat up with a sudden thought. "I've got an idea on how to help you read."

"But you haven't eaten your soup yet," Rasia pointed out, blinking innocently.

Kai rolled his eyes, braced himself, then drank down the remaining contents all in one go. He moved to his feet and motioned her to follow him outside. Rasia grumbled, but she was too curious not to follow. He led her outside of the canyon to where Kai practiced his running. His endurance hadn't improved much over the past two days, but at least now he looked like he was running instead of flailing pitifully about.

Kai dragged his feet through the sand to make several large

circles. He continued like this, sometimes skipping a foot over to seemingly start again.

". . . Are you dancing?" Rasia asked, confused. "Because no offense, you suck."

When he finished, Kai declared proudly, "It's a ka-kata."

Rasia tilted her head at the symbols he'd carved into the sand. If she squinted, they sort of looked like the same ones he wrote on the parchment earlier that morning.

"Try to follow them," Kai suggested.

Skeptical, Rasia stepped to the center of the first symbol. With her feet, she tried tracing the lines Kai made, but she was unsure where on the curve to start. Kai moved forward, reaching out to correct her and aborting his movement. "Think about it like a kata. The movement order and the strokes matter. Do it with intent."

"But I don't remember the order. You went too fast."

Kai reached out and once again faltered before touching her. He backed up. "I'll do it over here, and you can follow my movements."

"The fuck, Kai. I can't see all the way over there. Get your ass over here and touch me."

"Oh—o-okay," Kai said as he awkwardly came behind her.

Rasia would bet anything that Kai had never initiated contact with anyone but his siblings. Technically, one could argue that Rasia hadn't either. The Grankull forbade casual touch among the underage with the exception of supervised sparring. Rasia had sparring partners aplenty. She had shoved at bullies and had punched Nico in the face. She didn't consider herself some fresh-faced butterfly. Unconsciously at times though, Rasia found herself treating Kai like her jih. She couldn't stop nudging or shoving at him with a tease. He reacted awkward and stunned by her touch every time. It was hilarious, and Rasia couldn't pass up this ripe opportunity for a little bit of fun.

Rasia grabbed his hovering hand and placed it on her hip, then pressed her back against his chest. He wore her worn linen shirt, and through it she could easily feel the suggestion of his sternum. Kai immediately stiffened, his chest no longer moving.

"Like this?" Rasia asked, faux-innocent. She didn't bother tracing any of the lines as she circled her hips into his.

Kai jerked away so fast you'd think she was on fire. Rasia spewed with laughter when he spun away, back to her, but not before she saw the tent that had formed in his pants. He crumbled into a crouch, where his shoulders hunched, and his ears burned red.

She sniggered. "Stop being so dramatic. It's a boner. It happens."

Kai glared at her over his shoulder. "You did this on purpose. You're not taking this seriously at all."

"I am! It's not my fault you're so sensitive. I barely touched you, and you're practically at full mast."

Kai tucked his face into his knees. While he was busy drowning in his misfortune, Rasia dropped down and crawled up behind him. Then she popped up at his shoulder to whisper a suggestion in his ear, "Think of Nico's lone strand of boob hair."

Kai released a strangled, prolonged whine from the cover of his knees. It sent Rasia rolling with laughter. By the time she came back up for air, she found Kai pouting and glaring at her.

Rasia asked cheekily, "It worked, didn't it?"

"You're a menace."

"I am the best thing to ever happen to you." She slapped at his leg and rolled to her feet. "Come on, let's do this thing. I'll be on my best behavior this time. I promise."

He glared daggers at her.

"*Promise*."

Kai adjusted his pants as he stood. Rasia couldn't help but to slide her gaze to the previously provoked area. Considering how tiny the rest of him was, that tent was bigger than she'd figured it would be. Just sayin'.

Then, Kai touched *her*.

Kai had never initiated contact with her before, and it threw her for a loop when he knocked atop her forehead as if she were a misbehaving bud. Despite the brief tap, touching someone's face in any manner was understandably intimate. It seized Rasia's attention.

"One useless thing for another, that is what you agreed to. I've done my part. It is time for you to do yours. You're afraid to try because you've failed before, and you're afraid to fail again. But you aren't stupid, Rasia. Perhaps you learn better the same way you teach: not by rote memorization or tedious lectures . . . but by doing. Either you really try, or you let this be the one thing that defeats you."

Rasia's brows rose to her hairline because that was a challenge he had just thrown at her feet, and it wasn't in her bones to let it go unanswered. Who knew Kai had that in him? She shook out her limbs as if preparing for a fight.

"You're on."

Rasia charged back toward the first symbol.

Kai returned a determined, clammy hand to her hip but kept the rest of himself at a distance. He pulled her along the lines curved in the sand. At first, it felt like some nonsensical dance without pattern or reason—motions for the sake of movement. But as they hopped from one symbol to the next, she found herself anticipating the next step with increasing ease.

It did feel like some strange kata. Katas, at their core, were about repetition and patterns. She'd mastered so many over the years that her body understood the pattern first before it all coalesced into one brilliant epiphany. The downward stroke came first. The curved flourish came last. Every symbol was a deviation from the one that came before, like katas in a series.

Rasia moved with more confidence, accelerating with every motion she anticipated correctly, and began adding twists of her own.

"Rasia, you're going too fast." Rasia tripped over Kai's ankle, and they tumbled to the ground.

Rasia angled to avoid falling on her right side. Kai apparently had the same concern, as he braced an arm around her waist and put himself between her ribs and the ground.

Rasia thought it ridiculous. She could defeat a gonda single-handedly while Kai could barely face a grubworm. She knew how to fall. What did she need him throwing himself on the ground for?

"You alright?" Kai asked, loosening his grip and running his eyes over her with concern.

Rasia scoffed. "I don't break easy."

"Your ribs don't know that."

"Hey," Rasia said, shoving playfully at Kai's chest. Rasia had meant to push him away, but her hand sort of flopped against the line of his pecs, which she could feel through the linen. If she moved her pinky finger over just a little, she'd brush a nipple. She never understood the point of them for males . . . decoration, maybe. Like pretty baubles on a sword hilt.

She snapped her hand away from his chest before it refused to unstick. To distract both him and herself from the slip, she said quickly, "You're right. I was getting it at the end. It's the first time any of this made sense." She slowed, sincere. "Thank you, for throwing my words back at me. I'll never give up again."

People had tried to teach her to read for years and failed. Her teachers berated her. Kiba-ta had lost her patience. Even Ysai had gotten frustrated. Rasia had refused to care anymore. But Kai had helped her make sense of it all in the span of nothing but a drum. Rasia could never fully convey how much this meant to her.

Kai absentmindedly scratched at his chest where Rasia's hand had been moments before as he mused over the symbols they'd carved through the sand. "I was thinking of punctuating the completion of each symbol with its sound."

"Oh, that's brilliant. Then I can tell everyone you taught me a super-secret fighting style and see how long it takes for people to realize it's the kah. I cannot wait to show Ysai-ji. It's going to be hilarious."

The corner of his lips tilted into a half smirk-smile. "Exactly what I was thinking."

Rasia's stomach swooped. She smiled, bashful and unable to pinpoint the last time that had happened to her. It didn't help that his gaze melted hot, and she swore with the sun shining to their left, his eyes began to glow. Both his irises and pupils were normally gold, but they've never outright glowed before, producing their own light. They reminded her of elderfire at high noon, irises harsh and bright and so dense with heat she could barely breathe.

She lifted her face toward his.

Kai flinched as if she had thrown a punch at him instead. He stared, frozen, before his face reddened for the second time that day.

He bolted downhill. With pretty good form too.

Rasia shook her head and collapsed to the sand, both disappointed and mildly amused. She hadn't felt this way for someone in a while. Immediately, she began to consider angles of attack. He was physically attracted to her, that much was apparent, but Kai was more akin to a wild, skittish animal than anything else. She risked scaring him off. She didn't have patience for much, but she'd learned patience for the hunt. She had to lay her bait and wait for him to come to her.

This was a hunt that could very well take forever.

Good thing Rasia never gave up.

Not anymore.

CHAPTER FIFTEEN

—

Kai thought Rasia had tried to kiss him yesterday. Maybe. He wasn't sure. It could have been a figment of his imagination; she could have meant it as a joke, but it didn't seem the same as when she had been goofing around earlier. If only Kai had been brave enough to stand his ground and find out.

Kai jolted out of his reverie to find Rasia staring at him from where she stretched one leg atop the windship railing. All throughout the day, she'd been scrutinizing his every move and action. He thought about the almost-kiss again. Was he crazy to consider the possibility that Rasia, maybe, had a flame for him?

Rasia asked, "Are you magic?" Kai's stomach plummeted at the question. "I thought I was crazy at first, but your eyes glowed yesterday. And today, I noticed you adjust the sail before the wind."

The dragon-wing sail snapped overhead. Kai had no idea what she meant. ". . . is that a bad thing?"

"Steering a windship is reactionary. The wind shifts and a windeka adjusts the sail. But when *you* get caught up with multiple tasks at once, you adjust the sail for a wind change that happens vibrations later. Famed windekas who have studied wind patterns and seasonal charts their entire lives can't anticipate such minute wind shifts as you do. It's not . . . *possible*. I thought you didn't have magic like your jih, but I don't know how else to explain it."

"That's not magic. I feel the wind like everyone else," Kai said, becoming more and more uncertain as he watched the rising skepticism on Rasia's face.

Rasia lifted from her stretch. "*No.* What do you think the flags atop the windships are for? Windekas check it for wind direction, or they lick a finger and stick it in the air. They do these things because they can't anticipate something that hasn't happened yet."

". . . you don't do any of those things."

Rasia paused, squinted at him, and then explained. "I use my hair."

She tossed a hand through her hair as some sort of demonstration, then frowned when her fingers got caught on a knot. She tore at it. A strong breeze swept through, waving both her and Kai's shoulder-length hair to the wind's mercy. Kai got the general idea.

"I always know which way the wind is blowing, but for how it's going to blow . . . I can make reasonable guesses on how the currents are going to act in a certain season, but I don't actually *know*."

Kai's frown deepened as he absorbed the implications. They both terrified and angered him. He'd been aware of shifting wind currents his entire life, but that wasn't how magic was supposed to work. The magic-born didn't come into their powers until at least five years-till, but inexplicable strange phenomena had been happening to Kai all his life. Kai was partly convinced that all the strange occurred only in his head, and it wasn't something real and physical like tah's magic. She could grow trees from barren ground. For Kai, magic wasn't literal rainbows like it was for Nico. Kai lost days.

How was he supposed to know if he was magic or just crazy? He never would have known what happened at the oasis if Zephyr hadn't been there to anchor his sense of time. Magic was terrifying; it was out of his control. And if he had no control over it, how did Kai know that the things he hoped to accomplish in life were done by his own hands?

"*Are you crying?*"

Kai hid his face in his hands and ran. He fled down the stairs and slipped down the last few rungs. He searched for someplace to hide, but everything felt too open. He scurried into the cave and farther into the gloom, into the tight tunnels of rocks where the ground slipped wet and dipped into a silent pool of water. Kai crouched in the darkness, trying to hold it together and failing so abysmally as he croaked out sobs.

"Kai?"

Kai jumped at the sound of Rasia's voice, which echoed louder off the cave walls and ricocheted around him.

"I want to be alone," Kai mumbled.

Whereas Nico would have honored his request and given him the space to work through his ugly tangle of emotions, instead, the darkness shifted. Kai sensed Rasia coming closer. She patted her hand along the cave wall until she slapped down on his head, his face, then his knee. She sunk right next to him, and Kai tensed, irate by her refusal to leave.

"Look . . ." Rasia's disembodied voice rang out from the blackness beside him. "Ysai-ji has made me well aware that at times I can be quite, a little, just a touch, insensitive. I don't know what I said wrong. Actually, I'm really fucking confused here. *What did I do? Why are we in the dark? Do you hate me now?*"

"No, Rasia. It's nothing to do with you. It's me. It's . . . I . . ." Kai pressed his hands to his eyes with the sudden guilt caused by Rasia's confusion. He sucked in a breath, but the admission came no louder than a reedy whisper, shaped into words for the first time in his life.

"I have magic," Kai said, unable to run away from it any longer, "but it's broken. It's never worked right for me. I can't control it, and I hardly know when it's happening. This is the first time I've gotten any sort of chance to do anything worthwhile, and *it's all a lie*. All the progress I've made with the windship has been my magic all along. How can I ever accomplish anything if the magic accomplishes it for me? How can I possibly know what's me and what's not? I'll never know who I am, or what I'm capable of, because I have this stupid broken magic I can't control."

"O . . . kay," Rasia said slowly. Kai heard her shift her legs, stretching them out to rock a foot against his. "I . . . have mixed feelings about magic. It's not fair. Nico's magic gives her this huge advantage compared to everyone else in the Forging. Is she all that amazing if she was born with this innate ability others don't have? I don't think so, but everyone else is always so fucking impressed."

"Then I met you, and I realized I have a sort of magic of my own. Compared to all the others in the Forging, I began much further ahead of the starting line than everyone else. I know the Desert. I know windships. I know all these things because Shamai-ta taught me to know all these things. It's why I needed to break his record or why I have to hunt a dragon, because doing the same things expected of everyone else isn't a challenge. I *need* to challenge myself. I always *need* to be better. I hate standing still most of all."

"We all have magic in our own sort of way. The small little things that make up you—the way you remember and observe details, your smarts, and your magic—all add to the fact that while others might have the potential to be a good windeka, you have the potential to be a great one. But all that potential means nothing without hard work. You've still got to put in the work, Kai, no matter where you're starting from. And that hard work is on you. It'll always be on you. That's the only thing any of us can ever truly control."

Rasia's words felt like a lifeline tossed into a sea of storm clouds. They buoyed him out of the waters of his insecurities and self-hate.

"And no offense, but Nico can summon rainstorms and Avalai Ohan had human-eating plants. In comparison, you're essentially a human weathervane. While it's an everyday type of useful, it still sucks. I'd want fire-breathing or something. You've been rolling nothing but reds your entire life, Kai."

Kai found himself smiling at her dark observation. He tensed a moment when her head dropped on his shoulder, then he slowly decompressed under the anchor of her touch.

"Once," Kai whispered softly to Rasia, "Suri complained how easy it was to get lost in the Grankull. I told her to just listen to how the bones sing. She looked at me like I was crazy. I told Nico about it, and she looked at me like I was crazy, too. Nico didn't hear the bones until she was three years-till. I've never not heard them, and I never knew I was the only one who could. It's terrifying to think the world is one way when it isn't, and to be uncertain of it every day afterward. For so long, I've tried to ignore the magic and pretend it wasn't there and hope it was all in my head."

"You're smart enough to know that won't work," Rasia said. "Perhaps it's time for you to stop thinking of your magic as this separate thing that needs controlling and accept it as a part of you."

"It's supposed to be controlled. That's how it's supposed to work."

"Is it, though? There's a lot of magic out here in the Desert, and as far as I can tell, what defines magic is the fact that it doesn't have any sensible rules. I can't possibly understand what you're going through, and I can't imagine what it's like to have no control over something so . . . big, but it's got to be tiring fighting that every day."

Kai dropped his face in his hands. Rasia was right about that part—that it was a fight. Every. Single. Day.

He had plenty more secrets, and Kai couldn't hold their oppressive weight any longer. He needed to release them. "I want to tell you something, but promise not to tell jih?"

Rasia laughed at that. "To this day, Nico still doesn't know I'm the one who cut her hair first day of school."

"*That was you?*"

"Focus. You were going to tell me super-duper secrets."

Kai drummed his fingers along his thigh, grounding himself. "I hear the bones of the Elder sing. I apparently track wind like a sixth sense. I don't sunburn. I've never gotten heatstroke. High noon doesn't bother me. I drink less water but have formed the habit of drinking more because Nico worries. Sometimes, I lose track of days. Recently, in the last day or so, I know where you are. I wake up and know you're outside running beyond the canyon or on the windship. I have a better sense of it when you're exercising. My eyes glow. I don't know for what reasons, but it happens enough that little jih was surprised to learn no one else's eyes do the same. Those are the things that I know. The things I've kept in my head."

". . . I'd still prefer the fire-breathing."

A laugh burst from Kai's chest. It echoed and echoed and echoed, circling around them like draining water. Kai's lips twisted into a wry smile. "No, you don't. Because then it'd be too easy."

Kai figured she'd have a sharp comeback in response. Instead, a thoughtful silence ensued until Rasia admitted, like her own secret, "Yeah, you're right."

They sat in that darkness for a while, comfortable in it now, until Kai gathered all the courage he possessed in every grain of his body and whispered, "I think . . . I think you tried to kiss me yesterday, but so often for me the world seems one way when it isn't. I have difficulty discerning reality on my own, and even more so now, because you constantly challenge all the truths and expectations of what I thought I knew. I don't know what the world is supposed to be anymore."

Kai could feel Rasia's smile curl against his shoulder. She stood with mischief and teasing and an island of airy delight. Full of any and everything Kai never thought possible.

She declared, "The world is what we forge of it."

CHAPTER SIXTEEN

From the beginning, Kai knew the sixth rock would be the toughest, for it required the sharpest turn. Kai sailed around the fifth, and the sixth was coming on him fast.

Kai hesitated the first time he approached the sixth rock. His head got in the way. Was he strong enough to turn the ship? Would he need something to supplement his weight? What if he applied too much force? Multiple failures later, Kai thought he'd found the answer to all those questions.

Kai raced across the railing, caught the rope, and used all his momentum to slam atop the outrigger. The entire ship shifted. He adjusted the strength he applied—not too much and not too little—enough to feel the ship rock in its rut and turn. By now he'd gotten used to the feeling. He welcomed the whirlwind toss of his stomach and the ground turning over his head.

The ship cleared the sixth rock. One rock left.

All Kai needed to do was straighten the ship. He climbed up from the outrigger, caught his foot on the railing, and flipped over, landing hard on the deck. He flung himself across the distance to reach the steer. He slid, caught the bone lever, set his feet, and pulled.

The ship cleared the last rock.

Kai breathed, chest tight and throat burning, hugging the steer as he laid on his back.

He did it.

No matter what people said or what they called him, no one could ever take this achievement away. Kai hugged the steer and smiled.

Rasia yelled at him from above. He spotted her racing atop the canyon, waving and jumping in excitement, and didn't slow as the canyon opening neared. Wait. She wasn't going to . . . of course she was.

Rasia jumped with arms and legs splayed out like a falling star. She slid down the dragon-wing sail—the only thing that hadn't ripped, torn, or been crushed these past four days—and landed crouched, featherlight, onto the ship.

She raced to meet him. Kai scrambled to his feet, and the force of her hug toppled him straight down back to the deck.

"You did it!" Rasia exclaimed. She pounced off and set her knee to the front railing. Her hair flapped wild. The narrow sandstone opened dramatically to a sea of gold. She matched his excitement and energy twofold. "What do you say, windeka? Let's go for a ride."

Kai didn't know smiling could hurt your face so much.

"Understood, Han," Kai responded. He adjusted the sail's angle and, as he had often seen Rasia do, gave the ship to the wind.

They zipped across the Desert. The bone steer shook in his grip at the blinding speed. Kai wondered if this is what Rasia felt when she ran, when she was pure speed and flight. He'd never felt anything like this before—so weightless, so boundless—as if any moment the windship would veer off a sand dune and fly into the sky.

The wheel hit a divot.

Kai planted his feet and gripped the steer with both hands, straining with all his strength to stabilize the ship. If the steer snatched away from him at this speed, the windship would topple and no doubt flip. Kai held fast, his arms shaking, until the resistance slackened and the windship straightened out.

Heart racing, Kai skidded the windship to an uneven stop.

Rasia laughed, eyes sparkling, nonchalant at the fact Kai had come close to irreparably crashing the ship. The whole thing had happened in the brief span of a vibration; Rasia had been too far to help even if she'd wanted to, thus the only thing keeping them from disaster had been the measly, laughable muscles of Kai's arms. Kai bent back in relief, his arms still sore and shaking, as a breathless laugh broke out of his chest. Kai never thought himself capable of conquering this hulking mass of a windship. They'd diverted disaster on Kai's mere strength alone, and that more than anything left him awed and stunned.

Rasia slapped the railing. "That was fun."

"Yeah," Kai said, breathless. "Fun." He said the word as if putting it to an emotion he'd never felt before. Kai tried scanning through his memories, but he couldn't remember anything similar. Had he truly never had fun before? Certainly not with this mix of pounding adrenaline and triumphant accomplishment.

"We should celebrate!" Rasia suggested. "When we get back to the gorge, let's break open the alcohol and have us a feast."

"A feast?" Kai asked. He'd never experienced one for any other reason than a holiday. "We don't have much food supply left. You want to use all of it?"

"Now that you've proven yourself a solid windeka, tomorrow we'll go on our First Hunt to make this kull official. Food won't be a problem."

Kai's throat tightened with emotion. Rasia didn't use the term "kull" lightly, but she wanted to welcome him officially into her kull. For the first time, Kai found a space for himself, here with Rasia.

Together, they could do anything.

"I look forward to it."

Rasia certainly couldn't let Kai show her up.

She snatched a dagger from her belt and lowered her stance. She brushed the tip of her toe across the deck, completing a full circle before shouting the first sound. She'd been practicing the past few days, adding little twists of personality to the movements. She caught the letters one by one, and one by one, she pinned them to the mast.

Shamaijen Windbreaker.

The absence of her tah's name had felt like a bent wheel. You never sailed right until you fixed it. Ysai might have been too busy with Jilah to notice the mast had been replaced, but Rasia had also never outright asked for his help, either. She shouldn't have needed to. Ysai should have noticed, and every day he hadn't, the angrier Rasia had gotten. Why was she the only one who cared anymore that tah was gone?

Rasia carved the last letters larger and more crooked than the others, cutting deeper from the force of all her building anger and frustration. She snapped back with a huff to inspect her handiwork. Her chest heaved with a rage that blindsided her. The entire kull should have been here. She shouldn't have to do this alone.

Rasia looked down, startled, when Kai took a hold of her hand. The fog of her anger dispersed, and she remembered. Kai had steered tah's windship out of that gorge like a true windeka. Rasia hadn't thought that anyone could possibly deserve to occupy any space on her tah's windship, but she knew in her bones that Shamai-ta would have liked Kai.

Rasia plopped her head on Kai's bony shoulder and turned to the mast. When someone died, their bones were sealed in an urn inscribed with their name in the Heart Temple. Her tah's name didn't belong in that dank, dark place. It belonged here, forever sailing sun and sky.

"It sucks. If it weren't for Nico, if the bones had landed differently, I would have broken the Forging record my tah set. I would have earned the same Last Name. It was supposed to be ours to share. But . . ." Rasia sucked in a breath and expended all her leftover bitterness. "I'll earn my own."

Rasia tightened her grip on Kai's hand. He didn't flinch, cringe, or recoil but instead melted into the mold of her fingers.

"Do you know the kull's goodbye?" Rasia asked him.

"I don't think so."

"Pay attention. These are words all hunters know." Rasia then recited, "Paths diverge, and split, and end. Till we meet once more again. Forever this ship carry your name. All hunters are hunted, but the kull remains."

The kull remains.

CHAPTER SEVENTEEN

—

Kai noted Rasia's head on his shoulder and her hand tight in his. She shifted balance to her right foot, and the increase press of warmth up Kai's arm tickled at goosebumps.

Their eyes met.

And Rasia's gaze flicked down to Kai's lips with single-minded intensity.

Rasia was not subtle. For days now, she'd been tossing Kai the first move pretty unambiguously, and all Kai had needed was the confidence to catch it. He needed to get out of his head and stop being afraid of disappointing her. With the high of their wild ride still in his chest, he felt windblown by a foolhardy boldness. Kai turned toward her, and Rasia's smile sweetened with every vibration of space erased between them.

Kai leaned forward, toward the sun on her lips, then abruptly stopped. He had to ask, in case this was all a mirage of his own making.

"Can I kiss you?"

Rasia charged his mouth in the same manner she'd charged into his life: with confidence, and fearlessness, and a whole lot of tongue. The force of her charge stumbled him back. Rasia didn't care to be gentle. She didn't treat him like some fragile thing broken at every slight touch. Noses and teeth clashed. She clawed her fingers through his hair and carved her name into his throat.

Kai had thought his tastebuds dead until Rasia ignited in him a hunger. Determined to match her fire, Kai devoured her. They consumed and chewed at each other, and the kiss was a hot gooey mess.

Kai's chest tightened—a brutal reminder that not even his first kiss could make him invincible, and the pain solidified, hardening into a solid knot stuck in his throat.

He couldn't breathe.

Kai broke the kiss. "*I'm sorry*," he gasped out.

Kai tucked his face into the dip of Rasia's shoulder and clutched at his chest, willing the pain to subside. He feared Rasia's anger and disappointment. More so, he felt embarrassed, for he had idiotically thought himself strong enough to keep up with her.

"I'm so good I literally took your breath away," Rasia teased against his hair, dispelling his doubts and insecurities. She nibbled at his neck, notably too unbothered to pity or worry over him.

Still, Kai wanted to do better. And he was pretty sure that kissing required more finesse than eating each other's faces off. He dared to clutch clammy hands around Rasia's hips. He still vividly remembered how she'd guided his hands to her hips a few days ago while they were tracing "kah" in the sand. He'd never touched anyone like this before, and like then, she trusted him to guide her.

Kai pressed her against the mast. Rasia's eyes twinkled, no doubt curious at where this was going.

Kai gripped the date wood right under her tah's name for leverage. His other hand hovered in the air, briefly, before touching first underneath her jaw, then cupping her cheek in his palm. He hadn't touched anyone this gently since he'd held his youngest jih as a newborn. To Kai's surprise, Rasia softened. Her eyes drifted closed. He wondered if anyone had ever dared touch her with gentleness and care.

Kai kissed her again and molded her mouth with ease. He

set the pace and took his time savoring her. Rasia smelled of jasmine and rice bran, the sunscreen mixture she applied in the early mornings now slicked with sweat in his hands. She tasted melon sweet. The kiss turned into two into three into many, into punctuated smoldering pecks, to long boiling waves of heat. Savory moans and sour hitches vibrated to the back of his throat. This time, Kai remembered to breathe.

After they finished their prolonged kiss, Rasia clutched him tightly about the waist, her head bowed to his clavicle. It was so much: touching someone else. Being touched.

Then Rasia pressed forward, already ready for more. She whispered, sour-sweet into his ear, "I've got a vial of gonom in the windship hatch."

WHAT?!

Kai jolted back several paces, putting space between them. "That's illegal."

Very illegal. Gonom was a poison diluted from gonda venom that adults used as a contraceptive. It was illegal for any child to possess. Even the recipe was a Grankull secret.

"You can never be too prepared," Rasia said matter-of-factly. "But we've only got one chance at this. I only swiped one dose."

She grabbed at the end strings of Kai's waistband and pulled, popping the knot. Kai's pants loosened, but he quickly caught them before they sunk down his waist. Kai said, strangled, "*Rasia.*"

"Are we having sex or not?"

Sound fogged in Kai's ears at the outright question. Kai hadn't considered anything further than kissing; he'd never considered anything further an *option.* Kai honestly thought that once Rasia had gotten a taste of him, she'd lose interest. But standing in the middle of all the heat created between their bodies, Kai found the idea that she wouldn't pursue more laughable. He asked, to be sure. "You want to have sex with me?"

"*Yes.* Am I not obvious?"

To be fair, never in Kai's wildest dreams did anyone proposition him for sex. He honestly thought he'd die without ever having it.

(He honestly thought he'd die without ever being kissed too but, well, here he is.) But what if he was terrible at it? What if he couldn't physically accomplish the task? He was pretty sure this would be her first time. He couldn't ruin that.

"Are you sure about this, Rasia?" Kai asked. Most first times happened while drunk on one's Naming Night, usually during the bodika. "You could wait until after the Forging, then choose anyone you want."

"You mean choose between all the fuck-shits who've laughed at me? You are the one who is here, right now, on this windship with me hunting a dragon. I want *you*."

"Yes. Okay. Yes. Let's do it," Kai said, fumbling the words before he was fully aware of them. All he knew was that Rasia wanted *him*, and that knowledge alone dispelled the doubts. Besides, this could've been the only opportunity he'd ever get. He'd be a fool not to try. Kai cleared his throat and gathered the confidence to say, "Yes. I'd like to have sex with you."

Rasia's wicked grin curled. She told him to stay, then rushed toward the hatch and disappeared into the bowels of the ship.

Kai sucked in a shaky breath. *Okay.* This was happening. Kai caught his grip on the railing, just in case all the building anxiousness caused him to vomit. The vast expanse of Desert unfolded on all sides around him. Not a single rock or tree could be seen. Even sight of the gorge had disappeared behind a mountainous sand dune. Nothing existed in this place but Rasia and Kai.

Like some lewd adventure tale in the library, Kai's first time was about to happen on the deck of a windship in the middle of the Desert, with the most amazing person in the entire Grankull. Kai stuck his hands under his armpits, realized how sweaty they were, and frantically washed his hands. And his face. And his hair. He waited with all of this excited-panicked-joyous-anxious-aroused-terrified energy. Too much. Too many emotions.

Kai heard her climbing the ladder and stuck himself to the railing, trying to look nonchalant and knowing he was failing miserably.

Rasia returned waving a dragonglass vial, almost empty but for a swallow. Without hesitation, Rasia tipped the limpid green liquid into her mouth and immediately gagged on the taste. She scrambled for her gourd and swallowed down huge gulps of water. She wiped at her mouth with her arm, then tossed the empty vial over her shoulder, where it clinked rolling across the deck.

"All right. We've got one day to have as much sex as possible. Let's go."

"*What?*"

Kai had assumed a gonom dose covered each time. He hadn't realized he had just agreed to a whole day of sex. He wasn't sure his answer would have been any different had he known, but still . . . was he ready for this?

Rasia pawed at his shirt. Kai had thought he was prepared, but he was off balance now. Then he floundered further when he realized he'd forgotten something extremely, *extremely* important.

"Wait, Rasia, *wait*," Kai scrambled. He pressed himself against the railing and tugged the shirt, now only half-tucked in his pants, out of Rasia's grasp.

"Please tell me you haven't changed your mind. I've been hoarding that gonom for *two* years. There's no going back now."

"No, I . . ." Kai took a moment to slide some distance between them. He looked down at the clothes he clung to, pressed against his body. Logically, he knew he would have to strip to get to the sex part, but mentally, he'd hit a sudden wall. Out in the middle of the high-noon sun, he had nowhere to hide. Kai never had the choice when to expose his face, and ironically, it was Rasia who had taken that choice away from him.

But he had a choice in this.

"I need to do it. I need to be the one to take off my clothes."

Kai didn't undress around his jihs. He didn't visit the public baths or swim the Lakejaw. No one had ever seen him naked. He didn't even like looking at himself in the mirror. Kai didn't know why he'd forgotten such an important detail before he had foolishly agreed to this. And he knew in his gut that if he changed his mind and ruined her only dose of gonom, he'd never get this opportunity with her again. All those thoughts ran through his mind as he clutched at the linen fabric tighter and tighter. Every time he got close to deciding to go through with it, he kept remembering the moment when they were younger, when Rasia snatched off his shroud, and the disappointment on her face.

Rasia raised her chin. "I'll go first."

With the steer and all the adjoining contraptions in the back, the widest space of a windship deck was right between the mast and the front, before the head began to curve. Rasia planted herself at the center of this wide space, under the bright sun, with the windship her stage. She relished in the attentions of her audience of one.

She unbuckled the belt at her chest, slipped her shoulders out from the loops, and caught the sheaths crossed at her back. She sat her khopesh blades aside with reverence. She reached for the bottom of her shirt.

Kai had seen her without it multiple times the past several days, but this time when she tossed it off, it had more meaning. Rasia threw the shirt right at Kai's feet, the challenge clear.

Rasia glanced at him, to make sure he was watching, before pulling at the knotted leather ends and unloosening the waistband of her pants. The pants sagged, and even though they were loosened, the waistband caught on her curves. She had to wiggle them past her thighs to get them off. Three slight daggers hit the deck with a chime. She kicked them all to the side.

Rasia didn't wear any undergarments. Most of the Grankull used public bathhouses to bathe with no scrap of clothing in sight save for the children still required to wear their shrouds. Because of that, few adults were self-conscious about their nudity. Rasia didn't flinch from Kai's curiosity. He was unsurprised to find the pubic hair at her crest was as wild and untamed as the hair on her head. From thighs to ass to abs, Rasia was all muscle, and Kai found himself fascinated as his eyes traced her curved lines. Females were often considered physically softer compared to males, but Kai would never describe Rasia as such. She was curved toughness and explosive power.

Rasia moved her hand to the bandages wrapped about her waist. She had taken a lot of care to rest and avoid undue strain these past couple of days. He wished he had considered her ribs when he first agreed to this, but Kai had resigned himself to the fact he wasn't thinking with the right head. He'd have to be extremely careful not to worsen her injury.

Kai remembered waking up after the disastrous incident with the skinko to see a lower rib protruding from Rasia's skin. Now, a bright red scar had replaced the protrusion, healed closed with stitches almost ready to take out. A bed of withering bruises pillowed the scar. She didn't need to remove the bandages but had done so anyway to make a point: Rasia was not afraid to strip completely bare.

Last, Rasia reached for the bandeau the bandages had partly been wrapped over. Without the bandages, Kai realized it wasn't a bandeau at all, but several strips of cloth melded into one another. Rasia's fingers slipped trying to get a grip on it.

She frowned. Then reached around her back to find wherever the wrap started, but the beginning edge had merged into the rest of the linen. Rasia tugged and scratched and hopped around the deck trying to contort it off her. She laughed awkwardly. "I actually haven't taken it off in two years."

"Two years?" Kai asked, surprised by that revelation. Rasia eyed one of those knives she'd kicked across the ship. Kai lifted the dagger at his belt. "Do you need help?"

"Yeah. Get over here and cut me out of this thing." Rasia gathered up her hair as he approached, holding it atop her head with both hands as Kai came to inspect what he was working with. If there was ever a start or end to the wrap, the edges had faded a long time ago, as if she hadn't taken this thing off, *ever*.

He tested the bottom edge, looking for give. Kai gradually moved around to Rasia's back and found purchase right at her spine. When Rasia bent back her shoulders, there was enough room to wiggle the blade up. He cut through the multiple layers of linen. Some layers were tougher than others, as if strips had been applied at different times over the years.

"Why haven't you ever taken it off?" Kai asked.

"'Cause breasts are stupid. The fuck am I going to do with two sacks of useless fat growing out of my chest? I've trained my entire life to perfect my fighting styles, then everything is thrown off balance when these fuckers come in. I figure if I wrapped them tight enough, they'd stop growing."

"You're hurting yourself."

"You don't have boobs. You don't know shit."

"I know what it's like to hate your body, Rasia. That's what this is."

Kai snipped the last thread. Even though he had cut a vertical line up her back, the fabric didn't fall away on its own. Rasia reached back and stripped off the linen mold. The edges left behind angry red welts.

With her back turned to him, her bare shoulders visibly shuddered once freed.

"*They're bigger!*" Rasia snarled, spinning and hurling the mold at the windship railing.

Kai flinched at the sudden explosion, but as soon as her anger appeared, it receded. Rasia folded down to the deck with her arms crossed and hid underneath her hair.

Kai never thought Rasia could be insecure about anything. And yet, even though Rasia hadn't seen her own breasts for the past two years, she still had the courage to free them.

Kai glanced down at his uneven clothes and sucked in a determined breath. Kai pulled his shirt off over his head. He finished loosening the ties of his waistband, and the pants fell down his legs. He unfolded the front flap of his loincloth and took one more breath before shoving that down his legs, too. He stood naked on the deck of the windship. Kai resisted the urge to hide behind his hands.

Rasia peeked at him from under her hair. Her eyes scanned down his body, then she stood. Slowly, awkwardly, she unfolded her arms. It was the first time Kai had ever seen Rasia so unbalanced. She flicked her hair over her shoulders and straightened under his gaze. Her breasts were paler than the rest of her bronze skin. They stood out, not only because of their color, but how they were the soft parts of her, vulnerable in a way the rest of her wasn't. She wasn't all abs and muscle as he'd thought.

Kai and Rasia stood before each other, bare, in the bodies they were born in.

"I don't get it. What the fuck are you so insecure about? The scars?" Rasia asked. She waved her hand up and down her body, bringing attention to her own. She had a mottled burn on her shoulder, bites on her skin, and a vicious three-claw scar scraped from her back around to her left hip. She wore them all with the pride of namesakes.

"It's not the scars," Kai admitted, even though he did have a lot of them. The marks on his back, from when the Council had him whipped, certainly weren't pretty to look at. "You're not . . . disappointed?"

"Disappointed by what? You're pretty much the skin and bones I expected you to be."

"I'm . . . I'm . . ." Kai hid his face in his hands and said the obvious, "I'm small."

Rasia snorted. She crossed her arms under the weight of her breasts, unused to them, holding them up. "You don't look much different than Ysai-ji before he hit his growth. He was quite the scrawny stick too, till the day he shot up overnight like a rutting date palm. So, you're a late bloomer. Your dick is fine."

Kai's face flamed hot in embarrassment.

"I meant all of me," he mumbled. He meant the twigs of his arms, the stunted reach of his height, the sliver of space he inhabited, and yes, his dick too. "What if it's too late? What if I never . . ."

"*Eat*, Kai. Seriously. Fucking eat. Look at your tah, and your tajih, and grantahs. The males on both sides of your family are built well. You're capable of growing; you've just got to allow your body to do so."

"That's just it, Rasia. The healers say because of the sickness, I'll never grow right. Even if I slay a dragon and earn my face, I'll

163

never physically be an adult."

"*Fuck the healers.* They are wrong. Look at how these past few days have already made a difference. For one, you don't look so much like Death anymore. You are improving at the morning running exercises, and you've shown that you have far more strength than you think you do. Nothing is wrong with you."

"*There is,*" Kai said, frustrated. "I can't pretend it doesn't exist. There is an actual fire burning me up from the inside out."

Rasia approached him and poked right at the center of his bony chest. "Only because you've given up! You've stopped fighting and have allowed whatever this is to consume you almost hollow. I'm not saying it doesn't exist. I'm saying not to let it control you. Deny this sickness power over you and live your damn life. I think the healers are wrong, and you've still got growth ahead, but even if you didn't, this is the body you've got. And, no matter what anyone says, there's *nothing* wrong with it."

A knot formed in Kai's throat.

"I want your everything," Rasia declared. "Don't dare disrespect me with anything less than everything you've got to give. Everything is always enough."

Kai surged forward, to kiss her mouth, and pressed together skin to skin. He didn't hesitate to touch her, to squeeze her glutes in his hands and caress her breasts with his lips. He wanted to smear his everything all over her body.

"Show me what to do," Kai begged.

Rasia led him down to the windship deck and invited him between her legs. Poems and songs often described the vagina in metaphors—like the inside of a sweet fig, or the dark underbelly hatch of a windship, or the fragile petal folds of a garden flower. Kai didn't think it looked like any of those things, but perhaps all of them at once.

She showed him how she pleasured herself during cold nights alone in the Desert, when she gasped out with no one around to hear. But now she was not alone anymore, and Kai curled his fingers into her depths. In many ways, it felt like being handed the steer of a windship. At her helm, Kai felt even more powerful.

His hands not only held the power to stop a crash, but to steer her headlong into one.

Rasia's breath quickened. Her body stretched taut, lifting off the deck with legs wrapped around his waist. She collapsed a throbbing wreck.

"Fuck. *Fuck.*" Rasia pressed a hand to her ribs as she took in air. "That was good. That was really good."

"Yeah?"

"Don't get too cocky. You'll have to repeat that performance several times to make sure it wasn't a fluke."

"It wasn't. I had a good teacher."

"Damn right." Rasia snickered, then lolled her head toward him. "It's not sex till we both get off. Your turn."

"Are you hurt?" Kai asked instead. She was still clutching her ribs. He had been careful not to touch the wound but maybe he had pushed too far.

Rasia looked at him, defiant, jaw set. "I'm fine."

"Rasia," Kai said seriously. "What was the point of you taking it easy these past four days if you're going to ruin all that progress? You're right. We can't let pain control our lives, but that doesn't mean we shouldn't listen to it. *Are you hurt?*"

"A little," Rasia admitted softly. She reached out and clutched his hair, combing through it and clinging at different intervals. "But I haven't dislocated it, I swear. It just hurts when I bend. But I want to finish this. I'll tell you if it becomes a problem, I promise."

Kai didn't want to hurt her, but Rasia knew her body far better and for far longer than he did. She knew what she could handle, and all Kai could do was listen.

"Okay, but we should find a way to brace your ribs." Kai looked around the windship and caught his eyes on the name carved freshly into the mast. "I'm not sure Shamaijen Windbreaker would approve."

Rasia smirked. "Even better."

Kai repositioned her upright in his lap, pressed firmly between himself and the mast to give her better support. Kai gripped his

165

dick and found his nervousness bubbling up again. The Grankull often told parables of how awfully it could hurt to have sex when you were underage and unready. He licked at the sweat above his upper lip and aimed for her fig-hatch-flower entrance.

The heels of Rasia's feet dug into his ass and pushed him forward. Hot, smooth heat swallowed all six of his senses. Kai blinked, a little in shock at how easy it was to slide in.

"Are you hurt?" he asked quickly.

"Nope. Went in pretty easy," Rasia chirped. They felt impossibly locked together, like the windship knots Rasia taught him, strong and resilient but easy to unravel if you knew the trick.

Rasia pressed her lips against his ear with a demand. "Let's go for a ride, windeka."

Fuck, he almost came right then and there.

Kai lifted to his knees for purchase and thrust forward to chase his wind. The sun burned at his neck. Her fingers scrambled and slipped on his sweat-soaked back, often finding purchase on the scars. Kai reached for the mast with both hands for support, to propel harder and faster into her horizon. He had promised her his everything.

His chest tightened in pain, burning, and Kai unflinchingly met it head-on. He was done running away from it. He was done letting it control his life. If this killed him, if sex was the thing that finally did him in, he had no fucking regrets.

The pain exploded—or it was his orgasm—or both? It broiled through his limbs, seared his skin as if he had tumbled into a bonfire of his own muscle and bones and tendons. It melted everything out of him. *Excruciating*.

"Kai," Rasia whispered in awe. "Open your eyes."

Kai opened his eyes to find Rasia's lips bitten and swollen, her hair sweaty and stuck to her face, and her eyes bright in the sun. He turned to follow her gaze to the impossible sight around them, of sand spinning a vortex in the air as if they were caught in the heart of a sandstorm.

The breath he was holding dislodged from his chest, and all at once, the windship *fell*, out the clouds, crashing with a jolt and wheeling down sand dunes.

Rasia burst into gleeful laughter.

"THAT WAS FUCKING AWESOME!"

CHAPTER EIGHTEEN

—

A weight pressed against Kai's chest, and panic crawled with him out the depths of sleep. He worried his lungs had worsened and this was the day he would wake up unable to breathe. His heart raced, his throat constricted, he jerked his eyes open and froze, inhaling a trembling vibration of air.

Rasia laid sprawled on top of him, naked.

He collapsed back as the adrenaline and panic receded. It wasn't a dream. The soft crush of Rasia's breasts and the soreness from muscles rarely used was plenty evidence it wasn't. They hadn't managed to get into a bedroll, and the cave floor was cold and harsh under his skin. But Rasia's hair provided plenty cover for them both, and her heat kept him warm even when their fire had gone out overnight. Kai ruminated over yesterday's events while he watched her sleep. After their wild windship ride, they returned to the gorge and feasted and celebrated and drank too much alcohol. He was embarrassed about that. He didn't think he'd get drunk off of one drink. His head was still pounding.

He cast his eyes over Rasia's curved bum to the tangle of her legs in his. He flashed back to all the moans and gasps and breathless pants that had composed the unforgettable songs their bodies danced to all night long. *They had so much sex.*

Rocks scuffled outside the cave. Kai frowned, confused. At

first, he attributed the sound to one of the mountain goats. A voice soon popped his bubble.

"KAI!"

For one terrifying moment, Kai thought it was his jih. Then he registered the fact it was a male voice. *Zephyr.* A strong wave of relief surged through Kai's body.

Another consideration hit him. What if Rasia didn't want to be caught with him like this? It was one thing to fuck him. It was another thing for people to know.

Kai's panic returned with full force.

"Rasia," he whispered. "Wake up."

She turned over and her arm whacked him in the face. "Y*sai-jiii*, it's your turn for breakfast."

"Kai? You in here?" Zephyr's voice came closer now, at the mouth of the cave, his voice ringing and echoing loudly off the rocks.

Rasia jolted awake. She reached over Kai to search the cave floor. "Fuck, where are my swords?" Kai squeaked. "That's not my sword."

"Rasia?" Zephyr came rushing into the cave. "Where is—"

Zephyr didn't seem the type to be surprised by anything, but surprise smacked him in the face as he took in the scene. The cave had aired out overnight, so it didn't smell as thickly of sex as before, but there were empty gourds of palm wine and discarded clothes tossed around in a whirlwind. There was no mistaking the scene for what it was.

Kai's heart raced, thudding so hard it threatened to explode right out of his chest. Zephyr's invasion felt like an end to something. His abrupt presence shattered the dream Kai had been living for the past few days. Now it was time to wake up.

"Oh, it's you," Rasia said, breaking the tension before diving back under her hair. She curled into Kai's side. No shits or cares given.

"*Kai.*" Zephyr said his name like a stranger's. "*We need to talk.*"

Zephyr's tone cut Rasia the wrong way. Kai felt it when her body coiled against his. She popped up from her hair and hissed dangerously, "He doesn't need to do anything."

"I didn't ask you," Zephyr said. He set his feet and made it clear he wasn't going anywhere until Kai complied.

"*Leave*," Rasia snarled in turn. "Why are you here? He left your kull and joined mine. He doesn't want to be with you."

"It doesn't matter what he wants. I made a promise to Nico. Kai doesn't have a choice."

Rasia sprung. Kai moved to catch her, but she slipped right through his arms. Rasia charged at Zephyr, and there were some important facts to note:

1. Rasia was naked.
2. Her swords had been too far away for her to grab.
3. Rasia fought using speed and momentum to her advantage. She came at Zephyr at an angle, charging low to hit his knees to throw him off balance.
4. Zephyr didn't budge.

Zephyr scooped Rasia up by the shoulder, lifted her into the air, and slammed her with unrepentant force to the ground. Rasia landed on her right side, and the pain that twisted her face seared Kai's eyes.

Kai reached for one of the empty wine gourds.

Rasia lifted her legs to lock them around Zephyr's neck and bit down viciously into the arm that had her pinned. Zephyr slipped the other arm free of her leg and rolled forward, where they tumbled and wrestled out of locks and holds on the ground. Zephyr couldn't restrain her, but Rasia couldn't get a solid blow on him either.

Kai slammed the gourd atop Zephyr's head. It didn't knock Zephyr out, but he did pause in shock. Rasia used the interruption to slam her feet in Zephyr's face, kicking against it as leverage to create some distance between them. Zephyr pressed against the cave wall to wipe at the dirt from Rasia's feet.

"Stop, *I'll talk*," Kai said, forming a barrier of skin and bones between them.

Zephyr lifted his arm where Rasia had bitten him. "She's a

rutting animal."

"Mutt," Rasia spat.

"Rabid skink."

"*Stop!*"

Zephyr crossed his arms, then said pointedly, "I'll wait outside."

Kai shook with fury long after Zephyr had left the cave. Rasia grunted behind him, dropping atop a piece of pottery she had overturned to use as a chair. She lifted her breasts with one hand and inspected the injury at her waist.

Kai remembered himself, and so did his body. When he moved, his muscles blazed with soreness, bones creaking with belated ache. Kai pushed himself to help, even though all he wanted was to sleep off last night's activities. He rekindled the fire to help give Rasia light. He picked up her gourd of water, handed it to her, and crouched down to inspect the injury himself.

The fire lit yellow green over a bruised rib. On top of that, rocks had cut open an ugly gash. It was going to need stitches. They had been so careful last night so as not to worsen the wound, and now this.

Above him, Rasia swished the water around her mouth and spat a wad of blood to the ground. "You're not talking to him alone."

"It's better that I do."

"There's nothing stopping him from throwing you over his shoulder and running off with you. And look at this," Rasia said with a disgusted snarl, gesturing at her waist. "I might not be able to chase him down."

She did have a point. Kai left Rasia to stew while he grabbed some herbs and medical supplies from the kull stash. He returned and dropped most of the supplies at her feet along with one of the gourds of unfinished palm wine. Ample liquid still swished at the bottom. Rasia grabbed the wine and took a swig. Kai crouched in front of the fire to heat the tip of a porcupine belly quill.

"What we should do," Rasia said darkly, "is burn down whatever ship he sailed in on. Can't take you anywhere after that."

Sounded good to Kai. He nodded. "Let's do that."

Rasia squinted at him, surprised by his outright approval. Her rictus grin spread to reveal the blood red of her teeth. "Fuck yes."

Kai threaded the bundle of skinko sinew around the quill. He glanced at her, and Rasia nodded with a grunt. She upturned the wine and hissed as it washed over the wound. Kai weaved the stitches into her skin.

Before yesterday, Kai would have hesitated to touch her, but now he tended to Rasia without thought, and his hand lingered on her hip with too much ease.

"I grabbed all the herbs I could get my hands on. Which ones do you need?" Kai asked. Rasia pointed out the herbs that numbed the pain and reduced inflammation. Under her instruction, Kai ground the herbs and gently applied them over the stitches. Rasia realigned the broken rib carefully, afraid one wrong move could puncture a lung. Kai wrapped fresh bandages around her waist while she lifted her breasts, annoyed, so he could make each pass around.

Rasia didn't have anything to replace the former wrap Kai had cut her out of yesterday. She'd brought extra food, an extra pair of pants, and even gonom to the Forging, but she hadn't brought an extra wrap. After witnessing how her breasts flopped around in her fight against Zephyr, Kai understood her insecurities a little better now. Kai certainly wouldn't want his junk flopping around in the middle of a fight, either.

Kai sat back on his haunches once he finished, and he had an idea. He retrieved his shroud, the same one Rasia had snatched off twice now, from his belongings. It's a good thing he had brought two. He crouched in front of her with the strip of cloth.

"Arms up," he instructed.

She raised an inquiring brow and reached up, slow and hesitant to release the weight of her breasts. The once pale orbs had turned a crisp brown after only a few drums in yesterday's sun. Kai reached out to wrap his shroud around her breasts, to her back, and around again. He tied the ends into a tight bow. To secure it, Kai pinned the shroud with one of the bronze hooks from the kull stash the way he'd seen Nico do.

Rasia straightened her posture and stared at him intently, then drew forward and kissed him—hot and full of force. "Next time you take off my wrap, you don't go to sleep until you put it back on."

"Understood."

Rasia pushed to her feet and moved over to the tub of water they had drawn from the springs. Rasia scooped a calabash through the water and tossed it over her face. She wiped between her legs and at the residue Kai had left behind.

Kai moved to do much the same. He didn't know if he was sticky from the alcohol, sweat, or the cum; he didn't remember exactly how they'd passed out last night.

"What are we going to do about the hunt this morning?" Kai asked, considering her injury.

"We're still doing it," Rasia said, determined. "We don't have a choice now. We ate all the food."

"There are still some leftovers."

"Eat it for breakfast. We're going on this hunt," Rasia said, brooking no argument. Kai worried how this hunt was going to go but held his reservations. If Rasia said she could do it, then she could do it.

They bathed and dressed, and while they usually sat across from each other to eat their meals, Kai found himself surprised when Rasia dropped down next to him with her plate of food. She folded her knee against his leg and reminded Kai of another important topic he needed to address.

"What do you want to tell Zephyr about us?"

"What do you mean?"

"He obviously knows we had sex, but I can ask him not to tell anyone, especially if you don't want anyone to know . . . though he'll probably tell Nico."

"I don't give a shit what people think, Kai. And Nico can choke on her shroud." Rasia leaned forward and pressed a hand to his thigh. "The real question is: Do you think he's going to squeal to the Council about us? In that case, more than one thing needs to burn today."

Kai scoffed. "No. He's not going to risk my Forging. He and Nico are too close. He's not going to say a thing."

"Hmm . . ." Rasia sat back. "How does a tent kid even know your jih? I know Kenji-shi is friends with the foreigner, but what does that have to do with Nico?"

"The other tahs were friends. They struck up a friendship during their Forging. After"—Kai motioned to his face—"tah stopped associating with Zara . . ." Kai stumbled over her address. The Grankull revoked all Zara's earned names when they banished her. She didn't have any name but her First. Kai personally wasn't close enough to use -shi, but it was extremely disrespectful to address an adult by only their First Name. He felt uncomfortable disrespecting the person who had often supported his family. "There is fate between the families. Nico has been going in and out of the Tents for years."

"Huh, didn't catch that one," Rasia said. She leaned back with the information as she chewed, tossing thoughts around in her head.

Kai scraped the bottom of his plate and looked down, surprised. He had cleared it so quickly, and he was still hungry, which shocked him because he had eaten quite a bit last night, too. Rasia handed him her plate, which was about two-thirds empty.

"Rasia, I can't."

"I'm good. I don't like feeling heavy before a hunt."

She dropped the plate atop his empty one. With heavy reluctance, he ate the rest and even still, afterward, he felt hungry. He never thought sex would be the secret to building an appetite.

After he finished, Kai offered to help Rasia to her feet. She waved a dismissive hand. He watched her take a deep breath then pick herself up. She straightened, visibly sucking in the agony, then walked toward the mouth of the cave without a limp or hint of pain. Kai followed her.

They paused at the sight before them. A sandstorm had blown through. Everything, including the windship, lay half-buried. The rocks Kai had spent so painstakingly long trying to clear had disappeared under the sand. He thought he saw a few of their tips peeking out. It was a surprise the cave entrance hadn't been blocked in.

"I don't remember a sandstorm last night," Kai mumbled, confused.

"I do," Rasia said cheekily. She burst her hands open, imitating an explosion, and Kai blushed at the implication. She slapped Kai on the butt and winked before disappearing down a path that led around the gorge.

Just great—he did magic when he orgasmed. How utterly useless that was.

At least, from what he remembered of last night, the follow-ups were not as painful as that first time. Why had it felt so excruciating? Kai had no idea.

Kai shook his head and looked to where Zephyr sat atop an outcropping, watching the cave entrance and the whole exchange. Kai climbed the sandy hill that hadn't existed before yesterday and stood before Zephyr.

"What do you want to talk about?"

"You know exactly what this is about," Zephyr said, skipping right over all the small talk and greetings. "You know what's at stake. If Nico doesn't succeed her Forging, there won't be anyone on the Council fighting for the Tents. That's my family at risk, Kai. You're out here, literally fucking around, when lives are at stake. You had your fun, but this thing with Rasia has to end."

A thick oil of guilt flooded Kai's conscience. He crossed his arms and turned away, toward the mouth of the gorge and all he'd ever hoped for. "I told Nico to let me go."

"*She can't.* You know she can't."

Kai knew, and yet he had fled anyway. He squeezed his eyes shut and tried to ignore the fact that he'd been having the time of his life while jih was juggling her responsibility to the Grankull and her responsibility to him and the family. He'd been trying not to think about it. Was he the selfish one? His chest hurt. He could feel his resolve crumbling.

"I admit," Zephyr said, "you are the one person on the other side of Nico's life I wanted to meet the most. People hate us both for no reason other than the circumstances of our births. We have so much in common, and I want you a friend."

"We have nothing in common," Kai bit out. That could not have been more obvious at the oasis. Zephyr had stood his ground while Kai cowered. Zephyr demanded attention while Kai never received it. Zephyr was built like a fucking mountain, and Kai was the pebble Zephyr could easily crush underfoot. "Leave, Zephyr. Find Nico and convince her to let me go."

"Let you go where, Kai? Running off with Rasia and chasing her dragon is courting Death. You're steering yourself off a cliff. Do you really think Nico is going to let you go alone? You're her rock. You are the one she leans on. After Avalai Ohan died, you are the one who pulled Nico through the wreck of it."

"Because I'm the one who wrecked it in the first place!" Kai snapped. "It's my fault tah is dead. Was I supposed to stand by and watch it all fall apart because of me? Yes, I pulled Nico out of bed. I brushed her hair. I pushed her out the door. I took care of Rae when they cried and screamed and yelled for a tah they couldn't understand was gone. This family doesn't need me. I'm the one who broke it, and it would be better off if I had fucking drowned at the bottom of the oasis!"

Kai's chest heaved. He turned and buried his face in his hands and pushed against the tears. He didn't get to cry over it. He didn't get to mourn the tah he killed.

Zephyr sat with a stillness—like those large rocks of the gorge, tall and imposing and in the way. Zephyr said slowly, "Kenji-shi is either out hunting or at the bottom of a bottle. You are the one at home every day. You are more tah than jih. Nico needs you. Rae needs you."

"Shut up," Kai snapped. He hated Zephyr. He hated that this stranger knew all the intimate details of his life. It felt worse than Rasia snatching his shroud off in the market. It was unsettling, like a distant relative who knew your entire life while you'd never heard of them at all.

And now he couldn't get Rae out of his head. He couldn't stop thinking of Rae rushing through the hallways; turning the corner; looking, searching, and never finding. It crushed Kai's bones to think of Rae searching for him, to know no one would sing Rae to sleep or make sure they ate all their food.

Kai had almost torn his family apart all over again. He stared at that gorge opening, the same one he'd been reaching toward for days now, and clenched his fists in determination. "This is different. It's not the same. Rasia and I are going to slay a dragon."

"Are you listening to yourself? You and Rasia are only two people. It's not possible, and you've bought into her crazy scheme because you have a flame for her."

"You know nothing about her."

"It's been five days, Kai. *You* know nothing about her. In the Tents, they call her Rasia the Undefeated. She has a face in the Tents. She has a *name*. Think about that. After Shamaijen Windbreaker died, she brawled, undefeated, in tent matches for blinks. She's dangerous. And I get it, I know how utterly consuming a flame can be. It blinds you. It makes you do stupid and illogical things."

"Grief also makes you do stupid and illogical things," Kai said, remembering all the ways Rasia's voice softened when she spoke of her tah. The ways Rasia told stories of him and traced his footsteps on the windship. Kai shrugged. "Most people have blood on their hands."

He did. What did it matter if Rasia had killed a few people?

"It's not the blood I'm worried about. It's her temper. What if you get on the wrong side of that? What if you piss her off? You've got scars enough, Kai."

Kai grasped the subtext of Zephyr's words, and fog thickened in his ears. Kai seethed, his fury returning and completely burning all his guilt to ash. "*What has Nico told you?*"

Zephyr stared, implacable, and didn't answer.

"*That wasn't Nico's story to tell*," Kai snarled, furious at jih for the first time in his life.

"Nico thinks it was the one time. You've got a lot of scars,

Kai."

"Fuck you," Kai snapped, immediately wrapping his arms over his chest. He had clothes on now, but it was too late. "*Fuck you*. You think you know everything about my life, but you don't. You don't know shit."

"I'm sorry," Zephyr said, standing. "I didn't mean to overstep."

Zephyr reached to grab him, and all the emotions bubbling, boiling, basting inside of Kai exploded. Kai wrenched his dagger from his belt and the tip bled blood from the jewel of Zephyr's throat, daring Zephyr to test him.

Zephyr was too close to grab for his monstrous sword. He was completely at Kai's mercy and had no choice but to listen. And it scared Kai that Zephyr was looking at him as if he were volatile and dangerous, as if Kai had become a different person than that kid at the oasis . . . and maybe he had. It had only been five days, but time has happened all so fast and yet seemed to stretch on forever a vibration. He had gone from knowing Rasia only from jih's secondhand stories to knowing her as this unrelenting force of nature that had swept Kai into her grasp. Perhaps Kai had needed to be tossed, disrupted from the inside out, to finally understand what ground he stood on.

"No. I am staying with Rasia. No argument will shift my mind, and I will die before you physically lodge me from this spot. Return to your Forging and leave me to mine."

Now more than ever, Zephyr felt like a mountain: set in his ways and unable to change. Which was why Kai was so shocked when Zephyr shook the ground with a single word. "Fine."

"Fine?"

"I won't force you to leave. But I'll hang around for a bit. To make sure you're okay."

Kai withdrew his dagger and stabbed it back into his belt. They stared at each other. Kai studied Zephyr, suspicious of his motivations. "You do know that everyone has a flame for Nico, right? You're not special. This isn't going to change anything. You're wasting your Forging on her."

Zephyr crossed his arms, and they bulged the tighter he held them. "Your jih isn't interested in any flames, and I can respect that. I am here because your jih is my best friend, and I give a shit about you. Sorry if that's so hard for you to believe."

It *was* hard to believe.

"You don't know me."

"I hope to."

Maybe. Maybe he and Zephyr could become friends. Maybe he'd finally understand why Nico always came back from the Tents with all these new ideas and a righteous sense of justice. Like Rasia, Zephyr had been another character in Nico's tales. Kai had always suspected that Zephyr wasn't the hero that jih thought he was. No one could be that perfect.

"One condition," Kai said. "Don't you touch Rasia again."

"I don't make empty promises, Kai. Rasia goes for the kill. She's not the type of person you blunt your sword for."

"You broke her ribs," Kai snapped. An exaggeration, but Kai was too angry for nuance.

Zephyr searched Kai's face and picked his words carefully. "I didn't mean to. I'll be more mindful of my strength."

It was true that no one in their right mind fought Rasia without all they had to give. She hadn't attended school for long, but it was long enough to kick everyone's asses before walking away. She was infamous for storming the training fields and challenging anyone to a spar. Rasia was dangerous even when she was naked and unarmed. Kai knew that, and he also knew this was probably as good a promise he was going to get out of Zephyr. Kai pulled at his neck and admitted, "Rasia is going to burn your windship."

"What windship?"

Kai frowned. He walked to the edge of the sand hill and peered over to the other side.

At the bottom, Rasia glared balefully, miffed, at a camel. The camel glared balefully, miffed, back.

"You came here on a camel?" Kai asked.

"Why do you think it took me five days to find you?"

"Nico hasn't, and she has a windship."

"Yeah," Zephyr conceded. "I'm worried about that too."

CHAPTER NINETEEN

I

Nico pressed her shroud to her face in frustration. The piercing crack that sounded when they struck that unexpected trench still rung in her ears. The windship wheel had completely shattered around the axle. They hadn't made it but a day out of the oasis and already something had gone wrong.

Azan crouched down and studied the wheel. The blacksmith's child hissed between his teeth. "It's completely shot. The wood is ruined. Several of the spokes still look good, though."

Nico studied their surroundings for potential building materials, but this area was so unyielding—the ground cracked, parched, and gasping. The air was so dry it hurt the throat to breathe, and no tree or shrubbery was in sight. Just dry dust and heat. Nico was grateful they had refilled their water supply back at the oasis.

"Could we patch it with clay?" Nico asked.

"It'll get us back up and running until we can find an alternative. We'll be slower till then," Azan said.

"That'll have to be enough. What's your experience making clay?"

"Not much at making it. The shop usually imports clay from the brickmakers, but I've worked with it enough to guess at the sand-soil ratio," Azan said, a little uncertain. It was still better than the handful of lessons regarding clay-making Nico had in school.

Nico turned to Suri and Kelin, who waited for instructions on how to handle yet another disaster she had steered them all into. Her magic would help them little this time around. They were going to have to tighten their shrouds and get the hard work done.

"We're going to mix clay for a makeshift wheel, but we're going to have to sun-bake the mix. We're losing light, so time isn't on our side. Azan and Kelin, start digging a hole. Suri and I will sift the soil."

Nico unloaded her satchel and glaive, and the others followed suit. In one big pile, they discarded all the items they didn't want to get dirtied or weigh them down. They rolled up their sleeves and put up their hair.

Nico retrieved two large calabash bowls and the sift from the windship hatch. She leaned the sift against the hull and handed Suri the other bowl, but Suri grabbed at it blindly, distracted by Azan and Kelin, who were using the windship oars to break the hard earth and shovel out dirt into a gathered pile. Nico noted the frown that pulled Suri's bow lips taut.

They traveled off toward a nearby ditch of sand. Nico held her calabash atop her head to create a small measure of shade from the sun. Nico watched their shadows travel the hot ground beside them.

Once they'd left Azan and Kelin in the distance, Nico asked, "What's wrong?"

"I looked in Kelin's satchel."

"What? Why are you going through his things?"

Suri stopped. Her hair was curled and frizzed from the sweat on her forehead. "You can't trust him, Nico. You want to help them. That's who you are. But a tent rat will always be a tent rat."

Nico was jolted by the unexpected slur. That was the type of ignorance Nico expected of Suri's tah, one of the Council's most ardent proponents of wiping out the Tents, but Nico never thought Suri shared any of her tah's views. Where was this suddenly coming from? Or had it always been there and Nico had missed it all this time?

"You sound like your tah," Nico accused.

"There were herbs in Kelin's satchel for poisons."

"Neema brought knives."

"These are the type of poisons you slip into someone's drink. I knew you'd be blind to this. He is not to be trusted, Nico. None of them are."

"You're wrong. Tent kids are no different than any of us. There are good and bad on both sides, and I don't appreciate you calling them 'tent rats.' I have friends in the Tents."

"Kelin is trying to *kill* you, and that mutt bastard is only using you for your influence."

"Suri!" Nico snapped, aghast at Suri's audacity to drag Zephyr into the conversation. She'd spoken to Suri of Zephyr before, and Suri had never expressed such sentiments, but now, Nico was beginning to remember that they commonly had been one-sided conversations. Suri never inquired after Zephyr or asked questions, as if Suri didn't care but was only listening because Nico did.

Nico felt her world drying out. "You're wrong, Suri. You're wrong about Kelin, and you're wrong about Zephyr. You'll understand when you finally meet him. We won't talk on this anymore."

Nico whirled and stomped over to one side of the sand ditch to fill her calabash while Suri walked over to the other side. They'd been friends their entire lives, but they'd never had as many conflicts as they'd had during the Forging. Nico had been grateful that they had been had placed them on the same team, but now, she wondered if it was worth all these cracks rupturing their friendship. She doubted they were the sort of cracks that could be mended with clay.

When Nico and Suri returned with the sand, Azan was laughing at one of Kelin's remarks. Nico glanced at Suri pointedly, as if Azan's laughter proved Kelin's goodness, but it only deepened the mistrust on Suri's face.

BONES TO THE WIND

With a sigh, Nico plopped the large calabash of sand on the ground and shook out the strained muscles of her arms. She wiped at the sweat on her face and chest with her shroud and took a deep swallow of water before getting to work.

Nico and Suri worked in tandem, never needing to vocalize their actions or next steps. Nico wished it was always this easy. Suri held the silt, while Nico tossed in dirt from the pile Azan and Kelin had dug up. Suri shook out and flung the stones and pebbles over her shoulder. They repeated these actions over and over to thin the soil until it was fine and smooth.

"Is it true you eat people in the Tents?" Azan asked Kelin, both of them knee-deep in the hole. Nico immediately cringed at the question. "They say bodies disappear in the night because you eat them."

"Why do you think grub-mash tastes so strong?" Kelin smirked and leaned forward. His lips brushed against Azan's dusty cheek. "It's to hide the taste of what else is in it."

Nico recognized Kelin's answer as one of those brash tent answers common to such questions. Many tent folks believed the Grankull didn't have a right to tent business, and many embraced that mentality by perpetuating and exaggerating the very stereotypes they were often accused of. Others got tired of the same old questions and answered with lies and half-truths for the entertainment. A rarer few tried to educate, but they often got exhausted when their words bounced off dense ears. Whatever the case or reasoning, tent answers were never straight.

Kullers didn't understand that. They only heard the surface, as evident by the dawning horror on Suri's face. Azan laughed awkwardly. Nico could see his next question forming and subtly shook her head, but Azan couldn't stop himself.

"What *do* people taste like?"

Kelin's face was grave. "They taste like grubworm."

Azan laughed, though it receded when Kelin's face didn't change. "You're kidding, right?"

"No."

"Oh."

Kelin angled away from Azan and a roguish smirk pulled at his face. Nico shook her head. If the Grankull saw people living in the Tents as outsiders and the people in the Tents saw those in the Grankull as outsiders, how were they ever supposed to meet in the middle? Nico feared she was steering out of her lane, but nevertheless she felt compelled to speak the truth.

"They are called the Vulture Han," Nico said, "and none in the Tents have seen their face. At night, the Vulture Han's followers collect all the bodies fallen during the day, or those bodies of the dead given over, and their team of trappers use the bodies as bait to catch grubworms. It's one of the most important sources of food in the Tents. So yes, technically, all the dead taste of grubworm."

Kelin stopped and stared at Nico, surprised.

"Really? That's true?" Azan asked.

"I'm the Ohan."

Azan nodded, appeased by that explanation. Sometimes that line did come in handy.

"But why didn't Kelin just say that in the first place?" Azan complained, asking Nico the question, even though Kelin was standing right next to him. Kelin turned to Nico, amused, to see if Nico could tell him his own answer.

Nico didn't rise to Kelin's bait. She focused on Azan and chided, "Why should he have to?"

Azan looked between Kelin and Nico as if sensing he had done something wrong but unable to vocalize it. Azan said, hurt and defensive, "He's part of the kull, and he lied to us."

"He wasn't born of a kull. Why should he owe us anything? While the Tents have a clear purpose for their dead, cannibalism can still happen, as it also happens in the Grankull. Many in the Grankull do not have food. Those who fail the Forging do not receive rations. Those with no job do not receive rations. Cannibalism happens in the Grankull too, but we point to the Tents and vilify them and call them cannibals to make us feel inherently superior. But it's just a *story*, hiding the fact that we're not any better. The Grankull lies, too."

Azan, Suri, and Kelin were all staring at her now as if she had performed the most shocking of magic. The truth shouldn't be magic. Everyone was always so shocked to learn that all the stories, all the myths, all the legends, were edited.

"I didn't know," Azan mumbled.

"Now you do." Nico cleared her throat of her rant. She swallowed it down hard. "I think that hole is big enough. You both can stop now."

They were slow to move, but Nico continued and crouched before the hole. She drowned them out to focus on her magic and exhaled a deep breath.

Summoning the water for their dug-out hole was harder than the small lake she had previously made. No immediate water sources were in the vicinity to draw from, just the water that existed in their own bodies, gourds, and the supply in the windship. The Grankull often thought she summoned water from nothing, but that was an illusion. She *shifted* water. She moved it from one place to another, and it took far more magic to move it over large distances. She borrowed from the oasis a day away, and the water level of their dug-out hole began to rise.

"Okay, that's good," Azan said once the water hit his shins.

They added the fine soil and sand, then took off their shoes and blended the mixture with their bare feet. It squelched between Nico's toes, and her thighs burned at the pull of the thickening mud. They all worked in silence, and Nico admitted she might have soured the water with her rant. Her intentions hadn't been to splinter the group even further.

If the Tents and the Grankull were as sand and soil, could Nico be the water to mix them together?

After thoughtful deliberation, Nico reached out and slid her muddy hand across Azan's face. He looked at her, shocked, and Nico raised her brows in a teasing challenge. He grinned wide, then reached down to scoop up a handful of mud.

Nico ducked behind Kelin, and the ball of mud hit Kelin squarely in the chest. He gave an affronted yelp and didn't hesitate to seek revenge as he scooped mud in both hands.

Azan laughed as he raced toward the other side of the hole, splashing Suri on the way. Mud slid down Suri's face, and the sight resurfaced memories of Nico and Suri chasing each other through rain puddles. Nico wondered if those same memories had bubbled up in Suri when her face softened into a smile. Suri moved to grab for mud, and Nico grabbed her own. They each got caught in the crossfire between Azan and Kelin. Suri and Nico wordlessly agreed to join forces.

For a brief moment, the tension between the Grankull and the Tents was forgotten. They forgot about the Forging and the deadlines and the responsibilities. Nico forgot her worries of assassins and strained friendships and jih waiting for her rescue.

Nico let it all go.

And took the time to have a little fun.

The sun had set by the time they finished mixing the clay, which meant they'd be stuck out here at least till high noon tomorrow waiting for the sun to finish hardening the clay and set in the mold.

Which, in the end, was probably a good thing, for it took some time to scrub the mud from their clothes. They hung their wet clothes to dry along the sail line. Suri had won the first hand of rattle-bones, so she took her bath first, behind the windship and out of sight of the camp.

The shrouds might have been optional now, but it took longer than a few days for kids participating in the Forging to grow bolder with their bodies. Nico certainly didn't feel comfortable stripping in front of everyone, so she helped set up camp while itching in all sorts of places and waiting her turn at the water barrels.

Kelin, on the other hand, had no such compunctions. He stripped naked right there at camp and started washing off. At least he had the decency to move far enough away so as not to splash them with dirty water, but he was still close enough so that Nico and Azan couldn't miss the knowing smirk he tossed in their direction as he judged them both for their innocence. Kelin had a wiry build, with the sort of sleek muscle that was often underestimated and well-hidden under clothes.

Azan cursed when he cut his finger on the flint, a rarity for him. Azan always started the campfire on the first sure strike. He was so dependable that Nico envied his skill. It always took her at least a few tries to get the flame going. But tonight, Azan found himself distracted, constantly glancing over at Kelin. Kelin did nothing to help Azan's focus as he scrubbed at his skin, slowly and sensually. Flirting.

Nico had noticed it for the past couple of days now and even today while Azan and Kelin were digging the hole. They might become a problem.

"You seem to know a lot about the Tents," Azan said, curving the statement into a question while turning to her. He unconsciously scratched at dirt on his arm.

". . . yes?" Nico said, already knowing she might not like where this question led.

"They say tent kids have a lot of sex. Is that true?"

Nico groaned. "It's true that they tend to have more sexual experience than we do at this age, but not because they're undisciplined or deviant," Nico said the latter quickly to dispel those assumptions, "but more so because they aren't disallowed from having it. They don't risk banishment and shame like we do. They have no face to lose. That said, every person is different. For all Kelin's . . . bravado, he's a flock kid. They're protective of their investments. I'd guess he hasn't had any."

"What?" Azan asked, shocked. "But the Flock . . . they're whores, right?"

"Calling the Flock a group of whores is the same as calling dragonscale iron," Nico explained. "From what I understand, the Flock began generations ago when a group of whores decided they could better protect themselves by working together. Today,

I'd compare it to the sophistication of any of our merchant guilds. Kullers in need of extra money for whatever reason don shrouds, go into the Tents, and ask the Flock for work. The Flock dresses them as one of their own, with feather masks and all, and sells them to the next shrouded kuller looking to buy sex. Little do people know, the Flock is selling kuller to kuller and taking a percentage of every transaction. Are there people in the Tents who also work for the Flock? Yes. But in the Tents, the 'Flock' more accurately refers to the group of people who manage the Tents' empire of selling bodies."

"Spill all our secrets, why don't you?" Kelin said from over Nico's shoulder, more amused than angry. The Flock liked lying to the Grankull. They liked their reputation. In their opinion, it kept them protected. Kelin threw on his clothes and said more haughtily, correcting her, "I've had sex."

"The tahs don't know about it, do they?" Nico asked.

Kelin grinned and didn't answer. He sat next to Nico at the fire and glanced over at her. "I've never heard a kuller speak about the Tents the way you do."

"I support Tents' rights," Nico said. It was a controversial thing to say, and the importance of it went right over Azan's head. Azan was too busy staring at Kelin's face. "I'm probably the only ohani to do so since Sola-granta. I can only hope to build on her accomplishments."

Kelin scowled at that. "No Ohan has ever supported the Tents."

"Solaria Ohan is the reason you're sitting here right now. She is the one who advocated for tent kids to be able to participate in the Forging, arguing that kids born in the Tents shouldn't be judged on the mistakes of their parents, that they should have the chance to become a part of the Grankull just like anyone else."

"I've never heard that."

Nico shrugged. "Not many people have. It's not the type of history they teach in the Grankull, either."

Nico only knew of Solaria Ohan because her many writings overflowed the personal library of Nico's home, but these writings were practically absent from the temple. They were banned reading and inaccessible to anyone who wasn't a scribe.

"The Grankull have turned the Tents into the villains of a carefully curated story told so many times the lies have become the truth. I don't blame the Tents' mistrust and intolerance of kullers. It was the Grankull who twisted Solaria Ohan's good intentions to justify the first purge. Allowing tents kids into the Forging gave the Grankull the excuse to claim 'innocents' are given a chance, that if tent children can't survive the Forging, it's further proof they don't deserve to make it. But it's never been equal opportunity. The Forging has always been stacked against you."

"That, I know." Kelin nodded. "Every tent kid knows the bones are weighted."

"Yet, you're still here," Azan said.

Kelin shrugged. "You do, every now and again, win a rigged game."

It was easy to take rations for granted, knowing you were secure in your next meal . . . that was, until Kenji-ta dumped you around a fire of tent kids who didn't know where their next meal was coming from. Tent kids spoke of rations like Grankull kids spoke of hunting stars. Even though Kelin was a part of the Flock, he had still been an orphan first. At night, in the dark, he too had no doubt yearned for the stability on the other side of those bones.

"Solaria Ohan died young. She had many dreams and many ambitions, but she died from poison in her water." Nico leaned toward Kelin, away from Azan, and emphasized her point low under the crackling fire. Suri had grown up around healers all her life; she knew what poison looked like. Nico didn't doubt her. "Currently, the Council is at an impasse. They are planning another purge, and when I succeed in my Forging, I'll have the deciding vote. But the Grankull has turned you into the villains yet again. They think so little of the Tents that they'll hire a tent assassin to take out the one person fighting for them, because they don't think an assassin will ever have anything in common with an ohani, that they'll never talk, and they'll never be able to think for themselves and their best interests. That is how little they think of the Tents, and it disgusts me. You aren't bones to be thrown in someone else's game. The bones are in your hand, and you decide how you play."

Kelin's eyes scrutinized her, calculating. "Everyone lies."

"I hope I have all the Forging to gain your trust."

They stared at each other, never breaking eye contact, weighing the other. Suri considered Nico naive, but Nico tried her hardest to keep her face clean. Perhaps if Nico were Ava-ta, she would kill Kelin right then and there to avoid his imminent betrayal, but Nico had faith he'd make the right choice.

That was the thing about kindness and trust and compassion. If kindness were easy, more people would do it. Anger was easy. Revenge and jealousy were easy. Ignorance was easy. But kindness and trust and compassion were hard. They required you to open yourself up, to stride into a fight without armor and stand there and be vulnerable, not knowing whether the other person would wound you with disappointment or worse.

Kindness was not for the weak.

After everyone finished washing, they ate dinner around the campfire. When the lively chatter of dinner faded, Nico spread the standard map issued to all the Forging kulls across her lap. They were somewhere dawnward of the skinko mating grounds. Nico admitted that she was a little frustrated by their glacial pace, and the air was so dry in this area that she was having a difficult time sensing Kai's whereabouts.

She spat on the map and willed her magic to find him. She watched the spit coalesce on a pair of squiggly lines on the parchment—the kull's gorge hideout.

Great acoustics, her tah's voice chimed in her head.

Nico returned the map safely to the cylindrical case where it had been stored. Suri sighed, disgusted. Nico looked up, and beyond the bright burn of the fire, found Azan and Kelin all over each other's faces.

"Azan! Kelin!" Nico said, alarmed. "We're underage!"

Kelin rolled his eyes as he pulled off. Azan pouted, but those round eyes weren't going to work this time.

"Come on, Nico," Azan dramatically complained. "Everyone kindles a little fire during the Forging. My eldest jih fucked his whole Forging kull during his."

"He's lucky he didn't seed anyone."

"Calm your nips. He fucked them all in the ass. It was fine."

"That's still not safe!"

One of the biggest unsaid facts of the Forging was that kids were dumb, and when there were no adults around, sex happened. Tent kids might have had more sexual experience, but kull kids were downright horny by the time of their Forging. The Council knew sex occurred during the Forging, but they couldn't punish anyone without evidence. For those who were caught, however, the punishment was severe.

Underage touching meant a season of lost rations.

Underage sex meant banishment.

Unapproved pregnancy meant a death sentence.

For a society with finite resources, every birth had to be planned. Every child born of the Grankull must be approved. Unbridled pregnancies put the Grankull at risk, and the Council did not hesitate to march any offenders through the streets and burn off their faces at the temple steps. The price of an unapproved pregnancy was the death of one female and one male, and if the female refused to give up their accomplice, the Council would take the nearest male relative as payment. It tore families apart. The consequences had been branded on Zara's face before she fled to the Tents with Zephyr in her womb. They burned Zara's siblings, a male and female, in her stead.

It was a topic Nico didn't treat lightly.

"I am to be the Ohan. When the Council interviews my story

of the Forging, they are going to scrutinize every little detail. It would be safer for you both to wait. You can legally fool around all you want after the Naming."

Azan huffed while Kelin rolled his eyes again. They looked at each other and Nico knew they weren't going to listen.

Later that night, Nico wasn't shocked to wake up to the undeniable sounds of Kelin and Azan going at it. She slapped her hands to her face and tried to fall back asleep, but how did one sleep to the enthusiastic exclamations of Azan's big dick? She envied Suri's ability to sleep through anything. Nico pushed up from her bedroll and went for a walk.

A blanket of stars spread endlessly overhead, and it reminded Nico of a song, specifically, one of the many tah had composed. She closed her eyes and imagined the deep tenor of tah's voice. She hummed the tune on her lips and danced atop the melody. She spiraled, round and round, and collapsed with a lament. He wrote songs under these stars, found inspiration in their tapestry of light.

Nico shook her head and the sand from her clothes. The same voice that had once sang her to sleep haunted her now. She'd tried to bury tah's voice beneath his starry muses, but she knew it wouldn't stay there. It was woven too deeply, buried in dreams and skirted the fading light of a once good person. The songs were too much a part of her now. She'd have to break her own bones to escape them.

Nico returned to camp and found it quiet once again.

Kelin stoked the fire, and he looked at her through the flames with a clever smirk. Nico crossed her arms, and he immediately raised his hands. "You didn't see anything. Plausible deniability, right?"

Nico sighed. At least Azan and Kelin were a seedless joining and didn't have to worry about the worst consequences. "Just be discreet about it."

Nico slipped back into her bedroll and listened to Kelin shuffle the embers of the fire with a piece from the broken wheel; he had rolled first turn at watch. He was an odd one when he was bored,

Nico thought. Or perhaps he didn't know to expect long stretches of idleness. Azan sharpened and cleaned his axe when he was on watch or entertained himself with the single-player version of rattle-bones. Suri oiled her bow and explored the landscape, looking for any materials to add to her concoction of medicines. Suri didn't actually like the healing part of medicine. She liked the mixing and inventing and finding something new. During watch, Suri sometimes read through her favorite tales she'd checked out from the temple library, the ones of healers and their recipes. Kelin, on the other hand, sat and listened.

"Why do you care so much?" Kelin asked suddenly, surprising her.

Nico stared up at the stars. She'd wondered that question her entire life, be it because of Kai and seeing all the different ways he had been treated, or because of Kenji-ta and his insistence on bringing her into the Tents to experience for herself the similarities and differences. Or perhaps because of Ava-ta and being burdened with all the people she'd hurt. Or because of her friendship with Zephyr and the insight he brought from lands beyond and how often the things you knew to be absolute were conditional elsewhere.

Nico had the great fortune of having access to worlds she wasn't born into and had always taken great care to walk these spaces as their guest. She wanted so desperately to show people the world she saw, but it was so hard to open doors that weren't hers to open.

Nico didn't know the answer to Kelin's question. No answer was easy.

This is what Nico did during watch when she was staring into the fire—she thought, she debated, she questioned, and still she never found the answers she was searching for.

Nico settled on, "I care because I know. I understand how unbalanced the scales are."

Kelin scoffed. "All the Tents know the scales are unbalanced. Doesn't mean we're naive enough to think anything will ever make a difference."

Nico combed her hands through her hair, looking for a way to explain, to help him understand. It felt like grasping water. Maybe Nico cared not because of any of those outside influences, but because of something inside herself. Something as much a part of her as rainchimes and bittersweet songs.

"You don't ever see a pair of off-balanced scales and need to correct them?" Nico asked. "I *need* to fix them. I *need* the scales to balance. It makes me feel balanced in turn. What kind of person would I be if I don't use all this power I'm born with to try and right the world? Even if it's pointless, or naive, or people don't understand, that compulsion to balance is a part of who I am."

Her ponytail needed to be exactly at the center of the top of her head. The campfire needed to be made out of a perfect ring of rocks. Nico needed a certain harmony in the group. She needed the world to balance, and she'd spend her entire life making it equal. It was the only way she'd ever know peace, she thinks.

In the end, like everyone else, she was selfish too. If there are no villains in the Tents, there are certainly no heroes in the Grankull.

CHAPTER TWENTY

—

"*You* know how to steer a windship?" Zephyr asked.

Kai hunched at the question; Zephyr didn't need to sound so incredulous about it. Kai kept his back to the tent kid and swept sand from a spot of the deck he had already gone over three times. He mumbled, "Rasia taught me."

"You learned in *five days?*" Zephyr triple knotted himself to the railing.

Kai hunched further.

"Maybe I'm that good of a teacher," Rasia said, popping up from the underbelly hatch. "Everything is tied down. We're good to go."

Rasia touched her tah's name on the mast for good luck. Kai did the same and shuffled over to the steer. The sweat on his hands slicked the bone lever and made it hard to grip. It rattled in its groove, shaking.

Kai pushed down on the steer.

His head whipped back. Rasia hopped and kept her balance. The ropes strained around Zephyr's chest and saved him from being thrown overboard. The tip of the bow dropped, landing stuck in place.

Kai had forgotten to raise the anchor.

"Are you sure Rasia shouldn't steer?" Zephyr asked.

"What's the problem?" Rasia snickered at Kai. "Performance anxieties?"

Kai blushed, and Rasia's eyes cut between him and Zephyr with a sharp knowing. "Turn around, mutt. He can't get it up while you're looking."

Kai had invited Zephyr on this hunt with the hopes that Zephyr would leave if Kai proved capable enough of taking care of himself. But with the rock obstacles earlier, he'd gotten multiple chances to succeed. With Zephyr, he would only get the one.

"Maybe," Kai said. ". . . you should turn around?"

"Seriously?" Zephyr asked. Kai gave his best pleading look. Rasia outright cackled when Zephyr wiggled around in his bindings. "This is ridiculous."

Kai raised the anchor until he heard the catch in the mechanism. He sucked in a deep breath and set his hand to the now-sticky steer. Even turned around, Zephyr's presence didn't burn any less, but the hilarity of the situation helped to disperse some of his nerves. Kai tilted the steer forward.

The windship moved uncertain, wading through the mounds of sand formed by the unexpected storm. Once in motion, Kai found himself flowing into the muscle memory that had been drilled into him these past few days. With each rock that Kai navigated them past, his confidence solidified more and more.

Kai proved yesterday wasn't a fluke when he sailed them out of the gorge.

Leaning against the mast, Rasia glanced at Kai with a pleased smile. Her eyes glittered with mischief, and her eyebrows wiggled. "It's so *big*."

Kai caught her intentions. He asked, in a faux-innocent voice, "I got it up. What should I do now?"

Rasia gasped his name the same way she had last night. "*Kai, faster. Go faster!*"

Kai sped up the windship, and Rasia moaned dramatically.

"I'm going as fast as I can." Kai pressed down with all his strength and pushed the ship to speeds it shouldn't be going. "Is this fast enough?"

"Yes! That's it! Right there!"

"*Are you two done?!*" Zephyr shouted at them from over his shoulder.

Both Kai and Rasia burst into laughter. It hurt his chest, but he felt lighter than he had in a long time.

The ship wobbled. Kai snapped serious and scrambled to slow down. Once the ship returned to a steady pace, Rasia pushed off the mast and sent him a wink before climbing up toward the scout's nest. Kai followed the curve of her ass up every rung until he lost her in the sun.

He'd tapped that.

With a grin, Kai steered the windship. He reveled in the wind tousling his hair and the ability to have an entire ship at his control. It would never not make him feel powerful, accomplished, and proud.

They sailed in the direction the wind carried them. A drum later, Rasia signaled using the kull signs she was teaching him. He didn't know all of them yet, but he could put together her meaning.

Gran-scorpions. Dawnward.

Kai slowed the windship at Rasia's command. They neared the edge of a tall cliff where a lake had carved out the terrain thousands of years ago. The lake was withered now, but Kai imagined that it flooded during rainy season. Rasia hopped down each rung of the scout's nest with the finesse of messengers hopping roofs in the Ribcage.

"Five scorpions are directly below us," Rasia said. Kai couldn't see them at this angle. The ledge dropped off quickly, but he trusted Rasia that they were there. "If we head straight down, the speed and momentum will crash the ship. You'll need to cut an angle right before you reach the bottom."

That seemed like a lot more than he'd learned thus far.

"Are you sure you don't want to do this?" Kai asked, but the question fell on dry air. Rasia had already dropped down into the underbelly hatch. Zephyr turned to Kai over his shoulder, wordlessly asking the same question.

Rasia dragged up an item out of the belly—a sand sled, like the colorful painted ones kids used to slide off hills that formed off the Great Elder after a sandstorm. Rasia's sled lacked the color and fine details of those in the market, and the rough shape reminded Kai of Nico's, which was handmade by Kenji. Rae sometimes slid around the house on it.

Nico's sled didn't have a hole like the one drilled into the edge of Rasia's, though. Through the hole, Rasia tied and knotted a piece of rope.

"What are you doing?" Kai asked.

"It's difficult to kill a scorpion because of the hard carapace covering the top of them, so getting a good angle atop the windship is near impossible. But with this, I can come underneath." Rasia slung a bow around her chest, placed her foot on the rail, and looked at Kai with unbridled glee. Rasia's excitement converted Kai's nerves into a crackling sort of confidence. "I haven't had a chance to do this in a while. It's sort of a two-person job."

"This is insane," Zephyr said. Zephyr tested his ropes again to make sure he was properly secured.

That was probably a good idea. Kai snatched up a strip of rope from the tool hatch and tied himself to the steer as well.

Just in case.

"Okay, ready," Kai said, determined. He let up on the steer, and the windship tipped over the sharp rock face. This side was much steeper than the far side. The speed pinned Kai against the steering headboard as the windship plummeted.

Rasia slid alongside the ship on her sand sled, with a piece of rope connecting her to the railing. She cheered as her hair flagged behind her. At least *she* was having fun; Kai, on the other hand, was out-of-his-mind terrified. The bottom raced to meet them fast. Rasia's warning sat in his chest along with his fear, and Kai fought the forces of gravity to wrap both arms around the steer and jerk right.

The windship curved. The wheels audibly cut through the rock at a screech till they reached the bottom. They whipped past the band of scorpions, and Kai steered a circle around, closer and tighter, to get Rasia in range.

Rasia locked her legs around the rope, sat back against the sled, and drew back her bow. She loosed an arrow as they passed one of the scorpions. It struck the soft underside with a *thwick*, and the scorpion shuddered to collapse with a strangled squeal.

"She killed it in one shot," Zephyr said. He leaned forward against the railing in wide-eyed disbelief.

Yeah, she was kind of awesome.

"Kai," Zephyr snapped. "Watch out."

Kai jolted in alarm and barely evaded the cracked eggshells from the scorpions' breakfast. The movement yanked Rasia violently backward and trapped her leg in the rope. She cut her sword through the restraint and slid free. She rolled to her feet and surveyed the scene.

She scooped up the sled, ran a few feet up the incline, jumped on top of it, and went sliding toward another of the scorpions. She dropped to her knees, leaned all the way back, and brandished her swords like fangs. The dragonsteel flashed briefly before Rasia slipped underneath the scorpion's pincers and slid back out covered in blood and guts and a prowling smile.

She rolled to her feet and turned to the next scorpion. There were two left, one at her front and another at her back.

"Kai, bring the windship around," Zephyr told him, fumbling to loosen all his ropes. Kai steered toward the scorpion at Rasia's back. Zephyr cursed. The knots had tightened too much for Zephyr to get his fingers around them, and he couldn't reach his sword. Kai rigged the steer and ran over with his dagger to cut Zephyr from the ropes. The ropes snapped in quick succession.

Freed, Zephyr jumped from the windship and landed with a roll. He cleaved his heavy sword through the stinger Rasia had dodged moments before, and it snapped off in a spray of blood. For a moment, Zephyr and Rasia glanced at each other, then they turned back-to-back to focus on their respective scorpion.

Zephyr fought differently from Rasia. Whereas Rasia fought with speed and exploited the opponent's weaknesses, Zephyr was all patience and efficiency. He literally dismantled his opponent, starting with the stingers, then the pincers, until it was a flailing non-threat. But while Zephyr took his time, Kai worried for Rasia when she evaded a pincer a little too slowly, favoring her right.

Kai had to do something. He felt helpless stuck atop the windship, but he had no doubt that if he went down there, he'd be a liability. He looked around for something to use. Then he had an idea.

He re-tied his ropes extra tight.

Kai aimed the windship toward the incline, in much the same way Rasia had done with her small sled, to gain speed and momentum. He turned when he couldn't get any more height, then charged straight toward the scorpion. Kai shouted at the top of his lungs to give Rasia warning. She looked at him and baited the scorpion into the path of the ship before lunging out of the way at the last moment.

The windship and scorpion collided with a crash.

The cordage tied around Kai's waist held, but his head snapped back against the headboard. Kai looked up, shaking off the echoing pain, to find the scorpion flipped onto its back.

Rasia raced forward, vaulted herself up one of the pincers, and planted her swords into the scorpion's belly. As Rasia did so, Zephyr cleaved the head off his own opponent, spurting blood in the air. Rasia surveyed the field with the maddest grin.

"YES!" She cheered. "Now that's a fucking kull!"

CHAPTER TWENTY-ONE

I

Nico perched atop the cramped scout's nest and scanned the endless waves. Kelin lounged about the railing, and Suri adjusted the sail. Azan steered over the crest of a large sand dune and sped down the other side.

The next dune *moved*.

It shifted and uncoiled. Scales transformed from unsuspecting brown to gold in the sun.

Nico leaped toward the edge of the nest and shouted, "DRAGON!!!"

Azan swerved the ship, veering left to the nearest sand dune for cover, but the dragon had already raised their head and spotted them.

Nico rushed down the mast and scraped her hand against the foot grips in her haste. She dropped to the deck and the windship tilted, caught by the strength of the dragon's exhale.

Alarmed, Nico took an exhale of her own.

Nico erected a wall of water as bright white flames exploded, cracking the air. Hot steam blasted her skin. Sweat drenched her face. Her feet squeaked back across the deck, losing ground against the hammering force of the dragon's fire. Nico shook to hold the magic.

Azan tucked them behind the dune.

But the flames followed. They all fell flat to the deck, covering their heads at the sounds of harsh crystallization, then a hiss. When the flames stopped, the crest of the sand dune had hardened and supercooled to glass, twinkling and shimmering citrine in the sun.

Wings beat the air.

Nico lifted her head and met Suri's wide, terrified eyes from where she lay a body length away, pressed to the deck. Nico commandeered the lingering steam and congealed the water into a fog so thick it swallowed Suri whole. Nico couldn't see her own hands in it. Hopefully, the dragon couldn't see them, either. Nico held her breath and listened. The wings beat once, pounding against Nico's chest like a physical punch, and beat again. Then the drum-beats faded farther and farther away.

The fog thinned and ice plunged through Nico's veins. She curled, shivering, to the deck. Suri rushed over and pressed the back of her hand to Nico's forehead.

"You're freezing," Suri said. "Azan, we need to get her out of the dune shade. Get her into the sun."

"On it."

Nico felt slightly better once the rising heat of high noon touched her skin. Nico soaked in the sun while Azan looked around and asked, "Where's Kelin?"

Kelin popped his head out of the underbelly hatch. "Is it gone?"

"You hid in the hatch?" Azan asked, shaking his head, disapproving. "That's boneless."

"That was a fucking dragon. I didn't sign up for a fucking dragon. Did you sign up for a fucking dragon? I sure as fuck didn't sign up for a fucking dragon." Kelin climbed out of the hatch and tucked his hands under his armpits to stop them from shaking. He nodded toward Nico. "What's wrong with her?"

"She used her magic. She needs sun. Like a plant," Azan chirped.

"That's not how her magic works at all," Suri corrected. "Her magic affects her body temperature. When she expends it, her body temperature drops. She needs heat the same way you need heat if you were suffering from hypothermia. She's not a flower."

"Oh." Azan scrunched his face. "So . . . she's more like a dragon then?"

Suri's face crunched. While lying splayed out on the deck, Nico smiled at Azan's surprising insight. She explained, "Yes. If you cut open a dragon, there's not actually fire inside of them. They exhale magic the same as I do, but dragon bodies are better at regulating their temperature than human ones are."

"The stories are *actually* true?" Kelin asked. "I thought that was some made-up kuller shit."

"Of course, it's true," Suri argued. "The Great Elder gifted the Grankull with magic."

"The Great Elder is a pile of fucking bones."

"The Great Elder protects us."

"The Great Elder protects *you*."

"That's enough," Nico interrupted. "There are . . . half-truths to the story, but it is widely accepted that human magic came from the dragons. The Great Elder gifted the Ilhan, the first Ohan, magic."

"Sure," Kelin said.

Nico raised her hand, and Suri immediately helped Nico to her feet. Nico grabbed the railing for support and peered out toward the bent ruins the dragon had been gnawing on for lunch. Looked like a windship, or what was left of one. "We should go investigate. There might be survivors."

Suri looked askance at Nico, doubtful.

"What about the mountain of dragonglass?" Kelin asked. He flung his arm out behind her, at the glass quarry formed in the wake of the dragon's fire. "That could make us rich."

"Kelin," Nico said, "the Grankull will confiscate anything you think you can smuggle into it, and your entire Forging will be voided for the attempt. We'll mark it on our maps, and the kulls will come for it later."

"Why do we have to report it at all? I could tell my people instead. Granted, they'll take a cut of it, but they could get this hauled back to the Tents and smuggled through the Grankull if you all want a piece of it. We could make a good chunk of chips off this."

"Kelin, we'll investigate the windship first. We'll discuss this later."

Kelin grumbled and looked to Azan for support, but Nico knew that was the wrong horse to hitch a saddle to. Azan's family was pretty well-off, and he wouldn't risk his Forging for a complicated smuggling scheme. Sex, apparently, was a whole other matter.

Azan shrugged and tilted the tiller forward. They sailed toward the wreckage.

Kelin crossed his arms and leaned back against the railing across the deck from Nico and Suri. His face turned distant with thoughts, but his next question surprised her.

"If all is as true as you claim, why don't more people have magic?" Kelin asked. "We're all descendants of the Ilhan, are we not? Why, then, are you the only one capable of it?"

"Huh. I've never thought of that," Azan said, looking to Nico for the answer.

Magic had always been centralized within the Ohan's family. It was such a widely accepted fact that many in the Grankull rarely questioned *how* the magic was inherited, but the truth was always more complicated.

"Magic isn't genetic," Nico confirmed. "I have magic because Avalai Ohan went through the bloodrites and tied herself to the Heart of the Great Elder. The rite is so powerful, it often affects any children who come after. That is why I and all my siblings have the ability to manifest magic. When I go through the bloodrites, my children will also be able to do the same."

Kelin squinted. "So . . . anyone and their children can have magic if they go through the bloodrites?"

"Technically. And technically not. Magic is difficult for a human body to contain. Because I've lived with magic since I was five-till, I've grown accustomed to it, and thus I'm more likely to survive the bloodrites. There was a time, after the War of the Bloody

Siblings, when no ohanis were left alive. This power vacuum birthed the creation of the Council, whose original purpose was to find a new heir. The Council threw almost everyone at the Elder Heart, killing hundreds before they gave up and attempted to govern themselves. Two generations later, a weaver heard the bones sing. They survived the bloodrites and the magic was restored, but it was the Elder who chose them in the end, not the Grankull. If you have the arrogance to believe you are the one who is going to survive, you won't. So. Magic isn't genetic, but because the Ohan's children have the highest probability of surviving the bloodrites, it's easy to believe that it is."

"How does it work?" Kelin asked. "When you manifest your magic? How do you know?"

"You know," Nico said sourly. She'd never forget the day she woke up screaming in her bed. She'd thought she was dying. It was the worst pain she had ever experience in her entire life. "Feels like someone threw you straight onto a bonfire."

Then there was Kai, whose body couldn't handle the manifestation at all, or at least that's what Ava-ta had concluded before she died. No one really knew when it came to him.

As they neared the wrecked windship, Nico recognized the sail. The sail was the same translucent blue as their own. All Forging ships this year had been cut from the same dragon-wing. This had been a ship full of Forging kids, but now it was completely cracked in half. They could see no bodies save for an errant arm.

"They've still got a good wheel," Azan said slowly.

"No," Nico said. "We honor the dead before scavenging for supplies. Search for any personal items or affects. We'll burn those in place of bodies."

Azan and Kelin followed her instructions, but Suri hesitated, studying the setting sun. "We don't have time for this," she said. "We're losing light. At this pace, we're never going to catch up to your jih."

"We will. Kai has been in the same place for the past few days." Nico placed a hand on Suri's shoulder. "Besides, there is always time to honor the dead."

Suri sighed and went to help sift through the wreckage.

Nico searched the bow, which had broken away completely from the rest of the ship. She picked up a sandal some distance away, toward where the dragon had flown off. And then another. She realized abruptly that the dragon had taken someone. Could Nico have saved them if she hadn't been too busy hiding? Before she could spiral down that rabbit hole, her foot hit a golden item poking out of the sand.

Thinking it might be a shield of some kind, she pulled. As she held the piece in her hands, brilliant gold turned white, as it did when a dying dragon lost its color. Her eyes widened at the large dragon scale she held. It was a little chipped at the bottom, but still far more valuable than a mountain of dragonglass. Dragon scales were melted down to forge the dragonsteel weapons sharp enough to wound a dragon.

"Kelin! I need help!" Nico shouted.

Kelin came over, curious. He knew that if Nico wanted heavy lifting, she'd call for Azan, and if she'd found someone dying, she'd call for Suri. Kelin looked over Nico's shoulder at the scale, and his brows raised twofold. Nico dropped it to the ground and kicked sand over it.

"Tonight, you're going to bury this deep and mark it on your map. After the Forging, you tell your people where it is, and they can have the whole of it. Do it while you're on watch when everyone is asleep. Plausible deniability."

One dragon scale could far easily go missing than a mountain of dragonglass.

"So, what? You're buying my trust?" Kelin asked.

"I doubt that can be bought. The scale is a compromise."

Nico extended the middle and forefinger of her right hand—a sign of truce used in both the Tents and the Grankull, although under differing circumstances. Tent truces were always temporary, and thus used more frequently. Grankull truces were rare but permanent, often marking the end of bloody conflict in a bloodprice war between families. As the story went, the War of the Bloody Siblings ended with both magic-born found dead with their fingers locked in a truce.

"We're in this Forging together," Nico said. "After, feel free to reassess."

Kelin scanned her face, then locked his forefingers with hers. They shook on it.

As Nico excavated the rest of the area, Kelin stalked her shadow. Nico crouched when she caught a glimpse of something, and when she brushed away the sand, she found it only to be a multi-colored rock.

"What are the bloodrites like?" Kelin asked.

"You are full of questions today."

"It's not every day a tent kid gets to interrogate"—Kelin bit on that last word cheekily—"*ask* questions of an ohani."

"I talk to tent kids every day. They just don't know it."

Kelin paused, brow quirked up thoughtfully. "Have we spoken before?"

"Maybe, but we occupy two different territories."

Kelin's eyes lit up with revelation. Nico had walked too far from the crash site now. She didn't think she would find anything else out this far. She turned and walked back, with Kelin quick on her heels.

"You have the Scorpion Han's protection. That's why you could read the—Zephyr's language. Is that what his involvement is about? You and the Scorpion have some sort of deal?"

Of course, Kelin was convinced that an ohani couldn't be involved in tent life if it didn't involve a conspiracy of sorts. He couldn't believe that Nico just *cared*.

"Kelin," Nico said, exasperated. "Ava-ta and Zara-*shi*"—Nico stressed Zara's address—"were Forging friends. They remained friends even after Zara-shi's banishment. I often ran errands and messages between them because tah couldn't politically be seen fraternizing with her. That's it. There's no secret conspiracy."

"Sure."

"Fine." Nico crossed her arms. "Not one that I am aware of, and if so, most likely it died with tah. Satisfied?"

"You never answered my original question."

"I don't know, Kelin. I don't know what the bloodrites entail."

"Then how do you know you'll survive it?"

Nico gritted her teeth, crunching on the ever-present sand in her mouth.

"Because I have to."

They found the following items: a bloodied shroud, a clean pair of pants, one sandal, a molded clay figurine, and an arm. Azan struck sparks atop the pyre of personal affects, and they watched the items burn.

Nico offered the parting words: "All hunters are hunted, and Death is the greatest hunter of them all. Some are lucky to evade Death's clutches but never for too long. You've died faceless but not forgotten. All hunters are hunted, but the kull remains."

Suri and Azan repeated, "the kull remains."

". . . and everyone's got to eat," Kelin added, a tent addendum. Suri and Azan looked at him strangely, and he shrugged. "One of 'em could have been a tent kid."

They waited for the flames to die, for the items to curl and turn to ash, with only the bones left behind.

Nico scooped the blackened ulna and phalanges into her shroud, accepting the responsibility of delivering them to the Heart Temple once the Forging ended. Nico couldn't save this Forging kull, but at least she could put their bones to rest.

"If I die out here . . ." Kelin said softly to Nico.

"I know," Nico said. The bones of those born in the Tents never returned home. Instead, their corpses fed the Desert, providing life for the next. Everyone's got to eat.

Nico stepped forward, grabbed a handful of ash, and tossed the souls to the wind.

CHAPTER TWENTY-TWO

—

Butchering gran-scorpions was back-breaking work. Not only did it need to be done before the meat spoiled but also before the smell attracted the unwanted attention of predators. Kai had only ever cooked scorpion meat from rations, where they were already cleanly cut and packaged. This was the first time he'd ever butchered anything, and they had five gigantic scorpions to dismantle.

Thankfully, Rasia knew the work and jumped right to it. She chose an area away from the kill site, so they had to wheel over their haul. Zephyr and Kai helped separate the appendages, crack open the pincers, and cut edible meat into portions. According to Rasia, they'd eat a good amount of the meat fresh for dinner and smoke the rest into jerky overnight.

Rasia hung thin meat slices on a rope she engineered over a dense smoke cloud. Kai always folded into coughing fits when he neared her operation. Instead, he helped Zephyr with one particularly resistant mesosoma plate. Kai braced it, pushing at it with his legs while Zephyr pried at it with his sword.

The plate popped off with a grand thwump.

Kai tumbled to the ground. Before Kai had much time to realize what had happened, Zephyr automatically reached down and set him back to his feet.

"Thanks," Kai mumbled, brushing away the sand.

Zephyr grunted before chugging several swallows of water. He wiped at his brow with the shirt he had taken off and swung around his neck. He had a bite scar on the other shoulder, but the rest of his skin was unmarred. His skin color was distinctive in the Grankull. It was neither the clay pottery of his tah nor the cobalt night of his father but almost a combination of both, with smoky overtones and red undertones in his highlights.

Kai envied the comfort Zephyr had in his own skin and the ease with which hard work rolled off Zephyr's broad shoulders. For once, Kai wanted to breathe without his body feeling like it was stretched too thin. Kai couldn't feel his arms after all this work. His legs burned. If Zephyr hadn't picked him up, Kai probably would have stayed lying in the dust and the dirt.

"You did good," Zephyr said suddenly. "What you and Rasia did, what we did, taking out five gran-scorpions in one sweep, is the sort of feat only accomplished by the most experienced of kulls. Yeah, a lot of it was Rasia, her ego is well-deserved, but you rammed a scorpion with a windship. I wasn't fair to you this morning. You don't need, nor do you deserve, to be treated like a budchild. I'm sorry, Kai."

Kai kicked at the sand and watched it funnel through his sandals. You'd think he'd be happy for an apology, but it made him feel shameful, and like a lie. He whispered, "You were right to be concerned. I was tired of being a burden on the people around me. I was tired of being so helpless. *I was tired.* I ran from you because I was looking for an end. Instead, I've found a beginning. I'm not in that place anymore . . . but I can't go running back to Nico, either. I need to do this my way."

Zephyr expelled a beleaguered breath and rolled his shoulders. The muscles of him shifted, and it was so apparent that he ate far better than those on stable rations. Both he and Rasia shared that commonality—this swagger and energy that most of the Grankull lacked. As if their bellies were always full.

"Okay," Zephyr said, then repeated the word to himself. "Okay. Is she still trying to hunt this dragon?"

"Yes."

"Do you two have a plan?"

"I'm sure Rasia does."

"Kai," Zephyr said, unimpressed by Kai's blind trust. Kai braced himself for the criticism. "I'm concerned how shrouded you are by her. I'm from the Tents. I've seen how these things go wrong. You're not the only one who's messed around during a Forging, but you two are a seed-joining. You have to be careful. Unapproved pregnancies happen more often than you think. Either the female risks her life aborting it in a back alley, flees to the Tents, or the Grankull finds out. And you know what happens when the Grankull finds out. Tah is what happens when the Grankull finds out. You deserve to make your own choices but *be smart about it.*"

"Oh."

Zephyr surprised Kai at times. Kai had expected Zephyr to be an extension of Nico, but unlike Nico, sometimes Zephyr yielded. Sometimes Zephyr was willing to wait and see. Maybe Kai's initial impressions of him had been wrong.

"Rasia used gonom," Kai said, hoping to prove he wasn't careless. He knew the risks.

Nico would've gasped and clutched her shroud, but Zephyr nodded. "Good. And you do know, once the Forging is over, Rasia will move on to the next thing that catches her attention? People like Rasia don't stick around for long. Don't fall face first into the fire. Forging flames never last: Isn't that what you kullers say?"

Technically, that's an older saying poets penned to mean hardships eventually end, but after one drought too many, it's been cynically given new meaning over the generations—a phrase of hope turned to one of heartbreak.

"I know what this is. I'm not asking for more than she is willing to give."

Kai knew that most likely this flame with Rasia was a brief romp. He wasn't an idiot. He knew Rasia would eventually find something better than the pathetic runt of the Grankull, but he was determined to enjoy every moment of the heat. Even the inevitable burning. He wasn't afraid of charred bones. At least that he got to choose.

"Nico is going to rip her tent when she finds out about the two of you."

Kai wasn't looking forward to that. Maybe this thing with Rasia would be over by the time Nico caught up to them. For all the difficulty it took to sway Zephyr, he was a breeze compared to the storm on the horizon. ". . . you're not going to tell her, are you?"

Zephyr's shoulders rose at the force of his snort. "What for? Rasia will rub this in Nico's face the first chance she gets."

"You're wrong. That's not Rasia."

Zephyr gave him a flat stare. "Sure."

Zephyr turned back to their scorpion to finish their work. He twisted off the arms and legs with enviable ease and didn't have to cut through the tendons first, like Kai did. They sliced at the meat and laid the organs out along a heavy gonda-leather tarp Rasia kept in the windship for such bloody occasions.

"Zephyr," Kai said. He couldn't bring himself to face Zephyr as he asked the question. "Can you not tell Nico about the scars, either?"

Kai waited for the argument, for all the reasons and justifications for why Nico needed to know.

"It's not my business to tell. That's on you."

That was too easy.

"Promise on your tahs' names."

"My tahs don't have names."

"You know what I mean."

"I promise you a meal," Zephyr said.

Kai thought that was the tent equivalent to the same phrase, but he wasn't sure. ". . . what does that mean?"

"If I break my promise, you can take my corpse to the grubworm trappers . . ." Zephyr began explaining, then shrugged. "It's a tent thing. Know it's the sort of promise a person keeps."

"Thank you," Kai said, with a weight slipping off his shoulders.

Kai liked Zephyr, despite everything. Despite a loyalty that leaned in jih's direction. Despite Zephyr's misgivings about Rasia. Despite all their differences, Kai grudgingly admitted that he liked the way the world seemed more grounded in Zephyr's presence.

"You should hunt a dragon with us," Kai suggested.

"I'm not that sort of crazy."

"We made a good team, and aren't you tired of being at the mercy of other people's decisions? You're relying on Nico to become the Ohan and the deciding vote on the purge, but what if someone on the Council changes their mind? What if her vote doesn't matter in the end? If we kill this dragon, the Grankull's food supply will no longer be at risk. It would invalidate the need for a purge in the first place. Don't you want to ensure the safety of your family?"

"Several experienced kulls have tried to take that dragon down, and they failed. How would we be any different?"

"We have Rasia." Zephyr's face fell. "I'm serious. You've seen what she can do. Even if it's a sliver of a chance, don't you think it's one we should take? Slaying this dragon would help Nico, your family, and everyone in the Grankull. Rasia might be in it for the glory, but that doesn't mean it isn't worthwhile. People can't keep starving."

Zephyr stilled. His eyes lit green as he gazed at the horizon, thinking. Kai found no outward evidence of the shift, no change of expression or poise, but Zephyr's insides were made of softer stuff. His bones moved.

"Fine, let's hunt this dragon."

"I don't know, Kai. Do we really need him?"

Zephyr raised a brow, unimpressed, when Rasia's head popped up over the spine of the dead scorpion. She pouted, disappointed that she hadn't elicited a bigger reaction. She crawled forward and hung from the spine, looking down at them both.

"I trust him," Kai answered, also unfazed by Rasia's sudden appearance. He had sensed her creeping up behind them. "Besides, our kull of outcasts isn't complete without him."

Rasia blinked at him. "Shit, you're right. Fine, let's bring the mutt."

"Zephyr," Kai corrected.

"*Ze-fer*," Rasia said dramatically.

"What's the plan?" Zephyr asked.

"What do you think we're doing? After we get all this meat prepared, we'll have enough food to last us the rest of the Forging without wasting any more time hunting."

"What's the plan for the *dragon*? How are we going to slay it? How are we finding it? What route are we taking?" Zephyr asked all the questions Kai never bothered to.

"What's with the interrogation?" Rasia asked sourly.

"I like to know what I'm getting into. I don't follow anyone on blind faith."

"You follow Nico."

"I follow Nico because she wants to protect the Tents."

"Does *she* have a plan for that?"

No answer.

"That's what I thought. Now, are you two done gossiping like a gaggle of tent whores or are we getting back to work? The vultures are circling."

Rasia swung down from the scorpion spine. She grabbed the ends of the gonda tarp and dragged the meat Zephyr and Kai had butchered over to her smoke station.

Zephyr crossed his arms and glared at Kai. "She has no plan."

"She has a plan." Kai remembered all the considerations she poured into her preparation for the skinko. Rasia was not the sort of person who strolled up to a dragon with no daggers up her sleeve.

Or at least, he didn't think so.

CHAPTER TWENTY-THREE

I

Nico sliced open the sky, so thick with stars they spilled out over her head. She traced her glaive around the gibbous moon and through the constellations, from the brightest point of the scorpion tail to the nose tip of the howling jackal. Nico landed back on the ground with a shout. She lifted her leg and froze in poise, glaive held against her forearm. A cold wind blew across her heated, sweat-dampened skin.

Back in the Grankull, Nico often practiced her katas in the early morning to the sound of utter stillness before the world woke. In the Desert, however, she practiced to the loud and obnoxious sounds of Kelin and Azan having sex on the other side of the windship hull.

They were hardly ever discreet, so Nico might as well get some practice in while she was waiting them out.

Light footsteps curved around the hull. Nico settled out of her stance and planted the end of her glaive. The gibbous lit the soft roundness of Suri's face as she came into view.

Nico asked knowingly, "Couldn't sleep?"

Suri cringed at a particularly loud and reverent exclamation. Overhearing Kelin, you'd think Azan's dick was some perfectly crafted gift to the world. But if it was, did it really need all that stroking?

Suri asked, wincing, "They do that every night?"

"*Every. Night.* I was convinced you could sleep through anything."

Suri twiddled her fingers, embarrassed. "I only woke up because I had to pass water. Guess that's the problem of sharing a room with two jihs most of your life. You learn to sleep through anything, and all the flames they sneak through the window."

"You were always the good one," Nico said. They both smiled at the inside joke. Suri's siblings had always been the chatty bedside manner to Suri's solitary experiments, the boisterous conversations to Suri's whispered suggestions. Despite all the partners her siblings had brought in and out of the household while underage, Suri never said a word. Suri's tah thought of Suri as the good one, but Nico had always known there was a quiet rebel in Suri's bones.

Suri brushed her hair behind her ear. "Would you like a sparring partner?"

"Sure."

Suri retrieved a spare spear from the windship and hiked up her sleep robe to tie around her thighs. Suri's legs were long and reedy. Many of the Grankull considered persons too thin and narrow as unattractive, a clear marker of someone without a job and no rations. But Nico thought Suri beautiful, even when the spear didn't sit as comfortably in Suri's hands as her longbow. Suri tapped the polearm with fidgety fingers.

The wind whistled as they both dipped and circled their hands to their faces, signing "ready." Both dropped into fighting stances.

In school, they were taught how to use the most basic weapons of the Grankull: a spear, a sword, and a bow. Suri hadn't held a spear since those classes. Her basic forms couldn't keep up with the fighting styles Ava-ta had drilled into Nico as a young child. But neither cared much for winning; the spar, for them both, was a means to waste time. They flowed through the motions like a duet, acting and reacting, building atop each other's notes.

Nico made the mistake of performing a note too hard for Suri to follow. Suri's spear rattled from her hand, knocked away by

Nico's reverse-grip thrust.

Nico shoved her polearm against Suri's chest, pinning Suri to the hull, ending their song. Despite the light spar, Suri breathed heavily under the pole, her breath hot in the cold air. Suri licked her lips, and Nico's eyes couldn't help but to flick toward the motion.

Kelin and Azan had finished. The night finally quieted save for Suri and Nico's hot puffs of breath.

Suri touched Nico's face with long, graceful fingers, and Nico tracked their delicate touch along her cheek, tracing at the moles.

"I've longed to touch you for so long," Suri whispered, so soft and so gentle. Nico couldn't describe Suri's expression in words, only sensations—dancing in rain, the smell of petrichor, and spring water. Had Suri been hiding all of this under her shroud all these years?

Suri leaned forward slowly, asking for permission.

Nico shouldn't. She was the ohani. She was supposed to be a leader all others looked up to. She was supposed to wait until she was an adult.

But no one was around to know whether Nico folded to temptation this one time.

Nico surged forward and kissed Suri right this time, no holding back. Suri kissed back with equal fervor. They danced to a different song now. Nico tossed her glaive and brought her hands up to cup Suri's roundness, holding her soft in hand, like a flower.

But a tent rat will always be a tent rat.

Suri's voice clashed in Nico's head.

That voice of hatred and derision wasn't the Suri that Nico knew, but no matter how hard Nico tried to bury the words beneath soft, pretty lips and caresses in the dark, she couldn't do it. Thrown out of the moment, Nico grew numb to Suri's touch. It was too cold.

"Suri, stop," Nico croaked out.

Suri pulled back and searched Nico's face. "What's wrong?"

Nico squeezed her eyes shut. "Why haven't you ever said

anything before? About how you feel about the Tents?"

Suri's delicate expression retreated inwards, folding with the speed of day flowers at dusk. Suri stepped back. "You don't want me?"

"Depends on how you answer the question."

"I never said anything because I knew how you felt about the Tents. Maybe I never should have said anything at all, but they're trying to kill you, Nico."

"I've talked to Kelin, Suri. I don't think he *wants* to kill me. We're coming to an understanding."

"So, he *is* an assassin?! I told you. *I told you.* We should throw him overboard right now."

"We are not throwing anyone overboard. This is why I can't be with you, Suri. This is the problem. I have spent my entire life watching people hate Kai for no good reason. I've watched people hate Zephyr for no good reason. I never thought that you . . ." Nico stumbled on her words, tears blurring. "I never thought that you could be so hateful, too. I can't have a flame for someone like that. I can't."

"I'm trying to protect you."

"From what? Kelin has done nothing."

"But he will. You can't trust any one of them."

"No, Suri. I can't trust *you.*"

Suri's hate and prejudice had infected everything between them now, and there was no going back to the innocent children they once were. Nico had rejected flames before, but this one was certainly the hardest.

"Please," Nico pleaded, and closed her eyes to the pool of Suri's tears, "don't touch me again."

Clouds smothered the constellations and drops of rain fell from the sky, crying for her. Nico walked away into the cold biting darkness.

CHAPTER TWENTY-FOUR

—

Rasia raised a cup of palm wine to the sky, and moonlight spilled from the gleaming calabash. The meat smoke billowed upwind and flapped a cloak of storm clouds behind her. "I raise a toast to you—to our blooded kull, to our first hunt, and to a good day's work. Drink deep, drink well, for tomorrow the hunt begins anew."

"Oi-yo."

The sip of palm wine slid warm and sweet down Kai's throat. With the huntpour toast complete, they attacked the veritable feast before them—a spread of scrambled brains, a blood soup of kidneys and bones cooked slowly over the fire, poached pancreas, raw livers, and grilled hearts.

It was the first time Kai had tasted any of these dishes, as eating hunting game fresh was rare. It was a luxury afforded only to hunting kulls or reserved for guests of honor during a feast. And a feast it was. It was five times more food than Kai had eaten last night during his celebratory "dinner," when he'd thought that was the most food he would ever consume at once.

The quickening night chill bit harmless, negated by the lingering heat from the large cooking pit, the gut-warmth of alcohol, and the crush of Rasia plastered to Kai's skin. She leaned across him to shovel the fist-sized roasted scorpion heart into her bowl.

At first, Kai didn't think he had the energy to eat after all the day's work, but he quickly surprised himself as the tender meat slipped down his throat. The soft, squishy liver tasted of iron. The three of them chewed and spat out bones and drank in a voracious silence.

A good dinner needed no words.

"Shit, Kai. You've eaten a whole scorpion."

Kai blinked, pausing with full cheeks to look where Rasia had slithered down into a contented repose, her face smashed into his thigh. Kai felt bottomless. No matter how much he stuffed inside himself, none of it made up for all the meals he'd missed over the years. Kai wondered if maybe he didn't know what "full" felt like and didn't know when he'd made it there. Embarrassed, he slowed and felt shameful for eating more than his allotted portion.

"I didn't mean for you to stop," Rasia chided as she twisted under his arm, making herself more comfortable as she crossed her ankles. "I intentionally portioned dinner for more than we needed since you ate a bunch last night, too. It's for you, and Zephyr." She peered over at him. "Those muscles don't feed themselves."

"She's not wrong," Zephyr said. "Eat, Kai. Few have the luxury of eating till they're full. Never take that for granted."

Zephyr and Kai split what was left, but Zephyr soon followed Rasia into a pleased food stupor while Kai wiped every bowl, every palm leaf, every pot, and finger clean.

"It's always the tiny ones who surprise you," Rasia whispered conspiratorially. "Ysai-ji's like that. He'll eat a whole gran-scorpion by himself and still be nothing but a stick the next day, and that was before he shot up like a fucking date palm."

For the first time in Kai's life, he thought he was full. The heaviness hit him like a physical thing, and the sharp knife of his hunger had dulled. His exhaustion became much more pressing. All the bruises, falls, and physical demands of the past few days hit him over the head all at once. He folded and toppled brick by adobe brick to the ground.

Kai finally understood why Rasia didn't like to feel too full. It weighed you down, and he couldn't imagine how many grand meals like this one she'd eaten to develop such self-control.

For one glorious moment, they all basked in the stillness. The hanging scorpion tails rattled and drummed against each other on the line. Even upwind, Kai smelled the sausages and jerky drying over the smoke cloud. The stars twinkled overhead, dancing around a gibbous moon.

Rasia flipped to her feet.

"That's enough, you two. We need to get all this clean before the grubworms come grubbing around. Get up. Move it."

Kai mule-dozed his way through the chores, only halfway able to focus on anything but his own actions. Rasia attacked the plates with a kull's brew of salt and ash while Zephyr dried and stacked them into neat towers.

"What are we going to do with all the excess materials?" Zephyr asked. "Can't we fashion the carapace into shields against the dragon?"

"Sure. If you want to die. Speed, not defense, is our best weapon against a dragon. And a scorpion shield isn't much deterrent against dragon fire. It'll melt in your hands, then scald your skin off like tar. Haven't you learned anything from the hunting legends?"

"No, Rasia. I'm not allowed in the temple. I'm not allowed in any part of the Grankull."

Rasia scoffed. "Horseshit. Tents kids smuggle in all the time."

"On errands for their Tent Han, and if they get caught, they die. Tah would never take such risks with me."

"But she'll risk others." Rasia disapproved.

Zephyr's expression darkened. "I am not boneless and tah does not coddle me, but I face far more risks than the others. I still have family members on the other side of the Tail who will not hesitate to kill me. Unlike most, I don't blend in."

"You've really never stepped foot in the Grankull? How? How are you not curious?" Rasia asked, baffled, utterly unable to comprehend how Zephyr had never given into the temptation of his curiosity.

"Curious about what? About a place that scarred my tah because she had the audacity to choose my life?"

"Then why are you here? What's the point of the Forging for you, then? You could have kept wandering the world with your foreign-ta and never returned."

"Because I am both my tahs. And ultimately, I want the Grankull to see my face."

Rasia conceded, "*That* I understand."

"So. I don't know anything about dragons. I haven't read the legends. I haven't heard the stories. I know nothing, and I'd appreciate some sort of plan."

Rasia sucked in a breath. "We've got a lot to cover."

With a whip, Rasia swept all the cleaned dishes into her cloak, threw it over her shoulder, and delivered them back to the ship. She returned with an armful of weapons. Rasia produced a whetstone and eyed the blade edge of a spear. She detached the spearhead from the stem.

Rasia carried a different type of alertness out here in the wide-open Desert than at the gorge. With sandstone at their back, the gorge had been more defensible, but out here, a pack of wild dogs could easily make off with their hunt if they weren't careful. In response, Rasia was always moving from one task to another with a deadly steel-focused efficiency.

Kai didn't think she'd been still all day. He worried about her ribs. A small part of him worried how he'd ever keep up with her breathless pace. It was no wonder why Rasia had thought herself taking it 'easy' at the gorge.

Rasia slicked the spearhead across the whetstone. "First rule in dragon-hunting: only a dragon can defeat a dragon, which means that the only weapons effective against a dragon are those made from dragonscale. This includes my twin blades, Kai's dagger, and your big-ass sword."

"That's it? Those are all the options we have at killing this thing?"

"Yep. In all the history of the Grankull, there have been

nine successful dragon kills. I know all nine stories, and anyone hunting a dragon should know them, too. Listen up. It's going to be a long night."

Kai knew the stories. He'd read them all in the temple library, and even the youngest Grankull child knew the story of the first dragon hunt. The scribes recited the story in the form of an epic poem for every holiday and every namepour. Kai curled up in the dancing shadows of the campfire. He listened to the slick of steel across whetstone and Rasia reciting the poem in perfect rhythm, no word out of place.

He woke up around the seventh story. Rasia still spun words overhead. He snapped into full awareness when he couldn't mentally track her sentences. Usually, the windeka chronicled the hunt, but Rasia added anecdotes and differing perspectives that had gone unrecorded in the temple.

Kai stretched awake and rubbed at the eye crust. Rasia had finished sharpening her stock of weapons and laid them out within easy reach. She'd moved on to stitching a tear in her pants. Across from her, Zephyr lay with his bedroll bundled under his head.

"How do you know so much?" Kai asked. "That's not in the legends."

Rasia leaned back on her elbow and glanced at him with a clever smile. "I grew up around my tah's kull. Listen to the hunters enough and you realize that windekas don't always chronicle everything. They miss things. Sometimes important things. You've got to talk to them all."

"That's a sort of obsessive fascination with dragons," Zephyr said.

"I always knew I'd kill one. It was only ever a question of when. The Forging isn't what I consider the most ideal conditions, but what's life without a little challenge?"

"Not dead," Zephyr grumbled.

"You're no fun." Rasia rolled her eyes, but the previous tension seemed to have thawed between them. They spoke to each other with a little more respect than before.

"The eighth dragon is Anumis, the wing of my sail and the dragon that gave Kai and my tahs the name of Dragonslayer. They took it down a few hunting seasons into their first kull, with Shamai-ta acting as scout and Kenji-shi as windeka." Rasia chuckled with an added smirk. "Back when they were fucking."

"What?" This is the first time Kai had ever heard of such of thing. Rasia scrunched her face at his confusion.

"Of course, they fucked. Kulls fuck each other *all* the time. What else is there to do during high noon of a hunt?"

Kai had honestly never given it much thought, but it didn't surprise him. It was a common adage that new faces should fuck the entire Grankull, then twice over again, before deciding on a kulani. Up until now, Kai had thought Kenji one-sided. He knew little of the legend he shared a household with.

"We need to start charting our course," Rasia said, moving on. Zephyr shifted over when Rasia spread out her map in the fire light. Kai also rolled over curiously to trace the path of her finger across the worn, pictograph-marked map.

"I hope you've noticed the pattern by now: You don't happen upon a dragon and expect to kill it. You've got to plan for it. You've got to bait and trap it, but it's almost impossible to track a dragon in flight. When a kull kills a dragon, they plan around the dragon's den. It'll take us about half a blink to reach the Dragon's Coast. We're about here," Rasia said, pointing to the dawnward corner of the map. She slid her finger tailward. "To reach the dragon's den, we'll need to go through the Lake of Yestermorrow, then through the Graveyard, and on to the Dragon's Coast."

"The Graveyard? How are we avoiding the scavengers? Are we going around?" Zephyr asked.

"That will take too long. If we trade some of our supplies to the scavengers, we can negotiate for safe passage. I've done it before. We'll be fine."

Zephyr didn't look convinced.

"If you're so worried about scavengers, why don't you use your big ass impractical sword to scare them away?"

"It's only impractical against people."

"Then what's the point of it?"

"Dragons, apparently," Zephyr said, then further explained, "I need it when I'm traveling with my father. The Desert isn't the only place with giant monsters. I've seen winged beasts lift whole trees, dragons swimming the oceans, and predators turn into shadows. The locals call them Behemoths."

"Do they have hunting kulls as well? People who go out and hunt them?" Rasia asked, twisting forward, intrigued.

"Not really. People outside the Desert are different. They hide underground or build walls. But they still need to trade with other communities, and my father is one of the rare few brave enough to dare the roads."

"Huh, didn't realize he was such a badass."

"Why do you think tah had his children?"

"Well-pointed." Rasia plopped an elbow across Kai, tilted her head, and said, "I tried going beyond the Desert once."

It wasn't an easy feat to reach the edges of the Desert. The oceans dawnward and tailward were beset with dragons and even greater monsters that prowled the waters. The shadowed forests headward were almost a two blinks ride away from the Grankull, and no one survived the deadlands, where the absence of water made it untraversable. No one knows how far the deadlands stretched. Reaching any edge of the Desert required a vast amount of resources and food that few could afford.

"I managed three vibrations into the trees when I got this scar." Rasia pulled up her shirt and showcased the three claw marks scraped from back to hip.

"You encountered a shadowcat and lived?" Zephyr asked.

"Your tah gets past them all the time."

"Because he knows how."

"If he figured it out, I'll figure it out too."

"You're going to get yourself killed."

"We'll see." She yawned, then shook herself awake and bounced to her feet. "I'll take first watch."

Before Kai could argue, Rasia had already marched off to check on the progress of the smoked meat. With a sigh, Kai reached for his bedroll to actually fall asleep in it. Once settled, he glanced over at Zephyr, who had wrapped himself in the fluffy blankets of an animal Kai had never seen before.

"That wasn't a plan," Zephyr said, after a moment.

Kai sighed. "Let's just get to the Dragon's Coast, and we'll figure it out from there."

Both Zephyr and Kai jolted awake at the sound of whining hyenas. Before either could get their wits about them, the yips and howls were chased away.

"That's what I thought," Rasia said as she emerged from the other side of the windship, unharmed and spear bloody.

Zephyr relaxed back in the bedroll, but Kai remained tense. Rasia slung her bow and quiver over her shoulder then marched off into the darkness. They heard one more painful yip before the Desert fell silent again.

Awake and unable to go back to sleep, Kai watched as Rasia reemerged on their side of the windship. She took a drink from her gourd and leaned her bow against the side of the hull. Not once did she look in their direction to see if the commotion had woken them. Instead, she remained close to the food.

Kai watched her lower into a fighting stance. She moved gracefully through the motions of her katas, flowing and weaving through the wind-shifts of smoke. So fluid and certain of every step anyone could have mistaken it for a dance. Meanwhile, Kai had always felt uncomfortable in his body. His lungs were not enough. His skin was too tight. Everything fit uncomfortably. But Rasia had such finite control over herself—from the tip of her toes to the twist of her hips. She was always aware of her balance, never falling unless intentionally giving herself over to gravity. Rasia even stopped with purpose. Kai could watch her all his days.

"Why don't you go fuck her?" Zephyr grumbled out.

Kai's face heated in embarrassment, and he turned away in his bedroll. He crossed his arms over his chest; he didn't think he had been staring that hard. But his dick said otherwise.

"She's not going to say no," Zephyr said. "She's been over you all day."

"Rasia's like that. She's touchy."

Kai heard Zephyr shift, and he peeked over his shoulder to meet Zephyr's flat stare. "Kai. I don't know if you were paying attention to the conversation earlier, but 'kulls fuck each other all the time', was an invitation to *you*. When we get back to the Grankull, once she earns her names, everyone is going to be hunting after her. You two have a whole Forging together. Enjoy it."

"She's busy."

"Tell her I'm awake for my turn at watch. She won't be busy then."

Kai hid in the leather and linen of his bedroll. How was he supposed to stroll up and ask for sex? It seemed a little entitled.

He heard the crunch of sand, and Kai sprang up to stop Zephyr from going over to Rasia. But it had only been a trick. Zephyr stood over him with his arms crossed, then crouched to stare until Kai broke into a frustrated sigh. Kai dragged his hand down his face. "I've never initiated. I'm not sure how."

"Stand up, walk over there, and ask. You already know she's interested, so a little self-confidence isn't too misplaced."

Zephyr was right, of course. Kai and Rasia had had sex multiple times at this point. The only block was in his head. He'd gotten so accustomed to not wanting things. To want, and have that want immediately satisfied, seemed unattainable. But he'd had Rasia before. It wasn't unreasonable, Kai convinced himself.

Kai shot to his feet. Then, he crouched down to fix his hair, brush sand from his sleep robes, and wash his mouth out with charcoal.

Zephyr snorted at him.

Kai gathered his courage and walked over to Rasia, like

approaching a skinko with a bow he couldn't use. She high-kicked, twirled her blades, and spun them around to meet him. Kai froze when the sharp dragonsteel stopped a grain from his skin. She laughed and lifted out of her stance with smooth ease.

"Did the hyenas wake you? I took care of them."

Kai scratched at a mosquito bite on his arm and recited the words he'd rehearsed in his head on the way over. "Zephyr is awake, too. He's volunteered to take second watch."

"I should tell him about the hyenas. Three of them were sniffing around. I got one, but they might be back." Rasia buckled her blades to her back. She grabbed her gourd and moved past Kai to meet with Zephyr.

"Wait, Rasia." She turned. Kai's mouth instantly dried. She raised a questioning brow. There was nothing to be scared of. The worst thing that could happen was a "no."

Kai faced Rasia, squared his shoulders, and asked, "Do you want to have sex?"

"Fuck yes."

Rasia snatched Kai's hand and dragged him behind her. Zephyr passed them with a knowing look, nodded about the hyenas, and took up guard by the food.

Rasia dragged Kai past the bedrolls out into the open Desert, where she pushed him into the soft, gravelly sand at the bottom of a hill. The hill's crest blotted out all light from the campfire, and thick clouds blanketed the moon and hushed the stars. The inky blackness felt so impenetrable that you could float off and get lost in it. Rasia threw a leg over his waist and anchored him down.

"What if the hyenas come back?" Kai asked, despite this being all his idea.

"I'll protect you."

They'd had sex for the first time in the heat of high noon. This time, in the cold biting darkness, he had no choice but to be guided by his hands, the scent of salted smoke in her hair, and the taste of her skin. In the darkness, he discovered her mouth all over again.

Rasia panted above him, pressing her face, searching, until their foreheads aligned. She rested there to catch her breath. "You don't have to ask every time you want me, Kai."

"I don't want to presume."

She grinned into his neck. "I'm always down to fuck. It doesn't have to be any more complicated than that."

They pawed off each other's clothes in frantic haste. It truly felt if either of them paused, or faltered, or slowed, they'd freeze and die. Moving, seeking each other's heat, making their own warmth against the friction of their skin, became a matter of survival.

"There's no more gonom, but we've still got plenty of options." The cheekiness of Rasia's grin streaked hot across his hip bone. "What are you *up* for?"

This time, Kai didn't hesitate to tell her what he wanted.

"I want everything."

"Fuck yes."

CHAPTER TWENTY-FIVE

O

Well, maybe not everything.

Rasia and Kai stared at each other, wide-eyed, in shock. They scrambled apart. Rasia into the shade of a thorny euphorbia and Kai against the ochre cliffs of the gorge.

He was supposed to have pulled out.

"*I'm sorry,*" Kai stammered, "I didn't mean—I was trying . . . will this seed you?" Kai asked, panic shredding his voice. His breaths wheezed out of him until they became whining whispers, and Rasia grew alarmed at his failure to draw in air. She grabbed him by the face and demanded that he breathe.

"Calm down, Kai. Don't be stupid. This little bit won't do shit. It's fine."

"Kenji-ta is going to murder me."

"He won't," Rasia said, certain. "Because nothing is going to happen. All those horror stories of getting seeded after one time are just what the Grankull tells to scare people. They're horseshit."

Kai expelled shallow breaths, jerkily nodding his head.

"Good. Now, I am going to go wash off." She patted him on the cheek, got up, and headed toward the springs. When she was out of Kai's line of sight, she broke into a sprint and proceeded to bathe more thoroughly than she had in her entire life.

Rasia returned from bathing to find Zephyr slumbering

unaware in the shaded coolness of the cave. She'd missed him the first time she came rushing through. They all had spent the morning unpacking yesterday's hunting haul, and for high-noon break, Zephyr had dropped down for a nap while Rasia and Kai snuck off somewhere private.

Rasia jumped over Zephyr. She found Kai outside in a fresh loincloth, washing both of their soiled clothes in the water basin. There was quite the pile, clothes from the past three days now being tended to. Rasia slid her fingers over the thin pickings on the clothesline. On a mere whim, Rasia plucked off Kai's old caftan and tossed it on.

"I see why you like it so much. It's crazy comfortable," Rasia said. She gathered the bottom to crouch beside Kai and dig her chin into his shoulder.

Kai vigorously scrubbed at the clothes with soap, bubbling the water. The soapy mixture smelled fragrantly of olive oil, lime, and lavender. Rasia noted that Kai's skin smelled much the same. He had bathed as well.

"When was your last deathsblood?" Kai asked.

"Seriously?"

"Yes. Maybe you're right and the odds are low, but we need to keep track. It'll be just my bad luck that I seed you. Leave it to the runt of the Grankull to not be able to do anything right but that."

"I think all my good luck balances it out in our favor."

He glared at her.

"Fine." Rasia squinted and tried to count the days in her head. "I think seven days before the Forging? Calm your nips, Kai. You worry too much. *You pulled out.*"

"*Halfway.*"

"You're being dramatic. I'm Rasia. I don't let stupid things happen to me, especially something as stupid as getting seeded."

Rasia hopped up and snatched the pants out of his hands. She moved to wring them out while he washed another piece of clothing. "We'll be more careful from now on. We've still got plenty of options, and after the Naming Ceremony, it won't matter no ways. Then, we can fuck any way we want. And let's not forget about the bodika. We can't miss the free-for-all orgy."

Kai scoffed. "No one is having an orgy with me."

"But by then, you would have slayed a dragon! I'd have sex with anyone who slayed a dragon."

Kai broke into a wry smile. "I know."

Rasia had just clipped the damp pants to the clothesline when a cold drop of water fell sharp on her forehead and slid down her face. Rasia frowned when the pitter patter of water became more frequent. It never rained in this area outside of rainy season. "This isn't normal."

Kai's eyes widened. "It's Nico."

Rasia tossed the pants at Kai's face and leaped toward the nearest rock wall. She climbed to the top of the gorge and spotted a Grankull ship on the horizon. Judging by the distance, Nico would be on them by sunset. Nico was a problem, but Rasia was more concerned by the rain. The wellspring was going to spill over into a whole river soon. They needed to get out of the gorge *now*.

Rasia dropped back to the ground where Kai was scrambling to get on some clothes. Rasia pulled off his caftan and snatched a pair of pants and shirt off the clothesline. The shirt was still damp, but it didn't matter in the thickening rain.

"What the fuck, Kai? I thought you could sense her location," Rasia said as she hopped into her pants. "You were supposed to be tracking her."

"*I've been distracted.*"

"Really? You're really going to blame this a-*mazing* wet ass pussy? You had one job."

"I blame it on everything!"

Rasia barked out a laugh. "You damn right. Okay. Get the ship ready to sail. I'll grab what we need from the kull supplies." Rasia turned in the direction of the cave and paused. She looked over her shoulder at Kai. "What do we do about Zephyr? Think we can trust him?"

Kai snorted. "No. He'll want to *talk* to her. I'll get the ropes."

They nodded at each other and got to work. Rasia smiled at

the way she and Kai worked together like an experienced kull. They clicked in a way she hadn't with another person since jih. She enjoyed every moment of the situation, from restraining Zephyr in his sleep, to hauling him tied-up onto the deck of the windship, to the anticipation of Nico's impeding arrival.

"You need to talk to her," Zephyr insisted to Kai, grumpily awake now. Rasia loaded the windship with extra supplies from the kull stash. She even grabbed all Zephyr's belongings and his huge-ass sword because she was nice like that.

Rasia laughed when Kai stuffed Zephyr's mouth with Zephyr's own shroud. Kai secured Zephyr to the railing, then crouched in front of Zephyr and told him solemnly, "Nico isn't going to listen to me. She never has. We both know that. Sit tight, and I'll release you when we lose her."

Rasia did a cursory check of the gorge. She peeked her head into the cave and noted the rising water. Kai came through to grab more rope and paused at the sight of the ilhan in the corner before rushing back to the ship. Rasia glanced after him, then grabbed both the ilhan and as much olive oil as she could carry. Luckily, they had the majority of the scorpion's jerky and sausage already stored in the hatch. Once Rasia was satisfied she hadn't forgotten anything, she signaled to Kai "ready."

Kai steered the ship through the rocks. Once the ship broke the gorge's mouth and settled into a consistent speed, Rasia whipped out her map and slapped it atop the deck.

"Here's the plan." Rasia pinned the corners with her knees to keep the edges down in the wind. "Nico's ship is faster than mine, and the terrain this way is pretty flat, which means she's going to catch up. I'll serve as the distraction, but I need you to steer the ship"—Rasia pointed to a sizable hole marring the map—"to the Sand Bowl. We'll lose her there."

Thunder rolled through the sky. Dark storm clouds blotted out the sun and swallowed the Desert in darkness.

Kai blanched. "She's more pissed than I thought."

"The rain is going to be a complication. It will soften the sand and make it harder to maneuver."

"We could use her magic to our advantage," Kai suggested. "Nico loses control of her powers when she's emotional. If you can get her to expend her magic quickly, she'll pass out. Then she won't be able to follow us."

Rasia grinned. "Perfect."

The sharp rain drenched Rasia's clothes and plastered her hair to her face. In all her time exploring the Desert, Rasia had never experienced rain like this—a rain so cold it knifed through her skin. The sand softened and sloughed beneath them.

Through the heavy sheets of rain, Nico's windship drew nearer.

CHAPTER TWENTY-SIX

I

Rasia stood unflinchingly atop the bow of her windship, and the rain battered that infuriating smirk. Nico wanted the rain to slow Rasia down, to be so cold it stabbed Rasia's skin, but Rasia bore the rain shower without a hint of discomfort.

"Nico, it's freezing," Azan complained from the tiller, his shroud wrapped around his face and cloak tight about his shoulders. Suri's teeth chattered from where she sat atop the scout's nest, and Kelin shivered despite the extra layer of clothing Nico had warned them all to wear.

If Rasia was unaffected, maybe the rain wasn't worth it.

Rasia hefted a spear over her shoulder, and Nico jolted out of her thoughts. She leaped to the deck to avoid the spear aimed in her direction. In the last vibration, Rasia changed targets, and the spear sailed harmlessly over Nico's head.

Azan jumped to evade the spear, and the tiller sprang free. The windship tilted, and Nico slid into the railing. Suri's arrow missed Rasia by a foot.

When they finally got the windship back under control, Rasia's ship had drawn farther into the distance. This time, Nico switched places with Azan at the tiller. For so long, Rasia had always been a step ahead of Nico. Not anymore.

Rasia readied another spear when they came close again, with an even more infuriating smugness to her smirk. Rasia hurled the spear and, with a whip of water, Nico swatted it from the sky.

"Everyone, grab ahold of something," Nico ordered.

Nico exhaled, and the rainclouds condensed into a mist so thick even dragons couldn't see through it. Nico sensed Rasia like gonda vibrating for prey. Nico curved the ship, aiming to hit the hull head-on, to flip over Rasia's smaller windship and stop her in her tracks.

Rasia's windship came into foggy view, then disappeared. Nico blinked in bafflement until a shadow swept across the deck. Nico looked up to find Rasia's windship pass overhead, turning almost vertically on its stern.

Rasia smirked at her with two fingers raised in a v shape, and her legs gripped tightly around the ship's railing. Nico caught sight of Zephyr, eyes wide, tied to the ship. Then Kai, throwing his weight against the outrigger so far that he hung upside down. An image of Kenji-ta doing the same maneuver, the infamous Blindside, flashed in Nico's head. Nico found herself thrown so off-balance by the sight of it that she stood there, frozen, while Rasia's windship landed with an audible thud and shot off in the opposite direction.

Since when could Kai steer a windship?

"Nico, they're getting away," Azan said.

Nico quickly directed the others to help her turn the ship around. It took too long. By the time they were facing the right direction, Nico and her team had dropped behind five whole vibrations. Nico pulled her face in frustration. At least she could still see Rasia's ship, but it was so far away now, just a black speck on the horizon.

Nico didn't understand why Kai was helping Rasia. She didn't understand why he'd run off with Rasia in the first place. What could Rasia possibly offer him?

Whatever the promises, Nico was determined to get him back.

"Azan, grab the tiller. I need to focus."

Nico moved to the bow and conjured another storm. The rain poured hard over Rasia's windship and slowed it down enough to give Nico the chance to catch back up.

The edges of Nico's vision faded, and she caught herself against the railing, faint and dizzy. Nico knew she was expending a lot of magic, but every time a shiver zipped up her spine, so did the flash of Rasia's smirk. Rasia's cocky voice, *"Feel free to use your magic"* plugged Nico's ears. As if, even with it, Nico didn't have a chance.

Nico refused to let Rasia outsmart her again.

"Azan! Get us as close as possible!" Nico shouted over the wind. She'd jump ships and take the fight to Rasia personally. She'd see if Rasia was singing the same tune after Nico had washed the full force of her power against Rasia's stupid smug face.

Nico drew nearer and nearer, and Rasia just lounged against her ship with a self-satisfied smile. Nico stepped a foot onto her railing as the windships drew parallel to one another. Nico crouched, prepared to jump once they cleared the stern, although a little wary because Rasia hadn't bothered grabbing for another spear.

Instead, Rasia winked and stepped several paces back. She spun on the balls of her feet, right into Kai, and swallowed him down in a filthy, open-mouthed kiss.

Nico's brain stopped.

Rasia and Kai were both drenched from the rain, and the thin linen showed way more than Nico ever wanted to see. When Rasia outright shoved a hand down Kai's pants and enveloped the suggestive line of his—Nico wrenched her shroud up to her eyes, scandalized.

It all made sense now—why Kai had been so willing to run off with her, what Rasia could have possibly promised him. She was *using* him! She was pretending to care about him. She was taking advantage of him to get revenge against Nico for ruining her Forging. Rasia was a disgusting, selfish, manipulative . . . *skink*!

The world darkened. Blood drummed in Nico's ears. The air thickened, tight, humid. The oil in the mast lamp boiled. The water barrels in the underbelly churned.

Nico was flung back when the windship plummeted down a sudden incline. Nico fought gravity and a strong urge to vomit as she climbed to her feet to the sight of Rasia now at the windship's tiller. Rasia took a curving path to the bottom of a large spherical depression. She steered circles around them, coming to one side, cutting a sharp angle out of the other, and riding the speed around to pop free of the basin.

"I can't hold it!" Azan shouted, right before he lost control.

Nico scraped what little magic she had left to splash them safely to a landing.

The world tilted sideways. For a moment, Nico thought her magic had failed her and the windship had gone rolling, but then Nico hit the deck with the cruel reality that it was her body that had failed her. She crashed into an icy lake and sunk into darkness.

Nico stared blankly at the speckled bumps of the carapace deck. She tucked her arms around her knees, indifferent to Azan's failed attempts to mimic Rasia's technique and get them out of this infuriating Sand Bowl. Nico should have recognized what it was, the kulls used it to test their most advanced windekas. They weren't getting out of here until Nico's magic recovered.

Nico further ducked under the cloak Suri placed around her shoulders. Azan eventually gave up and collapsed cross-legged to the deck.

"Well," Kelin said as he looked around to survey their surroundings. "Can anything eat us down here?"

"If so, you're the first one we're throwing overboard. You didn't help at all," Azan complained.

"I know nothing about windships. I'd only be in the way."

"You know nothing about windships because you don't want to know nothing about windships. You could have tried to learn at any time," Azan said.

Kelin scoffed. "It wouldn't have hardly mattered. We were played the entire way here. There's no catching up to her."

"Maybe if you had pulled a bit more of your weight," Suri bit out. "Another person with a bow, and we could have had her pinned down."

"Enough," Nico choked out. "He's right. I threw everything at her. And it still wasn't enough."

It hurt—that bitter realization that Nico would never be as good as Rasia. Nico dropped her head atop her knees, throat heavy. Their hostile relationship had only ever been a game to Rasia. Now Kai was caught in the crossfire, and Nico felt helpless to do anything about it. Kai deserved better than to be manipulated against Nico in some foolish childhood competition. Nico refused to allow her jih to be reduced to some bone piece to bet on.

"So . . . are we hunting a gonda now?" Kelin asked. "Doesn't seem your jih wants any saving. Who are we to stand in the way of wetting dick?"

"*No*," Nico snapped, unable to break her brain further to imagine anything more than that lurid kiss. Kai and Rasia didn't make sense together. They had nothing in common. They were nothing like each other. Rasia was a selfish, egotistical hazard, and Kai deserved far better than that kulo. The sheer imbalance of it all shook Nico to her core.

"No," Nico repeated. "That was for show. That's how Rasia operates. She's only using him to throw me off."

Kelin and Azan looked at each other. It was Azan who broke the news.

"Rasia's hot. She's got that energy about her, you know? Like hold-on-this-is-about-to-be-the-wildest-time-of-your-fucking-life type of energy," Azan said, flailing his arms, trying to explain. "She walks around with it. It's hot. She's hot." After a pause, Azan blurted out, "You're hot too, but in a different way. And Kelin! And Suri! And Neema!"

Azan dropped his red face into his hands.

"Very eloquent," Kelin said with a snicker. "What Azan is

trying to say is that your jih and Rasia have spent several days alone together. If Rasia is willing to kiss him like that, no one who rolls in her direction is going to pass up an opportunity to do more. They're fucking."

Azan nodded. "They're fucking."

Nico turned to Suri. Suri gave a brief, hesitant nod in agreement.

Nico couldn't imagine it. Kai knew all about her history with Rasia, and more worrying, Kai knew how the Council was eager for any excuse to get rid of him. One mistake, and Kai could have his face burned off with Nico powerless to stop it.

"Kai's not that stupid."

Azan barked out a laugh. "We're *all* that stupid."

Nico glanced at Suri, remembering when Nico had briefly given into temptation. She feared what sort of devastation Rasia could wrought with that sort of power over Kai. Rasia was going to get her jih killed.

Nico rose to her feet, determined, and done moping about her failures.

"I don't care if jih is working with her. We still have a chance. If she's seriously hunting a dragon, she's headed toward the Dragon's Coast. To get there, she must cross the Lake of Yestermorrow. It will take days for Rasia to cross it, but for me mere vibrations. That is where we'll catch her. This doesn't end until I bring jih home."

Nico refused to let Rasia win.

CHAPTER TWENTY-SEVEN

O

Rasia tossed her hair, laughing, as dusk fell behind her. Nothing felt better than getting one over on self-righteous play-by-the-rules Nico.

So fucking easy.

Rasia turned to Kai, who paid her no attention at all as he stared out at the dust billowing behind them in their wake.

She jumped at him. Startled, Kai tumbled to the deck and landed awkwardly halfway against the railing. Rasia slapped his face with both hands and shook him. "*Kai*, you did it. You were fucking amazing."

He'd managed to pull off the Blindside in the middle of a chase!

Rasia snatched for the ties of his waistband, but Kai caught her wrists. He slanted his shoulders and slid away. His face scrunched as he said, accusatorily, "That wasn't part of the plan."

Rasia blinked. Using her momentary confusion, Kai slipped from underneath her and shuffled back on his knees. "You didn't tell me you were going to use"—Kai motioned between the two of them—"*this* against her."

Huh. Kai was angry at her.

Rasia sat up and crossed her arms. "It was your idea. There's no easier way to rile Nico up than to mess around with you. I thought that was the plan."

"You groped me in front of my jih!"

"And it clearly worked!"

Kai grabbed the top railing and pulled himself to his feet. He looked down at Rasia, frustrated. "I should have been the one to discuss this with her. She's my jih, and now you've gone and flung it in her face."

"What's there to discuss? We're just fucking."

Kai grimaced at those words and rubbed harshly at his face. "You know how she feels about you. Now, she probably thinks you're taking advantage of my innocence or naivete or some shit."

"Aren't I?" Rasia said, wiggling her eyebrows as she stood. She scrutinized Kai from head to toe. There was a lot she'd rather be taking advantage of right now than having this stupid conversation.

"I'm serious, Rasia. I know Nico. She's going to blame you for this."

"So? I don't care. Nico is nothing compared to me. Her best can't keep up with my worst. Apologize to her and do whatever you need to do after the Forging, but right now, let's get back to what we came out here to do and hunt this fucking dragon."

"It would be great if someone could untie me."

Both Rasia and Kai turned to Zephyr, who was still tied to the railing and clearly as disinterested in Rasia and Kai's argument as Rasia was. Kai left to untie Zephyr while Rasia harrumphed against the railing. This wasn't the victory celebration she'd imagined. All she wanted was a few orgasms. She didn't think that was a lot to ask for.

"This is why you should have talked to Nico," Zephyr told Kai once the knots were loosened.

"I'm sure that would have gone even better," Kai said.

"So, what now? You're going to continue letting her chase you halfway across the Desert?"

"Maybe she'll give up."

Zephyr gave Kai a flat stare. "After that stunt Rasia pulled,

Nico is going to drag you back home, Forging or not. I didn't think this could get any worse. We need to turn around, Kai."

"No," Kai bit out, storming to the other side of the deck.

Zephyr looked to Rasia as if she were the sensible one on this ship, and she laughed at his desperation. She informed him, politely, "We turn around over my dead body."

This morning, they had been working as a team offloading their well-earned spoils and generally getting along, and now they all stood on three different sides of the windship after what should have been a victory.

"All right, you two," Rasia said, tired of the dramatics. She walked toward the center of the ship. "What's done is done. We need to reach the Dragon's Coast with enough time to do what we need to do and make it back to the Grankull by the end of the Forging. Zephyr, do you know how to steer a windship? Doesn't your tah have one?"

"I don't know how to steer *your* windship," Zephyr said, implying something was wrong with it. If she had a choice, Rasia wouldn't let him within five vibrations of her steer.

"Good enough. To reach the Dragon's Coast with plenty of time, from here on out, we're sailing without break. We are not stopping to make camp. We are not resting for high noon. We are steering straight to the coast. We'll each steer in three shifts. I'll steer at night because I know the terrain. Kai will steer from morning to high noon. Zephyr will steer after Kai, till sunset."

"You're forcing Kai to steer *through* high noon? That's a heatstroke waiting to happen."

Rasia waved her hand between Kai and Zephyr. "Are you going to tell him, or should I?"

Zephyr turned to Kai, and Kai ducked his head, embarrassed for some reason Rasia couldn't begin to fathom. It's not as if Kai were still quaking the world at every climax. Kai discovered the night of their First Hunt that he could avoid that problem if he held his breath at the right moment. (If only he had been less focused on holding his breath and more focused on pulling out this morning . . .)

Kai took too long to answer, so Rasia wiggled her fingers and revealed, "He's magic."

Kai cleared his throat. "That."

"Come on, Zephyr. You're on shift first. I need to show you how things work. Kai, go below deck and make sure none of our supplies toppled over in the chase."

Kai scampered down the hatch. Zephyr, on the other hand, planted his feet and refused to move.

Rasia stared him down, planting roots of her own. "Stop being a kulo. We're not turning around, so you might as well pull your weight."

"I want to make clear the only reason I'm here is because of Kai, to make sure he doesn't end up dead. If anything happens, know I've killed better people than you." Rasia showed her teeth as Zephyr drew near, and their shoulders clashed when he passed by. He kept his back to her and studied the rigging. "Now, how do you steer this stupid ship?"

As Rasia had assumed, Zephyr did have experience steering his tah's large windbarge. He knew a lot more than those kids who thought they could pull off tricks after one measly class. Teaching Zephyr was as simple as showing him all the small details specific to her windship.

"Why did you bring it?"

Rasia paused in her explanation of the rigging. She turned to Kai, his chest halfway out of the underbelly hatch, glowering at her.

"Bring what?"

"Why did you bring the ilhan?"

". . . you were looking at it, and I figured maybe you thought we didn't have any room, so I grabbed it." Rasia shrugged, not understanding why it mattered. It was a vibration of a decision. "And you seemed to know how to play it, so. Yeah."

Kai stared at her, uncomprehending. "I don't know how to play the ilhan."

"Yes, you do. I don't remember if you were any good or not, since we were both definitely drunk, but you played it."

"It's not mine. We can't just take things that aren't ours."

"But it's your tah's. I'm sure he won't mind. He has hundreds scattered out here."

"It does not belong to me!" Kai snapped, harshly. "*We have to bring it back.*"

"The gorge is washed out by now, and no, we're not turning back around. What the fuck is wrong with the both of you?" Rasia asked.

Kai stared at her sourly, then pulled himself out of the hatch and stomped over to the front of the ship. Rasia glanced at Zephyr for some sort of explanation, her turn desperate for some sense. She was not the crazy one here.

Zephyr crossed his arms, unimpressed.

"You're a thoughtless idiot," Zephyr said. "Kenji-shi *disowned* Kai. Everyone knows that. Of course, they wouldn't have the best relationship."

Rasia knew that. The Grankull didn't allow people to disown infants, but Kenji-shi was the one notable exception. But that was a long time ago, and Rasia didn't understand what bearing that had on the now.

"This is Kenji-shi we're talking about. He gives water to strangers."

Zephyr stared at her, his eyes narrowing as if he were trying to drill information into her head. But if it was so important, why didn't Zephyr just tell her? Ugh. Whatever.

Rasia crossed her arms and huffed. It wasn't Rasia's fault that Kai was all stupidly sensitive about it. She paced. In bored frustration, she looked over at Kai, who was hunched to his knees.

Annoyed, and without any sort of plan, Rasia stormed over. She hovered over him and audibly stomped her feet to get his attention. Kai peeked out of his arms with a dark pout.

"If it's going to get you in trouble with Kenji-shi, I'll tell him I took it."

"No, it's not that. I . . ." Kai dragged a hand over his face, then bit out, "You remember more of that night than I do."

"It's not my fault you're a lightweight."

Kai glanced down at his hands. They drummed a specific tune on the deck. He asked softly, "That night, did I hurt you?"

Rasia blinked, thinking she might have misheard at first. She ran the words through her head a second time. Then she laughed. That was the most preposterous thing she had ever heard. "*You* could never hurt me."

Kai was bowed away from her, so she couldn't parse why he would ask such a question. She found Kai extremely puzzling at times. First Nico, then the ilhan, then Kenji-shi, and now a question about a night she thought had been fairly great. At least what she remembered of it. Rasia couldn't find the thread connecting any of those topics. Maybe Kai remembered something she didn't?

Rasia unfolded her arms and sat next to him. She stuck her legs through the railing and, testing her boundaries, leaned against his shoulder. She waited for him to shift or move, but he didn't.

Rasia asked, concerned, "Did I hurt you?"

According to Ysai, she was usually a giggly, dancing drunk. Although there had been that one time that she had gotten it in her head to dance with her swords. Not bad dance partners, in Rasia's opinion.

"No, not at all," Kai said. He gave a minuscule shoulder lift. "Some people can be angry drunks."

"Ah." Rasia leaned forward, more than happy to dispel that worry. She poked his cheek. "You're a touchy . . . oddly boastful drunk."

Surprised, Kai swiveled his head so fast their faces almost collided. Rasia took advantage of the sudden closeness and leaned forward to say, "It was a *good* night. The best night."

Kai leaned further back, catching his weight with a hand on the deck, and Rasia chased him until she stretched across the whole of him. "We're going to be stuck on this windship for several days, and all I want to do is spend it all with you."

"Rasia." Kai's voice was hoarse, strangled. "*I* messed up this morning."

"And it won't happen again," Rasia soothed. She stroked a

hand up his length and whispered, "I really want to suck your dick right now."

Kai's face pinched in consideration, and Rasia grinned victoriously when all his reservations gave way. Rasia fell over laughing at the sudden strength Kai pressed to her mouth. He grabbed her by the hips and led her to her feet. They tossed off clothes and stumbled down into the underbelly. Then Kai stuffed them into the small bunk slat that connected the triangle lead of the ship.

Rasia tugged Kai's loincloth down his thighs and popped free Rasia's new best friend. She smiled cheekily. "Poor innocent Kai, utterly at my mercy. Oh, whatever will your jih think?"

"Oh no. I'm so helpless."

Rasia laughed, dunked down, and thoroughly corrupted whatever innocence he had left. One thing was for certain: Rasia was determined not to give him back to Nico the same.

CHAPTER TWENTY-EIGHT

O

It had been three days so far stuck on the windship. Of course, Rasia had been confined to a windship plenty of times before with only herself for company. She could usually find something to occupy her time, but today nothing satisfied her. Kai had passed out earlier that day, and she longed to shove him awake and demand his attention. He'd give it, too. He'd look at her with that sleepy pout, then shatter her apart piece by piece to politely put her back together again.

But she'd had him up the shift before, and the shift before that, too. She should probably let him sleep eventually. Rasia hung upside down from the railing, uncertain about what to do, buzzing with restless energy. In a rush of blood to her head, an idea came to her.

And let it be said: All Rasia's best ideas happened when she was bored.

Rasia kicked her legs and spun, landing in a crouch to the deck. Rasia traversed to the other side of the ship where Zephyr had staked his corner. His eye twitched as she neared. Rasia and Zephyr's steering shifts were often two ships passing in the night. It was rare for them to be alone together on deck without Kai around to mediate.

Rasia planted her feet and declared, "Let's spar."

"No."

"Why not? Don't think you can beat me?" Rasia had been hankering for a rematch for a while now. She couldn't believe Kai had distracted her from it for this long.

"We're on a windship," Zephyr said. *Lame.* He was most certainly one of the most boring people Rasia had ever met. Even when it came to steering the windship, he refused to leave it rigged and unattended.

"So, you're a mutt and boneless?" Rasia taunted.

Zephyr's heavy brows smashed together, forming a rather impressive glare, but he refused to rise to the taunt. Rasia reached for Zephyr's large sword where it rested against the railing. She lifted the hilt and cursed at the sheer weight of it. She dragged it over and threw it carelessly at Zephyr's feet.

Zephyr crossed his arms. "I am not Kai. I am not your entertainment."

Zephyr's snark cut so deeply it only made Rasia want to fight him more.

"You're really going to do nothing? Did your tah do nothing when they stamped whore on her face? Must be true then, even if a skink paid for it." Rasia waggled her tongue suggestively through the v-shape of her fingers. No one, tent kid or kuller, could allow such blatant disrespect.

Zephyr reached for his sword and Rasia hopped back with anticipation itching the bottom of her feet.

"I hate to give you what you want," Zephyr said, grim, "but you brought my parents into this."

Rasia threw up her dual blades, caught them behind her back, and spun them in her grip. Zephyr reacted to the showmanship with a flat stare. No appreciation at all.

Using the spins and tricks to distract his eye, Rasia attacked first. And it worked. Zephyr barely evaded, caught off guard by the sudden attack. He countered, quicker at swinging around that heavy sword than most. It was still too slow to catch her, but if Rasia made one small mistake, Zephyr's sword could do some serious damage.

The windship allowed very little room to maneuver. The limited space constrained Zephyr's sword swings, and Rasia took full advantage of it. She cornered him and guided his attacks against the railing, by the mast, or near the steer. It wasn't really a fair fight. This was Rasia's ship, her terrain, she knew all the cracks to trip an opponent and how much space she needed to make a move. She fought circles around his heavy swings.

Zephyr lunged, an attempt to force Rasia into a corner. She skipped back and hopped atop the railing. She balanced with ease along the rim. The ship rocked and wobbled under the momentum of Zephyr's lunge, which left him open. She touched his side playfully with the flat end of her khopesh, then skipped around him.

"What's going on?"

Kai poked his head up from the underbelly, hair all tossed and silky even after sleep. Sometimes Rasia ran her fingers through Kai's golden strands in fascination. Somehow, it never tangled. Kai should add that to his list of superpowers.

"Shit," Rasia cursed, losing pieces of hair as she ducked under Zephyr's attack. She caught herself in a crouch and shook her head, reprimanding herself for getting distracted. Rasia gave Zephyr a wink for the cheap shot and decided to pay it back in turn. She rolled backward and slammed her hand down on the steer.

The windship lurched, coming to a stop so fast that it tipped on its side and skidded in the sand. Zephyr went flying, but much to his credit, he rolled to his feet upon landing and blocked Rasia's downswing.

Zephyr took advantage of the open space the sands provided, and the balance of power shifted toward a fairer fight. Rasia enjoyed the change in environment, and it allowed her the opportunity to prove that no matter where, even at his best, he couldn't defeat her. He'd gotten lucky the first time.

"Why are you two fighting?" Kai asked, climbing down from where he had grabbed onto the mast at the last moment.

"We're sparring!"

"No, we're not!"

Now that Zephyr had full range of motion, Rasia found it harder to get through his defenses. He took advantage of his considerable bulk and rooted himself to the spot, deflecting and blocking as Rasia tested his defenses from every angle.

Zephyr heaved his massive sword, and Rasia lunged right into the attack. It'd kill her, most likely chop off her head in one clean stroke, but Rasia was willing to roll that bet.

She won when he changed angles. The sword sailed over her head. She kicked the back of his knee, and his bulk came tumbling down. She planted a decisive foot on his chest and crossed her swords at his neck.

"You're fucking crazy," Zephyr spat out.

"Zara might be the Scorpion Han of the Tents, but you have none of her ruthlessness. Not once during the battle did you press for the wound at my right. You must get that softness from your foreign-ta."

"I didn't kill you because you're fucking my best friend's jih," Zephyr growled out. "I swear, if you were anyone else . . ."

"Mutt, you still wouldn't be able to beat me."

"Don't call him that."

Rasia turned to Kai, who stood behind her. His voice had lowered a register, and it sent a shiver up Rasia's spine. Rasia released Zephyr and turned to Kai with a roll of her eyes. "I was just egging him on."

"She called Zara-ta a whore, and implied my father is a skink," Zephyr said.

Snitch.

A hard storm swept through Kai's eyes, and in that moment, Rasia knew she'd miscalculated. When had Kai and Zephyr gotten so close?

Kai untied his spare shroud from around his waist and threw it down at Rasia's feet.

"I challenge you on the honor of Zephyr's parents. I demand a blood price."

Rasia laughed, and laughed, and laughed. Kai was hardly a

threat to anyone. She should know. She knew the exact width and breadth of his shoulders. She'd traveled the low hills of his muscles. She'd traced her lips down his thin frame and intimately knew the physical limits of his body. What's more, when it came to sex, the playing field was equal because of their shared lack of experience. This was different.

Kai didn't even know how to hold that dagger of his correctly.

"Sure. Whatever," Rasia said, more amused than anything else. She dropped into position with her swords crossed in front of her.

Rasia attacked.

Kai anticipated. In the last breath, he shifted, barely, but enough for Rasia to lose the angle on him. With her weight already thrown into the attack, Kai flipped his dagger and stabbed it straight into Rasia's thigh.

Oh.

Rasia stared at the blade protruding from her leg in shock. He'd used her expectations against her, knowing she'd underestimate him. He knew she'd attack first and had used her momentum against her. She'd been outsmarted.

It's not a tactic Kai would ever be able to use against her a second time, but Rasia hadn't lost a spar since Shamai-ta. It'd been much longer than that since she'd felt steel in her flesh.

This changed everything.

Rasia thought she'd explored all Kai's mountains, the dips of all his valleys, and the topography of his scars. She thought him a land well-traveled and conquered, a landmark to be soon crossed off her map, but she was *wrong*.

There was an infinite more undiscovered.

From behind her, Kai snatched the dagger from her thigh, then pressed the bloodied blade against her throat. Rasia leaned back into his chest, forcing him to tighten his grip.

"You little shit," Rasia said, breathing hard, "You pretended not to know what you were doing."

"Concede," Kai whispered into her ear. Rasia melted in surrender, more than willing to concede in any way he wanted her. "Words, Rasia. I know you can use them."

Rasia squeezed her eyes shut. There was a literal dagger at her neck, but she was so fucking wet right now. "*I concede.*"

A cold chill washed over her when Kai stepped back. He swept his shroud from the ground and used it to wipe the blood from the dagger. He presented Zephyr the bloodied shroud.

"I offer this blood price on your parent's honor."

"I accept on their behalf."

Kai returned to Rasia. He ripped the bottom of his cloak, crouched down to his knees, and began to bandage Rasia's thigh.

"Maybe no one taught me how to steer a windship, but before Ava-ta left this world, she made sure I knew how to protect myself," Kai said, refusing to look at her.

It made sense. The dagger was an efficient weapon for him. It wasn't too heavy to slow him down, nor did he have the luxury of stamina. He would have learned to strike as quick and dirty as possible. In order to protect himself, he didn't have a choice but to go for blood, and despite everything they'd done together, Kai hadn't hesitated.

Kai tightened the bandage and rolled her pants leg back down. The moment he stood up, Rasia grabbed for him to defile the fuck out of his mouth.

He pulled away.

"What's wrong?" Rasia asked.

Kai took several agonizing vibrations to find the words, but when he said them, they lacked any hint of softness. "Zephyr is my friend. He has agreed to hunt a dragon with us, and how you've treated him is unacceptable. You've insulted him and his parents to taunt him into a fight. You could have asked."

"I did. He said no."

Kai frowned, and you would have thought Rasia had pushed him off a cliff, for the betrayal and disappointment in his eyes. Rasia had thought she could depend on Kai to follow her no matter what. Where others would have long balked, he understood and accepted her. Or so she'd thought.

Kai narrowed his eyes, then said, pained, "I don't think we

should sleep together anymore. Let's just hunt our dragon."

The weight of a gonda toppled on top her.

"*No*," Rasia scalded. Kai didn't get to end this. Rasia was the one who was supposed to get bored of him first. She was the one who decided when this should end. "I paid the blood price. That should have been enough."

Kai shook his head. "What you said was unforgivable. You don't treat me like that."

"Yeah, because you're fucking me!"

Kai's face completely shuttered.

"*Not anymore.*"

Anger coiled in Rasia's limbs as he turned to walk away from her. She exploded forward, shoving at his shoulder to turn him back around. Then she slammed a fist in his face.

Kai went sprawling to the ground, and Zephyr stormed forward in a fury. Rasia spat. "At least Nico could take a punch."

Kai grabbed at her ankle and twisted, sending Rasia folding to the ground on top of him. She moved to knee him in the gut, then yelped when his fingers tickled her sides. Rasia curled, batting him away, before she succumbed to helpless giggles. Kai pulled out from under her, and Rasia glared at him, outraged.

She reached out to wring his fucking neck and blinked when he whipped a strip of cloth around his arm. Rasia slapped a hand to her breasts, pinning in place the makeshift wrap on the brink of unravelling. She lunged for him, but Kai whipped up his end of the linen strip to trip her. They rolled. Kai on the bottom, then Rasia, then Kai again.

"Ha!" Rasia said triumphantly, pinning him to the ground. Her breast-wrap had loosened further and was now tangled between the two of them. Kai's eyes narrowed.

"*Fuck!*" Rasia screeched, when Kai mercilessly twisted her nipple. She oomphed, thrown to her back on the ground.

Kai stood up over her and sucked in raspy breaths. "That's for punching my jih. I'm sure you deserve it."

He walked away.

Rasia rubbed at her poor abused breast and pressed her other hand to her racing heart. That's twice now she's lost to Kai. And Zephyr, fucking Zephyr, towered over her as if *he* had won.

Rasia is not fucking losing again.

CHAPTER TWENTY-NINE

—

The windship remained where it'd landed, turned on its side. Zephyr and Kai used it as a barrier against the wind and huddled around their small campfire. Rasia had run off after the argument. She hadn't returned since.

It was a Hunter's moon that night, and they both wore their shrouds under Death's gaping eye. Even Zephyr, who had traveled many lands, couldn't shake the superstition. Kai hoped Rasia had remembered to bring her shroud. They said Death favored the hunters, for better or for worse.

Bowed under the full moon's weight, Zephyr and Kai ate scorpion sausage for dinner. They crunched on doum palm cores while the dunes sang eerie songs.

Zephyr retrieved their store of kindling from the windship underbelly and fed the fire. He stared hard into those flames, light dancing on his shroud, and warned, "If she hits you again, I'm killing her."

"No," Kai said. "You stay out of this. Your involvement will only antagonize her and escalate the situation. This is my mess that I've steered myself into. This is between me and Rasia." Zephyr opened his mouth to argue further, but Kai cut him off. "I don't want you touching her."

Kai hadn't forgotten when Zephyr slammed Rasia to the

ground. He had also almost taken her head off today. And while yes, Kai had stabbed her in the leg, he had been careful to avoid serious injury. Zephyr didn't *care* about Rasia. He respected her. He was wary of her. But he didn't *care*.

"You're in way over your head, Kai. Every time we're on deck together, she drags you away until she's the center of your attention. Rasia barely allows us to have a conversation without her butting in and interrupting. I don't think she realizes what she's doing, but if you think she's going to let you go, you're wrong. I first thought you were just fun to her, but she has a flame for you, and she has a shit way of showing it."

Kai had noticed Rasia's monopoly of his time, but he hadn't exactly complained about it either. He had bent to her whims, did what she wanted, shifted topics of conversation to include her interests, and dedicated his entire everything to pleasing her. But there's a line. There has to be a line. Nico should have been that line, and he had allowed himself to be pulled right over it.

Despite how much Kai had tried to forgive the incident, what happened with Nico had never sat right with him. He should have been the one to explain to Nico his relationship with Rasia, nor should it have been used for shock value. The Elder knows jih doesn't react well to surprises. The magic could have killed her. He doesn't know what he would have done if he hadn't been able to sense her alive as they sailed away.

The situation with Zephyr had also been line, and Kai could not compromise another one. Perhaps Zephyr had been right all along. Did Kai really know Rasia? Had he been this blind to her faults, or had it taken time for the cracks to show?

"I didn't have a choice," Kai said. "She shouldn't have said those things about Zara—" Kai stumbled over the address, uncertain.

"Zara-shi," Zephyr told him. "*You* can address her as Zara-shi."

Kai nodded, honored by the permission. "Who would I be to let those words go unblooded? I know what Zara-shi has done for my family. Rasia might have paid a blood price, but I doubt she'll ever apologize for it."

"No, I'm grateful for what you did. I'm not saying you should have ignored it. I'm saying we should *leave*. We tie *her* to the railing and turn this ship around."

"Mutiny? I'm not going to betray Rasia like that. She considers too many people to have abandoned her, and I'm not going to be one of them." Despite it all, Kai couldn't help but to defend her.

"Exactly. There is a reason she has no friends, Kai. She's selfish, she's spoiled, and she's dangerous."

"She's *lonely*. Of course, she's not going to want to let me go."

"I could say the same for you."

"Fuck you," Kai bit out. He turned away, arms crossed, to the howling winds of the Desert. The wind was so strong, the air had become thick and hazy with sand.

What did Zephyr know of loneliness? What did Zephyr know of what it was like to be born so broken no other half could possibly fit all your edges?

Rasia could be all Kai got to have, and he'd given her up for blood honor. For Nico. And ultimately, for himself. This ride had always been headed for a crash, and he knew it. Deep down he knew it.

Kai shrugged and muttered, knowingly, "Rasia is all I'll ever get to have."

Zephyr gave a hard, aggrieved sigh.

Then Zephyr cupped a hand behind Kai's head and kissed him.

A shroud kiss.

Kai's eyes widened as Zephyr deepened the heat against the linen and pushed Kai to the ground. Kai clutched at the edges of his makeshift shroud, his heart racing out of his chest, as Zephyr looked at him with intent.

"Get that stupid shit out of your head, Kai. Rasia is not your only option. You've got bones of dragonsteel, and anyone would be lucky to have your favor. Rasia doesn't deserve you. But I'll show you what you deserve right here, right now."

Dumbfounded, Kai stared at the wet stain on Zephyr's shroud, where his lips had been, and heat curled in his belly. But he couldn't bring himself to move beyond this indescribable weight pressed against his chest. In that moment, all Kai could think of was Rasia. And how she would react, and all the ways he could hurt her even though she claimed he couldn't. Rasia and Kai were *just* fucking. Rasia had repeated the phrase often enough, but it was more for Kai. It had always been more.

Kai pressed his hands to his shroud-covered face, a makeshift one he had ripped from the bottom of his old caftan since he had given his last over as a blood price. He rubbed at his face, again and again. "I can't."

"Let me know the day you can," Zephyr said. Then he withdrew, as if nothing had ever happened.

Kai sat up, suddenly exhausted, and wiped at his eyes. He felt frustrated by everything—by Zephyr, by Rasia, by his own stubborn morals and stupid feelings and the constant self-discoveries that were upending his world. Before the Forging, Kai had never thought his sexuality worth exploring, until Rasia had blown in and irrevocably captured his attention. Now, this.

"Are you okay?" Zephyr asked, concerned. "I apologize. I should have asked first."

"No, I . . ." Kai stumbled to gather his thoughts. Zephyr had admittedly thrown Kai off balance. "I don't know. I don't know how my bones roll."

How could he not know? He'd jerked off before, but it had always been more of a challenge to make sure he could do it. He had never dared to want or hope for something he could never have.

"Sometimes you *know*," Zephyr said, gentle, "and sometimes it's an exploration. Don't stress about it, Kai, and feed the flames as they come."

Kai drummed his fingers on his knees, which he had bent to his chest. He undoubtedly had a flame for Rasia and didn't know anything at all on how to contain that fire. "Then, what do you do to get over one? How did you get over Nico?" A stiffness froze over Zephyr's shoulders. Kai asked softer, more tactfully, "What happened between the two of you?"

Zephyr shrugged. "The day my father asked if I wanted to join his caravan, I told Nico my feelings for her. I didn't want to leave if maybe she wanted me to stay." He shrugged again. "She turned me down. Told me she's too busy, and how it had scared her how much of a wreck Kenji-shi had become after Avalai Ohan was gone. It's not something she could afford to worry about. She told me to go with my father and not to waste my life waiting on her."

Zephyr shrugged again. Kai had suspected, but now he was certain that Zephyr was still carrying a huge flame for Nico. He sorely regretted his words back at the gorge, when he'd told Zephyr how he wasn't special.

Kai hadn't been fair because his words had been untrue.

"For what it's worth," Kai said softly, "she has a flame for you, too."

But tah had died. Then Zephyr, the tent kid, had also disappeared from Nico's stories.

"I know," Zephyr said, pained, "she told me that too. I was so angry about it for a long time. My parents are the type of kulani that legends are written of, the ones who found a way despite all the odds against them. Just the same, I thought Nico was the one. It never crossed my mind that I'd be rejected, especially by someone who felt the same way. I went away on that trip with my father angry, and devastated, and stupidly foolish. After a year, I thought I had figured it all out, and then I get back, and see her again, and it still hurts just as much. I don't know, Kai. I'm still trying to move on from mine. They say forging flames never last, but I think, the first one . . . leaves you burned forever."

CHAPTER THIRTY

O

Rasia hummed a jaunty shanty. She sat atop the windship railing with one foot looped through the vertical pole to keep her steady. She unraveled the twine of previously cut pieces of rope to weave back into one longer whole. She gripped the end between her toes, weaving with such practiced ease that she didn't need to look at her hands. She glanced intermittently at the windship steer, but Rasia's attention was on the horizon.

The first few rays of sunrise, which had glowed first across her cheek, brightened the dark early morning. She'd waited a long time for daylight. She clutched the rope gleefully to her chest and stared at the hatch door in anticipation. Yesterday might not have gone down like Rasia had wanted, but today Rasia had a plan.

The door flew open and banged with force against the deck.

"*What did you do?*" Kai accused, head popping up from the underbelly. Dawnlight crawled across the deck, not yet reaching his nebulous outline.

Rasia bit down hard on her mischief and forced a nonchalant shrug. "You're going to have to be more specific."

"Zephyr wanted me to wake him at the start of my shift." Rasia might have overheard something of the sort. "He's not waking up."

"And you think I have something to do with it?"

Kai crossed his arms and glowered. Rasia tried so hard to keep the curl from her lips but broke in the span of a vibration.

"Geez, calm your nips. I just put a little sleeping powder in his gourd. He'll be *fine*. Besides, the morning is our time. Now we have the deck all to ourselves."

"Rasia, what do you want?"

Rasia hopped down from the railing. She tossed her unfinished project over her shoulder, letting it sprawl to the deck. Kai would inevitably pick it up anyway. He was big on the whole "not leaving things out so people can trip over them later." But people wouldn't trip over them if they looked where they were going. Cough-Zephyr-cough.

"Who says I want anything?" Rasia asked as she prowled around the deck. She pressed her back against the mast and motioned to the unattended steer, available for Kai's shift.

Kai glared at her, then habitually went through the steps of preparing for his turn at the steer. He double-checked the knots and adjusted the sail for windshifts even Rasia couldn't predict coming.

With Kai's back to her, Rasia popped her hip. She twisted and angled her body the way she'd seen tent whores do. Awkwardly, her arms dangled, and she tried to assemble them in a more appealing manner.

Kai looked up from where he was adjusting the rigging. "Rasia, what are you doing?"

Rasia had never tried to intentionally be sexy before, so forgive her if Operation Seduction had a few kinks in it. She stared at him, holding eye contact, and placed two fingers in her mouth. She swirled her tongue around the digits and popped her fingers out wet and glistening with spit. She pulled the leather strings of her waistband.

Kai left.

Rasia hadn't even gotten to the good part!

The wind blown out of her sails, Rasia crumpled to the deck, legs and arms flopping, and hit her head back against the mast in frustration. She peeked around the mast to where Kai had swiped her undone rope from the deck and stuffed it away into the equipment hatch.

Rasia knew she should have put it away.

Kai continued to shuffle through the hatch, his back turned to her, denying Rasia the audience she wanted.

It wasn't *fair*.

After sitting up, Rasia planted her chin in the palm of her hand and pouted, blinking pathetically and hoping he'd take pity on her. She whined, "I get it. You've made your point. Can you let it go, and we can get back to having fun again? We haven't had sex in *forever*."

"We literally had sex yesterday morning."

"Exactly! It's not healthy to break routine."

"Enjoy your fingers, then. By all means, don't let me interrupt."

"Fuck you."

Rasia launched to her feet and stormed to the other side of the windship. She crossed her arms, embarrassed and feeling like a fool. She paid the fucking blood price. What more did he want from her? She didn't get it. They had been having a good time. Why ruin that?

Rasia glanced over at him. He had walked back to the other side of the ship, having taken nothing from the equipment hatch. Now he was standing there steering her windship how *she* taught him, wearing the clothes *she* gave him, ruining *her* kull.

"Take off *my* pants."

Kai glanced up from the steer. The sun reached his face, and dawn broke hard over his expression. "You gave them to me."

"I want them back. *Take them off.*"

Kai clenched his jaw, then yanked at the belt cords. Kai pushed down the pants and kicked them across the deck. He pulled the shirt over his head and tossed it over too. It wasn't exactly the striptease Rasia had planned.

Rasia charged, scooped up her clothes, and threw them overboard. They fluttered, traveling quite a distance in a hard gust of wind.

"Real mature," Kai said, crossing his arms over his bare chest to ward off the cool morning air.

She hated him. She hated his stupid face and his stupid hair and his stupid eyes and . . . it occurred to Rasia in that moment that Kai was stupidly handsome. He'd grown half a hand taller than her. Or maybe he'd stopped hunching his shoulders smaller than he actually was. Or maybe the sky had finally grown tall enough for him to stretch out and stand. He's taller, somehow. Kai's cheeks didn't look so sharp and sunken anymore. His sharp angles had rounded. Lean muscles wired his arms. Kai stood before her, bright and full like someone had stuffed him with elderfire. His own brilliant sun.

Rasia had done that. She made him eat. She taught him how to run. She had claimed all his firsts. The fact Kai stood there looking *so* pretty boiled her nerves.

In blinding fury, Rasia stampeded forward and slammed her hands down on either side of him, trapping him between the railing and the anchor mechanism. Kai never flinched or stumbled back in fear. He never went for his dagger. He confronted her without a single quake, far braver than anyone else would ever dare to be. Fuck. It was kind of hot.

"You want me," Rasia insisted.

"No."

Rasia was so used to people telling her that word and was used to doing what she wanted anyway. That word was often a boundary or a restriction placed on Rasia for no good reason. Well-meaning family members limited her for her own safety, because they saw nothing beyond the edges of their small mental maps.

But it sounded different when Kai said it. For one brief moment, Rasia considered barreling over his defiance and taking what she wanted. But her not listening to Zephyr was exactly what got Kai mad at her in the first place. What was the worst that could happen if she didn't listen to him? Would he leave her?

She was up against a border that was illegal to cross. Kai didn't belong to her, and his body wasn't a territory anyone could explore without his permission. Rasia had been invited in as his guest. It might be hard to accept that she had to leave this brand-new terrain she'd barely gotten the chance to map, but to lay claim to something that wasn't hers, to steal landmarks for souvenirs, would make her a skink. That was the worst sort of person to be.

Rasia pushed away. She crossed her arms and turned her back. Whatever. She didn't need him anyway. She had been fine before Kai, and she'd be fine after Kai.

"Rasia," Kai said, gently. "I haven't abandoned you. I'm still here. I am still your *friend*, and I hoped you'd still consider me so even without the sex. I still want to hunt a dragon with you."

Rasia yelled. She yelled some more, then ran and jumped off the windship.

Too many emotions huffed through her chest. Rasia laid where she'd landed, covered in sand, and stared grumpily at the shifting clouds. She heard the windship stop. Rasia ignored Kai's shouts.

Kai wasn't her first kiss.

That honor went to fucking Faris.

And it utterly sucked. Faris laughed afterward, thinking someone had put Rasia up to it as some stupid prank. He hadn't taken her seriously because she was *Rabid Rasia*. But she wasn't anyone's joke. Rasia had promised herself then she wouldn't waste her time chasing empty hunts.

If Kai didn't want her anymore, that was his problem.

Rasia wiped at her cheeks and stomped off. She kicked at the sand and scanned the indiscriminate brown. She snatched up the shirt and pants. She trudged back, climbed the steps of the windship, and slammed the clothes down at Kai's feet, sending up clouds of dust. The sun shone, blinding.

"Let's hunt our fucking dragon."

THIRTY-ONE

—

The Lake of Yestermorrow encroached closer and closer, spilling molten gold over the horizon. Kai had read so many stories of dangerous lake crossings. In the legends, something bad always happened when a kull was suffering from conflict and discord. They never crossed to the other side intact.

"Rasia told me to wake her when we reached the lake," Kai said.

Zephyr glared at the approaching waters, considering whether they could transition the ship to the water by themselves without involving Rasia.

Rasia and Zephyr weren't speaking to one another. Zephyr was understandably pissed when he woke from the sleep powder incident and had thrown all the remaining supply off the windship. Kai convinced Rasia not to retaliate (primarily because she had more hidden in the smuggler caches), but Zephyr thought she was biding her time. The past two days had been stressfully spent keeping the two apart.

The tension reminded Kai of boiling liquid, taking a while to heat but threatening to bubble over quick. Rasia and Kai might have established a tentative understanding, but the easy camaraderie from the gorge had never returned. They were all on the edge of a boiling point, and Kai didn't think a magic lake would help lower the heat. Perhaps he'd read too many stories. Perhaps he'd been applying too much narrative symbolism to real life, but Kai had a bad feeling about this.

But what else were they expected to do? Go around?

Kai sighed out. "I'll go wake her."

Zephyr grunted in reply. Kai climbed down the ladder into the ship's underbelly. Sunlight peered through the deck cracks, which provided enough light to navigate around the maze of barrels, baskets, and supplies netted in the upper corners. He found Rasia awake, fingers scraping the bottom hull as she lay atop the bunk. Her eyes immediately rolled at the sight of Kai standing there in his old, ripped caftan. She did it every time she saw him, ever since he'd returned her shirt and pants, washed and folded. Those clothes felt tainted now with the anger and humiliation of that day.

"We've reached the lake?" Rasia asked sharply. She didn't wait for his answer. She strapped on her swords, tied up her boots, and swept past Kai to the ladder. When Kai returned to the deck, the lake had clawed closer.

Rasia stood with her back to him, notably ignoring Zephyr at the other corner of the ship. "Kai, take the steer," she ordered.

"Shouldn't you steer?" Kai asked. Rasia's eyes cut in his direction, and her judgement scraped across Kai's bones. He quickly took up position at the steer.

"When we reach the water line, steer it in gentle and slow," Rasia instructed. "We want to make sure none of the water splashes on deck. You know about this lake, right?"

"What I've read in the library," Kai specified, knowing that meant nothing compared to Rasia's experiences. "The Yestermorrow Lake formed in the aftermath of the War of the Bloody Siblings, where they destroyed each other, but their magic never faded. They say the lake shows you what you want. That your happiness is at the bottom, but Death swims faster."

"That part is true," Rasia confirmed. "You get a drop of water on your skin, and you need to be tied to the mast to keep from diving in. When tah taught me and jih the eight dangers of the

Desert, this is the first place he showed us. He looked me straight in the eye and made me swear I'd never be stupid enough to touch the lake, right before he stuck my hand into the water."

Kai's jaw dropped in horror. The library scrolls clearly stated *never* to touch the water.

"That explains a lot," Zephyr grumbled loudly. Rasia tossed him the v of her fingers over her shoulder.

"Shamai-ta knew I was far too curious for my own good. So. Tah taught me a lesson. Afterwards, the pull was so strong he had to tie me to the mast for three days and three nights. Sometimes, I still smell the sweetness of those honeyed dates. I still feel the stickiness on my fingers and the crust of hazelnut and salt on my tongue. It's been years, but it lingers with you, even after all this time."

"Honeyed dates?" Kai asked. "That's your happiness? What Rajiani wants most in the whole world?"

"I was eight-till!" Rasia laughed.

Kai realized suddenly he missed her laughter and all the different versions of it. From short bursts and gleeful cackles to the sparkling mischief and long rib-aches strong enough to double her over. His breath caught when she glanced at him, smiling, blinding him with the flame-tipped edge of her star-whirling joy.

She frowned, remembered, and dimmed. Kai's shoulders dropped, mourning the empty space where her light had resided. Kai never thought maintaining his distance would be so hard. He noticed the tenseness in Rasia's shoulders as she drew forward and clutched the railing.

Her back to him, Rasia shrugged. "I've never touched the lake again. Why would I need to? I don't need a magic lake to get what I want. I can do that all on my own."

For once, she didn't sound very confident, and Kai felt guilty for shaking what had been such solid ground.

"Stop the windship," Rasia said. "I'll go lock in the wheels."

Kai waited at the steer and heard the wheels lock and seal against the hull. When Rasia returned to deck, they were a windship length away from the water. She nodded toward Kai and reminded him, "Gentle. Slow. Remember, you control the windship. Don't let it control you."

Kai adjusted the sail enough to slow the ship but hopefully not enough to send them headlong into the water. Still, the ship's weight fought against him. Carefully, firmly, the ship moved forward. They hit the water softly, and the hull eased into the lake without a splash.

Proud, Kai smiled, but it immediately dropped when the Lake of Yestermorrow fully claimed them. The air stilled, and that sixth sense that tracked magic darkened so abruptly, the loss punched Kai in the throat. He wobbled, disoriented, and a nauseous dizziness overtook him. He needed to grab hold of something.

Kai hugged the railing and squeezed his eyes shut, hoping the nausea would pass. But the magic weighed the air so much that he found it hard to breathe. The lake wasn't bright or warm like the magic of the Great Elder. This bitter magic wailed a dark and sorrowful dirge.

Both Rasia and Zephyr moved toward him, concerned. Rasia ran and audibly skidded across the deck to reach Kai before Zephyr. She stretched to her tiptoes in an unsuccessful attempt to block Zephyr from view. Kai was too occupied trying not to vomit on his sandals to worry about the glares they sent each other overhead.

"Kai? Are you okay?" Rasia asked.

Kai kept a tight grip on the railing, afraid if he let it go, he'd fall. Rasia gripped the back of his caftan, apparently holding the same concern.

"The wind is gone," Kai said.

"Yeah," Rasia said, confused. "The wind doesn't blow over the Yestermorrow Lake."

Kai glanced back at the steer. "Then how do we *sail*?"

"We don't. The ship will float on its own."

"But what if we need to maneuver? What if we need to turn around?"

"There won't be any of that turning around business, but if you're so worried, it is possible to use the oars if we need to, but that risks splashing up water if we're not careful. Better to let the lake move us."

It shook Kai to his core to know they had so little control out here. Kai looked down at the murky water, full of sand and dirt and bones at the bottom. He wouldn't dare try to boil this water clean.

"There are pockets of magic like this in my father's lands," Zephyr said, crossing his arms from where he maintained a foot of distance from the railing out of caution. "But they exist at the edges. It's rare you need to traverse them. It's odd. There is considerably more magic here in the Desert."

"That's because of the dragons."

Rasia and Zephyr both gave Kai blank stares. Kai asked slowly, "You don't know?"

"I must have missed that lesson in school."

Kai rolled his eyes and nudged at Rasia's arm. Rasia brightened at the touch and stared at the point of contact like a voracious hyena, all ravenous and sharp-toothed. Kai reminded himself he should be careful how he touched her. Every touch carried too much meaning now.

Kai retracted his arm. He explained, "The Desert has magic because of the dragons. My family is born with one element of magic because that's all a human body can take. But a dragon has two elements, usually consisting of their breed-element: fire, storm, ice, or whatever surprise they have for you, and the second element of wind. It's impossible for creatures of that size to fly, so they breathe magic to get airborne and glide on their wings. It's why the Desert is so windy and windships are a viable form of transportation in the first place—because their magic saturates everything. Dragons limit us, but we need them as well."

"I've never heard that before, not even from the most veteran windekas," Rasia said. "Did you read this in a scroll?"

Kai narrowed his eyes, unable to properly express feelings and sensations none had yet captured in words. "*I know.*"

Rasia pursed her lips thoughtfully and leaned her weight against the railing. His heart jumped in his throat at the creak, but Rasia reclined fearlessly as if they weren't traversing the most dangerous lake in the entire Desert.

"Your element of magic is wind, right?" Rasia asked him. "It would make the most sense and explain why you have such a hard time perceiving it, because you can't see it. Wind can only be felt."

Kai never considered himself having an element before. His magic did crazy things. He accepted that. But the way she spun facts into truth amazed him. It made so much sense. Why hadn't he realized it sooner?

Kai wanted to kiss her. That was probably a bad idea.

"I guess so," Kai said. *Wind*. His element was wind. But even as he thought it, something didn't feel all the way right. It didn't explain everything.

In the corner of Kai's eye, something floated by. He didn't have time to further consider his magic as windship wreckage and bloated bodies swept past. Out in the distance, a ship bobbed in the water. It haunted closer and closer.

"Is that a scavenger ship?" Zephyr asked. The ship was a lot smaller than the standard Grankull ships, with a sail stitched and patched together from various scraps of linen.

"Odd. They don't usually cross these waters." Rasia lifted her foot to the railing, and Kai snatched at her shirt, alarmed she might accidentally fall in. He belatedly realized she had moved intentionally.

"I'm going to go investigate," Rasia explained.

Their windship was going to pass close to the other, but not that close. She would have to jump across, and for one terrifying instant Kai imagined her going down in those waters that sang of Death songs. He imagined her bloated body floating. All her light gone. Kai clutched her shirt tighter.

"Let me go, Kai. The ship is almost near."

"Is the risk worth it?" Kai asked. Sometimes, curiosity had too high a price.

Rasia grinned and leaned mischievously to whisper, "I don't learn my lessons easy."

She licked his cheek. Kai jerked back, shocked, and wiped at the wet streak with his sleeve. He inadvertently let her go and, without hesitation, Rasia leaped.

The other ship wobbled when she landed, and Rasia stepped around the murky puddles with a dancer's grace.

Kai crossed his arms and stuffed his hands in his armpits. He watched nervously as Rasia investigated the ship.

Rasia nudged her sword at a sopping linen on the half-destroyed deck and dipped her head into the underbelly hatch. From the looks of it, the entire bottom half was flooded. The floating dead stared at him. Some were scavengers, and others were Forging kids judging by their clothing. The right thing to do would be to recover the bodies and return the bones home, but that was nigh impossible. Kai suspected many restless spirits haunted these waters.

The distance between the ships was increasing at an alarming rate. Rasia spun on her heel at the last possible vibration, winked at him, and made a running jump. She caught the railing, sticking heels to hull, and flipped her hair while hopping over.

"Looks like scavengers are rounding up Forging kids," Rasia said. "You rarely see scavengers on this side of the lake though, and even if you do, they're more likely to go around."

"What about the codes?" Kai asked.

Rasia scoffed. "Those codes are more suggestions."

The codes were informal rules that governed scavenger and kull relations out in the Desert. If scavengers stole gonda from hunting kulls, then fair, those hunting kulls weren't good enough to keep what they'd gotten. But if scavengers killed a kull member, there was a blood price to pay. Kai didn't know all the codes, but he'd picked up a few from reading windeka reports. Generally, Forging kids were off limits.

Rasia bounced from one foot to the other. "Scavengers don't usually bother Forging kids unless they're stupidly wandering around scavenger territory. If I had to place my bets, the scavengers are desperate and starving too. Which might become a problem. I really don't want to deal with their antics. We seriously don't have the time."

Death songs played as they glided along the lapping strings. The water hazed murkier, denser, with magic and sunken corpses. An awful sort of beauty threatened to consume them on all sides. Kai found it hard to worry about scavengers right now. All he wanted to do was cross this dismal lake alive.

CHAPTER THIRTY-TWO

I

Nico traced the lines of spit on her map. The glob pulled incrementally away even as she stood there and gawked at it.

"That can't be right."

At Nico's disbelieving mutterings, Suri ventured out from under the overturned wing-sail to join Nico in the high-noon heat. Suri crouched, careful to cast her shadow away from the map. "What's wrong?"

Nico couldn't explain the impossible distance Rasia had widened between them. Nico reached for a writing utensil, but her charcoal stick was in her bags under the sail. Nico unbuckled her glaive and used the blunt end to calculate the distance in the sand.

Five vibrations equaled a kull. Five kulls equaled a drum. Eighteen drums in a day.

"I don't understand." Suri studied Nico's calculations. "Rasia is already this far from us? We weren't that far behind."

Nico stood over the results. The numbers seemed impossible at first, but she had no choice but to accept them. The truth cracked dry out of Nico's throat. "She's not stopping. To get this far ahead, Rasia has to be sailing through both the night and high noon."

Nico should have caught this sooner, but because she didn't,

Rasia was now too far ahead. They barely had the skills to match Rasia's pace, so how were they supposed to sail twice as fast as her? Nor were they experienced enough to sail through the night. They could barely sail through the day without hitting a ditch and losing a wheel. Even with Nico's advantage at the Lake of Yestermorrow, it still might not be enough.

Suri's eyes begged Nico to see the truth written in the sand. This was the point where Nico should quit. This was when Nico should give up and let Rasia win.

"No," Nico said, snatching up the map. She slashed her spear through the calculations in defiance of their undeniable truth: Rasia had outsmarted her again.

When Nico straightened, she found Suri barring her path, bow readied. Suri reached for an arrow and nocked it to the bowstring. "Nico, it's time to let go."

"I still have time. I can still catch her, Suri."

"How? We can't compete with her out here. You've got to recognize this for the empty hunt it is. We're outmatched, and if you don't turn back now, you put your kull, and the Grankull, at risk. Don't you want to save the Tents?"

"Don't use that against me as if you care."

"But you care. Or so you claim."

"We've still got half our Forging left, Suri. We've still got time. I can save Kai. I can save this kull. I can save the Grankull and the Tents."

"You can't save everyone, Nico. That's the whole point of the Forging. There are too many kids for the Grankull's resources, and some must die. The Forging cuts down the weeds."

"I don't believe that."

Suri raised the bow and pulled the bowstring taut to her mouth. She aimed it toward Nico's leg. Nico watched the sweat gather in the dip of Suri's lips and the heat plaster her hair to her face. But Suri's arms stayed steady and true.

Nico marched past Suri. Nico listened for the quick *thwimp* of the arrow, but the sound never came.

Nico dipped under the sail and found it emptier than she had left it, nothing but a scattered, unfinished game of rattle-bones and the dirty wrappings from the scorpion jerky they were all getting tired of eating. It didn't take a genius to figure out where Azan and Kelin had gone.

Nico beat her fist against the hatch door and gave the two a moment to gather themselves before ducking her head into the coolness of the underbelly. It smelled of sex, with notes of salted meat and Suri's pungent herbs. With the windship turned on its side, Nico navigated the hatch upright when usually she had to shuffle through bent over. Sunlight filtered through the cracks, and Nico spied the shadowed lines of Azan and Kelin's bodies pressed into the hatch bunks. The barrels, bound by the side netting, blocked most of the view. Not enough, in Nico's opinion.

"We're kind of in the middle of something," Kelin croaked out.

Azan giggled. "*I'm* in the middle of something."

Nico lips twitched, fighting the smile at the crude joke. "Finish up. I'm righting this ship whether you two are done or not. We're headed out."

"Shit," they both cursed.

Nico stepped out of the hatch and into the blast of high-noon heat. Even under the shade, the sun boiled hot and stifling. Sweat dripped from every pore, and the crown of Nico's hair frizzed with unruly strands. The sunblock she'd pasted to her skin earlier that morning slicked almost slimy. Nico leaned against the hull and swallowed a liberal amount of water from her gourd, then unstaked the sail.

Suri watched, bow in both hands and her lips pressed in a thin line. No doubt disappointed in herself.

Both Kelin and Azan emerged from the hatch half-dressed. Kelin reinserted his earrings as he walked. Azan had disregarded his loincloth. In this sweaty heat, the weighty line of his dick printed obvious in his linen pants. Azan caught her staring. His eyes brightened as he asked, "You interested?"

"No," Nico answered. Azan had too much jih energy for Nico

to consider him as anything more than a sibling.

"Got it," Azan said, leaving it at that.

Kelin squinted. "Why is it still high noon?"

"We can't afford to linger here any longer. Rasia has gotten too far ahead. We need to leave now," Nico said.

Kelin and Azan looked at each other. Nico didn't miss the doubt on their faces.

Nevertheless, they helped her push the windship upright. Nico adjusted the sail while Kelin and Azan dressed more fully for the worst of the sun. They applied a liberal amount of kohl soot to their eyes and slathered each other with Suri's sunblock mix, snickering and flirting all the while. It was hard to get them focused once they'd been distracted.

"Group up," Nico ordered, demanding their attention. Everyone trudged over to meet Nico at the center of the mast.

"We have fallen too far behind. Apparently, Rasia is sailing through the night and high noon without stopping."

Azan's brows raised. With a jih in the hunting kulls and another in the supply kulls working the mining route, Azan knew how rare and dangerous such a nonstop flight could be. And how utterly unprepared their own kull was for the task.

Azan asked, "Are *you* steering through the night?"

"I'm not Rasia, and none of us can steer a windship as well as she can. But there's one last option we haven't taken. I have magic. She doesn't. It's time we used it to our advantage."

Whenever an Ohan over-exceeded, there was always fear, always consequences. Coming into the Forging, Nico had promised herself to use her magic only when necessary, but it was all the more apparent she wasn't going to catch up to Rasia if she kept holding back.

"That could kill you," Suri said. Her hand twitched around her bow.

"That's a risk I'll take."

"No, it's not," Suri argued. "Your life is worth far more than Kai's. He wouldn't want you to do this. He wouldn't want you to throw your life away for him."

"To you and everyone else in the Grankull he might be worthless, but to a few, he means the world. Just because you don't see his worth doesn't mean he doesn't have any. Kai is worth fighting for."

"At what cost, Nico? At the cost of your Forging? At the cost of the Grankull? You can't afford to put family above the Grankull. You are the *Ohan*."

"I am Nico!" Nico shouted, frustrated.

Nico stormed away from the huddle and toward the bow of the ship. Was being Ohan even worth it without family? Nico had spent the last two years fighting to keep it from falling apart. With Kenji-ta's absence and Kai's apathy, she often felt like she was alone in this fight. As if she were the only one who cared, but Nico didn't know how to give it up. Because if she did . . . if Nico couldn't save her own family, how was she supposed to save anyone else?

Nico stared down the distance with a headache pounding behind her eyes. If she didn't do something drastic, the distance would soon become insurmountable. Then all this chasing, all this time, and all this effort would have been meaningless.

Nico probed for water in caches throughout the Desert—the springs, the kull cisterns, the oasis, and even the water hoarded by succulents. She borrowed from them. She pulled water from the air and squeezed droplets out of the clouds.

The windship was propelled forward on a wave of water, gliding on a river over dunes and ditches.

CHAPTER THIRTY-THREE

O

Rasia yawned as she climbed the underbelly ladder to the deck. She wasn't getting much sleep lately, but that was nothing new. Either her mind whirred too fast, too used to the constant vigilance required of the Desert, or her body buzzed with too much energy. Sex with Kai had helped with both. Rasia hadn't realized how much sleep she had gotten until he was gone.

No, not gone. Just out of reach.

Rasia popped her head out of the hatch and frowned at the sight of Zephyr and Kai sitting against the front corner. Zephyr read aloud from the leatherbound scroll he carried in his satchel: first a sentence of unfamiliar sounds, then a translation of the same sentence into an oddly terrible song.

Neither had noticed her yet.

Kai pointed at something inside the leather-bound parchment. Zephyr leaned forward at the question, and their shoulders pressed together. Rasia didn't hear Zephyr's response, but Kai looked up, and Zephyr smiled, and their eyes met with all the soft light of impending dusk.

The bottom dropped out of Rasia's stomach, a chilling lurch that no amount of speed or danger could elicit. Her guts churned with anger and realization and fury.

Rasia had been willing to give the "just friends" thing a

chance, but she hadn't known that meant losing to *Zephyr*. She hadn't considered Zephyr competition. Quite frankly, she hadn't considered *anyone* competition. She had arrogantly assumed Kai couldn't possibly be attracted to anyone other than her. Who could possibly compete?

And yet, she was never chosen. She'd been abandoned time and time again—by Ysai, by stupid kids at school, by her tahs.

Rasia stormed across the windship, and her feet beat the deck so loudly the sound had Kai and Zephyr scrambling to their feet in alarm.

"Rasia, what's wrong?!" Kai asked.

A knot welled in Rasia's throat as she looked between Zephyr and Kai. She didn't know how to put this ugly, blinding rage shaking through her into words. What ended up cracking from her throat cut her raw.

"*Why doesn't anyone want me?*"

Kai's face fell. He bowed, staring at the deck. His silence stabbed at Rasia's worst fears. Was there something more going on between Zephyr and Kai? Were they having sex?! It didn't seem possible Rasia could have missed such a thing on this small windship, but she had obviously missed the fact that Kai was double-sided.

"Are you and Zephyr fucking?" Rasia demanded.

"Wouldn't be your business if we were," Zephyr grumbled from behind her. Rasia spun on her heel to confront him, and Zephyr tensed, ready for her to make a move. Rasia would shove him overboard if she could, but she doubted he'd budge much. She hated him more because of that.

"Zephyr, do you mind giving us a moment?" Kai asked.

Zephyr's brows furrowed. He released a heavy sigh as he retreated to the other side of the windship, out of earshot. But Zephyr leaned against the back railing, facing them, to threaten Rasia with a glare. Rasia honestly thought she'd never hate anyone more than Nico. But her hatred for Zephyr was certainly coming close.

"No," Kai said, answering her. "Zephyr and I aren't having

sex."

She believed him, if for no other reason than this windship really was too small for any sort of covert shenanigans. Still, she knew what she just saw. She was certain something was there. Rasia asked, "Do you want to have sex with him?"

Kai shrugged. "I don't know."

"You don't know?"

"I don't know, Rasia."

It fogged Rasia's brain to think of Kai being with Zephyr in the same ways they had been together—how Kai lazily picked things out of her hair while she was falling asleep, how Kai kissed her as if they were the only ones in the world who mattered and everyone else were grains of sand to their bright stars, and how he would tie on her wrap with increasingly intricate linen flowers. She refused to give that back to him.

Rasia didn't know when Kai had gone from the obsession she needed to flush out of her system to the hands that put her to sleep. All Rasia knew was that "just friends" wasn't enough. But seducing him hadn't worked. Yelling and screaming hadn't worked. Patience hadn't worked. She didn't know what else to do.

"Is it so hard to give me a second chance?" Rasia asked, desperate.

Kai rubbed his face. "It's just . . . Rasia, you can be a real asshole at times. It's a lot. It's a lot for me."

People had criticized Rasia all her life—from Kiba-ta, to Ysai-ji, to other members of her family.

Rasia is too wild. Rasia is too rough. Rasia is too curious for her own good. Why can't she sit down? Why can't she pay attention? Raj, why can't you be nicer to Jilah?

Rasia had long learned to ignore those voices, and Rasia had never in her life bent for anyone. Rasia hissed, low and defensive. "Who are you to demand that I change?"

"I'm not. I'd never assume I'd have the right to ask, and I like who you are, but . . . *I* can't. I'm sorry. We don't work, Rasia."

But they did work. That's what frustrated Rasia the most. Rasia pressed at her eyes, thinking, trying to find a way. She could compromise, maybe a little. "I'll be nicer to Zephyr. I can do that."

"This isn't just about Zephyr, Rasia."

"O*kay* . . ." Rasia waited, but Kai didn't elaborate further. "How am I supposed to make this right if I don't know what it's all about? What else is there if it's not about Zephyr?"

Kai's lips thinned as he bit down. Then he sighed. "It's about Nico, too."

Rasia's face fell, confused, and a little blindsided. "What the fuck does this have to do with Nico?"

"She's my jih, Rasia. What happened during the chase never sat right with me. I tried to push it aside, but I can't."

"We settled that forever ago!"

"Nico is risking her entire Forging for me, and I do feel a little guilty and selfish about it all. I don't want to hurt her any more than I already have. Nico has sacrificed so much for me and you . . . you feel like a betrayal."

"I don't believe this," Rasia fumed, pacing. "That skink is cockblocking me, and she's not even *here*."

"You just called my jih a skink! That's exactly what I'm talking about."

"Yeah, 'cause she's a sk*iiii-ink*," Rasia sang and crunched the end with satisfaction. "Clean your fucking face, Kai. Nico is the selfish one here. She's the Ohan, and she's out risking her kull, and the future of the entire Grankull, chasing after *you*. You'd think she'd get the message after you ran away from her the first time, but she's so far up her own ass that she can't see you are perfectly capable of deciding where to point your own dick! She's not saving you, Kai. She's the one wrapped up in her own doomed, tragic quest. Nico is the villain here. Not me!"

"You don't know everything, Rasia. She's only trying to protect me."

"You are plenty strong enough to protect yourself, and you shouldn't have to feel guilty and selfish for going after what you want. If you want something, fight for it. *Do you want me, Kai*?!"

Kai dropped his eyes to the deck and brooded in his silence

before releasing the most horseshit line Rasia had ever heard. "Doesn't matter what I want."

Rasia understood when someone wasn't interested in her, but she couldn't wrap her head around the fact that Kai clearly wanted her but was holding himself back for these flimsy, ridiculous excuses. She waited for Kai to say something more, but only the lapping waves against the hull filled the air.

Fuck it. If she couldn't have his everything, she would rather have nothing at all.

"You know what? If you want Nico so much, you can have her. Once we cross this lake, get off my ship—and take your mutt with you."

Kai scoffed. "So that's it, Rasia? You're going to push me away like you've done everyone else?"

"*Excuse me?* You think I chose this? You think I chose Shamai-ta, the only person who ever truly understood me, dying from a fucking rock to the head? You think I chose jih abandoning me for that insufferable shroud? They left *me*."

"You're wrong. All Jilah has ever wanted is to be your friend, but you've never given her the chance. Kibari Oshield cared enough to be at your bone toss. And your jih didn't abandon you. He offered to go out on the windship with you that day. I remember. You are the one who refuses to forgive *him*, all because he chose to carry Jilah-shi's name."

"Keep Ysai-ji out of your fucking mouth," Rasia snapped, then shoved at him in her anger. Jih was none of Kai's fucking business, and *he was wrong.*

Zephyr dropped an arm in Rasia's path, grabbed her by the shirt, and threw her.

Rasia slid across the deck, and the great palm mast caught her, shaking. The ship dipped, and a large splash of water hit against the hull, splattering droplets along the deck.

All three of them watched the water roll, sliding into bumpy grooves, and stretching to the other side. They watched, frozen, as the water dried out in the sun.

"You are going to get us all killed," Zephyr accused, turning to

Rasia as she pulled herself to her feet.

"You're the one who threw me halfway across the deck!"

"Zephyr," Kai hissed, "*stay out of this.*"

"Kai and I are not waiting until we cross this lake to get off this ship," Zephyr said. "We are turning around right now."

"*Over my dead body.*"

"Done."

Metal whistled through the air as Rasia unsheathed her khopesh blades, and Zephyr lifted his sword from his back. Rasia had already proved she had the advantage on the windship, so no doubt Zephyr had some trick up his sleeve. Kai shouted something, but Rasia wasn't focused on him anymore. She was focused on the distance—how many bounds it would take to reach Zephyr, the range of that sword, and played all manner of approaches through her head.

Zephyr grabbed Kai by his caftan and slid him back, before lunging forward.

Rasia spun around the mast to avoid his attack. She whirled with her own blades and missed his head, cutting into the wood. The blades stuck, and Zephyr rammed his knee straight into her injured ribs.

Rasia heard a crunch. The pain knocked the wind from her, and she bit down on her lip to keep lucid. She released the hilt of her blades, still stuck in the mast, and grabbed her dagger from her belt. She stabbed her dagger into the flesh of his thigh. Once. Twice.

Zephyr took a hopping step back. He pulled the dagger out of his leg and tossed it across the ship.

Released from where Zephyr had her pinned against the mast, she landed on her feet with a hiss. Her lower rib might have broken, *again*. She felt the bone move when she grabbed the handles of her swords, and with considerable exertion, she pulled the blades out of the wood.

Zephyr wasn't playing around this time, and that one blow might have won the fight. Rasia wasn't going to be able to slip through his defenses with speed anymore and would need to use the windship to her advantage. But she'd already shown her hand days before, and Zephyr knew it.

"*Zephyr!*" Kai snapped at him, furious, as he rushed between them.

Zephyr shoved Kai aside and pursued Rasia relentlessly. He battered her back against the railing, pressing his blows toward her right side. Each time, the rib pain stabbed sharper and sharper, and each time Rasia got slower. Their swords clashed, ringing through her arms, and Zephyr's sheer strength overcame her block to send Rasia sprawling to the deck. Her swords slid from her grip out of reach.

Zephyr lifted his huge sword, casting a shadow.

Hands hooked under her armpits, and Kai dragged her out of the path of Zephyr's blow. That big, stupid, monstrous sword stabbed a hole through her poor windship.

Kai stood in front of her, arguing with Zephyr, but Rasia only heard the rush of blood in her ears. She seethed as she climbed to her knees and grabbed two daggers out of her sandaled boot. This close, Zephyr couldn't swing his sword, leaving him wide open.

She rose, and unabashedly, used Kai as a shield. She thrust the attack under Kai's outstretched arm and ripped into Zephyr's bicep. She attacked with the second dagger, aiming to slice across Zephyr's stomach. Kai turned to stop her, and she pushed him out of the way.

It happened in slow motion.

Kai's feet slipped.

His eyes widened in surprise.

He reached for her as he toppled back.

The moment Rasia's brain calculated the angle of Kai's fall to "oh shit," she dropped her daggers and grabbed for his outstretched hand, missed, wrapped her arm around a leg only for it to slip through her fingers.

Kai disappeared into the murky waters of the Yestermorrow Lake.

The shock of it all would hit Rasia later, but she had never been a person to stand around when the ground vibrates.

Rasia raced toward the equipment hatch and pulled out her longest strip of rope. She knotted one end to her waist, ignoring the pain of her ribs, and tied the other end to the windship mast.

Zephyr's big dumb block of uselessness stood there, horrified.

"*Move*," Rasia demanded. Zephyr got out of her way. Rasia ran forward, vaulted her foot against the railing, and dove into the water.

The Grankull cheered Rasia's name through the streets, over the rooftops, and across the wingfields. Rasia had done it. She'd slain the dragon, and now the Grankull was singing her name-songs. She dropped down from the deck of the ship, and strangers patted her on the back, gave her tearful hugs, and wreathed her with adoration. They draped her in flowers and silk. Rasia danced. She twirled on the haters, the naysayers, and the disbelievers who called her Rabid Rasia. Now, they'd never call her out of her name again.

The crowd parted, and Rasia stood face to face with Kiba-ta.

"I'm sorry," Kiba-ta said. "I was wrong."

Rasia grinned, then continued to dance.

The crowd parted, and Ysai swept her up in a spinning hug. Jih apologized for ever doubting her. He promised that he would never ever, ever leave her again. They danced in the alcoholic rain showers and feasted their bellies full.

The crowd parted, and Rasia's breath caught in her throat.

"TAH!" Rasia shouted, sprinting forward, and the crowd and all its strangers melted into a wave behind her. Rasia tackled Shamai-ta into a hug. He smelled of dust, fresh air, and honeyed dates. His laughter boomed like wind during high speeds. He held her, his most precious thing in the whole world.

"I'm so proud of you, Raj-po. So, so proud."

The Grankull inked her legend into the papyrus scrolls. Then, gleefully, Rasia made dust of their heroes. That night, when they slept with throats hoarse of her name, Rasia climbed into her windship and sailed away.

Fuck 'em all.

Wait.

Shamai-ta was dead, his name written by her own hand into their windship mast. His voice, the distant one she was beginning to forget, came back to haunt her, to remind her: *Always remember, the lake is a lie.*

Rasia opened her eyes to the opaque waters of the Yestermorrow Lake. Her eyes burned at the sight of Kai's hazy figure falling deeper down the impenetrable depths. She swam toward him.

"Han, permission to set sail?"

Rasia stood at the helm of her own kull. She didn't recognize the faces assigned to the scout and oars position, but she knew they'd all fought and bled together on many hunts. They followed her command without hesitation. She smiled to see Kai standing behind her at the steer, bright and brilliant. They all waited for her response, all waiting on her permission to begin yet another adventure. Where would the wind take them this time?

No.

Rasia batted away the image. She wanted only one thing right now. Rasia fought the weight of the water. She fought the burn searing her lungs. She fought the deceptions of the lake. Each battle took more and more energy out of her, but each victory brought her closer.

Rasia reached out.

"I'm sorry, Raj," Ysai said as they sat atop their rooftop. *"You were right about Jilah. It's over now. I should have never let her come between us. I should have listened to you. Let's return to the Desert, just you and me. What do you say?"*

Ha! Like that was ever going to happen. Ysai was far too up Jilah's cunt to climb back out of it now. Stupid lake. *Is that all you've got?!*

Rasia sailed a windship on the ocean. No! *Rasia hiked distant white-capped mountains.* No! *Rasia discovered lands beyond her wildest imaginations.* No! *Rasia saved the world.* No! Rasia knew what the fuck she wanted.

She closed her hand around Kai's wrist.

Kai smiled at her from the railing, and his eyes forged gold. His hair flied around his face like a bright stream of fire. The wheels creaked beneath them. Their breakneck speed drummed the wing-sail. The entire Desert and beyond, waiting for them to explore.

Together, they laughed. And Rasia was happy.

The lake surrendered. The weighted resistance lifted from Kai's body, and Rasia yanked him into her arms. She spun, toward the nebulous sun, and threw the rest of her strength into one great tug of the rope.

Her vision blacked out, and water filled her lungs. Drowning.

At least Rasia got what she wanted in the end.

Rasia searched through the training fields looking for tah, all while hiding from the sentries. The kulls were practicing pitching and unpitching a wing-sail, competing against each other for the best time. Tah always said that drilling the motions into your body was important so that when you were out in the field and the ground vibrated, you reacted without thought.

Rasia sprinted under the sails.

"Hold on, you little colt." A hand grabbed the back of Rasia's shirt and lifted them into the air. Rasia kicked the air, ready to bite, then grinned cheekily to find it was Kenji-shi. "Aren't you supposed to be in school?"

"School is dumb. Where is tah?"

"Apparently, you're not the only one skipping today. Your tah decided to drop in on Kiba-kull at work."

Rasia scrunched their nose. "Nasty."

Kenji-shi chuckled and tossed them over his shoulder. He signed "water break" to his kull.

"But I don't want to go back to school," Rasia whined.

Kenji-shi rummaged around the bins where the kulls placed their belongings. He reached into his packed lunch, and Rasia brightened when he procured a bright orange apricot.

He handed Rasia the fruit and sat beside Rasia while they ate it. Rasia munched at the apricot gratefully. This is why they liked Kenji-shi. He didn't try and drag them back to school like their tajihs.

"Why don't you like school?" Kenji-shi asked. He shielded Rasia when a gust of wind swept up from the pitching of a nearby windship. Rasia continued to munch happily.

"The teacher says I'm dumb, but tah says they don't know shit. Tah says he didn't need school to make a name for himself, and they don't teach anything important no ways. Tah says once the hunting season is over, he's going to take me out to the Desert and teach me himself. So, if school don't matter, why I have to go?"

"Hard to argue with that logic," Kenji-shi said, nodding his head. "What about friends?"

"They're stupid too. They're mean and think I'm weird. But tah says to fuck the little shits. I don't have to change for anyone. I'm perfect just the way I am. I asked Ysai to skip with me, so we can play together, but he's still mad at me for breaking that stupid basket he made. Said he was going to give it to some girl at school, but why? That girl is ugly and has stupid hair."

An amused smile stretched across Kenji-shi's face. "I worry about you sometimes, kid. Between you and me, I think your tah spoils you way too much."

"Tah says I'm hi-lar-i-ous."

"That you are."

Rasia crunched the last of the apricot, spraying juices in the air. When they finished, Kenji-shi held out his hand. Face wet and sticky, Rasia placed the apricot seed into his palm.

"No one is perfect, little stallion. We all start off like this seed here. We're planted in the ground, then we grow. But the apricot isn't any more or any less because it has changed shape. It's still an apricot. It's still itself. That goes for you too, Rasia-po. Life *is* change. There are times where you'll have to grow and change shape, but that doesn't make you any less yourself. The bad changes you prune off, and you let the good changes bear fruit. Grow what makes you happy."

". . . but I'm not an apricot. I'm Rasia!"

Kenji-shi smiled, and asked, patient, "Will going to school make you happy?"

"*No*," Rasia said. Definitely not!

"Will being nice to those kids who are mean to you make you happy?"

"No!"

"Will apologizing to your jih so he'll play with you next time make you happy?"

Rasia blinked. "Oh."

Rasia liked talking to Kenji-shi. Kiba-ta always forced Rasia to apologize to Ysai whether they wanted to or not. And Shamai-ta always told Ysai to forgive them because Ysai was the oldest. But Kenji-shi always explained why things were important.

"I'll apologize to jih," Rasia promised.

Kenji-shi beamed, and Rasia dipped their head, suddenly bashful. With a thumb under their chin, Kenji-shi raised their face and wiped at their sticky cheeks with his dampened shroud. He adjusted Rasia's own half-shroud, and then when finished, knocked Rasia on their forehead.

"Grow what makes you happy, and you'll always be yourself."

Rasia sucked in air.

She tightened her grip around Kai's chest as the rope pulled her up, and up, and out of the water. With leather gloves, Zephyr hefted them both over the railing. A burn, something sharp, scratched her thigh, as she flipped over and flopped onto her back, coughing up water, with the sting of it in her nose and burning through her lungs. Kai lay motionless in her periphery, and she crawled, ribs in agony and body rattling, to reach him.

Zephyr pumped at Kai's chest, each compression a forceful pound Rasia feared could crush him. A gurgle, then Kai coughed up water. His eyes snapped open, glowing gold for a flash before burning out white.

Panicked, Rasia lunged for his wrist. Kai's heart thudded against her fingers, but Kai failed to respond to either Rasia or Zephyr's pleadings. Rasia feared the lake had given back a shell and stolen all the good parts for itself.

Kai was always warm sleeping next to her, grinding against her skin, at night without a fire. But he was shock cold now. Empty. As if all the light of him had been left behind in the lake's murky depths. His eyes gazed lost, and Rasia remembered tah's eyes after they dug him out of that collapsed building—alive but not alive.

"He's still breathing," Zephyr said, singularly focused on the rise of Kai's chest. But breath was not life. Rasia knew that intimately.

Her tah had been breathing through the coma, but he never woke again. The strongest person she knew, who cherished her more than anything in the world, couldn't make it back to her. What chance did Kai have?

Rasia stared down at Kai and shivered at the ghost of his lips on her skin. She bent over at the sore memory of laughs curled tight under her ribs. Even when they were fighting, even when they disagreed, he still considered himself her friend. Her first friend. And she'd killed him.

Rasia hadn't meant to push so hard.

She hadn't meant to.

"He's not waking up," Zephyr said, frustrated. "Rasia, what do we do? You have more experience with the lake than anyone else. Why isn't he waking up?"

Zephyr reminded Rasia she couldn't afford to break down now. When the ground vibrated, all Rasia knew how to do was act. Rasia forced herself to look at Kai as a problem to solve.

"His clothes are still drenched. We need to take them off. The water might still be affecting him," Rasia said.

Zephyr immediately stripped him, then Zephyr pulled off his

own torn and bloody shirt to dab the water from Kai's skin. Rasia stripped out of her own clothes, just in case.

After Kai was laid out dry in the sun, they both stared at him, watching, hoping. Kai didn't look right, lying like that. Kai always curled up in deep sleep. She'd often woken to Kai coiled in the smallest corner possible. Looking at him now rubbed Rasia the wrong way. He was laid straight out on his back as if someone had arranged his corpse on a funeral pyre.

Rasia shouted at him, "Kai! Wake up!"

Kai didn't move.

Angry, frustrated, and a little scared, Rasia slapped Kai hard across his face. No movement. She raised her hand again, but Zephyr caught her by the wrist.

"Rasia, that's enough."

Rasia fought against Zephyr's iron grip until all the heat drained out of her and she surrendered. For the first time in Rasia's life, she didn't know what to do. She'd never encountered this in any of the legends. As far as she knew, Rasia and Kai were the only ones to have ever escaped the Lake of Yestermorrow after being fully submerged, and the closest analogy she could find were the faded memories of her younger self at five-years till.

"Why aren't you like him?" Zephyr asked.

Rasia didn't have the answer to that question. Kai was the magic one. He was the one that weird and unexplainable shit happened to.

"I don't know. I think . . . this isn't a physical problem. It's a mental one. When tah put my hand in the water, I had dreams after. Maybe that's why Kai won't wake up. The dreams are too strong. We need something stronger to pull him back. Do you know his favorite food or song or something?"

"No. Don't you?"

Rasia blinked, blankly.

"You've been fucking him and didn't care to learn anything about him?"

"Aren't you supposed to be best friends with his jih? Why don't you know anything?"

"I know *Nico*'s favorite food, and *her* favorite song." Zephyr paused, in realization. "We need Nico. She'll know how to pull him out."

"Without Kai, we don't know where Nico is. She could be days behind us."

"We need to turn around," Zephyr argued.

"*No*. We are closer to the other side than back the way we came. I know a place with water, and it's defensible. We make camp there."

Zephyr's eyes hardened as he loomed over her with all the immensity of the mountain he embodied. "How do I know you're telling the truth? How do I know you're truly willing to stop?"

Rasia sneered, showing her teeth. "You think I dove into those waters just to watch him die? Fuck you."

Rasia turned on her heel and stomped away, pacing, where Kai still lay composed like the dead. In her periphery, she caught sight of tah's name carved into the date wood. Was Rasia going to have to carve Kai's name there, too?

Sight blurring, she screamed. Rasia went running and slammed her shoulder into the mast. The ship shook.

"Why the fuck did you leave me!?" Rasia demanded, collapsing in a heap that hurt her ribs. She clawed at the deck and glared at the bright gold waters of the lake.

Taunting her.

In a mindless rage, she grabbed at her swords and raced toward the waters. As if she could stab the lake. As if she could wrestle it, and slay it, and rescue back Kai's light.

She hit the deck hard when Zephyr tackled her, one bound from the railing. She fought at him blindly but found herself pinned to the deck, her wrists bruised and twisted till she let go of her blades.

"Let me go," Rasia screeched. "Let me go!"

Zephyr held her even tighter. With nowhere to go, and nothing to do, it hit her like a storm. Rasia broke into tears, sobbing and quaking in Zephyr's stupid arms.

What had she done?

The storm left her drained and limp under Zephyr's hold. She couldn't even muster the energy to knee him in the dick, so she lay there, numb. Through the flood, Zephyr had maintained an iron hug around her. Rasia didn't know when she'd begun hugging him back.

"I'm sorry," Rasia whispered. "I'm sorry. For everything."

Zephyr's grip loosened. Pain flared in the absence of his weight. She had all kinds of tricks and maneuvers to take down mountains like him. But Zephyr looked at her, the same height as she, just as broken and crumbled and humbled into dust.

"Me too," Zephyr said, crying ugly. "I'm sorry too."

Sometimes, no one won.

CHAPTER THIRTY-FOUR

O

Rasia perched atop the rocky mountain crest. The winding mountain range marked the beginning of scavenger territory and offered a view of the Graveyard, the gonda breeding grounds, and the dark waters of the Dragon's Coast. When confronted with the vastness and sheer size of the Desert, some people felt small and humbled. But from this height, Rasia could reach out and touch every place she'd explored on her map and feel taller.

Or at least she used to.

Rasia had hiked all the way to the crest hoping it would make her feel better, but instead, for all the immense size of the Desert, she felt crushed. The air was noticeably too thin, making it harder to breathe. Knowing the disappointment waiting behind her and the impossible drop before her, she felt cornered. For a brief vibration, Rasia considered vaulting off the mountain to please the frantic panic clawing at her ribcage. But her bones were too strong for her not to turn around and see her mistakes to their bitter end.

Rasia gathered the pouch of figs and hunter berries and swung the fox corpse over her shoulder. She retreated down the steep, rocky path flattened by the hooves of mountain goats. The campfire glowed, an almost hazy light, as Rasia walked into the camp they'd established halfway up the mountain. At this elevation, they could spot any windship coming at them, be it Nico or scavengers.

Rasia approached Zephyr, who sat reading a rhythmic narration over Kai's prone form. Rasia hefted the fox from her shoulder, then dropped her bags, and the bountiful figs spilled, rolling out. They weren't pressed for food, but Rasia needed something to do. She crouched and scooped the purpling fruit back into her satchel. "How's he doing?"

"I got more stew down his throat today."

Rasia knew it wasn't enough. Already, Kai's frame had begun to wither. He'd been unconscious for two days on the lake and two days on the mountain. Nico had better hurry and get here soon.

"You should talk to him," Zephyr suggested.

Rasia's thoughts flashed to a memory seared behind her eyelids: Shamai-ta bleeding out, cradled in his kulani's arms, a knife stabbed decisively into his chest. Rasia had arrived after it happened, but to this day, she dreamt of that blade going in. Kiba-ta made a choice, and Rasia had never forgiven her for it.

"I'll go scout around. This is scavenger territory." Rasia motioned to the fox and the additional results of her foraging. "Do with it what you will."

"I never thought you to be boneless," Zephyr flung at her fleeing back.

Rasia froze at the accusation. She twisted on her heel and glared at Zephyr. He stood sentinel over Kai, his tiny bound parchment clutched in his hands and his eyes red with exhaustion. Increasing hopelessness and too much time thinking carved tired lines into his face. Unlike Zephyr, Rasia refused to watch Kai waste away.

"What's the point? Me talking to him won't change shit. Nico is the only chance we've got."

"I don't know if she is," Zephyr said quietly, uncertain.

"What are you talking about?"

"Nico is the one Kai ran away from. Who's to say he won't flee deeper into his mind? Nico is always frustrated by how he keeps secrets from her. Even she might not know how to wake him."

Rasia had never considered that—that even Nico might not be enough.

Zephyr looked down at Kai, haunted. "I think it's you. You're the one he agreed to throw his Forging on. You're the one who convinced him to hunt a dragon. Maybe you can convince him to wake up too. Rasia, you pulled him from the Lake of Yestermorrow. No one fully submerged in the waters has ever lived to tell the tale. That has to mean something."

Rasia sneered. "It means the lake has a cruel sense of humor."

"What if . . ." Zephyr paused and looked at her, that same dense look he'd been throwing her the past couple of days. "What if you're his kulani?"

Rasia laughed. How absurd. "Of course, you'd be a damn romantic. There are plenty legends of kulani going into the waters after one another and never coming back out. It doesn't mean shit."

"I think it's you. I think he'll come back for you."

"I already tried waking him up. It didn't work."

"You slapped and yelled at him. *Talk* to him."

Rasia couldn't vocalize why she couldn't sit there and talk to Kai, for him never to respond. She couldn't sit still in that desperation again, to be torn apart again, and infected with an anger that had throttled her the past two years. She couldn't breathe sometimes for how angry she was. Sometimes she woke to it on her chest, and she'd have to run it out of her. But no matter what she did, it always returned to weigh her down.

"Zephyr, I can't."

"Yes, you can. You're the one he has a flame for."

"Yet it didn't matter," Rasia bit out. "He still chose Nico over me."

It was mind-boggling. Rasia had never met anyone who so wholly denied himself what he wanted.

Rasia froze; an idea struck her.

Rasia raced down the mountain to the windship. She dropped down into the underbelly hatch and searched through the supplies to stop at the sight of the ilhan, sitting in a corner, never touched.

Kai had made such a fuss over it, but he never played it and had hidden it behind the water barrels like an inconvenient eyesore.

Kai denied himself what he wanted.

Rasia grabbed the ilhan, carried it up the deck, and paused at the mast. She placed her forehead to tah's name. She was so tired of losing people.

Rasia charged back to camp with the ilhan carried in both hands. When she got in hearing range, she yelled, "Wake the fuck up Kai! If you don't, I'm going to break this thing. It's important to you, right? Kenji-shi's ilhan? I'm going to smash it."

Rasia lifted the ilhan over her head, and all her anger and frustration and guilt gave her strength as she slammed it against the rocks with a mighty clang.

The strings snapped. The neck splintered in two. The gourd cracked. It dangled, off-note, and she raised it back up to bring it back down again.

"Stop!"

Kai woke up.

CHAPTHER THIRTY-FIVE

—

The ilhan strings snapped. The sharp twang clawed into Kai's chest and popped against his sternum. He sucked in air. At the sudden lunge of shadows, he jumped but found himself pinned, trapped. His bones seized with panic and fear.

Kai blinked, owlishly, at Rasia overtaking his vision. She sat atop him and clutched at his face, holding on.

"The lake is a lie," Rasia said, clutching him harder. Kai gazed into the glittering hunter's cloak of her eyes, across the hills and valleys of her face, tempting him back to this side of the world.

"Fuck the dragon," Rasia declared. "Fuck the Forging. Whatever the lake promised you, I will give it to you for real. Wake up, and I will not stop until you have what you want most in the entire world."

Rasia shook him.

"*What do you want?* Tell me what you want, and I'll stop at nothing to give it to you. Help me make this right."

It hurt to breathe. Images of the lake rushed at him. Kai squeezed his eyes closed but found no reprieve in the darkness of his thoughts. He wanted to shrink from it all, to flee, to hide away. But Rasia refused to let him escape. She pressed their foreheads together and kissed him with a fierceness and desperation he felt in his bones.

"Don't fall for the horseshit, Kai. Nothing worth having comes easy. We get what we earn. So, tell me, what did the lake promise you? All I need is an ember, Kai, and I'll build you a bonfire."

Kai shook in her grip. He didn't want to think of the lake. He wanted to forget and crawl inside her, but Rasia gripped him fiercely and impaled him in place, a shrike's prey to her thorn.

It was stupid. Kai could want anything in the world. Rasia imagined things he could never dream of, and yet all he'd ever wanted was this small, insignificant thing. Kai felt like a melon smashed to the ground, cracked apart, with all his secrets and guts leaking out of him. All those wants Kai had buried deep down, the lake had yanked free and wrestled out from under the lies and lies Kai had piled atop them over the years.

He couldn't stop the tears. He couldn't gather the smashed, sloppy guts of his insides and put them all back. He was messily stained with his dreams. He knew the colors of himself, and he grieved for all the things he wanted and would never have. He shut his eyes, squeezing them. The lake spun visions around him like a too fast foe, feinting at the corner of his eyes, and if he let down his guard, if he gave in, it'd smash him again and again into pieces.

"It's impossible, Rasia."

"I do impossible things every day. If you think you'll ever be satisfied after this, you won't be. You've had what you've wanted most in the world, and nothing else will ever be enough. So, let's go fucking get it and deny this lake any power over you. Tell me. What are the dreams pulling you back? WHAT. DO. YOU. WANT?"

Kai trembled, and broke, crumbling apart in her hands. The truth burst out of him, agonizing, tearing at bones and tendons to claw from the deep pit where Kai had caged it for years. He smashed himself to the ground.

"Kenjinn Ilhani says my name."

One change had the power to upend his entire world, and the lake showed him exactly what sort of power it could have. Kai no longer looked from the outside in. He no longer crept through the hallways of his own home as a roach skittering at every sound. All he ever wanted was a fraction of the attention Kenji gave to Nico and Rae. He wanted that warmth, like a struggling melon root waiting for water to flourish and grow. Kai feared Rasia's judgment for his small wants. He feared her condescension for how such a little thing could render him so helpless to the lake's illusions. He wished his wants were grander, and yet he felt them more impossible than slaying a dragon.

"Done," Rasia announced. "I'll make it happen."

Kai laughed, in hysterics. Kai was the reason Kenji's kulani was dead. No forgiveness existed for that, and after everything he'd done to ruin Kenji's life, he shouldn't want it in the first place. Kai felt guilty and angry for the wanting. It wasn't something Kai got to have. "Forget it, Rasia. It's not important."

"Absolutely not. If this is what you want, you fight for it. You never give up."

"You can't change people, Rasia."

"Nonsense. This is Kenji-shi we're talking about—the one who gave water to a stranger in the Desert, the one who learned to sing from flock whores, the one who's slayed dragons and brokered truces with scavengers. He's not unreasonable or uncompromising. Kenji-shi always listens."

Rasia stood, hands on her hips, and declared, "There's only one surefire way to get your tah's attention: We slay a dragon."

It was no coincidence they were already on the path.

Kai stared at his hands, biting his lip and clenching at this heat in his chest. As the days wore on, when he learned how to steer a windship and they got closer and closer, Kai thought—no, he was beyond lying to himself now—Kai *knew* there was a small part of him that hoped slaying a dragon might matter to the person who had killed one himself.

Kai tried not to feed those hopes. Hope had betrayed him before, so he kept them small and easy to extinguish.

"The dragon might not matter," Kai said finally. "He might not care at all.

"If a dragon isn't enough, then you keep trying. You do the

next thing. Kenji-shi is overseeing the kull tryouts this year, isn't he? Tryout as windeka. It'll give you the chance to *show* him what you can do. Become so big, so brilliant, that he'll have no other choice but to pay attention. Outshine his ass."

"I can't enter the kull tryouts. I'll make a mockery of myself."

Rasia threw her arms up. "Kai, you've already got the windship part down. We've still got the rest of our Forging, and some time after the Naming Ceremony until the tryouts. That's enough time to whip you into shape where you won't embarrass yourself. It's not as far out of your reach as you think it is. It's *possible*, Kai." Rasia crouched and poked him in the chest. "First, you've got to want it, and let yourself want it. Then you fight for it. That's the secret, Kai. Impossible is just the next foot in front of the other."

You couldn't miss something you didn't have, but Kai knew what it would be like to have it now. And he knew that, fundamentally, at his core, there was no going back to before the lake. He'd never be satisfied with anything less than everything.

"Okay."

Kai shoveled down his plate of freshly cooked fox and wild figs, stubbornly focusing on his food while Zephyr sat hunched beside him. Kai could feel the unsaid words between them hovering in the air. Rasia, on the other hand, was a flurry of motion Kai could barely keep track of. She cooked him dinner, and now she'd gotten it in her head to boil him some tea. Before Kai could stop her, she marched down the steep path to fill their water pot from the mountain creek.

She'd left him alone with Zephyr and all the words waiting to be said. Zephyr rubbed at his eyes, full of tired brambles.

"I'm sorry, Kai," Zephyr said. "I should have listened. I should not have gotten involved between you and Rasia. You handled it far better than I did."

Kai could hardly muster up enough energy to be angry about it right now. He shrugged.

Zephyr wanted to say more, but he bit down on his words every time they rose to the surface. His hesitance itched at Kai's skin, and Kai had an anxious idea of what Zephyr wanted to say. Finally, Zephyr said, choosing each word carefully, "You've been through a lot, and I don't want to add any more stress, but I have to say it. You've got to tell Rasia about Kenji-shi."

Kai knew it had been coming, but he still went cold—with annoyance, rage, and frustration all at once. Kai didn't want Rasia to know. Not because Rasia might not help him if she knew Kenji struck Kai in drunken rages, but because he didn't want to ruin her relationship with a face she considered kin.

"I don't need to. When Rasia and I kill a dragon, I'll have proved I'm not such a waste of space. Things will get better after the Forging."

"That's not how that shit works, and you know it."

Kai turned to argue because how could Zephyr understand? But Zephyr understood annoyingly too much.

"Listen Kai, hate is ugly. Hate poisons good people and sharpens bad ones into worse. Kenji-shi is family to me, too. He found a stranger, a foreigner, dying in the middle of the Desert and gave him water. He's advocated on my father's behalf time and time again. He speaks my father's language better than my tah does. But Kai, people are not perfect." Zephyr, shrugged hopelessly. "None of us are."

Kai blinked blankly and crossed his arms. He hunched his shoulders, cold and drowning and—Zephyr clutched his shoulder with a rough hand, grounding him.

"It's your decision," Zephyr said, "but if you're serious about pursuing this, at the least, you've got to tell Nico. She needs to know about all the other times."

"No." Kai snatched his shoulder away from Zephyr. Kai sorely wished Zephyr hadn't seen the scars and hadn't known what they meant.

"You've got to tell her the truth," Zephyr insisted. "Nico can admittedly be too overprotective, but you're no better either. Denying her the truth is denying her the chance to make her own decisions. She should know her tah for who he is. You're not being fair to her either. I understand if you're not ready to tell Rasia, but you've got to tell Nico. Why are you so scared of telling her?"

Kai's hands tightened on his empty plate of food, searching himself for an answer he'd never sought before. "Because . . ." Kai said slowly. "Because if I ruin Kenji and Nico's relationship, he'll hate me for that, too. I'll never even get the chance."

"That's not on you. If the truth ruins their relationship, that's dirt on his face. He is at fault for his own actions. You shouldn't have to hide or cover for that. I get it. I do. My tah still has family on the other side of the Tail. Cousins I've never met. I would like to know them, but at what cost? Either they accept me, or they don't. Family shouldn't be conditional."

"Sure, idealistically," Kai argued. "But the truth is that I failed my Forging last year. I've brought in no rations, and I *have* been a burden on my family. How can I judge him for his hate if I hate myself too?"

"*That's* the problem. You hate yourself so much you don't think you deserve better. The lake gives you what you *think* you want, but you don't need Kenji-shi's approval."

"Are you done?" Kai asked.

"I'm trying to help."

"You've helped enough!" Kai spat out, bitter, finally feeling all the anger that had been building since the lake. Kai had told Zephyr he could handle Rasia, but again and again, his words were treated as cricket noise. At least Rasia listened when he told her no. Zephyr didn't, and Kai found that betrayal hard to forgive.

"*I'm sorry,* Kai."

Kai got up and marched away, more hurt than he thought he'd be. Kai didn't care what Zephyr had to say anymore. Zephyr didn't have any right to stick his nose in Kai's business. If Kai wanted to hunt a dragon, that's what he'd do. If Kai wanted to prove to Kenji he was not a worthless piece of shit, that's what he'd do. Kai was done holding himself back from the things he wanted.

Holding a pot of water on her hip, Rasia tensed in alarm when Kai came around the trail curve. Before she could ask what was wrong, Kai shoved her against the nearest rock. The pot clanged against the ground and splashed water all over their feet.

Perhaps it was true that the lake offered only what Kai thought he wanted, full of secret cravings, half-truths, and desires. Perhaps Zephyr was right and Rasia's promises were empty hunts. But at least Rasia's world was full of stars, dreams, and impossible things. They both might be lies, but he knew which one he preferred.

Kai dove for Rasia's lips, ready to drown.

Kai glanced down at Rasia in his arms, where she curled against him, bundled up in his bedroll. The delicate light preceding sunrise softened the sky. Zephyr snored across the fire from them, out like a rock ever since Kai and Rasia returned to camp after their lengthy detour down the mountain trail.

Rasia's cold toes rubbed against his legs. She woke, blinking at him with a smile, and hugged her arms about his waist. She mumbled into his clavicle, "You didn't wake me for watch."

"You seemed tired, and I've had enough sleep," Kai said.

Rasia scrunched her nose, smelling his horseshit. Kai rolled his eyes and admitted, "What if I don't wake back up?"

All through the night, the visions weighed on him like a thick blanket, trying to lull him back to the lake.

"The dreams become less powerful over time. They will fade," Rasia promised, then kissed him soundly on the lips and pulled out of his arms. He watched her as she boiled water, naked except for the wrap he had tied back on her last night.

"Here."

Kai gratefully retrieved the calabash of tea Rasia handed him.

Rasia sat next to him, with their thighs flushed together. She lifted her own cup of the same drink and clicked it against Kai's in a toast.

He twisted his face at the bitterness of it. It had a distinct earthy fragrance. He looked down at the crushed grounds sunken in black water. "What is this?"

"It's the Hunter's Drink. Kulls drink it to stay awake for late night watches. It's to keep you awake until the visions weaken."

Kai took sips of the bitter black tea. Almost instantly, it perked him up with energy.

He asked her, curious, "How come you weren't affected by the lake? Or were you, and I'm the weak one? I'm sorry for not being stronger."

"Many never make it back out, Kai. You were plenty strong. As for me? Maybe because it was my second time the lake wasn't as powerful. I don't know, Kai." Rasia grinned and tossed a hand through her hair dramatically. "I'm invincible."

Kai probably should've scoffed at her oversized ego, but he was beginning to believe her. He finished his drink and focused on Rasia with a sharp, undiluted attention. She met him with that same intensity, and the moment of staring stretched indefinitely.

The campfire cast flickering shadows across her bronze skin. He asked, almost outside of himself, "What is it that Rasia, the invincible, wants most in the entire world?"

Kai figured her response would be one he could never imagine on his own. She laughed and curled over her knees with a soft crescent smirk.

"You."

Kai blinked. He must have misheard.

She nudged him with her foot. "Why else do you think the lake gave you back to me?"

Kai blushed, unable to comprehend. Perhaps that was the trick. Somehow Rasia had deceived the lake.

Rasia placed her empty cup down and left to shuffle in her bags. She returned with a set of folded clothes—the clothes she had first given him, and Kai later returned.

Rasia glanced at him, almost shyly. "You can't practice for the tryouts in that caftan of yours. What I did was really shitty, and I won't ever do that again. I regret a lot of the things I've done, and I'm sorry. For all of it. I'd really like a second chance at not being an asshole and a better friend."

She offered the clothes, hoping.

Kai hadn't expected it, especially considering they had sex last night, which had pretty much reestablished their friends-with-benefits relationship. Rasia had nothing to gain by apologizing, and Kai felt surprisingly touched by the act. Rasia was a beautiful, complex creature *and* an asshole. He appreciated her trying.

"Thank you, Rasia."

Kai accepted the clothes and brushed his hand over the folded linen shirt. Something shimmied on the edge of his senses. He glanced over at Zephyr, still snoring, and wondered if the lake had further thrown off his already erratic magic. That was a problem he didn't feel like dealing with. Kai longed for those simple days from the gorge when it was just him and Rasia alone.

Kai asked her, "Want to go for a ride?"

Rasia smiled, that beautiful wind-tossed grin of mischief and adventure. The lake, despite all it had offered, never conjured visions of Rasia. Perhaps it knew nothing could ever match the imperfect real thing. She existed here in Kai's waking, this irresistible energy and strength of will that continued to toss him like a whirlwind. If acknowledgment from the parent who disowned him was what Kai wanted the most, then Rasia was what he needed.

Even the Lake of Yestermorrow never saw her coming.

CHAPTER THIRTY-SIX

I

"Campfire!" Suri shouted down the hatch.

Nico woke with a start from the hard plank of the windship bunk. She didn't remember falling asleep. She must have strained her magic propelling across the Lake. It was hard not to keep going when Nico was so close.

Nico rushed up the ladder to the deck and peered through the morning haze. Her chest tightened at the sight of smoke and flickering firelight, a glowing eye blinking atop the encroaching mountain range.

For the past two days, Nico had wondered why Rasia had broken her pattern. Had Rasia finally stopped because she thought herself secure enough to make camp, smug in the knowledge Nico would never catch up? If so, nothing felt more satisfying than determination and dedication finally triumphing over carelessness and complacency.

Kelin joined Nico by the railing and mused, "Awfully bold of her. Anyone can see that fire for drums around."

"It doesn't matter. We did it. We finally caught up."

"Could be scavengers. Could be a trap."

"It's her," Nico said, confident. "Azan, approach the range at an angle. Hopefully, they haven't seen us just yet."

Nico feared another chase. The campfire left Rasia exposed,

but no doubt the high elevation offered greater visibility. Rasia might be expecting them, and Nico needed to be ready to cut her off.

They anchored the windship out of sight of Rasia's campfire, hugging the rock-shadow. They readied their weapons.

Suri slung her quiver and bow over her shoulder. Azan hefted his great fan axe, and Kelin dripped sharp with his talon dagger.

They walked the rest of the distance, hoping to maintain the element of surprise. Eventually, they came upon a trail leading farther up the mountain. Nico noted signs of recent passage. She crouched to the grass and listened to the plant water.

"No one has come this way since this morning. If they sighted us, they're no doubt rushing down the mountain now. Suri and Azan, see if you can find their ship and commandeer it. Kelin and I will go up the mountain path."

Suri hesitated. "You're choosing him to go with you?"

"I need you to find Rasia's windship, Suri. If we can cut off her means of escape, she'll have nowhere to go." Nico hastened up the trail to avoid further argument.

Kelin followed behind her and fell in step once the trail wound out of view.

"She really doesn't like me, does she?" Kelin asked.

"You haven't bothered to make any effort to change that."

"Seems like a *her* problem to me."

"You don't give her the chance to know you," Nico said, but perhaps Nico was being unfair. Who would want to play nice with someone who regarded you with such open disdain? "No, you're right. Besides, it's not about you anyway."

"You mean, since you rejected her?"

Nico paused and spun to face Kelin. She hadn't known anyone had overheard that conversation. Kelin gave a slick smile and an exaggerated shrug of his shoulders. Nico rolled her eyes. "That's enough talk of Suri. We need to focus on the mission at hand. I'm relying on your help with Rasia. Ready?"

"Always."

Nico might not trust Kelin in a dragon fight, but he'd been

trained by the Flock. Nico hoped Kelin could be the edge Rasia didn't see coming.

Nico hiked around rocks and scraggy trees to encounter a tower of shadows. The bright sun framed the obstacle. Kelin tensed beside her. Nico squinted. The shadows came into view as Nico drew closer. The shapeless mass solidified into the hunch of shoulders and a familiar face Nico knew all too well.

Zephyr slid from the rock where he sat waiting for her.

They stared at each other, like one would test a mirage. Then Nico and Zephyr rushed forward, and Nico found herself swallowed by his hug. He smelled of figs and fire smoke. She plastered herself against his brick chest and was swallowed by bicep walls. She was so relieved to see him.

An incredulous scoff interrupted their hug.

"And here I thought I had discovered some secret tent faction conspiracy." Kelin rolled his eyes with such sass. "Nope. Just a pair of flame-whipped kids."

"I *told* you," Nico said, as she separated, then blushed. "Wait, not the flame-whipped part, just the . . ." Kelin's brows raised, and Nico didn't have the time to argue over a point she might be lying about anyway.

Zephyr looked more than a little amused by her fluster, with a smile showing off the dimples. Every time they met, it was as if the breath was knocked out of her.

A few years ago, when Ava-ta died, Nico had told Zephyr she feared becoming Kenji-ta, so crushed by the loss of his entire world and unable to function. Zephyr could be that possibility, and it frightened her, that potential for wreckage and destruction. It was why, out of self-preservation, she'd always kept a certain distance. She was reminded of that choice every time she saw him.

"Where are Kai and Rasia?" Nico asked, trying to get herself back on track.

Zephyr crossed his arms, his biceps bulging. "Gone. Snuck off while I slept. Missed them by several drums."

No. That can't be right.

Nico snatched the map container from her belt and shook the papyrus out of the oblong gourd. She tucked the container under her arm and shook out the map now marred by permanent stains.

Nico spat. She watched in horror as the line of spit fled further and further away from her position.

She should have checked the map when Suri woke her. Nico had been so sure. Nico had thought she'd finally caught up, that Rasia's arrogance had been her downfall, but in the end, Nico's downfall had been her own. Even with all Nico's determination and all her effort and all her magic and every ounce of everything she had to give, it still wasn't enough.

She wasn't enough.

Nico and Zephyr started down the mountain path, but somewhere in the middle of Zephyr's tale, Nico had to sit down to process it all. Zephyr joined her atop the wide rock shelf.

Nico listened to Zephyr's stories of Kai ramming a gran-scorpion with a windship, to Rasia and Kai's apparent relationship, to Kai falling into the Lake of Yestermorrow, to the promises Rasia made him.

Nico stared blankly down the trail, toward the direction where she had sent Kelin ahead to update Azan and Suri while she and Zephyr privately caught up.

Loose strands of hair itched at Nico's neck. She pulled off the dragonglass holder and corrected her ponytail, thinking. Nico battled and warred with her thoughts. Emotions stormed through her chest. She didn't know what impossible place to start first. After several failed attempts, the first question finally dropped from her lips.

"*Rasia has a flame for Kai?*"

"So massive you could probably see it from here. Kai had

broken things off with her, but I knew that wasn't going to last long. Caught them making out right down the trail yesterday."

"I just . . ." Nico shook her head, unable to visualize Kai and Rasia *together*.

"They *can* be good for each other," Zephyr admitted. "When Rasia is on deck, she's everywhere. She doesn't stop moving. It's exhausting watching her all day. But if Kai is there too, she orbits him. She sprawls, springs, and laughs all over him. He anchors her, and Kai flourishes at the center of her attention. The flame between them, I don't know if it's going to burn them up or forge into something. I'm certain it wasn't Rasia's idea to leave me here. That was Kai."

"You're suggesting Rasia is a good thing? She pushed him into the Yestermorrow Lake. He almost died because of her!"

"It was an accident, and there's fault on both sides," Zephyr admitted. "Rasia is the one who dived into those waters. She's the one who brought him back out, and ultimately is the one who woke him up. For all Rasia's faults, she does care about him in her own way."

Nico shook her head. This Rasia who put someone else's life above ambition wasn't the one she knew. Nico wasn't sure she recognized Kai, either—this jih that laughed, and smiled, and could steer a windship.

Nico glanced back at Zephyr. He had told her everything, or at least everything he felt was within his right to say. She didn't know how she felt about the kiss between Zephyr and Kai. Maybe she was a little jealous, even though she was the one who had told Zephyr to move on. She did think Zephyr could have been good for Kai and wondered how things could have been if the bones had landed differently, or at least, unmanipulated. But instead . . . it had to be Rasia.

Nico pressed her lips together and remembered Azan's and Kelin's certainties after the chase. She ventured to ask, "Are they having sex?"

Zephyr put a little too much effort at keeping his face blank. Anyone else would have missed it, but Nico knew the signs of

Zephyr gliding over a lie. He sighed, knowing he'd been caught out. "Kai promised they were being safe."

"*Safe?* Kai didn't go to school. What does he know about safe?"

"I didn't go to school either, but it's not all that complicated. You put a dick in a vagina and a baby comes out nine blinks later. Do you really need to know more than that? Kai will be fine."

Nico rubbed her eyes. She understood tent kids had underage sex all the time, that if you were smart about it, it wasn't a big deal. But kullers had so much more to lose if they were caught. Kai could lose his life. She worried. "You think this is going to continue? Even after the Forging?"

Everyone knew Forging flames didn't last.

"I don't know, Nico."

"It doesn't matter," Nico said, shaking her head. "Regardless of their relationship, it does not change the fact Rasia has got it in Kai's head to slay a dragon. We ran into that dragon. Even with my magic, I could barely hold my own against it. Someone needs to get a hold of Kai and pull his head out the clouds."

"Nico. I know you don't want to hear this, but Kai is not going anywhere without that dragon. If you aren't careful, you're going to push him away. This is what Kai has chosen. This is what he wants." Zephyr's voice gentled, that soft, patient voice he so often used with his little jih. "It doesn't make sense to chase after him anymore. He's on his Forging path. It's time for you to sail yours."

"But do you truly think they can slay a dragon alone?"

Zephyr grew quiet at that. "I don't know."

Perhaps Nico could finally accept this was what Kai wanted, but that didn't mean Nico should let him do it by himself. He needed help. The chase wasn't over. She still needed to find him.

"I'm sorry," Zephyr said. Nico turned, alarmed by the distress breaking through Zephyr's voice. "I failed my promise to you. I promised to protect Kai, but because I couldn't listen, he almost died. I failed him, and I've failed you."

Nico pulled herself out of her own problems and fully studied her friend. Zephyr wasn't the sort of person to beat himself up over things out of his control. That was normally Nico. She pressed a hand to his back because she sensed he needed it. He'd gotten so much bigger than her over the years, and it was so easy to forget how Zephyr was the one who always craved the hugs and comfort.

People looked at Zephyr and saw a mountain, but she remembered when he was soft-clay and mud. The exterior might have hardened over the years to protect those soft insides against spiteful strangers and a hateful world, but Zephyr had always let his guard down around her. The protective shroud Zephyr wore unraveled, and exhaustion and guilt overcame his face.

Nico asked, softly, "Are you okay?"

Zephyr opened his mouth to answer, then closed it after a long moment. He dropped his head in his hands, like a kuller, like his tah. "I don't know. I . . . no. No, I'm not. I should have told you that night before the Forging, but I feared you'd look at me different."

"Zephyr, what's wrong?"

Nico dragged her hand up his back, to his neck, and patted her lap in suggestion. Zephyr resisted only for a moment before his head bouldered down onto her thighs. The rock shelf wobbled under his weight, then settled. They used to sit like this when they were younger, venting and ranting about life.

As Zephyr stared out at the breathtaking view, the words rolled out of him. "Before Father and I set out for his caravan last year, he warned me that his people didn't approve of same-side relationships. I didn't listen. I fooled around with a boy who had joined our caravan. They caught us, and they . . . they *stoned* him dead in front of me."

Nico grew horrified at Zephyr's description of the event.

"I would have been dead too if my father hadn't gotten me out of there. And I . . . ever since I've felt so fucking helpless. I couldn't protect your jih. I almost got him killed because I couldn't listen, *again*. And every time I think about the purge, I get so angry because there's nothing I can do to protect my family from it. Sometimes it feels as if I'm there again, watching that boy die, and helpless to do anything about it. It was all my fault, Nico."

Zephyr pressed his hands to his face, and Nico held him as he cried into her lap. Nico felt partly to blame for this. She had stretched him too thin. She never would have asked so much of him had she known. She should have been there for him. She should have been a better friend.

"Why didn't you tell me the night of the Forging? Why would you ever think I'd look at you differently?"

"Because now you know my father's people are pieces of shit too, just like my tah's. There's nothing good about me."

"Zephyr," Nico said softly. She combed her fingers through his coiled hair. He didn't like anyone but family touching the curly strands, but the tension leaked from his shoulders when she massaged her nails through his scalp. "You know that's not true."

Zephyr wiped at his face and sat up hunched beside her. "All I've ever wanted was to be your equal. To no longer be stuck at the border. I wanted to be someone you can be proud of, and not the tent kid, or the halfling, but someone who can help you change the world. But I've messed everything up. Forgive me."

"No, Zephyr. Forgive *me*. I have been the selfish one. I have been the one wrapped up in my own shroud. You are good. You've done good," Nico insisted. "Now it's my turn."

Nico had been chasing after someone who didn't want her help and hadn't asked for it, all while there were lives depending on her actions. Maybe this hunt wasn't a failure after all.

Nico had finally caught the person who truly needed her.

CHAPTER THIRTY-SEVEN

1

Nico and Zephyr reached the bottom of the mountain trail, where Kelin, Azan, and Suri had pulled the windship closer. They stood on deck at the railing, ready for orders to sail through high noon and continue the chase.

"I've made a decision," Nico declared. "Break down the sail. From here on out, we hunt a gonda. We'll rest here for a few days to gather our strength before turning for the gonda breeding grounds."

"About time!" Azan cheered and hugged Kelin in his excitement. Suri, who Nico thought would be overjoyed the most, stood with a shadow over her face.

"You sure about this?" Zephyr asked at Nico's shoulder.

At some point, the chase had stopped being about Kai and what was best for him and had become more about Nico. Nico had needed to prove herself better than Rasia, but eventually you had to realize that there were some people in life that are just . . . better. It was time Nico considered what was best for her kull, and the people at home depending on her.

Nico reached into her belt for Zephyr's dagger, back from the oasis, and handed it over. "I'm sure. Come on. Let's introduce you to the kull."

Kelin climbed down the stairs and gave them a cocky smile in acknowledgment. The tent kid teased, "Sure did take a while up there."

"Perhaps you and Azan could learn a thing or two," Nico said, biting down a smirk. Kelin squawked out a laugh and gave her a cheeky wink as he walked away.

"I hope he's been minding himself," Zephyr said pointedly.

"We've come to an understanding."

Azan and Suri unhooked the sail from the deck. Azan lowered it and Nico reached up to catch the edge. She stretched it over the ground, and Zephyr staked it with an effortless stomp of his foot. Azan jumped from the stairs to meet them.

"Azan, this is Zephyr. A good friend of mine. He's here to join our kull. I know we've been rather short on a fifth member for a while now."

Azan glanced over Zephyr, curious. "You look different than what I imagined."

Zephyr glowered. "What did you imagine?"

"My family fulfills quite a few orders for your tah. Figured you'd be as dark as him, and short and small, but you're not. Well met."

"Well met," Zephyr said, wary. Azan left, walking toward Kelin to help build the campfire. Zephyr looked to Nico for an explanation, no doubt expecting a worse reception.

"He's good bones," Nico explained.

One more introduction, and it was the one Nico had been imagining for years—the moment when she introduced her best friends to each other. Except now, Nico wasn't that same wide-eyed, optimistic little kid. While Azan had made his greetings, Suri had curved past to disappear into the underbelly of the windship.

"Wait here," Nico said, walking over to peer inside the hatch. She found Suri sitting atop the water barrels, staring at nothing. "Suri, you can't hide in here forever."

"Did you fuck him?" Suri whispered.

Nico's shoulders tensed at the accusation. Suri's tone was completely different from when Kelin had teased Nico about her relationship with Zephyr earlier. "Even if I did, that's none of your business. Can't you get past your hate for just a moment and meet him?"

"Fine." Suri pushed herself off the barrels and shuffled past.

Nico followed Suri out the hatch, hoping Suri would talk to Zephyr and find all her fears about him were unfounded. Those hopes were quickly dashed when Suri spat on the ground at Zephyr's feet. Zephyr's jaw tightened, and for a moment Nico thought Zephyr might retaliate, but Zephyr did nothing. Very few kullers would have let that go. Suri moved past without a second look.

Nico rushed forward, outraged, but Zephyr stopped her with a touch on her arm. "Nico, it's whatever. It's okay."

"No, this is not okay. You two are my closest friends. It's not supposed to be this way."

Zephyr rolled his shoulders. "For what it's worth, I've been jealous of her too."

The admittance took Nico aback. Zephyr had never spoken of Suri with ill will. She had naively hoped they had been as excited to meet each other as Nico had been excited for them to meet. But like Zephyr, it seemed Suri had always been jealous of the other best friend.

"That's no excuse not to introduce her name to you," Nico said. Perhaps Zephyr could shrug it off, but Nico was done with this behavior. She marched after Suri.

"Suri, we need to talk. *Now.*"

Suri followed after Nico. They stopped close to a rock wall. The campfire cast their shadows tall against the mountain, like some sort of play cast along the sides of adobe houses. "Apologize to Zephyr."

"I'm not apologizing to a tent rat."

"*That is enough!* Zephyr has never done anything to you. Nor are you competing against each other. A no to you doesn't mean a yes to him. And even if I did choose him, that doesn't give you the right to treat him so poorly."

"Clean your face, Nico. These tent kids aren't to be trusted, and he's been playing you for years. He's using you. You're just some prize to him. You're the Ohan, and you deserve better. Look at how he's already changed you. Now, all of a sudden you stop chasing after Kai? I begged you for days. What could he have possibly said or done to change your mind?"

"That Kai is happy!" Nico snapped.

Nico could change her mind, and it frustrated Nico that Suri couldn't change hers. Nico was willing to give Rasia a chance, so why couldn't Suri give Zephyr one? Suri's jealousy had morphed into this thing that was so intractable, and Nico was done ignoring her behavior in the hopes she'd get better. Nico was done giving Suri's hate space with her silence.

"I promised you success in this Forging, and I will keep that promise. But I will no longer tolerate your hate. Our friendship ends here."

"You don't mean that, Nico."

Nico reached for her magic and slapped Suri in the face, splattering clods of grass and dirt, with the wad of Suri's own spit.

Nico felt the devastation she'd always feared, that terrifyingly loss that cut organs out of her body, the crushing of her entire world. But she fought through the pain. She was stronger than her parents. She refused to break.

Some friends weren't forever.

CHAPTER THIRTY-EIGHT

I

Nico flowed around Zephyr's massive sword swing, focused more on evading rather than blocking his powerful strokes. He lost control of a swing chasing after her. His balance crossed his center, a mistake ringing in her ears like off-key notes. Nico lunged through the opening to stab the sheathed glaive into Zephyr's chest. Zephyr nodded, conceding.

Both Nico and Zephyr collapsed down into the sand, exhausted from their spar. Nico wiped at the sweat with her shroud and took a chug of water. She pulled back the sweaty strands of her hair into a neat ponytail. Despite making camp in the mountain's shadow, the sun's heat seeped through her clothes.

"Even after all these years, you still beat me," Zephyr huffed.

"I only beat you when we were little because you could barely lift that sword." Zephyr splashed water into his hair, and Nico watched the drops drip down his bare torso. She'd been taller than him once. "You've gotten a lot faster since then. I guess all those muscles aren't for show."

Zephyr raised his brows at the compliment, and Nico blushed at the unintended suggestiveness. Nico turned and fanned air to her overheated skin.

Zephyr broke the branch off a nearby tamarisk. Nico laughed when he fanned the leaves and sent swooping air in her direction.

She closed her eyes for a moment to enjoy the cool air, then peeked an eye open to Zephyr enjoying the view even though she was all sweaty and gross.

"Stop," Nico said, swatting at the makeshift fan. Stop looking at her like that. Stop making her feel so hot. Stop flirting with him, Nico, even though she couldn't seem to stop herself.

"You messed up my hair," Nico complained. She pulled off the hairband and shook out her hair, glancing over at him as she did so.

"Need help?"

Nico turned her back to Zephyr, almost in relief. She closed her eyes to his fingers combing through the thick mass of her hair.

"You've gotten better," Zephyr noted as his fingers massaged through her scalp. "I couldn't land a hit on you."

"I've been sparring with Azan and Kelin. They're great practice. I just . . . I wish it was enough to catch up to Rasia."

"You're just as good as Rasia."

Nico laughed at his attempt not to hurt her feelings. Zephyr finished with her hair, not nearly as perfect as Kenji-ta used to, but it would do. She turned back around to find Zephyr frowning at her.

"Seriously, Nico. Your technique is perfect. When you fight, there's no move or action wasted. You suck at fighting Rasia because she treats a spar like a damn fight, and you're never looking for a killing blow. If I have any criticism, you react slower to things you don't expect. It's clear you've studied every fighting style, but Rasia often throws styles together and thrives on the unexpected. Lastly, Rasia has always been the one able to get under your shroud." Zephyr shrugged. "She's your worst match up, that's all."

Nico's head tilted. "I've never thought of it that way."

"You're both also extremely competitive, have strong personalities, and two very different approaches to the same problem."

"Okay. I get it. We are destined to be at each other's throats."

"Are you? You stopped complaining about Rasia after your tah died."

"Because there were bigger things to deal with it. The little things weren't important anymore."

"Exactly."

Nico considered Zephyr's words. Had she been letting every little thing trip her up when she had so many bigger things to tackle?

"And it's not about Rasia," Zephyr said. "It's never been about Rasia. Nothing has ever come easily to you. You've worked hard and endured a lot to master your technique. You pride yourself on the hard work but resent all that hard work as well. You've grown to hate Rasia because you've never been able to hate the person who deserves it."

Nico narrowed her eyes at him, knowing exactly where he was going. "Ava-ta wasn't that bad."

"She refused to let you sleep until you memorized every argument put forth to the Council. She made you practice your magic until you were blue. She forced you to train through broken bones. You never had a problem standing up to Rasia, but you were never able to stand up to her."

Nico stood, taken aback by such an old argument. Zephyr had always gotten angry on her behalf when she told those stories, but tah was dead, and she'd figured that old anger had died with her.

"She did what she had to, Zephyr. I'm the heir. It made me strong."

"The only difference between you and Kai is that people can see his scars."

"*What does it matter*?! She's dead. All of that was a long time ago, and it didn't make a difference anyway. I'm still not strong enough. I'm still not good enough. I'm still a fucking failure," Nico croaked out.

"Nico-"

Nico walked away and needed some space to gather herself. She walked past one of the hare traps they laid for gonda bait and slumped against a large boulder. She'd forgotten how unerringly direct Zephyr was at times. It was useful when Nico got too much into her head, but more often than not, it was a punch to the gut.

Nico tensed when Suri leaned against the same boulder.

"He touches you," Suri observed.

"Doesn't mean anything. I grew up touching him. They don't care in the Tents," Nico said, unapologetically.

Nico refused to shield Suri from her friendship with Zephyr, nor had Suri any right to know that Nico had already rejected him and now they were trying to reach some sort of normal in the aftermath. Nico, admittedly, wasn't doing a very good job of it.

"What do you want, Suri?" Nico asked.

Suri pursed her lips. She murmured, "He's right. You never complained of what your tah put you through, but I noticed too."

"What did I have to complain about? At least I was healthy. At least I had Kenji-ta. I had you, and Jilah, and Zephyr, and the rest of my friends. Kai had no one. I didn't have the right to complain."

"For all of Kai's weakness, you were expected to be stronger. It wasn't fair to you." Suri looked at Nico, bright eyes asking for forgiveness. "It's okay to be flawed, sometimes. No one is perfect. I am sorry, Nico."

"You are not forgiven," Nico said firmly. It was not Nico who Suri needed to apologize to.

"NICO!"

Both Nico and Suri swiveled to attention as Kelin came racing toward them, notably without Azan. Kelin and Azan were supposed to be checking the traps. Judging by the balled caftan Kelin clutched to his groin as he ran, they had gotten distracted by other things.

Nico raced out to meet him, and Kelin's momentum had him slamming into her. His bare chest heaved against her, and his eyes contained a frantic terror.

"B-big f-fucking spiders," Kelin stuttered, then forced himself to snap out, barely more coherent, "A big fucking spider!"

"I warned you about having sex outside of camp. Put on your

clothes," Nico commanded and immediately turned on her heel. Both Zephyr and Suri came to meet her from opposite directions, drawn to the commotion. "Ready your weapons. Azan has been nabbed by silk spiders."

Without hesitation, despite all the drama, both Zephyr and Suri immediately did as Nico ordered.

Nico scooped up her glaive. She slung her canteen and preparation pack around her shoulders. Ready, Nico searched for Kelin. He was dressed now, and his perpetual swagger had burst into a mere stuttering, wide-eyed child of sixteen years.

"Where did it happen?"

"This way," Kelin said. He held his arms crossed in front of his chest in a terrible attempt to disguise his shaking hands. Nico placed a firm hand on his shoulder as they walked.

"We'll get him back. Silk spiders can't digest solids, so they don't feed on their prey immediately. We have time. But not much. What happened?" Nico said, partially to get information and partially to keep him calm.

"I think Azan heard or felt something. He threw me off, and then he was gone." Kelin hunched forward. "He saved me."

They arrived at the scene of the incident, where sand swirled down a depression caused by the silk spider's tunnel. Silk spiders resided in the silk mines, but they often hunted from burrows to capture unsuspecting prey and drag it into their lairs.

"Follow five vibrations after each other," Nico ordered, and Nico moved toward the sinkhole.

She made to step toward the center when Kelin clutched at her arm. "What are you doing?"

"It'll take us forever to find the right entrance to the silk mines. We have no choice but to go the way of the spider. I suggest you hold your breath."

Kelin held a death grip on her.

"You're all I've got left," he hissed.

Nico softened. "Kelin, this is what it means to be a kull. When the ground vibrates, there's no time for self-doubt or fear. You do what you've got to do. You put it all aside, and get it done."

Nico offered her hand.

"You're all brave idiots," Kelin whispered. He grabbed ahold of her forearm with both hands. "Don't let go of me."

"I won't."

Nico turned back to that whirl of sand. She held her breath and jumped into the whirling pit. She and Kelin sunk into the darkness. Their backsides hit dirt and slid down until the angle of the tunnel evened out.

The deep darkness swallowed all light. The air tasted thin and clogged. Nico searched her rucksack, easily navigating through the myriad of items she always had at the ready in the event of such a disaster. She counted the time in her head as she pulled out a small clay lap. Soon the lamp glowed with a fire and battled the darkness of the tunnel.

At once, Nico lunged toward the mass of items that had also fallen down the hole—Azan's canteen, a shroud, a strip of underwear, a shoe, and most notably, Azan's fan axe, waiting to cut anyone who unknowingly tripped over it. She grabbed the hilt and dragged the weapon out of the way as Suri came to a sliding stop.

Zephyr followed soon afterward.

Kelin gathered up all the fallen items, throwing Azan's canteen over his shoulder, wrapping Azan's shroud around his neck, shoving Azan's shoe in his bag, and stuffing the loincloth in his belt. It wasn't Kelin's underwear since he didn't wear any (and it was ridiculous that Nico knew that).

Nico motioned to Zephyr, and he came over to shoulder Azan's axe with ease.

Nico pulled a rope out of her rucksack. "We'll use this to keep from getting separated, but we also need to keep our hands free in case anything attacks. Wrap it around your waist. Me first, Kelin, Zephyr, then Suri."

Kelin between Zephyr and Nico to keep him calm. Suri, the ranged fighter, at the back.

They tied themselves to each other then continued down the tunnel with careful urgency. Nico led, holding the lamp in one hand and her glaive in the other, guiding them onward.

Rarely did surface dwellers dive into the Desert's various underground mazes, built by the silk spiders, gondas, and all the creatures who made a living hiding from the sun. Nico could sense them at her feet sometimes. She never thought one day she'd be in the belly of them.

"Silk spider venom isn't like gonda venom," Nico warned, both for Kelin's benefit but to also fight back against this suffocating darkness. "While gonda venom kills slow, silk spider venom is a paralytic. Most likely Azan won't be able to move when we find him. Zephyr, it will be your job to grab him. The rest of us will back you up."

The tunnels grew thicker and thicker with spider webs until it was almost impossible to avoid them. Silk spiders sensed movement based on the vibrations of their webs, which made any element of surprise impossible.

They stepped into a cavernous space filled thick with spiderwebs crossing each other in a mad tangle even the greatest weaver could never mimic. At the center, a massive spider was cocooning Azan in silk, almost covering his entire head. Azan's eyes widened at the sight of them.

The shadows moved, or at least that's what Nico thought at first, before realizing they were surrounded by hundreds and hundreds of smaller silk spiders, traveling with silent deadliness toward the intruders in their home.

"Elder protect me," Kelin breathed out.

"I thought you didn't believe in the Elder?" Suri asked.

"I do now."

"Suri, target the Han. On my signal," Nico said, while untying the rope that held them together.

Suri drew her bow and aimed toward the spider at the center. The leader was so large each one of its legs spanned two lengths of Nico's glaive.

"Hold this," Zephyr pressed the fan axe into Kelin's chest, and Kelin toppled back into the nearest wall at the weight of it. Zephyr reached for his large sword and swung it over his shoulder, so big it scraped the tunnel's low ceiling.

Nico glanced at Zephyr, he nodded, and they moved back-to-back.

Nico smashed her lamp against the web-covered wall. The clay cracked, splattering oil. Fire blazed up the silk.

Suri released her arrow, and Nico and Zephyr pushed forward into the cavern. Out in front, Nico carved the path. She whipped water from her canteen and swatted at the small silk spiders closing in.

In her periphery, a furred shape hurled toward her.

Azan's fan axe cut through the air. Limbs flew, and a severed leg brushed Nico's face. The silk spider fell twitching, and Kelin stomped it still.

Nico grabbed Kelin by the arm and dragged him into her and Zephyr's formation. Behind them, Suri remained at the entrance protecting their exit. The smaller silk spiders shied away from the fire, and Suri dipped her arrows into the flames to shoot chaos into the thickest parts of the cavern.

Suri's initial shot had failed to kill the massive Han spider. It dropped down atop their heads. Nico spun. Zephyr slammed down all his weight to cleave the enormous spider, halfway. Zephyr hefted up his sword again and sliced through the other half. Nico winced at the warm splatter of blood and guts.

Azan dangled too high in the air to reach him.

"We're going to have to get on each other's shoulders," Nico said. "Kelin, you're the lightest. You're on top."

Zephyr bowed down, and Nico climbed atop his shoulders. Zephyr took hold of the fan axe while Kelin climbed up, onto Zephyr's shoulders, and then up Nico's torso. Nico gripped Kelin's thighs as he reached to rip the webs from Azan's cocoon.

The flames that had once been their shield began to thicken, and the smoke burned Nico's throat. They didn't have much time to make it out before the entire cavern went up in flames.

Most of the spiders had fled now, disappearing into unseen cracks and crevices.

"Got him," Kelin cried triumphantly as Azan sagged and

floated to the ground with stray webs still attached. They scrambled down, and Zephyr threw Azan over his shoulder without looking back.

"Grab hands!" Nico shouted when they reached Suri and the exit.

Nico grabbed Suri's hand. Suri's grabbed Zephyr's. Zephyr grabbed Kelin's.

Water flooded the cavern.

It took a while for Nico to move the large body of water from its deep underground aquifer, but it answered her summons exactly when she needed it.

The flood swept them off their feet. It carried them with force down the tunnel, spinning them around the walls at a speed that roared in their ears.

They shot out the ground atop a geyser. Nico tucked in her arms and landed, rolling in the sand.

Nico spit out dirt and water and coughed on the smoke still stuck in her throat. She picked herself up, drenched and covered in sopping silkwebs, careful with the wiggling weight in her arms. She unwrapped the baby silk spider out of her shroud.

Their hare traps had been coming up short, and they needed bait for the gonda.

The sky had transitioned to night, even though they had dived underground only a little after high noon. Kelin and Zephyr ripped away the rest of the cocoon to free Azan. Once freed, Kelin tackled Azan and sobbed. Even though still affected by the paralysis and naked as the day he was born, Azan managed a smile.

"Nico," Suri said. In that tone. When someone needed her.

What now?

Nico blinked at a sudden windship on the horizon. She couldn't tell if it was friendly or scavengers. Exhausted, she handed Suri the baby silk spider.

Nico cleared the spider webs from her face and dug her glaive out of the sand. She used it to stand and face the next storm on the horizon.

CHAPTER THIRTY-NINE

—

The kull tryouts consisted of three tests: a test of physical endurance, a test of weapon proficiency determined by a tournament of duels, and a test of windship knowledge that culminated in a windship race around the Grankull. Kai was optimistically hopeful for the latter, but the other two . . . were a work in progress.

Swords clashed, and the blow echoed down Kai's arms, so hard the scimitar twisted from Kai's grasp and went spinning toward the deck.

Kai shook out the lingering pain in his arms and rolled his shoulders. He attempted to catch his breath on his knees and pressed a hand to the painful stitch in his side.

"No break." Rasia slapped him on the butt with the flat side of her blade. Kai grunted and waddled bruised and sore legs over toward the fallen sword.

When Kai wasn't spending every vibration of the day getting the shit knocked out of him, or "sparring" as Rasia called it, she drilled him through various kull exercises. Even though Kai had maintained his routine of morning laps from the gorge, he felt ill-prepared for Rasia's grueling training regimen. More than once, Kai thought he was going to hack out a lung or stop breathing. Somehow, he wasn't dead yet.

Honestly, Kai wasn't sure he'd made up his mind about the kull tryouts. He felt like a windchime at times, sometimes blowing in Zephyr's direction when it came to tempering his expectations, and at other times he was wrapped up in Rasia's can-do-anything attitude. He felt one strong wind from being jostled solidly to one side or the other.

Kai bit down on a wince as he reached for the fallen sword, then paused and looked toward the hatch, half-expecting Zephyr to appear up the ladder. The lake was still messing with him. Kai didn't know why, but he kept sensing a third presence on the windship.

Kai noted the lengthening shadow crossing the deck and barely evaded the attack Rasia launched at him from behind. Rasia never gave him time to *think*.

Rasia came up with her sword, and Kai defended to the right. He stumbled to the left. Blocked right. Slashed horizontal. Blood splattered the air.

Kai stared at the cut on Rasia's arm.

Any other time he would have considered it a victory, but Rasia herself had paused. She pressed a hand flat to her chest, to the shroud-wrap because she didn't bother wearing a shirt while sparring.

"Rasia?"

Rasia gave a hard swallow, then bit out. "Fifty push-ups."

Automatically, Kai dropped to the deck at the command. Kai pushed his wobbly arms underneath him. Sweat dropped from his nose when he raised himself to the height of the first push-up.

Rasia rushed across the deck and threw up over the railing.

Kai stopped.

Kai didn't miss the perplexed expression that crossed Rasia's face as she wiped at her mouth. She hid it quickly and narrowed her eyes at him. "I didn't tell you to stop. Fifty push-ups."

Kai tried to focus on the second push-up, but his mind was a wreck now. He was concerned. Ship sickness wasn't normal for Rasia, not for someone practically born on one. She threw up yesterday too, around dinner, when he cooked their last supply of sausages. She complained the soup had smelled wrong, but Kai had found none of the ingredients spoiled.

Kai tried to remember all the potential illnesses he'd read of in the temple, but what stuck in his mind the most was the image of his tah, shroud to her mouth, the first blinks pregnant with Rae.

Rasia gurgled water and spat the taste of vomit out over the railing. Kai looked at Rasia, at her bare abdomen, overcome with dawning horror. He'd gone from trapped within his own dreams to spiraling down a horrific nightmare.

"Rasia, you're pregnant."

Rasia looked at him and laughed, tossing her hair with the movement. She said dismissively, "I'm not fucking pregnant."

Kai dropped to the deck, no longer focused on the push-ups anymore. He did the math in his head. He was unconscious for four whole days. Two days since leaving Zephyr atop the mountain. Fifteen days in total since they left the gorge behind. Her deathsblood should have come by now.

"You missed your deathsblood," Kai said.

Rasia opened her mouth to argue, then her face narrowed in calculation. She counted her fingers. "That doesn't mean anything. I could be late."

The third presence. The third presence. The third presence.

"Rasia, I know like how I know the Elder songs, like how I know the wind currents, or the breath of you. *I know.*"

Finally, *finally*, Rasia doubled over in realization, punched by it. The crippling blow blasted through her denial and left her trembling in shock.

One word spat repeatedly from her lips.

CHAPTER FORTY

O

"Fuck Fuck Fuck Fuck Fuck Fuck Fuck Fuck Fuck Fuck Fuck
Fuck Fuck Fuck Fuck Fuck Fuck Fuck Fuck Fuck Fuck Fuck
Fuck Fuck Fuck Fuck Fuck Fuck Fuck Fuck Fuck Fuck Fuck
Fuck Fuck Fuck Fuck Fuck Fuck Fuck Fuck Fuck Fuck Fuck
Fuck Fuck Fuck Fuck Fuck Fuck Fuck Fuck Fuck Fuck Fuck
Fuck Fuck Fuck Fuck Fuck Fuck Fuck Fuck Fuck Fuck Fuck
Fuck Fuck Fuck Fuck Fuck Fuck Fuck Fuck Fuck Fuck Fuck
Fuck Fuck Fuck Fuck Fuck Fuck Fuck Fuck Fuck Fuck Fuck
Fuck Fuck Fuck Fuck Fuck Fuck Fuck Fuck Fuck Fuck Fuck
Fuck Fuck Fuck Fuck Fuck Fuck Fuck Fuck Fuck Fuck Fuck
Fuck Fuck Fuck Fuck Fuck Fuck Fuck Fuck Fuck Fuck Fuck
Fuck Fuck Fuck Fuck Fuck Fuck Fuck Fuck Fuck Fuck Fuck
Fuck Fuck Fuck Fuck Fuck Fuck Fuck Fuck Fuck Fuck Fuck
Fuck Fuck Fuck Fuck Fuck Fuck Fuck Fuck Fuck Fuck Fuck
Fuck Fuck Fuck Fuck Fuck Fuck Fuck Fuck Fuck Fuck Fuck
Fuck Fuck Fuck Fuck Fuck Fuck Fuck Fuck Fuck Fuck Fuck
Fuck Fuck Fuck Fuck Fuck Fuck Fuck Fuck Fuck Fuck Fuck
Fuck Fuck Fuck Fuck Fuck Fuck Fuck Fuck Fuck Fuck Fuck
Fuck Fuck Fuck Fuck Fuck Fuck Fuck Fuck Fuck Fuck Fuck
Fuck Fuck Fuck Fuck Fuck Fuck Fuck Fuck Fuck Fuck Fuck
Fuck Fuck Fuck Fuck Fuck Fuck Fuck Fuck Fuck Fuck Fuck
Fuck Fuck Fuck Fuck Fuck Fuck Fuck Fuck Fuck Fuck Fuck

Fuck Fuck Fuck Fuck Fuck Fuck Fuck Fuck Fuck Fuck Fuck
Fuck Fuck Fuck Fuck Fuck Fuck Fuck Fuck Fuck Fuck Fuck
Fuck Fuck Fuck Fuck Fuck Fuck Fuck Fuck Fuck Fuck Fuck
Fuck Fuck Fuck Fuck Fuck Fuck Fuck Fuck Fuck Fuck Fuck
Fuck Fuck Fuck Fuck Fuck Fuck Fuck Fuck Fuck Fuck Fuck
Fuck Fuck Fuck Fuck Fuck Fuck Fuck Fuck Fuck Fuck Fuck
Fuck Fuck Fuck Fuck Fuck Fuck Fuck Fuck Fuck Fuck Fuck
Fuck Fuck Fuck Fuck Fuck Fuck Fuck Fuck Fuck Fuck Fuck
Fuck Fuck Fuck Fuck Fuck Fuck Fuck Fuck Fuck Fuck Fuck
Fuck Fuck Fuck Fuck Fuck Fuck Fuck Fuck Fuck Fuck Fuck
Fuck Fuck Fuck Fuck Fuck Fuck Fuck Fuck Fuck Fuck Fuck
Fuck Fuck Fuck Fuck Fuck Fuck Fuck Fuck Fuck Fuck Fuck
Fuck Fuck Fuck Fuck Fuck Fuck Fuck Fuck Fuck Fuck Fuck
Fuck Fuck Fuck Fuck Fuck Fuck Fuck Fuck Fuck Fuck Fuck
Fuck Fuck Fuck Fuck Fuck Fuck Fuck Fuck Fuck Fuck Fuck
Fuck Fuck Fuck Fuck Fuck Fuck Fuck Fuck Fuck Fuck Fuck
Fuck Fuck Fuck Fuck Fuck Fuck Fuck Fuck Fuck Fuck Fuck
Fuck Fuck Fuck Fuck Fuck Fuck Fuck Fuck Fuck Fuck Fuck
Fuck Fuck Fuck Fuck Fuck Fuck Fuck Fuck Fuck Fuck Fuck
Fuck Fuck Fuck Fuck Fuck Fuck Fuck Fuck Fuck Fuck Fuck
Fuck Fuck Fuck Fuck Fuck Fuck Fuck Fuck Fuck Fuck Fuck
Fuck Fuck Fuck Fuck Fuck Fuck Fuck Fuck Fuck Fuck Fuck
Fuck Fuck Fuck Fuck Fuck Fuck Fuck Fuck Fuck Fuck Fuck
Fuck Fuck Fuck Fuck Fuck Fuck Fuck Fuck Fuck Fuck Fuck
Fuck Fuck Fuck Fuck Fuck Fuck Fuck Fuck Fuck Fuck Fuck
Fuck Fuck Fuck Fuck Fuck Fuck Fuck Fuck Fuck Fuck Fuck
Fuck Fuck Fuck Fuck Fuck Fuck Fuck Fuck Fuck Fuck Fuck
Fuck Fuck Fuck Fuck Fuck Fuck Fuck Fuck Fuck Fuck Fuck
Fuck Fuck Fuck Fuck Fuck Fuck Fuck Fuck Fuck Fuck Fuck
Fuck Fuck Fuck Fuck Fuck Fuck Fuck Fuck Fuck Fuck Fuck
Fuck Fuck Fuck Fuck Fuck Fuck Fuck Fuck Fuck Fuck Fuck
Fuck Fuck Fuck Fuck Fuck Fuck Fuck Fuck Fuck Fuck Fuck
Fuck Fuck Fuck Fuck Fuck Fuck Fuck Fuck Fuck Fuck Fuck
Fuck Fuck Fuck Fuck Fuck Fuck Fuck Fuck Fuck Fuck Fuck
Fuck Fuck Fuck Fuck Fuck Fuck Fuck Fuck Fuck Fuck Fuck
Fuck Fuck Fuck Fuck Fuck Fuck Fuck Fuck Fuck Fuck *Fuck!*"

CHAPTER FORTY-ONE

O

Rasia leaped the ladder and bolted through the maze of supplies in the underbelly. She knocked into the kindling supply, tumbling it over, and the dry foliage rattled behind her. She tore at the netting that held safe a shelf of dragonglass jars.

"Rasia, what are you doing?" Kai asked. He reached the last rung of the ladder and rolled on one of the fallen branches, sending wicker baskets of scorpion fangs and leather falling one after another. Rasia didn't bother worrying about the mess.

"They test the kids after the Forging, Kai. We've got to get rid of this *now*." Rasia lifted the glass jars to the thin rays of sunlight coming through the deckboards. She squinted at the contents.

Rasia wouldn't have the chance to pay someone to cut it out of her. The moment the windship returned to the Grankull, they would march everyone to the healers for their annual medical exam. Rasia had planned to wash thoroughly beforehand, but how was she going to pass the piss test if she was actually fucking pregnant?

Rasia had done some dumb shit in her life, but she thought this time around, she had been *careful*. She and Kai only slipped up once. She should have taken Kai a lot more seriously when he claimed he had extremely bad luck. No shit. Lightning-strikes-the-same-place-twice type of bad luck. Rasia couldn't believe this.

Rasia finally found the jar she was looking for. Couldn't mistake gonda venom for anything else, the color was an unnatural green that reminded her of scarab beetles. Without hesitation, she popped open the lid and put it to her lips. The venom tasted even worse in its liquid form. Concentrated, it was all metallic bitterness. Rasia swallowed it down.

"Rasia!" Kai shouted. He dove forward and yanked the jar out of her hands. But it was empty now. Kai looked at it and sniffed. "What is this?"

"It's fine. It's gonda venom."

"*What?!*" Kai exploded.

Rasia balked at Kai's outburst. She'd never seen him this type of angry before, tinged with panic and fear. His irises whirled.

"Relax. It's practically the same thing as gonom."

"*No*, it's not! Gonom is diluted with other stuff to make it less deadly!"

"I've been poisoned before, Kai. I have some resistance to it, and . . ." Rasia lifted the jar that sat right next to the venom on her poison shelf. "I have the antidote."

Rasia loosened her pants and kicked them off. She settled back against the bunk with the antidote at her hip. Rasia glared between her legs and willed this seed to hurry and bleed out of her.

"Once the poison does what it needs to do, I'll take the antidote. It'll be fine. I know what I'm doing. Get above deck before we crash into something. Someone needs to watch the steer."

"I'm stopping the windship."

"*Don't you dare.*"

Kai stopped the windship.

Rasia hit her head back against the inner hull, annoyed. An odd sensation tingled through her legs and arms, and then—a sudden electric jolt. Her head tossed back, knocking against the hull as a seizure wracked her body.

She blinked, dazed, once it was over. Felt as if she had been ploughed down by a gonda. She shakily pulled herself up, where she had fallen cheek to the bunk, and looked between her legs.

No blood.

"Rasia, this is madness," Kai said, pupils blown and terrified. Rasia startled, not knowing when Kai had rejoined her below deck. He crouched beside her with the antidote jar cradled in his hands. "You need to take the antidote."

"No, not yet. Not until this thing is out of me."

"What if you die, Rasia?"

"I'm not going to fucking die. I've survived the deadlands. I've survived the shadowcats. I've survived the fucking Lake of Yestermorrow, and I'm not going to die of some basic ass gonda venom. Besides . . ." Rasia rolled her head toward him. "If Kibata finds out about this, I'll be dead anyway."

Rasia unknotted her wrap because it was getting harder to breathe. Sweat pooled in her cleavage as she shivered. It was so hot all of a sudden. She scrambled for Kai. "I can't breathe. It's too hot. Help me above deck."

Kai dipped his shoulder under her arm and grabbed her about the waist. For a moment, his other hand brushed her stomach and he paused, glancing down at her abdomen. Rasia never would have known anything was there and wondered what it was like for him, to be able to sense it.

"What does it feel like?" Rasia asked, accepting she'd regret the knowing but too curious for her own good.

Kai supported her through the maze of mess they made in the underbelly. Both the question and physical exertion had him quiet for a while, until he finally said, "A firefly. So small it's easy to miss, until it glows."

Uncertain emotions welled in Rasia's throat, and she swallowed them all down. Kai helped lift her up the ladder rungs and out onto the windship deck.

Kai laid her down in the same space where they first had sex. Then Rasia proceeded to immediately shit all over herself—the nasty, runny kind that pasted her bare backside to the deck. The name carved into the mast looked down at her with so much disappointment.

"I . . . umm . . . I'll go get something to clean you," Kai stammered.

"Wait, Kai, don't—" Rasia grasped his hand, right as a seizure wracked through her limbs, twisting the top half of her body one way, and the bottom half another.

The pain hurt as much as when that shadowcat almost sliced her in half. Rasia gritted her teeth, dazed, and foggily searched for the blood.

Nothing.

"Please, Rasia," Kai sobbed, still holding her hand. "Take the antidote. We'll keep the baby. We'll stay out here. We don't have to return to the Grankull. You don't have to do this, Rasia."

Huh. That sounded pretty nice . . . and absolutely fucking insane.

Rasia was going to kill her ta-fucking dragon. She was going to earn her face, and her names, and nothing was going to stand in her way, not even this stubborn-as-fuck piece of her that refused to come out.

"No," Rasia growled out. "I want my names."

The next seizure struck, so blinding it knocked her unconscious. She woke to the whiff of a sweetly floral scent, and something pushed to her lips.

"It's gone, Rasia. It's gone. Drink, *please.*"

Rasia tried to focus the triple vision that swam through her eyes and locked onto the red that smeared her thighs and the windship deck. It was a smear of deep black, easily mistaken for the clumps of blood that comes out of her during her deathsblood. It didn't look at all discernible to an actual baby from what Rasia could see. Just blood. She'd spilled so much of it in her lifetime.

Rasia fought for the strength to open her mouth. She swallowed the too-sweet antidote, then collapsed back into Kai's lap, an utter mess, exhausted, and smug in the knowledge that Death hadn't caught her today.

As soon as the thought crossed her mind, in vengeance, a seizure ripped through her body and squeezed out all her insides. Rasia vomited up acid and bile. More blood cramped past her thighs. Liquid leaked out her ears. Kai looked on with horrified eyes.

Something was wrong.

The symptoms weren't abating, but growing in intensity. She had taken the antidote too late. Or she had taken too much poison to begin with. Somewhere close, Death was laughing at her.

This sucked.

Rasia was a star pinned high to the Hunter's Cloak. She orbited a windship that belonged to a stupid, idiotic, dumb kid—a kid who thought themselves too skilled, too experienced, and too talented for Death to catch them. That dumb kid gazed up at her, as confused and terrified as a fallen star far from home. Tears fell, joining the mess of shit and blood, a sight so undignified the star felt embarrassed for her.

Kai, that shimmering wing-sail sunlight, cleaned the poor thing. He fanned her when sweat stuck to her skin. He poured water past her lips. He cried and held her while seizures ruined her body. Kai kissed her, and in a panic, the star realized this might be the last one. *Ever.*

The star hurled down from the sky in desperation, crash landing, exploding with pain all throughout Rasia's body. No longer floating outside herself, Rasia pressed her lips to Kai and tasted snot and tears. But she was remembering the first one, and the second, and all the ones in between.

The kiss ended all too soon. Rasia was supposed to have a lifetime for more. Kai gripped her tightly into a hug, and Rasia sobbed into his skin. The words cracked hoarse and sour in her throat. *"I was supposed to be invincible."*

This wasn't how her story was supposed to end.

"Kai," Rasia said with the last of her strength she could muster. She needed him to continue. She needed him to understand. "You better live with my death for the rest of your days. You live and see all the things I couldn't see and do all the things I should've done. You kill my ta-fucking dragon. Eat well, and laugh loud, and cry for me. I am not sacrificing myself for you. This is not for free. My death has a price and I fully expect you to pay it. Continue my story, Kai."

"Rasia," Kai sobbed, holding her. "I can't do this without you. I need you. You promised you weren't going to die for me."

Rasia blinked. "When the fuck did I say that?"

"At the gorge."

"Well, I change my mind."

"What if we turn around?" Kai begged. "Nico and the others are only a couple of days behind us."

"No. Turning. Around." What would be the point? Rasia wasn't going to last that long. Might as well keep sailing on.

"But, Rasia—"

"Stop arguing with me. I'm dying. You messed up my cool last words."

Kai's eyes narrowed at her. "You die on me, and I'm telling everyone your last words were a dramatic confession of your secret flame for Nico."

Rasia gasped. "*You wouldn't.*"

"Don't die."

Rasia would laugh if she could, but it hurt too much. She smiled at him and regretted nothing. It was fun while it lasted.

"Thank you," Rasia whispered. "I always thought I'd die alone."

"Wait, Rasia. You promised what I wanted most in the whole world. I want you. I've changed my mind. I want you. Don't you give up on me."

Tears rained down on her cheeks. Rasia felt another seizure coming, and she thought this was the big one, for she felt no pain. She turned and saw the face of Death, waiting for her, like an old, patient friend.

All hunters are hunted.

CHAPTER FORTY-TWO

—

Kai refused to lose anyone else. He had watched his tah's death and wouldn't do the same for Rasia. Kai was not letting her die today.

Rasia's breath whispered thready and weak after the last seizure. He needed to hurry before the next one hit.

Kai rushed to the windship steer and turned the ship around. He didn't care if Rasia was going to be angry about it, she could be angry at him alive.

He sailed the windship at full speed, toward a dark horizon crowned by stars. Kai hadn't been aware when the sun had set. The only passing of time he'd experienced was that of one dying breath to the next.

The Lake of Yestermorrow showed Kai many things. Kenji wasn't the first vision the Lake of Yestermorrow had used to tempt him down its dark depths. The lake also gave Kai the truth of his magic, but it had been so unbelievable, so impossible, Kai had dismissed it.

But if Rasia were going to live, he needed to believe in that dream. He needed to believe it was true.

Breath control was important for controlling magic. Physical resilience was important for enduring it. But to consciously use it—to summon rain, or breathe fire, or grow orchards—you simply must want it.

Magic had always come easily to Nico, someone who had never hesitated to fight for her goals. Kai, on the other hand, had never been sure he wanted magic in the first place. It had done nothing but complicate and ruin his life. Nor had Kai ever allowed himself to reach for his wants, not before the Forging, not before Rasia.

No more time for thinking. His body could endure—would endure. It had no choice not to.

Kai sucked in the deepest breath he could muster and wanted that horizon line like he'd never wanted anything in his entire fucking life. He wanted with a singular focus and fire. He wanted so powerfully the world bent to his will.

A suction of wind popped his eardrums.

Kai blinked and the mountaintop loomed overhead, filling his vision. Kai slammed down the steer, and the windship skidded to a stop. He scooped Rasia into his arms, wrapped her in his cloak, and hauled her down the stairs.

Kai slid to his knees cradling Rasia in his arms.

"Nico-ji, *save her.*"

CHAPTER FORTY-THREE

I

Nico finally stopped chasing Rasia, and now, here she was. Bloody and offered to Nico like some half-wilted flower.

"Nico-ji, *save her.*"

Nico didn't hesitate.

She ordered, "Kelin, grab water from the windship, and drag Azan out of the way. Suri, go get your supplies. Zephyr, carry Rasia."

Barely anyone had time to catch their breath before the next incident came ramming on top of them, but nevertheless, they pushed through Nico's orders.

Kai's arms shook. Whatever adrenaline had gotten Kai this far threatened to fail him at any moment. Kai buckled in relief when Zephyr retrieved Rasia's weight.

Nico directed Zephyr over to her bedroll. Zephyr placed Rasia atop the reed mat, and Rasia's arms and legs spilled out of the cloak wrapped around her. Rasia's weak breathing unsettled Nico. Rasia was nothing if not tough and near indestructible, and it was hard to reconcile that with this image of sickness and naked vulnerability.

"Zephyr, we need light."

Zephyr relit the campfire, which had burned out while rescuing Azan from the silk spiders. Faint strings distracted Nico's vision, glistening off the firelight. She snatched the spiderwebs from her hair.

Suri walked out of the darkness with her bag of medical supplies. She crouched and pressed the back of her hand to Rasia's forehead.

Rasia smelled horrendous. The smell should have warned Nico what to expect when Suri tossed aside the cloak, but she found herself startled to spy the chunks of vomit in Rasia's hair, the sticky sheen of sweat, and smears of blood. She looked like Death.

"I've been cleaning her between seizures, but I ran out of water. I did the best I could," Kai said, defensively.

"Poison?" Suri asked. Before Kai could confirm, she began digging in her satchel for her stash of antidotes. Zephyr handed Nico a torch, and Nico moved over to give Suri more light to aid her search.

"Yes. Gonda venom," Kai said.

"This looks like a severe reaction, even for gonda venom. How much did she breathe in?"

"It was the liquid form. She ingested it."

Suri's eyes widened.

"With all due respect, Suriyah, I'm not here for your expertise. It's too late for that." Kai turned to face Nico, full of fire. "I need *you*, Nico. Your magic allows you to control anything in liquid form. You can get the poison out."

Kai was talking but Nico's brain was still stuck on the first part. There was absolutely no reason anyone would ingest undiluted concentrated gonom venom, unless they didn't have a choice, and there were no better options. It was the type of stupid desperation someone would do if—if—Nico's mind blanked to a startling silence. Before she could get her thoughts that far, Kai formed the words for her.

"I accidentally seeded her."

Nico slapped him.

The strike echoed off Kai's cheek. It echoed off the boulders and howled in the wind. Nico stared at her own hand, stinging, with absolute horror and clutched at the rebellious limb.

"I'm sorry. I didn't mean—I . . ."

She wasn't sorry. She was so sorry. Nico had never struck Kai in her entire life. How could she have done such a thing? Anger choked her. Disappointment flooded her senses. Both at Kai, and at her own reaction when that first strike of fury zapped through her.

How could Kai do something so utterly stupid? This wasn't just a mistake of one. This was the sort of mistake that could affect and ostracize an entire family. One male. One female. That was the cost of an unplanned seed. That was the sort of cost that ripped families apart. If Kai had died out here, and Rasia made it back to the Grankull pregnant, someone would still have had to pay that price.

Nico had spent so many drums of planning, and so many days of other people's Forging trying to protect him, trying to make sure he survived, and here he was practically spitting in her face.

And for what? *For what?*

For Rasia?!

That kulo could burn.

Kai grasped her by the arms. "Nico, please. *She's dying.* I need you. *Help me.*"

Now, he was asking for her help. Nico squeezed her eyes shut and tried to get all her fury, dark thoughts, and worst impulses under control. There was no time for anger or regret or forgiveness. When the ground vibrated, you did what you had to do. You put it all aside and got it done.

Nico crouched in front of Rasia's prone form and confronted the monumental task Kai had asked of her. Nico could barely control anything other than water. And she was drained from the silk spiders. And all the bruises, the demanding heat, and the relentless pace of the Forging suddenly weighed on her shoulders. She was *so* exhausted.

What if she wasn't enough?

Rasia's body shuddered, then quaked as Rasia arched off the ground with a breathless scream. Suri and Kai pounced to hold

Rasia down.

"*Nico!*"

The poison stopped. A breath from Rasia's heart. Nico licked her lips in concentration.

It was so much easier to call upon the full might of her magic, but to control it so precisely, to move it through branched veins, had Nico's nerves churning. All Nico's life, control and perfection had been battered into her bones. Nico couldn't afford to fail the moment it mattered the most.

The vacuous venom weighed heavy and thick. Flush out the digestive tract. Collect all the strays. Coalesce the poison particle by particle, one by one, like counting fine grains of sand. Nico was moving not just venom, but also water and blood, breaking apart infected cells in the bloodstream.

Nico was so focused, for once she didn't feel the loose strands of hair at the back of her neck, or the spiderwebs she missed on her shoulder, or the sweat dripping and stinging her eyes. Nothing mattered but the work, particle by particle.

Nico willed the poison through Rasia's veins, up and up, through the digestive tract, then the throat, until a thick tar cloud came vomiting out.

It hung suspended in the air, and Nico swatted that black cloud into the fire.

Nico tilted forward.

She blinked, finding herself collapsed over Rasia. Nico was so cold she couldn't feel it. She saw her breath when she breathed. But Nico scraped dirt under her fingernails to push herself back up. She scanned Rasia again to make sure she had gotten all the poison. Rasia's breathing evened out.

"She's clear. It's gone," Nico croaked out.

"Thank you," Kai whispered, hoarse. "*Thank you.*"

Nico surrendered to the unforgiving chill, and Kai caught an arm around her waist. As long as Nico had known Kai, he had always been warm, but depleted of magic, Kai felt like a fire. Like falling into the sun.

The next time Nico opened her eyes, she found her cheek

laying on Kai's thigh, and the sight of Rasia slumbering on the other.

Rasia's eyes peeked open.

Nico and Rasia stared at each other, blinking, and both at once, went back to sleep.

CHAPTER FORTY-FOUR

—

There were two waking Rasias. The one who woke lazy and slow after Kai had fucked her brains out, and the other one, the Rasia who immediately woke alert and grabbed for her swords. On this morning, Rasia's swords were far away on the windship, but Kai certainly opened his eyes to the latter. Kai didn't know how long she'd been awake, but he had no doubt she'd been listening and taking stock of the situation.

Behind where Rasia and Kai lay, Kelin and Azan talked over the morning campfire while stirring grain for breakfast. As usual, Zephyr slept heavy, and his familiar snores reverberated like first drum at rising dawn. Kai knew Nico was staring at them, her eyes burning into his back and waiting to strike the moment he and Rasia moved.

"*You turned around,*" Rasia accused.

"And I'd do it again," Kai defended. "Nico saved your life. She's the only one who could have."

"Considering she's been staring daggers at me, I assume she knows."

"She knows."

Rasia clicked her tongue. "We'll eat breakfast because that shit smells good, but then we're sailing on."

"You almost died, Rasia. We can afford to take a break."

"You turned around, which means we've lost two whole days." Rasia scrunched her face. "How long have I been out?"

"We haven't lost as much time as you think. I magicked us here. Grew wings, then lifted the entire windship. You wouldn't have missed it if you weren't too busy dying on me."

Rasia cracked out a laugh. She smiled at him, eyes melting warm as she scanned his face, then pulled forward.

Kai raised a hand to block the kiss.

"I don't favor vomit for breakfast."

Rasia snorted. She attempted to leverage on her forearm to get upright. At her visible struggle, Kai helped her sit up, and a shadow immediately loomed over them. Nico glared down at the two of them, hands on her hips.

The slap last night had startled Kai. He'd never seen Nico strike *anyone* in anger. Nico prided herself on her self-control, and Kai hated that he was the one who'd cracked it. He was pissed at her for hitting him, a line Kai didn't think Nico would ever cross, but if Rasia had died, if she had died . . . he would have been glad that Nico had. It was a messy tangle of emotions he was too tired to deal with. But Nico wasn't giving him the choice.

"You're awake. Good. We need to talk."

"Rasia needs to rest right now, jih," Kai said.

"I don't need no rest," Rasia declared.

Rasia pressed a hand down on Kai's shoulder to pull herself to her feet. She wobbled. Her legs folded, and Kai scrambled to catch her. She fell, curling like a snake into his lap. Rasia stared over his arm and blinked at the pallet of hair in the bedroll. She reached a slow hand up to her head and watched strands of her hair fall away in surprise.

"Oh."

"Kai is correct. She does need to rest," Suri said as she rushed over, tone angled sharply at Nico. Kai frowned and looked between the two friends. Suri crouched to check Rasia's heartbeat through her neck. "Rasia, your body has suffered significant trauma. Please, lie down."

Those weren't words Rasia accepted easily. He felt her

frustration coil against his chest. Rasia didn't like to show injury, and didn't like to feel helpless, especially in front of those who raised her hackles.

It didn't help when Nico demanded, "How did this happen? How could you have been so stupid?"

"It's my fault," Kai said, facing the brunt of Nico's wrath. "I forgot to pull out."

"*You forgot to pull out?*" Nico echoed in utter disbelief. "Rasia almost died last night! The Grankull would have had both of your faces, all because you *forgot* to pull out?!"

Suri asked, calmer and more professional. "Is that the only time? You've only had vaginal sex once?"

Kai blushed, embarrassed to talk about sex in front of his jih. Rasia had no such reservations. She shifted in Kai's lap and defended, "Technically no, but the other times we used gonom."

"*Gonom?!*" Nico slapped herself in the face. She peeked through her fingers and looked over her shoulder to make sure the others hadn't heard her outburst. She hissed. "If anyone reports to the Grankull that you are illegally in possession of gonom, your Forgings are over."

"Are *you* going to report us?" Rasia challenged.

That vein at the top of Nico's forehead pulsed.

"Besides . . ." Rasia shrugged. "It's all gone now. I drank all of it the first time we had sex. I didn't have much to begin with."

Nico froze. Suri's eyes widened in horror. That was the moment Kai knew he was missing something.

Suri said, "*Rasia,* that is not how gonom works. You don't drink it the day you have sex and that's it. For it to be effective, you need to drink it *every* day. You haven't been having safe sex *at all.*"

Kai stopped breathing. *Fuck.* Jih was right. He was stupid.

"How does that make any sense?" Rasia moaned.

"We learned this in school."

"I didn't go to fucking school! Excuse me if it's not all that intuitive!"

Nico clutched at her head, probably giving herself one of

those stress headaches. Nico pointed at Rasia and accused, "You don't even care. You're not even apologetic."

"What do you want me to say, Nico? That yes, we fucked up. What does it matter anymore? It's gone."

"All of this is your fault! If you hadn't seduced jih in your twisted game of revenge against me, none of this would have happened."

"The fuck you talking about?" Rasia laughed. She laughed so hard she threw up. She coughed out acidic bile into the grass. Kai pressed a supportive hand to her back.

"I'll brew her some tea," Suri offered. "It'll help stabilize her stomach. Then she needs to eat."

"She needs to have some self-control and stop hopping on every dick she sees."

Kai's brows rose. Even Nico paused, as if realizing she said that aloud. She didn't take it back but only dug in her heels further. Rasia was more than happy to attack bite for bite.

"Last I checked, being his jih didn't give you the authority to tell him where to wet it."

"I hoped he'd at least have the self-respect enough not to stick it in a public cesspit."

"This pussy is amazing!"

"That's what all tent whores claim."

"Excuse you, he got it for free."

"No one would want it if it weren't."

"ENOUGH!" Kai barked between them, standing.

Nico's mouth clacked shut in surprise. Yes. Kai and Rasia messed up, and Kai was willing to atone for that, but he was so tired of their petty fights. Rasia was not going to get any rest as long as Nico was in the vicinity.

"You want to talk, Nico? Let's talk. You and me. In private."

"Fine." Nico turned on her heel. Kai followed her up the mountain trail to walk straight into the conversation he'd been avoiding the entire Forging.

Nico stopped and rubbed at her temples. It was a Nico thing. She was the only one in the family who got such headaches, but she reminded Kai of tah when Nico crossed her arms and cut him with that sharp, cold anger. Kai approached her with his own temper, hot and quaking.

"Let's get a few things straight, Nico. One, Rasia did not seduce me. Two, I was not manipulated. Three, I know this might be hard to believe, but Rasia doesn't spend every vibration of the day devising ways to ruin your life. She is not the villain you always make her out to be."

"Kai, if she truly cared about you, she would have waited to have sex until the Naming Ceremony. Why do you think she didn't? She's using you."

"You're doing it again. You're imagining schemes where there are none. Rasia didn't wait because she's the most impatient person I've ever met. That's it. Doesn't mean she cares for me any more or any less."

"No one puts someone they truly care about in this position."

"I put myself in this position!" Kai snapped. "I am equally at fault. I should have known better too."

"How could you have known better? You wouldn't have known anything about gonom or sex. We've never—"

"We've never talked about these things because you didn't think I'd need to know," Kai finished for her. "Because Ava-ta is dead and no one thought to teach me, so I relied on Rasia to know what she was doing, but she didn't. My ignorance does not excuse my actions, as it does not excuse Rasia hers. We are both equally at fault. We both messed up, but Rasia almost died to fix it. She would have died if that meant one of us could walk away from the consequences alive. *She saved my life.*"

"After she's the one who put you in danger in the first place! Like the lake. She might have pulled you out of it, but she's the one who pushed you in. One of these days, there's going to be a mistake Rasia won't be able to fix, and I refuse to see you as her casualty. We are going home, Kai. We are going to hunt our gonda and *we are going home!*"

"No!"

Nico rubbed at her forehead and took a deep breath. She

shifted strategies and said softly, "You like her. I understand how a first flame can feel all-consuming, but life is full of flames, Kai. I assure you there is someone out there who is better for you, who will take care of you and treat you like you deserve. You shouldn't have to settle for Rasia because you believe it's all you'll ever get."

Kai hissed at that jab. "Why is Rasia worth less than some future hypothetical that might never happen? You have never given Rasia a fair chance."

"I've given Rasia all the chances! Time and time again, she has thrown them in my face. How am I supposed to trust either of you after Rasia turns up half-dead and seeded in your arms? I had stopped chasing you. I *stopped*, because I thought you responsible enough to make your own decisions. How am I supposed to trust you now?"

"It. Was. A. Mistake."

"YOU DO NOT HAVE THE LUXURY OF MAKING MISTAKES! The Council has been clamoring to kill you since you were born! You can't afford to mess around as if there aren't any consequences! One wrong move, and you're dead! This is exactly why Rasia is so dangerous. You're not thinking, Kai. This whole Forging has been a disaster since the moment you met her."

"Meeting Rasia was the best thing that's ever happened to me. Because of her, I want to slay a dragon. I want to be more than just a scribe and a life of empty pages. I want to try out for the kulls and be a windeka. I want Kenjinn Ilhani to see my face. I've never, in my entire life, gotten anything I've wanted. I want this."

Nico tightened her jaw and told Kai the awful truth. "You don't get to have this, Kai. You can't walk this world the same as everyone else. Your actions are judged more harshly than everyone else. While everyone else's mistakes cost an apology, your mistakes cost you your life."

"Then I decide what mistakes I spend my life on! I choose Rasia. I choose the only chance I'm ever going to get to be someone and do something worthwhile."

"Wake up, Kai, and stop living in Rasia's world! It isn't yours! You are *never* going to slay a dragon. You are *never* going to pass the kull tryouts. You are *never* going to be a windeka." Her voice watered on her own words. "Kenji-ta is *never* going to give you the chance you deserve. Those things aren't for you."

One strong wind.

Ever since the lake, Kai had been trying to make up his mind on which way he wanted to go. Kai's jaw hardened. His eyes tightened. He'd prove Nico wrong or die trying if she was right.

Kai stormed away. He descended the trail and curved into camp. He approached Rasia, who sat bent over washing her mouth out with charcoal. She looked at him as she approached, teeth black, and immediately tensed for a fight. Kai bent down and pulled her into that kiss. Kai had always kissed Rasia as if he'd never get another chance. He thought of her like wind, ample to blow away at any moment, but this time Kai stamped her lips with possessiveness, as if able to deny Death the power to touch her ever again.

Kai crouched down, and without question or hesitation, Rasia hooked her arms around his neck. Kai hefted her onto his back and carried her past the serving plates of porridge, past Suri's unfinished tea, and Zephyr's unsurprised expression.

Kai rushed Rasia over to their windship and up the stairs, then sat her down against the railing. He lifted the anchor and dug the oar into the ground to turn the ship. Right into Nico, standing in the way to stop him.

"I'm not letting you leave!" Nico threatened. "Get off that ship right now! I won't hesitate to use magic to stop you."

Kai pressed down on the steer.

He took a breath before Nico did. Nico's eyes widened and pressed her hands to her throat, choking on air. She fell to her knees gasping, and Kai steered around her.

Kai sailed on.

CHAPTER FORTY-FIVE

I

Nico needed some time alone. She hiked up the mountain trail and watched the murmuring mountain creek for a long time, trying to regain her balance. She focused on the water and practiced her breathing. Gradually, her pounding headache lessened. Her storms calmed.

A colony of bats filled the sky, marking sunset, and Nico picked herself up and walked back down the mountain.

Suri and Azan worked the cooking pit, their turns at preparing dinner. Kelin took advantage of his downtime to wash clothes. It was nice how they were all pretending nothing had happened, as if Nico hadn't made an embarrassment out of herself just that morning.

Except Zephyr. He couldn't let her get away with anything. His brows probably would have been more intimidating if he hadn't been talking to the inside of a wicker basket.

Nico sighed and came over to sit down beside him.

Zephyr reached into his satchel and lifted a squealing rat. He lowered it into the wicker basket between his legs. The rat screeched until the spider's paralytic got ahold of it. The baby silk spider happily wrapped its dinner.

Nico whispered between them, "I keep thinking . . . what if I never see Kai again? Will those be the last words I've said to him?

What have I done?"

"The whole situation came as a shock. It was a lot to process," Zephyr said, making excuses for her, then said gently, "I'm sure he knows you don't react well to surprises."

"You didn't hear the things I said. You didn't see his face. It crushed him. But how are he and Rasia supposed to take down a dragon alone? How is he supposed to try out for the kulls? Can you imagine how tah will react if Kai embarrasses him in front of all his friends? Tah is trying to *banish* him. The night before the Forging tah—he—" Nico choked and stuffed her face into her hands. She sobbed. "I just want to protect him."

"Nico . . . you can't," Zephyr told her. "When I left the Desert, my father had warned me about his people, but I didn't listen. I thought I knew what I was doing, and it almost got me killed. You can't sail Kai's Forging for him. All you can do is be there when he asks for help. And you were, Nico. You saved her, and he'll remember that."

Nico locked her hands together and crouched over her knees. "Tah and the Council never had the best relationship, and they doubted her when tah claimed something was broken with Kai's magic. Tah was dead for four days, when I returned from school to find Kai *whipped*. The Council had dragged him out of the house in front of Rae, left Rae home alone by themselves, and returned Kai whipped and bloody. And I thought, stupidly, naively, there must have been a mistake. I went and confronted the Council myself, and it was then I learned exactly how much tah had been protecting us. They made their excuses, but I know the truth. They wanted Kai *dead*. The only reason he isn't is because Rae ran to tajih's house, and tajih stopped it. Tajih ran for the Council after that to protect us, but that's only one vote. Kai makes one mistake, and they'll break him for it. They hate him. They hate him so much. And I don't—I don't know how to protect him from that."

"You can't keep him shrouded forever, Nico," Zephyr said. "People are always going to hate him. It's not fair, but that's the truth. He's got to learn to live with it. There's no choice but to learn to live with it. And it's not easy, but at least he's got one of the toughest jihs I know on his side."

Zephyr raised his arm. Nico sighed out and leaned into his shoulder. Next time she saw Kai, she'd know what to say. She'd practice her words. She'd be better. Nico glanced down at the open wicker basket and the silk spider climbing the sides looking for more dinner.

Unafraid, Zephyr reached down and petted the thorax. Nico hoped he wasn't getting too attached and this wasn't another puppy farm situation. Both Zephyr's dogs had been rescues.

Zephyr looked at her, eyes round, and Nico sighed before Zephyr asked the question, "Maybe we can find different bait for the gonda?"

Nico patted her hand on his knee.

"Everyone's got to eat," Nico said absently. Then after a pause, she said to him, "I am here for you too, you know. When the hate becomes too heavy, I am here."

"I know," Zephyr smiled. He held his hand out palm up, and Nico gripped it with both hands.

It was so hard for Nico—the fact she couldn't carry the weight for them. She hurt to watch those she cared for struggle. But there's no growth without rain, Kenji-ta used to say.

"You'll make it right," Zephyr told her. "You always do."

CHAPTER FORTY-SIX

O

Rasia smoothed a hand over her bare head. Most had molted off, but when Kai floored the windship away from Nico, the wind had taken the rest. Kai helped to shave the few stubborn patches left with his dagger. Rasia wondered if this was what a granscorpion felt like without its carapace, or a hyena without its pelt. She felt stripped of skin, exposed, and scratched raw by every brush of air.

Rasia had escaped Death before, but it had been so close this time, as if Death's claws had raked against her skin and taken chunks out of her. She felt porous and off-balance. Or maybe it was the lack of hair. Who knew hair could hold so much weight?

"Are you alright?" Kai asked.

Rasia turned to Kai, who sat behind her. Back on the windship, Rasia had struggled to stand for any length of time, so Kai pulled the windship over and made camp so they both could get some rest. Or so he'd claimed. He had probably done it so he could keep an eye on her without having to steer.

Kai leaned against a large rock formation that formed a hollow wrapping them in a hard hug. It was a good spot for a camp, and judging from evidence of past campfires, scavengers had thought the same.

"Am I still sexy without my hair?" Rasia couldn't help but to ask, self-conscious, finally feeling like all her peers taking off their shrouds for the first time.

"Of course you are," Kai said, too fast in Rasia's opinion. "I think all the insects and small creatures that made it home will miss it more."

Rasia pushed her hand into his face, smiling. She barely applied much strength behind the playful shove, but Kai dropped down on his side. He stared up at her, with an intense gaze, searching her face. Something uncomfortable twisted her stomach. Rasia used one of the nearby rocks to temporarily stand and brush off the snippets of hair.

"Remember the first time we had sex?" Rasia asked.

"I'll never forget."

"I hadn't taken my wrap off in years. It had sort of melded together and I couldn't take it off even if I wanted to. Then you cut me out of it, and suddenly I was exposed and off-balance and never realized how it had become a second skin. It feels the same without my hair. Dying sucks."

Rasia spread out her bedroll, weak kneed, and laid across the mat in painful relief. Kai joined her, and it felt good when he wrapped an arm around her waist. She stared at the stars, too tired to move her body and process all the tossed emotions the poison had left in its wake.

"I'm sorry," Rasia whispered.

"For what?"

"About the gonom. I thought I knew what I was doing. I never intended for this to happen."

"I know."

Rasia tangled their fingers and tucked his arm under her head. She was still feeling spasms through her body.

"Rasia," Kai said, after a moment.

"Hmm?"

Kai shifted onto his forearm. Rasia turned to look at him, with that intensity in his eyes again. He licked his lips. "I want more. I want to be more than just friends. I want to . . . court . . . you."

Rasia laughed, and immediately regretted it when pain stabbed through her ribs. That injury too, was annoyingly still there. At Kai's wince, Rasia realized Kai had been serious, and it wasn't some joke she hallucinated.

"I'm sorry. That was stupid." Kai laughed at himself, sharp and hollow, then turned and huddled away from her.

Technically, courting wasn't too different from what they were doing now, except that courting was a blatant declaration of intentions to pursue her in the hopes of a romantic commitment. It was the commitment part that was the problem.

"Kai, I . . . I almost just died," Rasia said, unable to be anything but honest. "I've only ever had sex with you. There's so much I haven't done yet. I want to kiss other people. I want to have sex with other people. The last thing I want to do is tie someone else's name to mine." Rasia stared at his back. "This doesn't have to change anything."

"You probably think me a fool."

"Not necessarily. I am awesome," Rasia said lightly.

"It's not awesome being on the other side," he mumbled.

"We can still fuck."

Kai turned at that and gave Rasia the most frigid, unimpressed glare imaginable.

Rasia quickly amended, "I *mean*—no sex until after the Naming Ceremony. I've learned my lesson. No more mistakes. No more accidents. We'll do this the right way."

"How mature of you."

"I know. It sucks. Try not to miss this ass."

"If only I had an ounce of your self-control."

"Ha! I have plenty of self-control."

"Your hand was once dipped into the Lake of Yestermorrow because you don't."

Rasia's smile warmed. "Kai, I like you. You're literally the first friend I've ever made other than jih, and he doesn't really count. Even beyond the Forging, and beyond the tryouts, that fact doesn't change. The lake tried to give me everything I could possibly want, but all I wanted was you. That's not fate, or bones thrown. I chose you. You and I, and our kull, that's forever."

CHAPTER FORTY-SEVEN

—

Kai slowed his lap of the windship, unable to keep his eyes off the mountain of bones growing ever taller.

The Graveyard was comprised of the dead bones of mythic dragons, hundreds of them that matched the size of the Great Elder, each one an entire mountain unto itself. Back atop the mountain range, the Graveyard had looked like a hill of bones, one shift of wind from toppling over. But now, as they crept into its shadow, Kai was awed by its monstrosity.

While the bones of the Great Elder were white and cared for by the scribes, the Graveyard had whole ecosystems flourishing in their shade. They were much larger than the dragon Kai and Rasia were currently hunting, like comparing a hill to a mountain, but both a task to climb.

"Sometimes I wish they were still alive," Rasia said as she joined Kai at the railing. "I've dedicated seasons preparing for a hunt, so much so that when it's all over, I feel empty. To defeat an elder dragon would take more than seasons, possibly even years. I'd dedicate my entire lifetime to defeating one, and I think I would be happy with that."

"What happens after?" Kai asked, never doubting that if Rasia put her mind to it, she could defeat anything. "When you've defeated the strongest predator the world has ever known, and everything else seems like grubworms, what then?"

"Then I'll have you." Rasia smirked. Her words brought his thoughts back to that night two days when Rasia turned him down. He knew it had been a long shot. She nudged him in the shoulder. "Hey, you've still got seventeen laps to go."

Rasia moved to slap him, aiming for the butt. She hesitated and lamely patted his back, afraid of sending mixed signals. She pushed him into movement, and Kai continued his jog around the windship.

It was weird. They were friends. But the boundaries were more twisted, looped up, than ever before.

Kai shook his head and focused on surviving the morning's exercises. He hacked his way through the lunges, and sit-ups, and pull-ups, and crunches until he collapsed.

"Stop being so melodramatic. Come on, eat." Rasia nudged her foot against his thigh.

He reluctantly bit into the sour gooseberries and wild celery cooked with their stash of dried scorpion meat. It made him sick to eat sometimes, not in the bubbling nauseous way it used to when he started eating full meals, but sick in his bones to know that his little jih was back in the Grankull eating rations that didn't fill their belly. Every time he allowed himself to think about the amount of food he consumed now, it gagged him.

Kai finished his meal as Rasia steered the windship into the shadow of a large sand dune, keeping them out of the Graveyard's line of sight. She crouched in front of him with her map spread across the deck.

Her eyes narrowed, like a jackal who'd gotten the scent of prey. Kai straightened to attention.

"We lose three days if we go around, so we have no choice but to go through. If everything goes according to plan, it should only take a day. There are trails large enough to bring in the windship, but they are few, and it'll make us a target. If we want to make it out alive, we have no choice but to strike a deal with the scavengers."

"What's it like in there?"

"There are only two places in the entire Desert with enough water able to support life, the Grankull and the Graveyard. But the Graveyard sits right at the crossroads of the gonda breeding grounds, the Dragon's Coast, and the silk spider mines, so you would either have to be desperate or crazy to live there."

"Would you?"

"Too crowded," Rasia answered, as if she had already given it some thought. "The scavenger bands are always at war with each other over control of the whole Graveyard. Last time I cut through this entrance, the Han in control of this territory was somewhat reasonable, but I can't say if that's the same or if the same scavenger group is still in charge. So. This is what we are going to do—we'll dig in and hide the windship here. Then we go in and make a deal with whatever scavenger group has control of this territory. Hopefully, it's the same group I encountered before. Better the enemy you know, than the enemy you don't. Once we guarantee our safe passage, we come back for the ship and continue through."

Rasia handed Kai one of the extra scimitars from the equipment hatch.

"I know you're still shaky with a sword, but we don't want to look like easy targets. If we look tough, they won't trouble us. We're just kids on our Forging. We're not worth the effort. And don't forget to hide the weapon you are good at under your clothes."

Kai nodded as he pulled himself up on aching legs. He placed his dagger under his shirt. He watched as Rasia strapped her double khopesh to her back, slung a bow over her chest, and buckled a scabbard to her hip. Kai's hands trembled with fear.

"Sometimes there's no avoiding a fight," Rasia said, mouth set in a serious line. "You ever kill someone, Kai?"

The situation required the question, but it still caught Kai off guard. It brought Kai back to that alleyway, helpless and afraid and suffocated by bodies trapping him in on all sides. He remembered the frantic way he washed his dagger of blood afterward. Unconsciously, he pressed his hand to the scar on his stomach, the one he had stitched himself to keep Nico from finding out.

"Yes," Kai told her. He waited to fold under her judgment. She glanced toward his stomach, where Kai held himself, over the scar she'd kissed on multiple occasions. She nodded in approval, jumped from the windship, and marched toward the Graveyard.

The road they entered had obviously been paved to allow for windships to come through. Trees and animals Kai had never seen were flourishing within the Graveyard bones. Flowers sprouted from cracks between the ribs. Large hawks made their nests in the broken hollows. Trees grew large and wild and untamed. Green had twisted and dominated this place. It looked more like a forest than a memorial to the dead.

"The stories say the dragons fought amongst each other. That this had been the battlefield marking the end of their age," Kai said.

"I don't know about that. There's no . . . wounds or scars on the bones," Rasia said. "Almost as if all the dragons laid down and died. It's weird. And look at the rate of decomposition. These bones are thousands of years older than the Elder."

It was all strange and a little fascinating.

"They don't sing like the Elder," Kai said. "These bones are empty. The magic has been stripped away from them."

Kai stepped toward one on a whim and touched his hand to the yellowed bones. He heard them, whispers, a warm greeting, a swirl of happiness, then warning, warning, dread.

Kai gasped when Rasia physically yanked him away.

"What was that?" Rasia asked, glaring at the bones with suspicion. "Your eyes glowed, and they never glow in this light."

"They don't?" Kai didn't feel when it happened and never knew what prompted it.

"Yeah, it's weird. They glow in the sun, but not in the dark. Come on, Kai. You can fondle the bones after we find whatever scavenger group is in charge of this entrance."

"Wait, Rasia." The air had shifted. Something had been displaced. "Someone spotted us. They've gone to get reinforcements."

"Scouts, no doubt." Rasia surveyed the area. "We don't know how many they will bring back. Even though we are on their territory, it's best to meet them on our terms. This is a good place. The growth covering the ribcage will protect us from snipers, and the space is limited here, which will help against multiple attackers if things go wrong. Here, help me set some traps."

Kai nodded, and they got to work digging holes to cover with brush.

"Maybe you can't control your magic, and it's not as big and loud as Nico's, but it is useful."

Kai hadn't yet admitted to Rasia that he had a bit more control over his magic than before. She was still under the impression that Kai's use of magic to reach Nico had been accidental. Despite the lake's bold declarations, maybe that was all Kai's magic would ever be—knowing the wind direction and sensing the occasional enemy's location. Kai would have missed the scout if he hadn't been so hypervigilant since they'd stepped into the Graveyard.

"What's the range on it? Can you sense animals too?" Rasia asked as they worked. Others would have been dismissive about Kai's "feelings" because it wasn't the sort of magic they had come to expect, but Rasia poked and prodded, interested in the mechanics to break down all the parts to find anything of value.

Kai concentrated on what he typically considered background noise. He tried to feel with the sixth sense that had been such an unquestioned part of his being. Once he gave it attention, the range widened and expanded so quickly Kai gasped at the sudden onslaught of information. He crouched, as if tightening himself into a ball could help him contain it.

"Focus, Kai." Rasia grabbed him by the face. He sucked in a breath and focused on the pressure of her hands. The startling noise dimmed to the background. Rasia asked again, her nose touching his, demanding, "What's the range?"

"No range." Kai elaborated after catching his breath. "It's everything. I sense everything. I sense all the way to the Grankull."

"Control it."

"I can't." Kai squeezed his eyes shut. "*I can't.*"

Nico would have given him space. The Council would have beaten it out of him. Rasia demanded better. "This could be life or death, Kai. You do not have the luxury of giving up. Try again."

It wasn't the pain that frightened him. It was the too much of it all. But Rasia was right. Knowing how many were coming for them could be the difference between life and death.

Kai braced himself for the onslaught of information. It was better, now that he was expecting it, but it was so much to sort through and make sense of—pebbles of sand, shifts of movement, intakes of breath, running, gasping, wheezing—Kai was a sweaty, shuddering mess by the time he reined in the range. "Three. There are three coming for us. Two vibrations out."

"Good." Rasia patted his cheek. She stood. "That is good. They sent five to welcome me last time. We can handle three. You okay?"

"Eventually." Kai dragged himself to his feet and eyed the trees. Two vibrations weren't that far out.

Rasia posted against a rib, waiting. She wanted to throw them off guard, to show them that she was expecting them. Unlike Rasia, Kai didn't know what to do with himself, so he stood there awkwardly when two scavengers finally appeared through the trees. Both scavengers wore elaborate, red-painted bone masks, broken off around the eyes. The third, a sniper, stuck to the canopy.

"Shit," Rasia cursed and drew her swords.

Kai didn't understand why Rasia's confidence had turned sharp and alarmed. They didn't look much different from anyone in the Grankull, other than the scarred lines etched onto their arms.

"Look," Rasia said, "we're just passing through on our Forging, and we have four bricks of scorpion jerky we are willing to trade for safe passage. I didn't think that required the attention of facehunters."

A chill ran up Kai's spine. He never thought they'd encounter facehunters, specialized scavenger assassins whispered of in stories. Kai stared back at those scars, hundreds of them, lining the facehunters' arms, marking the number of people they've killed.

"We're here for the runt," one of the facehunters said.

"What? *Why?* He can't do magic like the ohani. He's sickly and isn't worth anything. He has no value to you."

"It's none of your business what we want with him."

"My name is Rasia, child of Shamaijen Windbreaker. Your Han, Timar, knows me. We can figure something out."

"Move aside or die."

Rasia snapped so fast Kai barely tracked her movement. She threw one of her khopesh like a throwing knife, almost catching the front scavenger in the chest if they hadn't begun to evade. The blade thudded into their shoulder with a resounding, "no," in answer.

The facehunters tempered their surprise, and the first quickly faced Rasia as an opponent worthy of their attention.

The second scavenger came after Kai. Kai stumbled back against the rib, eyeing the curved sword in the facehunter's hand. The scavenger stumbled and buckled their knee in the hole Kai and Rasia had dug earlier. Kai dropped the helpless act, snatched his dagger from under his robe, and stabbed the blade under the scavenger's ribs.

Warm blood drenched Kai's forearm. Kai twisted the dagger free, and the scavenger slumped to the ground. At the same time, Rasia feinted, ducking underneath the other scavenger's wide swing, and thrust the khopesh's sharp end into their stomach.

An arrow flew out of the canopy straight toward Rasia. Kai sucked in an alarmed breath, and a gust of wind bounced the arrow away.

Rasia loosened her sword from her opponent's chest, and all in one smooth motion, unswung her bow and aimed it up toward the scout. "Kai. Where?"

"Two feet headward." The brambles were too thick for the arrow to get through. A branch wobbled, then stillness. "They're gone."

"We've got to get out of here," Rasia said, turning. She grabbed Kai by the hand and ran. "What do they want with you? And why would they send facehunters after you? It doesn't make any sense."

If it weren't for Rasia's preparation and foresight, Kai doubted he would have made it out of that encounter alive.

Despite all the drills and laps Kai had made around the windship in the past couple of days, his lungs burned at the edges as they ran. Kai fought through it, focused on placing one foot in front of the other until they shot free of the Graveyard's vines. Kai stumbled to his knees.

"We're not safe yet. We have to make it to the windship."

The distance between Kai and the sand dune where they hid their ship yawned further the longer he stared. Rasia studied Kai, analyzed the situation, and in an instant decided. "I'm going to run ahead for the ship. You keep running. Don't you dare stop, or I swear I'm going to kick you in the balls."

Kai nodded, unable to catch his breath enough to answer her. Rasia sped off, like lightning, revealing just how much Kai slowed her down. But he kept his promise. He forced one foot in front of the other, dragging them along like anchors.

Rasia curved the windship beside him.

She didn't slow.

Kai jumped using the last of his strength and caught the steps. Rasia grabbed ahold of his arms and helped him climb aboard.

Kai collapsed back, chest heaving, utterly spent. Kai was more than a little happy to put some distance between himself and the Graveyard.

CHAPTER FORTY-EIGHT

O

Rasia didn't know what to do. They could try entering the Graveyard at a different point of entry, but what if the facehunters weren't a coincidence? What if, for some unfathomable reason, all the scavengers were after Kai? Alternatively, they could go around, but that would lose them three whole days compared to the one if they went straight through. Depending on the moon, they had about twenty days of their Forging left, and Rasia needed at least twelve of those to get back home.

Kai sailed the ship at a parallel from the Graveyard at four vibrations, enough distance that if any scouts were looking, they were far enough away to be mistaken for a scavenger ship, an easy thing since Rasia's ship wasn't a standard of the Grankull.

"What do you want to do?" Kai asked.

"I want to try again," Rasia said with a sigh. "Timar definitely sent facehunters after *you*. If she were expecting me, she'd have sent more than three."

"What about a whole armada of windships?" Kai asked, straightening. Rasia followed Kai's gaze toward the armada breaking over the horizon. Red flags adorned their masts.

"Yep, that looks about right. Kai, full speed!"

Rasia grabbed her longbow and climbed the mast to the scout's nest. She nocked an arrow, but the scavengers stayed outside her bow range. They weren't taking any chances. This definitely felt like Timar. Any other scavenger would have underestimated her.

Rasia jumped back to deck. "They're playing it safe. Steer toward the gonda breeding grounds. We'll lose them there."

Kai curved around a sand dune to find another line of sails on the other side. The opposing ships formed a line with a chain-link of bones between them. Behind the link sailed a warship with a ram four carapaces thick and three times the size of Rasia's small ship. It too waved a bright crimson flag.

"We should probably turn around."

"On it."

Kai jumped the outrigger to turn, and set the ship at an angle, aiming for the hole between the ships at their front and the ones at their back. The scavenger ships moved to join with one another and close the hole. Kai and Rasia were going just fast enough to make it through, but it would bring them well within the range of scavenger arrows.

Rasia ran for the oil lamp jostling against the mast. She wrapped the tip of her arrow in linen, soaked it in the lamp oil, and set the arrow afire with the strike of a flint. Unlike Rasia's dragon-wing sail, scavenger sails were made of flax, easily flammable.

On the decks of the five windships across from her, archers lined up. She shot off her arrow before they got off a shot and set the closest of the five's sail ablaze. Rasia raced to the underbelly hatch and jumped inside.

"Kai, any moment now, the sky is going to be full of arrows. Get in here!"

"What about the ship?"

"Trust it to steer us straight, but you're not steering anything if you're dead." Dark clouds of arrows filled the sky. "GET IN HERE NOW!!!"

"Wait, let me just-" Rasia reached for him as he passed with the steer rope. She snatched him into the underbelly where they fell down the ladder. The air knocked from her as Kai slammed into her chest. Hundreds of arrowheads pierced through the deck, pinning sharp edges through the ceiling.

Rasia peeked her head out of the hatch and cursed at the sight of the chain-linked ships joined together, blocking off Rasia and Kai's escape. The ships slowly began curving, to trap Rasia and Kai at the center.

"I've got an idea." Kai squeezed passed her up the ladder. He sidestepped the arrows stuck to the deck and rushed over to the steer. He turned the ship toward the sand dune. Once Rasia realized his aim, she grinned. Then caught herself against the hatch door when the entire ship shook.

Sand exploded.

Rasia covered her eyes to avoid the sand shower. A massive dragon incisor had landed a vibration away from their ship, barely missing them.

The large warship launched another incisor in their direction, and Kai deftly steered the ship to avoid the projectile. Rasia grabbed a spear. They sailed closer and closer to the line of ships, speed increasing at every vibration.

Kai launched the windship off the sand dune's side, up and over the ship's bone link chain.

Rasia gripped the railing with her thighs, pulled back her arm, and launched the spear. She struck the windeka steering the ship below them. The scavenger ship careened into another, and another, and toppled their line.

Rasia and Kai landed with a heavy thud, safely on the other side of the chain. Kai got the ship under control as they sailed toward freedom. Rasia cheered in excitement, jumping at their victory, then fumbled her triumph when a large fang soared overheard and crashed in front of them.

Kai swerved the windship hard. Rasia flew off her feet, catching herself against the railing. Rasia's eyes widened, sighting the warship charging them at full speed. Rasia pushed herself off the railing to do *something*, but she knew it was too late. They couldn't go forward. The dragon fang had angled them right into the warship's path.

Kai met her eyes with the same realization, then his irises flashed gold, so bright it forced Rasia's eyes closed.

370

When she opened them, she watched an out-of-body experience as the warship rammed into her windship. The impact echoed like thunder. Her windship rolled three, four, five times. The mast cracked, the deck ripped open, and the carapace hull bent and folded unto itself. The wreck of her ship landed on its side. Through it all, the dragon-wing sail fluttered, unharmed.

Rasia sucked in a gasp at the damage, then realized in growing horror that she was *outside* the ship. She sat four vibrations away at the top of the sand dune Kai had jumped earlier. Below her, the scavenger ships had stopped to disembark. Somehow, she had been whisked to safety.

Rasia searched frantically for Kai. Finding no one, she swiveled back toward the wreckage.

Rasia could easily sneak behind the scavengers, steal their windship, and get the fuck gone. Maybe return for Kai with a grand rescue, but she didn't know if Kai were alive or dead. That was the sort of wreck people didn't get up from.

Rasia slid down the dune and sprinted toward the ship. She heard shouting over her shoulder. Surprise and shock stumbled the scavenger's steps, while Rasia beat them to the crash site and slid into a crack of the overturned hull.

"Kai?" Rasia called out. She crawled through tossed items and ripped deck boards. Any other time, Rasia would be mourning her poor mangled ship, but a windship could be fixed, Kai couldn't.

Rasia found him hanging limply, the steer of the ship pierced through his shoulder. At this distance, she couldn't tell if he was breathing or not. Rasia rushed over, broke the steer, and carefully slid the bone through his flesh. She found linen to staunch the blood, quickly binding up and under his underarm to apply pressure. Blood dripped down his face. The light was too dim to check for a head injury, and she prayed to the Elder he'd be all right. She crouched down and lifted him onto her back.

Carrying Kai, any possibility of escape was unlikely, and Kai might not survive if he didn't get help soon. Which meant Rasia was going to have to talk her way out of this.

Rasia crouched under the warped railing and rose to find

herself surrounded by two dozen archers all pointing arrows at her.

"A little overkill, don't you think?" Rasia asked.

The line of archers parted to make way for the Han. Bones rattled with every step as Timar, leader of the crimson scavengers, stopped before Rasia.

Timar wore an impassive bone mask, bone beads in her hair, tally marks down her arms, and a bone peg strapped under her right knee. She had a white dragonsteel sword strapped to her waist, unsheathed, showing it off.

"Shoot her. We're taking them both."

"Hey! Wait—fuck." An arrow pierced Rasia's thigh, and she buckled under Kai's weight. Although painful, the arrow was a good sign. It meant Timar wanted them alive.

Rasia snapped at Timar as she approached. "If you need us alive, why the fuck did you slam into us with a warship?"

"I never let anyone get the better of me twice." Timar paused, looked Rasia up and down. "What happened to your hair?"

"What happened to your leg?"

Timar cocked her bone leg back, and Rasia saw stars.

CHAPTER FORTY-NINE

O

Rasia came to while tied to the mast of Timar's warship. She peeked her eyes open, careful to hide the fact that she was conscious. They had chained her hands behind her back. A puddle of blood had grown underneath Rasia's thigh. They hadn't even bothered to take out the arrow.

Next to her, Kai struggled to breathe, lightheaded from blood loss and . . . what the fuck?

The scavengers had locked an iron choker around his neck. The metal cut into his windpipe, practically choking him every time his head lolled to the side.

When they reached the Graveyard, one of the facehunters kicked the arrow in Rasia's thigh to 'wake' her.

"Fuck you," Rasia spat as the facehunter untied her from the mast.

Another crouched down and pressed their thumb into the hole in Kai's shoulder, but Kai only flinched in response. Kai was pulled to his feet, groggy and dazed the entire time they forced him from the ship. Rasia limped next to him, trying to subtly keep him standing with her shoulder.

Timar sent her armada through an entirely different entry point and ordered a select few, including Rasia and Kai, to follow through a smaller overgrown animal trail.

Rasia took note of the path, dug in her feet at landmarks, and timed how long and in what direction they walked. She had her ropes loosened and a dagger they missed in her chest wrap, but Timar had the key to Kai's collar, and he was in no shape to escape. Still, Rasia kept her eyes sharp and observant.

The facehunters moved in a tight formation with Timar taking point, weapons out, which had all Rasia's instincts buzzing. They were in Timar's territory, and from the moment Timar caught Rasia, she didn't seem to be taking any chances with her or any other scavenger group. The more defensive Timar and her group became, the more and more Rasia wove the threads together.

"Kai?" Rasia asked. He tilted his head in acknowledgment. "How many people in the Grankull know how your magic works?"

"Just . . ." Kai struggled with his words, unable to take a deep breath. ". . . the Council."

"The scavengers put that collar around your neck to keep you from breathing deep enough to perform magic. How would scavengers know that? They also wouldn't have known you had magic until you blocked that sniper's arrow from earlier. But there's one person they do know who has magic, and I think every scavenger is out hunting for her. There's a bounty on Nico's head."

Because, of course, this was about Nico.

Of fucking course it was.

Timar's base was located strategically inside a large dragon tail that formed a natural defense around the camp. The shipyard, inside the jaw of a separate dragon nuzzling the end of the tail, had boats ranging from the smallest of rigs to stolen Grankull ships. Rasia and Kai walked through the skull, up through the path where the tongue once furled, and out into the ring of bones.

Rasia had never seen a scavenger camp before. Their location was a closely guarded secret and often moved within the territory every few years. It was deceptively small, but with closer inspection, Rasia spied dwellings hidden among the bones. Woven into the trees, the houses were built and shaped to fit and blend into their surroundings. Judging by the number of houses, Rasia calculated that hundreds lived in Timar's hikull alone.

One tree in particular stood out among the rest. Unlike the many other tree trunks sharing space with the bones, this tree bloomed mighty at the center. The scavengers had thoughtfully decorated its branches with severed heads.

Timar walked off, giving orders to the no-faces who served the camp, while Kai and Rasia were jerked in the other direction and thrown inside of a large wooden wheeled cage.

"Why am I not surprised?" said a familiar voice from the next cage over.

Rasia peered over into the cage next to hers, filled with dirty and smelly children. Rasia spotted a face she recognized, but for the life of her, she couldn't remember the name. The kid gave a flat look, and it was a wonder the cage could contain all that sass.

"Neema. The name is Neema. We were literally on the same Forging kull."

"Right. You."

"Rasia?"

Rasia turned to the other cage on her other side. She recognized this face, even though it was much gaunter and sallower than she remembered. "Faris? Looking pretty pathetic there."

"You know *his* name?" Neema huffed out. Faris was the child of Shamai-ta's old kull members, and the grandchild of the current Claws Councilor. Faris and Rasia ran in the same circles.

"It's nice of you to take a break from your dragon hunting to visit with all of us normal folks," Faris mumbled, eyes closed against the bar of his cage.

"You could have joined me."

"I don't have anything to prove to anyone."

"Certainly not stuck here in a cage."

Faris sighed. "You don't change, do you?"

Rasia rolled her eyes and turned her back to him. She motioned at Neema with her chin. "How'd you get here?"

Last time Rasia checked, Neema had been with Nico's kull. Rasia thought she saw Neema back at Nico's camp, when Kai was hightailing Rasia out of there. Had Neema been missing this entire time?

"Fucking Nico," Neema spat out. Rasia could relate. That was practically all the explanation Rasia needed, but Neema further elaborated, "I jumped ship back at the oasis, but a few days later, a bunch of scavengers came through looking for her. I told them Nico left. Guess they found the wrong one." Neema indicated where Kai was slumped against Rasia's shoulder, who was focused more on trying to breathe than following any of the conversation around him.

"They dragged me and everyone else across the entire fucking Desert. We've all told them everything we know. I don't understand why they can't let us go."

"They're scavengers," Rasia explained. Utter cluelessness crossed Neema's face. Wasn't it obvious? "Timar is waiting until after the Forging when you've failed and are less likely to run. Then, she'll determine which to make no-faces and which to coerce into her kull. She's starving you so that when she makes the offer, you're desperate for it."

Forging kids broke easily, especially once the Forging ended and children faced shame returning home. A lucky few were recruited, but most were branded as no-faces. Once branded with the X, there was no going back to the Grankull. No Forging or dragon large enough could ever earn back a face.

A facehunter approached Rasia's cage. Kai squeezed Rasia's arm weakly and shook his head. No doubt Timar planned to question her about Nico. Rasia might not personally like the stuck-up ohani, but Rasia was no snitch.

The facehunter reached for her, and Rasia kicked the facehunter in the face for the effort. She could get out without any help, thank you very much.

"Careful before you add to your collection," Timar warned, indicating the arrow still stuck in Rasia's thigh. Rasia should get the arrow out, eventually, when she had the time to make sure she wouldn't bleed out first.

Timar held court on a wooden throne under her rattling windchimes of skulls. Scavengers gathered to watch the interrogation. "I like you, kid. Don't make me kill you."

Rasia scoffed. "Let's make this easy then. The bones put me on Nico's kull, and we went our separate ways after some . . . differences, and I haven't seen her since."

"She never came after her sibling?"

"If she did, she couldn't keep up. Not my problem. I'm not her fucking keeper. Are we done?"

"We're done for now," Timar said. "I do want to remind you my original offer still stands. I am always in need of a capable apprentice, and you have the bones for this life."

"Or bones too many. I don't need you to earn my own."

"You are willing to risk your life for what? A test dictated by the Grankull as an excuse to cull an entire generation? You are smarter than that. Certainly, you see the Forging is nothing but a lie. Here, among scavengers, you need no one to determine that you are grown. Or would you rather die for their meaningless respect?"

"You're wrong to assume I do what I do for the Grankull. I act for my tahs, for my kull, and ultimately, for myself. What do I care that most won't survive? The Desert has finite resources. There will never be enough to go around. Let the weak die and the boneless join your merry band. Strength is those who survive."

"How strong are you in my chains?"

"Let me go and find out. I'm hunting the dragon Aurum for my Forging." Rasia paused and allowed the ensuing laughter to die down before she spoke again. Timar was the only one among the scavengers who didn't laugh. "Hunting this dragon benefits you as well as the Grankull. No more wings breaking your trees, no more fires razing your homes, and less competition to the gonda population. I can kill that thing, but I need my windeka to do it."

"It is my understanding that his jih can track him with her magic. She will come looking for him. He's bait."

"Can *I* go?"

"No, Rasia," Timar said, smiling. "I enjoy wasting your time. You can always kill dragons once the Forging is over."

At a signal from Timar, two facehunters approached Rasia. Rasia calculated her chances. With her wounded leg, Rasia wouldn't get far with all Timar's scavengers at the ready. She'd have to choose her moment, wait until night when they were asleep, perhaps. Therefore, she didn't resist when the facehunters pulled her to Timar's side. She wondered why they didn't put her back in the cage, until they dragged Kai out of it.

They dumped Kai to the ground, and he fell harshly to his knees. Timar's eyes narrowed. "The ohani can use magic to find you, and I imagine it can go both ways. Now, we can wait until she gets here, or you can give up her location."

Kai kept his face to the ground. Rasia didn't know if he was playing dumb, or if he was really out of it. She remembered the moment of lucidity from him in the cage and figured it was the former.

"This is pointless," Rasia complained. "He's the runt of the Grankull. He's dumb. He doesn't talk. You're not going to get anything out of him."

Timar gave Rasia an unimpressed expression. "He jumped my chain line. You're telling me a dumb mute can steer a windship as well as he did?"

"You're the Han of a scavenger band, and you've got one leg. Anything is possible when you put your mind to it," Rasia said, smiling.

"You're not the only perceptive one here," Timar remarked before turning back to Kai. "I know you're not as dumb as you pretend to be. I know Rasia had a chance to leave you behind, but she didn't. I know you whisked Rasia off that windship without any regard to yourself, be it a lack of control or a lack of time, but be it as it may, I am no one's fool. So, you can do this the easy way, or I can cut off Rasia's sword arm."

"What?! But both my arms are my sword arms!"

Timar gave Rasia a knowing look. "Exactly."

Rasia oomphed when a facehunter kicked her to the ground. Pissed, she spun on her back and kicked a knee out from under them. The facehunter folded over. Rasia locked legs about their waist, pulled up, then latched her teeth to their throat. The facehunter stood, snatching at Rasia's back to try and throw her off, but Rasia ripped at the larynx with her teeth.

She rode the facehunter to the ground. Then she picked herself up and spat out the vocal cords and cartilage.

"Touch me again, I dare you."

"Not easy, then."

Timar reached for her fancy white sword. The scavenger crowd cheered.

Rasia smiled, teeth stained red with blood. Rasia shook off her bindings. She broke off the arrow shaft in her thigh and tossed it aside, leaving some of the shaft behind to keep the wound plugged, for now. Rasia limped as they circled each other with the dagger previously hidden in her wrap finally in hand.

"Not much of a fair fight," Rasia said.

"I don't plan for it to be," Timar said, and signaled the archers. As Rasia expected, they shot at her wounded right. Rasia leaped out of the line of fire, landing to the ground at a roll.

Rasia swept a kick at Timar's good leg. Timar stumbled and stabilized her footing with her sword. Timar sneered. "That's what I like about you. Everybody always goes for the bone leg."

"I'd never be so predictable." Rasia leaned back as an arrow swept past her face. Rasia reminded herself not to have too much fun. This was a serious fight.

Rasia avoided more arrows, straight into the diagonal swing of Timar's sword, forcing Rasia to evade on her wounded leg.

It buckled.

Rasia fell and found herself slow to get up. Timar stabbed her peg leg into Rasia's hand, forcing Rasia to release the dagger. Timar raised her sword.

Kai tackled Timar to the ground.

Rasia blinked in surprise. She used the moment to grab the dagger, whirl it into one of those archer's faces, and retrieve Timar's dragonsteel sword that had fallen to the dirt. Rasia clutched both hands around the elaborate dragon hilt. The blade was sharp and beautiful. This baby had to have been stolen from the Grankull, right out of the temple no doubt.

Kai couldn't hold Timar for long. He was hardly a brawler and barely conscious. By the time Rasia found her feet, Timar had gotten the upper hand and had cracked her knuckles against Kai's face.

Timar rolled off him to evade Rasia's sword swing. The blade whistled sharp and clean, heavier than Rasia's custom dual blades. Rasia grabbed at Kai by the scruff of his shirt and dragged him up to his feet. He dropped against her back.

Hundreds of scavengers surrounded them with swords brandished and arrows pointed. Timar stood and wiped dirt from her face. Timar lifted her hand, and one of her apprentices tossed a spear into it.

Rasia knew she wasn't making it out of this alive, but she couldn't wipe the smile from her face. At least this was a better end than poisoning herself dead.

Kai collapsed.

"Shit," Rasia cursed, swinging around to check on him. His chest wasn't moving. "Fuck."

Kai had lost too much blood. He needed medical attention *now*. Rasia glared at Timar. "How the fuck is Nico supposed to track him if he's dead?"

Timar's eyes narrowed through her mask. Then the scavenger Han lifted out of her fighting stance and stamped her spear to the ground.

"Get him a healer."

CHAPTER FIFTY

O

They brought Kai to a small cone-shaped dwelling, hollowed out from an upright talon. Bright pink ivy curled around it, and blue wildflowers speckled this corner of the base. From the inside, a spot of light filtered down from the top, where the claw had been shaved down. Unfortunately, the hole was barely big enough to fit Rasia's head through.

The voices of the scavenger healers echoed round and round, rising like the chorus of a song, as they staunched, cleaned, and bandaged Kai's wound. Rasia circled, watching, and inspected their work. When they finished to Rasia's satisfaction, they glanced at Rasia's leg uncertainly, and Rasia threatened to break off their fingers.

The pair of healers couldn't get away fast enough, leaving Rasia with Kai and the facehunters guarding the entrance.

Alone, Rasia used the supplies left behind to finally tend to that arrow. The leg flooded with blood the moment she pulled out the remaining shaft. She cleaned the wound, sniffed at a jar of the scavenger poultice, and discovered it numbed the skin when she slathered it on. As she wrapped the bandages, she listened to Kai's breathing, which echoed around the hollow bone.

She looked over her shoulder at the sweaty sheen across Kai's forehead. He shifted and curled toward Rasia, and a tightness

Rasia didn't know she carried relaxed from her shoulders. They were certainly stuck in the middle of some shit, but at least they weren't stuck in too small cages like those other poor saps.

The heavy entrance curtain pulled back with an audible *thwick*, shooting sharp and ricocheting off the walls. Timar entered the small space, hand on her sword hilt, glaring. Rasia brandished the dagger she pickpocketed from the healers and returned Timar's glare with one of her own.

Why did this have to be so difficult?

"It had to be *your* Forging year," Timar bit out. "There's no more audience, no more need for dramatics, and no more games. Let's talk."

With Kai tucked safely behind her, Rasia waved the dagger to the empty space in front of her. Timar, the Crimson Han, swept aside her hyena pelt cape and sat cross-legged before Rasia with an exhausted sigh. Rasia wondered at Timar's angle by showing such weakness, but soon realized this was a Timar who didn't give much shits anymore. She had truly left all the theatrics and games at the door.

Timar spoke softly, mindful of the acoustics. "I need the ohani's head. I need the prize that it wins me. She's been following her jih, and thus following you. You know your own footsteps. You know the Desert. You can find her."

Timar cutting a deal made sense. If Nico came to the Graveyard on her own accord, Timar wouldn't know what section of the Graveyard Nico might enter through and whether another scavenger group would intercept her first. Even if Timar did torture out Nico's location, how many of Timar's scavengers would fall to Nico's magic with a direct confrontation? But Rasia, on the other hand, could approach Nico safely as a friend(*ish*).

"My people are making another collar for the ohani as we speak. I don't give a shit if you put it on her, or if she puts it on herself, but you will lead her here. Then you and your windeka can walk. We have a deal?"

Rasia ran through the possibilities in her head. There were too many scavengers, and their wounds made it difficult to escape on their own. It was the best option they had.

"Deal."

Rasia didn't trust the facehunters guarding the door. She watched the entrance with a paranoid vigilance as she rested her leg. It still hurt, but Rasia's splint took off some of the pressure and made it easier to walk. What was worse were the old aches and bruises pulsing from her ribcage.

"Rasia."

Kai placed a hand on her knee and rasped out a cough. She grabbed the gourd of water, one of the various items Timar had provided after Rasia accepted the deal. Timar had also delivered a basket of fruit and a thick mushroom soup Rasia hoped wasn't poisonous. She certainly ate all of it, and it would suck to almost die of poison again, but she was pretty sure Timar wanted her alive, for now.

Rasia pressed the water to Kai's lips. He drank in small gulps, careful of the tight collar. Rasia could barely get a finger through the thing. Kai tightened his grip on her leg once he caught sight of all Timar's presents. His expression shuttered. "What did you do?"

"I made a deal with Timar."

Kai pushed under him to sit up, first with his dominant hand of his bad shoulder, and flinched. That shoulder might become a problem. It might not heal by the time they got to the dragon. If they actually managed to get to the dragon.

Rasia moved to help, but he refused her assistance. He sat up on his own and demanded, "Tell me everything."

Rasia told him the details of the deal—about the collar, Timar's agreement to refurbish her windship, and the fact Nico would certainly follow Rasia of her own free will once Nico learned Kai was in danger. Rasia stressed how this was their best option, but she could see the silent fury growing on Kai's face, easy to tell because his eyes went from a warm light to a molten gold.

"You're sacrificing my jih?"

Rasia threw up her hands. "Did you hear anything I said? Nico is coming after you either way, at least now someone is there to warn her."

"She's not," Kai corrected. "Nico isn't chasing us anymore."

Rasia slapped a hand over his mouth. She looked over at the entrance curtain and the feet of the facehunters no doubt listening in. Rasia crowded into Kai's lap, hooked her hand behind his head, and pressed her lips to his ear. "Facehunters are at the door and sound echoes here. Don't ruin our only leverage."

Kai nodded against her cheek.

"Good. Now where exactly is your dear sweet jih?"

"I'm not telling you."

"Kai, we have no other options."

"You could leave me here. You've got your dragon, and Nico has her Forging to finish."

"I'm not finishing my Forging without you, and I'm not abandoning you here. I am going to go find your insufferable little jih, and we are going to figure out a plan to rescue you that keeps everyone's faces intact. You stay here and heal and rest. Watch for your opening. Watch for anything you can take advantage of and fight this on the inside."

Kai turned his face away, frowning.

"Don't tell me where she is then. Nico is excruciatingly predictable. I can find her on my own."

If Nico had stopped chasing after them, that meant she was going after a gonda. If she was going for a gonda, she was headed to the gonda breeding grounds.

"Just a few days ago you almost died in my arms," Kai said. "I don't want either you or jih risking your lives for me."

"That's life, Kai. Get over it. We're a kull. I'll always come back for you."

Rasia got it. She understood. When the windship crashed, she thought she had lost him. That had been happening a lot lately.

This Forging was stressing her out.

"Also, Timar is holding my dual blades hostage."

"I'm glad to hear it takes so little for you to sell out my jih."

"Hey. Those are one of the few items that can hurt a dragon. We can't exactly go hunting after a dragon without them." Rasia rested her cheek against his. "That's hardly nothing in comparison. I'd destroy the whole world for you."

"I'd never ask for that."

The entrance curtain swept open, and Timar dipped inside. She straightened and crossed her arms at the two of them. "It's time."

Kai looked to Rasia in alarm, and Rasia took that moment to steal a greedy kiss. Then in one smooth motion, Rasia stood and hopped over him, careful on her splint.

Timar glanced at her. "He tell you where she is?"

Rasia scoffed. "I'll find her."

The heat of Kai's glare burned her back.

"I'm coming," Kai bit out. He reached for his bloody shirt and threw it over his head, where it promptly got stuck. Rasia snorted and helped him put it on over the collar and his bandaged shoulder. Timar watched the whole scene amused, even when Kai grabbed Rasia by the hand. They walked together outside.

Timar led them to the shipyard.

"My baby!" Rasia cried at the sight of her windship. The poor thing had been revived scavenger-style, with materials slapped haphazardly atop to cover the holes, but it would do. She'd sail.

Rasia moved to throw herself against the hull and found herself stalled by Kai's tight grip on her hand; a hand connected to Kai's hand, which was connected to Kai's wounded shoulder where Timar dug in her fingernails.

"This is where you two embers separate."

Rasia glanced at those sharp nails and back at Kai's stubborn face. "Let me go, Kai. I know I haven't given you much reason to trust me lately, but I need you to trust me now."

Rasia could slip her hand from his grip, but she needed him to understand she wouldn't fail him or do what he feared most and give up his jih. Rasia knew she had made some missteps and he'd lost that initial faith in her, but she hoped to regain it.

"*Trust me.*"

Several times now, Kai had refused to let her go—back on the lake when she jumped ships, back when she was dying in his arms. She saw all those memories flash in his eyes before he yielded.

"*Okay.*"

Finally, Kai released her.

Rasia turned to inspect the windship. All the hatches had been stripped clean, but at least they hadn't taken the sail. That single item was the most expensive thing and the hardest to replace. No doubt the only reason Timar saved it was because she needed Nico to view Rasia as a friend.

Timar snapped her fingers, and one of the apprentices came running with the second metal choker. It was heavy and unyielding when the apprentice handed it over. Rasia chucked it behind her onto the deck.

"You've got three days. Then I kill him."

Rasia laughed at that. Look at Timar acting all big and tough in front of her scavengers.

Rasia threatened, "You put one fucking mark on him, and the Forging doesn't matter anymore. The dragon doesn't matter anymore. You'll be my next hunt, and it is your head that'll be hanging from that tree."

The worst part about dealing with people who knew what you were capable of was that they didn't underestimate you.

The best part was that they listened.

CHAPTER FIFTY-ONE

—

Rasia had barely disappeared into the trees when Timar locked a steel chain into the loose link of Kai's choker. She glared at her scavengers as she hooked the chain to her belt. Kai made a note of that, the fact Timar didn't entirely trust her own people.

"Strip."

Kai blinked. He glanced over at the no-faces waiting obediently for an order, or rushing around at tasks or errands, all naked. Despite Rasia's threat, he feared Timar might brand an "x" on his face, which would effectively raze all Kai's hopes and dreams to the ground.

Timar read his thoughts. "I know better than to court her fury. I'd make sure Rasia is dead first, then I'd do it. But I need her, so your face is safe, for now. Clothes. Off."

Kai gritted his teeth under the scrutiny of the surrounding scavengers. The longer he defied her, the more attention he attracted, but Kai stood firm in Timar's own admittance that he was safe from harm, *for now*.

Timar glowered at the blatant challenge to her authority.

"I wouldn't have thought the runt of the Grankull would be so prideful. You think you're better than our no-faces? You think because you're born of the Grankull that you're better than us?" Timar nodded to the scavengers behind him. "You're weak, and the weak serve."

The scavengers rushed him from behind. Pain lanced up his right arm from the shoulder injury. Kai grunted when his face hit the ground, soft with dirt and wet leaves. They twisted his wounded arm and pinned him, helpless.

They snatched the shroud from his waist. They ripped off Rasia's shirt, and pants, then his loincloth. All eyes stared at his scarred, whipped back.

Kai was so tired of never being strong enough.

The chain rattled as Timar's boots stepped into his line of sight. "Did you defy the Grankull too when they whipped you? Or did you let them do it?"

The collar tugged up, cutting into his neck, and Kai scrambled, half-dragged, onto his feet. He had no choice but to follow after Timar's departing figure.

Timar collapsed down on her throne, under her canopy of swaying heads. She glanced at Kai, with her eyes traveling up and down his scars.

"You could find a home here, you know. You could be free here. You could touch anyone you want. You can fuck anyone you want. You could choose any face you want. You could be and do anything you want."

"I want to go free."

"Tsk. This chain is for your own protection. You are the key to untold riches and all the food anyone could ever eat."

"You've been lied to. The Grankull doesn't have that sort of food."

"That I know, but the deal still has its benefits. Unfortunately for you, most scavengers are born here and don't understand the Grankull's subtleties. I'm the one person standing between you and their hunger. Undermine my authority at your own risk. I consider you under my protection, but I make no promises if you decide to leave it. No matter how much you have endured and suffered to get this far, there is always more pain. You can either break or harden. I suspect I know which one you are, but you could skip all those hard lessons and just do what I say."

Kai realized Rasia wasn't the only one planning to renege on their end of the deal. Kai accused, "You're not planning on letting me go."

"Ha! Of course not. I think you and Rasia will like it here."

"Rasia isn't staying here."

"Do you truly believe the Grankull is big enough for her?" Timar laughed at that. "The Grankull doesn't deserve her. Or you, for that matter."

Timar motioned to a no-face holding an amphora of water beside the chair. As ordered, the no-face came around and held the pitcher out to Kai.

Timar raised an eyebrow, testing him to see if he would obey this time. She was right that this could be a lot worse. Even now, Kai could feel the interest of the scavengers, some of them looping around more than once to get a look at his eyes. With a shoulder injury, no weapons, and stark naked, he had little chance of escaping on his own. Kai took the water.

Kai held the pitcher with his good arm, ordered to remain at Timar's side. He poured the water straight into Timar's mouth every time she asked for it.

When he wasn't busy following her every command, Kai studied that dragonsteel sword at Timar's side—tah's dragonsteel sword. Kai had never asked Nico about its absence.

From atop her throne, Timar talked to her facehunters about strengthening their defenses. She lectured her apprentices. She ordered around no-faces.

Kai often couldn't follow the thick scavenger's dialect. He didn't understand a lot of words even in context. Timar switched flawlessly back to the Grankull schoolroom-taught diction when she spoke to Kai.

Around sunset, drums banged throughout the camp. The scavengers gathered, and the no-faces ushered out dinner.

Dinner provided a good view of all the distinct scavenger groups. Both facehunters and the general scavengers wore tallies along their arms to mark their kills, but the facehunters wore sleeves of them. The apprentices wore unmarked arms and red accessories. The branded no-faces weaved through dinner, serving food and an alcoholic drink that, as Timar explained unprompted, was made by infusing a whole snake and scorpion in red wine, aniseed, and the blood of their enemies. Kai didn't know if she was joking or not, but the scavengers called the drink Deathsblood.

Timar stood and lifted the large goblet of red liquid in toast.

"To eating what we want! To fucking who we want! To killing who we want! And to Death, the one true god!"

The scavengers cheered and drank their goblets empty.

A no-face handed Kai a dinner plate. Timar gave him leave to sit and eat. Most of the fruit he'd never seen before. The main dish consisted of a mushroom he didn't think grew wild. The quantity of it suggested it might be cultivated in some manner. It would explain Timar's power if she had control over a food source.

Even though the food looked edible, Kai found it hard to stomach with the eyes of the oasis kids burning into his back. They watched him full of hatred, angry at the fact Kai got to eat instead of sitting starved in a cage alongside them.

A tray of food dropped after a no face tripped over a foot intentionally thrown out to stumble them. Then a facehunter came over with a branch and beat the no-face bloody to crude laughs and jeers, as if entertainment.

On the other side of the field, scavengers finished their dinner and, as if demanding a second helping of food, ordered naked no-faces into their laps. Their blank stares gazed out into the forested graveyard of bones. Some of them were young enough to be in shrouds.

Kai looked away. He glared at the white moonflowers around Timar's throne, feeling sick with revulsion.

Sex was an exchange, a physical bartering like trading items at the belly market. It might not always be an equal exchange, and the other person could cheat you, but the expectation was that both parties always gained something in the end. Even whoring was a mutually agreed-upon trade. But this violent robbing was something Kai didn't have a word for.

"Rape. The scavenger word is rape," Timar told him, reading the horror on his face. It felt right for it to be a different word. "The weak serve, and the strong choose their faces. That's the scavenger way."

"Some of them are children."

"Funny how the Grankull believes a shroud can protect them. It didn't protect them when their families sold them off. It didn't protect them from starving. It didn't protect the little orphan tents kids, or the unwanted, or the imperfect. The shroud is a lie. It's nothing but a tool the Grankull uses as a means to control. We aren't the Tents relying on the Grankull like an engorged tick on its host. Here, we are free."

It was no wonder why the oasis kids hated him. They had to witness this every night, knowing it could happen to them once the Forging ended, while Kai waited to be saved.

"A freedom at the expense of others," Kai criticized.

Timar laughed. "All freedom is at the expense of others. The only difference between a kuller and a scavenger is that we're honest about how our shit smells. The Grankull might not have a word for it, but rape happens within the bones. Just because there isn't a word for a thing, doesn't mean it doesn't exist."

Kai couldn't imagine it. The Grankull had only ever had two rules when it came to sex: no unapproved pregnancies and don't touch children. The rest was a free for all. Adults often had multiple partners and flames, unless they were in committed relationships, and even that was negotiable. There were always, of course, bad people, but the Grankull was a place where leaving someone sexually unsatisfied could be grounds for demanding a blood price. In more atrocious situations, it was the triarch of the family that would come collecting that debt. Bad sex could literally get you killed.

Kai tried to reconcile the things he understood with what he saw. Perhaps without a face you lost the right to a fair exchange. But no, Kai had to shift his understanding. This wasn't about the exchange. It was about control, and power, and one group asserting its dominance over another. It was about breaking bodies and souls and creating objects out of people. It wasn't sex at all. It was *rape*. Kai thought he understood enough to hold the word in his head now.

"Your freedom is a lie," Kai spat out.

"Oh yes, that's true."

The rest of the night, Timar reveled in the cost of her freedom. Kai would never understand how anyone could pay such a high price. No backstory could ever justify this.

Kai felt a nauseous combination of disgust and relief when Timar decided to retire for the night. He followed her into her personal dwelling built around the trunk of a large tree grown over the curled tip of the tail.

A furtive no-face lit candles in the rooms Timar entered. The entryway displayed a showcase of, as Timar boasted, an array of colorful bone masks from all her fallen enemies.

Timar's bed was the tail vertebra tip, decorated with pelts and woven feathers padding the dips. One of Timar's apprentices joined her on the bed. Curly blond hair sprouted from around the mask, and the young apprentice gently, almost reverently, removed the straps around Timar's thigh. Timar released a relieved sigh when the apprentice freed Timar of the bone leg. Timar didn't take off her bone mask or the belt that kept Kai attached to her.

The two began to whisper. They took off each other's clothes, and the candlelight flickered across the long-corded scars on Timar's back—*Wait*. This was really about to happen.

"Perhaps you want some privacy?"

Timar waved at him, dismissively.

"Open that chest."

Kai opened the nearest chest and found Rasia's two dual blades sitting at the top. He froze.

Was this a test?

Could he grab these blades, kill Timar and her apprentice, get through the scavenger camp, and find his way out of the Graveyard to freedom? Or would he get caught and be subjected to the tortures of the first scavenger he came across?

Did he trust Rasia enough to wait for her?

He glanced at Timar and found her watching him, amused by his indecision.

Freedom was a lie.

He was too valuable. She wasn't going to let him cut his way out. There were traps here, and he didn't know where they lay.

Kai wished he could be that brave hero in legends who slashed his way out of anything, but he had absolutely no idea how to use Rasia's khopesh, and his dagger had been confiscated. No. He needed to observe and listen and wait for his moment, as Rasia advised.

"What do you need?" Kai asked smoothly.

"Just underneath. You'll see it."

Kai shuffled past the blades and pulled out the item below. Kai stared confused at the buckled straps and the oblong bone piece at the end. He blushed in realization and quickly tossed it to the bed.

In the Grankull, to dare chip off the Elder cost death.

Here, they fucked with the bones.

CHAPTER FIFTY-TWO

1

The gonda breeding grounds didn't look much different from other barren stretches of the Desert.

But it felt different.

The ground vibrated underfoot, a buzzing sound at first, then a constant rumble of the deck, then a shattering that wouldn't leave your bones. They said the epicenter shook like an earthquake and rolled booming thunder in your ears. No one had ever crossed the epicenter alive.

Nico and her kull stopped at the edge of the breeding grounds when they felt the first sign of vibration in their legs. They were careful to speak in kull signs and move slowly, lest they draw the attention of a gonda before they were ready.

One wrong move could summon hundreds.

Nico looked at the faces of her kull—Azan at the tiller, Suri in the scout's nest, Zephyr at the oar-position. Even Kelin managed to stay above deck, though his shaking wasn't because of the ground.

Zephyr pressed a parting forehead to the baby silk spider and handed it over. Nico minded the fangs as she stepped down the windship stairs. She stopped at the second rung from the bottom and released the poor thing.

It scurried off.

The silk spider wasn't big enough to attract a stampede of hungry gonda, but it was small enough to tempt a curious one over.

Suri signaled from the scout's nest. *Two.*

Nico lifted her hand and waited. Two gonda ploughed toward the spider, cresting waves behind them. The waves raced toward the doomed spider, crashing closer and closer.

Nico opened her hand.

Azan pushed down the tiller, and they were off, speeding away from the grounds. One gonda chased the spider, but another veered and chased after them. Nico smiled, triumphant at how perfectly the plan was holding together.

"Ready your arrows!" Nico yelled.

Arrows fitted to bowstrings. Nico aimed at the gonda speeding toward them.

"Slow, Azan!"

The windship slowed, drawing the gonda into arrow range. Zephyr, Kelin, and Suri stood with their arrows at the ready, waiting for Nico's signal. Nico widened her stance and set her sights on the reaching tentacles.

A windship crossed their path.

"HOLD!"

What the Elder?!

Nico's confusion quickly turned to annoyance when the windship weaved between the tentacles like dancers weaving between flames on Naming night. The sail spun around, a feature Nico had never seen before, and the ship moved parallel to theirs, moving *backward.*

Rasia leaned one arm against her ship railing. Even without her signature flag of hair, that smirk couldn't have been more infuriating. "You busy?"

How come when Nico had finally stopped chasing after Rasia, here she was, showing up at every turn?!

"Rasia!" Nico yelled. "What are you doing here? Kai, why are—" Nico stopped and searched Rasia's windship deck for Kai.

"We need to talk," Rasia said.

Rasia pushed off her railing and guided the ship with one hand on the steer and the other arm around a rope, pulling and tugging it to move the sail. Rasia's windship veered off, away from the breeding grounds.

Nico turned toward her kull. The gonda was still chasing after them, vibrating in her ears. She saw her kull's disappointment and frustration reflected fivefold.

Zephyr stated Nico's thoughts out loud. "Rasia wouldn't be here if Kai weren't in trouble, *and* she couldn't handle it herself."

Nico rubbed at her temples. She had made her kull a promise, but something was wrong, and she needed more information. They still had time. The gonda could wait.

Nico couldn't abandon her jih.

CHAPTER FIFTY-THREE

I

Nico and her kull caught up to Rasia at a large limestone shelf. Azan parked the windship in the shade of the overhang, next to Rasia's. Nico peered up high, where Rasia sat atop the shelf, kicking her legs impatiently.

They hadn't been *that* far behind.

"We'll get our gonda," Nico promised her kull. "Let's meet with Rasia and break till high noon end."

"We're still close to the gonda breeding grounds. If we're going to break, we should do it atop the rock. It'll absorb our vibrations and keep the gonda from sensing us. She picked this place for a reason," Zephyr advised.

Nico nodded. "Don't bother breaking down the windship. Keep it ready for sail. Gather your supplies and any materials for shade. We'll take lunch on the rock."

They had to climb to reach the flat rock shelf. Nico took the lead, taking care to test the holds for those following behind her. Suri followed, then Kelin, then Azan, and then Zephyr at the tail. With their strength, both Azan and Zephyr carried most of the supplies and could reasonably take another person's weight if someone should slip. Nico reached the top and immediately turned to help Suri up after her.

Suri stared at Nico's hand. They hadn't talked much since their argument. It'd been a chilly silence since. It didn't surprise Nico when Suri pulled herself over the rock shelf.

Nico looked down at a freeze in the line, where Kelin stopped three quarters of the way up. The tent kid looked down at the ground, staring at the distance, huffing out.

"It's okay," Azan said from under him. "It's not any taller than spine street."

"I'm going to kick you in the face," Kelin snapped, clutching the rock face. Nico had never paused to consider this might be the highest Kelin had ever been in his entire life. Before Nico could think of a solution, Zephyr reached out and tested the rocks before climbing around Azan.

Zephyr tied one end of his shroud to Kelin's belt and the other end to his own. "Kelin, if you fall, you're attached to me, and Azan is right below to catch you. Nico is right there, waiting to pull you up. You're safe. We've got you."

Kelin jerked his chin. Zephyr pointed to the handholds Nico marked out earlier in her climb. Kelin moved to the one indicated, and hand by hand, he crawled higher and higher. Nico grabbed at him as soon as he was in reach and pulled him over onto the rock shelf. Kelin squeezed at her, sweaty, and Nico reached around him to undo Zephyr's shroud so it didn't trip anyone up. Zephyr waited for Azan before climbing up last.

"You did good," Azan said. He hooked under Kelin's armpits, pulled Kelin to his feet, and dragged Kelin away from the edge.

Nico placed a hand on Zephyr's arm when he stopped beside her. "Thank you."

"It's nothing."

They shared a nod. Nico turned to Rasia, standing there, waiting, with the most bored and frustrated expression on her face.

"Wow, you all are *so* slow."

Nico's entire kull stood at her back on one end of the rock shelf, while Rasia stood alone on the other. Nico noted the fresh bandages around Rasia's thigh and the splint. Rasia's khopesh were also missing.

"What is this about, and where is Kai?"

"Okay. Don't crash. *Listen.* Scavengers captured Kai and—"

Rain drummed atop the rock and drowned out Rasia's last words. The bright flash of lightning blinded Nico's vision.

It was always something with Rasia. First, Rasia stole jih to go chase after a dragon. Then she pushed him into the Lake of Yestermorrow. Then she got herself *seeded*. And now—*now*, jih was caught helpless in the hands of scavengers! Nico didn't think it was possible to hate someone as much as she hated Rasia in that moment.

"I *said* not to crash."

This time, Nico didn't rein in her magic. The initial scattering of rain thickened to a downpour.

The rain dripped around Rasia's growing grin. Rasia reached for her swords and paused a moment when she realized they were absent. Rasia didn't skip a beat when she spun the replacement scimitar from her hip and dipped into a fighting stance.

Rasia smirked. "Come on, then. Maybe you'll listen after I beat your ass *again*."

No. Not this time. Nico refused to lose. She'd learned her lesson. Nico wouldn't pull her punches. Not anymore.

Nico stormed forward with glaive in hand. Rasia sprinted to meet her in the middle.

Rasia's momentum stalled when she slipped on the puddle Nico summoned underfoot. Nico swiped overhand with her glaive and missed by a hair, if Rasia still had any.

The slippery snake rolled out the way.

Despite her anger, Nico took great care to maintain awareness of her breathing and environment. She remembered the windship chase and how Rasia used her emotions against her. That was another lesson Rasia had taught her.

Nico glided on puddles of water, almost dancing around Rasia as Nico's breath found rhythm, and the magic flooded her veins.

Steel clashed, and the force jolted through Nico's arms. Nico twisted, wrapped a whip of water around Rasia's sword, and yanked the weapon right out of Rasia's hand.

Rasia moved too slowly on her bandaged right leg. Nico swiped toward Rasia's right and too late did Nico realize Rasia had been laying a trap. Rasia wasn't as slow as she'd let on. Rasia pulled a dagger out of her belt.

Hot steel cut Nico's forearm. Her magic flared instinctively. Nico splashed and she reformed two puddles away.

Rasia grinned, smug. "Give it up, Ohan. You'll never beat me."

Nico stepped into the rain.

Nico jumped the droplets, bounced from the water in Rasia's gourd, and took hold of the liquid life that ran through Rasia's veins.

Nico gripped the rough fibers of Rasia's dagger-hilt in her—*no*, Rasia's—hand. The right leg did hurt, in such agony Nico almost hopped back to her own body. What Nico had thought a trap was a bluff. What Nico thought was Rasia's inevitable victory was, in fact, Rasia barely standing. Nico tightened Rasia's hand around the dagger hilt, added another hand, and turned it toward Rasia's chest.

Rasia stood her ground, mentally fighting Nico, but Nico pushed the magic more and tightened her control on Rasia's blood by sheer force of will. In the beating rain, Rasia stood frozen.

"GET THE FUCK OUT OF ME!" Rasia screamed.

Rasia dropped under her leg, folding to the pain, and went sprawling back to the ground. The dagger screeched a streak of sparks against the limestone. A sharp pain at the ribs screamed through the magic synapses. Nico jolted back, out, and hit against the rock, wet and reformed.

Rasia lay on the ground, heaving.

Nico stood over her, and even with the drastic difference of their positions, Rasia looked far from defeated. Rasia, secure in the fact that she knew Nico, she'd known Nico since they were children and how Nico cried when Rasia stomped on her favorite doll. Rasia said, "You can't save Kai by yourself. *You need me.*"

Nico's hands dived around Rasia's throat, then vengefully pushed Rasia down, down, down into the watery depths of Nico's anger. Nico rampaged with the destructive power of a flash flood. She was endlessly whirling seas and vicious storms. She struck with all the unforgiving destruction of a natural disaster.

Nico-ji, save her.

Nico startled at the sound of Kai's voice, echoing as desperate as when he had once offered up Rasia cradled in his arms.

What was she doing?

Nico was more than this. Nico was more than her anger, and her jealousies, and her insecurities. She was more than just Nicolai, more than the heir and a title she hadn't earned yet.

Nico was the rain shower.

She gave life to starved plants and barren earth. Children played in her puddles. Animals quenched their thirst. She was relief to a parched throat. She was the cycle. The condensation. The evaporation. The thunder. The pour. She doused. She cleansed. She sunk. She floated. She drowned. She soaked. She rippled. She was an oasis.

Nico's hold loosened.

Rasia sucked in a breath, gasping. A fist slammed into Nico's face, and Nico's head snapped back at the force of the blow. Nico thunked to the limestone, frozen.

A laugh flew from Rasia's lips, the sound of madness if Nico had to ever describe the word. Rasia pressed a hand underneath her, wobbled, and tried to stand. Rasia collapsed on her bad leg, and laughed again, and laughed some more, then laughed herself unconscious.

Neither could get back up on her own.

CHAPTER FIFTY-FOUR

I

"How is she?" Nico asked, tentatively approaching Suri standing at the edge of the rock shelf. Suri washed her hands of Rasia's blood.

"She refractured her ribs and needs to stay off her leg, but she's Rasia." Suri shrugged. "She poisoned herself with gonda venom and somehow survived. She'll be fine."

Nico sorely regretted her actions. Jih was out there in the clutches of scavengers, and Rasia was currently lying unconscious in a bedroll and unable to communicate any information. Nico turned to join the others by the campfire and paused when Suri bit out in a whisper, "Why is your hate for Rasia justified? How is my dislike of the Tents any different than your dislike of her?"

"It's different."

"I've known you since we were buds, Nico. You've always hated Rasia. Long before she ever met Kai."

"It's not comparable, Suri. You hate an entire group of people you don't know and won't give a chance. I've tried to get to know Rasia. I've tried to give her chances. I've tried to be understanding. But she makes being the better person *so hard*. I'm not going to claim that I am perfect. You're right, I should not have allowed Rasia to drag me into another one of her games, but I'm trying to be better. And you are better, too."

Suri finished washing the blood from her hands and turned away from Nico. "Maybe I'm not."

Nico wanted to continue arguing, but Suri had retreated. With a sigh, Nico dragged herself over to the campfire, into the shade of the lean-to they carried up from the windship. Under the shade, Kelin and Zephyr talked in low tones while Azan hummed a tune with his head in Kelin's lap.

Nico faced them all nervously. She feared their reception and how they would react to such a destructive display of her magic. But Azan looked up, with that handsome smile of his, and offered the bag of jerky he was snacking from. Azan was the only one not tired of the dried meat yet.

"Thank you." Nico reached for a jerky strip and dropped down with a sigh.

"You were pretty badass," Azan offered.

Nico scoffed at that. "Rasia was injured, running on scant drums of sleep, and did not have the use of her best weapon. It's hardly anything to celebrate. I let her get under my skin, *again*."

Nico glanced over at Zephyr, ashamed. He had tried to stop her, but she had been too angry with Rasia to hear him. Nico expected judgment, but Zephyr asked, concerned, "How are you feeling?"

"Cold," Nico said.

"I didn't mean your magic."

Nico wasn't sure her answer was any different. She hunched and bit her lip when Zephyr wrapped his cloak about her shoulders. "None of us are perfect, Nico."

"I hate who I am around Rasia. I've tried hard my entire life not to turn into tah and be feared for my magic. And I genuinely *try*, but she always brings out the worst in me."

"I don't have magic, and the Grankull fears me all the same." Zephyr shrugged.

"That's not comparable, Zephyr. My anger threatens to flood our entire way of life. My anger ruins crops and livelihoods. My anger drowns people. I almost let it win this time. I almost killed her."

"But you didn't."

"I almost did."

"I'm not scared of you," Azan said. "Because I know you, and I know you would never want to hurt anyone on purpose. Back at the oasis, when you gave me a choice to stay or follow you, I chose you. I have three older jihs, and they all are more skilled and better than me at everything. But you always made sure I felt part of the team. Like I matter. You're a good Ohan."

Nico found herself warmed by the words. "Thank you, Azan. Still, I want to say sorry to all of you for giving in to the worst of me."

"It was the best of you," said a fifth shadow.

They all turned to Rasia standing before the lean-to. Nico's jaw tightened at the sight of her. The bruises of Nico's fingers blossomed around Rasia's neck. Rasia squinted at Nico. "For the first time, you've given me all that you've got, and it was pretty damn amazing. Now, stop moping around. We've got your jih to save."

Nico could only stare at Rasia, uncomprehending. Nico didn't know if she expected Rasia to be angry or scared of her after what Nico had inflicted, but of course Rasia never did what Nico expected. The fact Nico might never understand Rasia settled like a stone in her chest. Nico didn't have to understand Rasia.

"Let's save my jih."

Nico stood and faced Rasia. Nico had hated Rasia for a long time. Long before the Forging, back when they were half-shrouded buds. Nico could never understand why Rasia seemed the only person in the world who didn't want to be her friend. Perhaps that rejection had colored and altered Nico's vision since. It had kept her from seeing Rasia as someone who genuinely cared for Kai. Nico and Rasia themselves might never be friends, and that was okay. *It was okay.*

Hate never dies.

You let it go.

CHAPTER FIFTY-FIVE

—

"Han, we're under attack."

Kai startled off the floor when a facehunter crashed into Timar's bedroom. The Crimson Han sprang from the tangled limbs of her apprentice, who moved several moments after, grabbing at weapons and clothes tossed on the floor. No-faces rushed in with Timar's armor.

"How many?" Timar asked, calm and collected as the no-faces dressed her.

"Both the Cobalts and the Serpentines are advancing into our territory. It's unclear if they are working together or have the same idea, but word about the gold-eyes got out."

"Hold our defenses, and once this is over, find the traitorous rat. I'll behead them myself."

Still chained to Timar's belt, Kai had no choice but to follow as Timar stormed outside.

Timar's scavengers attacked from defensive positions along the camp's tail. Kai didn't know how many scavengers advanced through the dark tangle of vines and bones, but he heard them dying. For the most part, the attack seemed like suicide from the opposing side; hundreds out there desperate to capture him on the off chance he'd reveal his jih's location.

But the hundreds must have been thousands, for they broke

through the tail's defensive wall with sheer numbers alone. The screams erupted closer.

Kai tripped over his own feet to avoid an arrow, only to be jerked in the same motion by Timar when one of Timar's own apprentices flashed a hidden dagger. Timar twisted the dagger out of the traitor's hand and swiped white dragonsteel cleanly across the traitor's shoulder. Their head rolled.

Kai dove for the fallen dagger and snatched it up. Timar turned to meet another blade at her back, and Kai flew backward. Kai was pulled into the motions of the fight, ducking under blades and narrowly missing having his head chopped off. Kai tried breaking the chain link with the dagger, but it refused to bend. Kai choked when a scavenger slammed into the line.

"Stop fucking moving," Timar snapped at him.

Kai brandished the dagger at her.

"Really?" Timar snapped. "Look around you. One of these rival clans gets a hold of you, and they'll torture you dead."

Timar whipped the chain forward, but Kai was already moving the same direction. The momentum gave him speed.

Timar stared for a surprised moment at the bloody slash across her waist.

Kai had managed to wound her when all others hadn't been able to. It gave Kai hope he might fight his way out of this, and maybe escape in the confusion. Rasia was still a few days out, and this could be his best chance.

Timar charged him in anger, and Kai's bravado was immediately proved overblown. The force of her sword stroke snapped back his arm. She tripped him with the chain. Kai lost his grip on the dagger.

Chink.

A large battle axe cut into the ground, severing the chain that connected Kai to Timar. Timar leaned back to avoid an attack from the largest person Kai had ever seen. If not naturally big-boned, it was rare to see someone with so much body weight in the Grankull, and the scavenger hefted his battle axe with trained ease.

Timar's crimson bone mask faced off against a cobalt black one.

"Timar." The opposing Han grinned. "I hear you've been a greedy thing, keeping the gold-eyes all to yourself."

Kai got to his feet and ran.

Timar gave chase but couldn't follow while avoiding the destructive power of the Han's battle axe. Kai wove and ducked through the battle, chain rattling behind him.

He had a clear path to the trees. If Kai could save himself, Nico or Rasia wouldn't have to risk their faces.

But Kai caught sight of the oasis kids, stuck in the cages. He recognized some of their terrified faces: Neema from the belly market, the female who tried to drown him in the oasis waters, and two of the kids from his initial Forging team who had pushed him off the windship.

Kai couldn't leave them to the fate the scavengers had planned for them. No matter how they'd treated Kai, they all deserved better than what he witnessed last night.

Kai curved toward the cages. He slipped on loose dirt and caught himself against the cage bars. They shouted at him as he pulled at the lock. It wouldn't budge, and he had no idea where the key might be.

In the corner of his eye, Kai saw a bloody spear lying in the hand of a nearby corpse. Kai grabbed the spear, jammed it into the hollow of the lock, and slammed down with all his weight.

"Come on, you fucking runt."

"We're so dead."

"Try harder!"

Kai's muscles strained. His shoulder ached. His legs shook and sweat dripped down his face. The lock refused to budge. Kai gave up that plan and grabbed the hook attached to the bottom platform, which was used to connect the wheeled cages to a windship. Kai pulled, and the wheels creaked and groaned.

Kai choked.

Timar stood behind him with a fresh head wound, and the collar chain wrapped around her forearm. Kai fought to stand his ground, but she jerked him back so hard, the hook snatched from his hands, and he flew off his feet.

She dragged him by the throat. Kai tried to reach some sort of weapon—a shortsword lying on the ground, but it brushed out of reach past his fingertips. He clawed against the ground, ripping a fingernail, cutting himself over dead corpses, while the chain rattled in his ear.

When they reached the trees, Timar curved her fingers into the collar link and hauled Kai to his feet. She pushed him toward a secret tunnel hidden beneath a door of vines. The ground cut his feet raw, and branches slapped at his bare flesh.

The ground led down and then up. Soft lush turned to hard stone, sharp twists, then cavernous, smooth bone. On the walls of the cavern, clinging along the damp and mossy bone neck, grew hundreds of clustered mushrooms.

After drums of hiking, they reached the cave opening, framed by teeth. A mountain had grown around the maw of this dragon, a part of the same skeleton where vibrations away scavengers slaughtered each other at the center of its tail.

Timar tied Kai's chain from around her forearm to an incisor. She dug up a secret stash of supplies, and Kai watched her, judging.

"You abandoned all those who follow you."

"I'm a scavenger," Timar said as she hunched down, then ate dinner all the while her kull burned in the forest below. "This isn't my first time I've had to start over."

"You cared about some of them."

Timar shrugged in response.

There was enough slack in the chain to allow Kai to reach the bushes at the cave's lip. He passed water, took a glance over his shoulder at Timar, and shuffled slowly to the edge. With the exception of the fire, it was a beautiful view with several ponds and lakes glittering through verdant green.

Looking down, the mountain wasn't so much a sharp incline but a rough roll to the bottom. The chain at his neck went taut.

"Don't even think about it. You're more than likely to break your neck than escape me."

Kai wasn't going anywhere with this collar around his neck. He backed away and was startled when his stomach growled. There had been a time when he had been so used to going without that his stomach hadn't known it could complain.

Timar tossed him a leather bag of nuts and dried fruit.

Kai looked at her quizzically. Timar answered his unspoken question. "You're the last play I've got, and your jih can't find you if you're dead."

Kai munched on the bag's contents, watching Timar. Now that the adrenaline was fading, all the aches and pains pummeled Kai. The dirt ground bit cold against his bare skin. Bugs he'd never seen had bitten red welts on his arms and legs.

Timar hunkered down, on guard as she watched the quietening of the forest. Kai watched her. Timar watched him. They watched each other.

Timar said, without prompt, "Most people believe in the Grankull's lie—that it'll take care of you, that as long as you work hard, you eat. But what happens when the Grankull doesn't have the resources to take care of everyone? People fall through the cracks. They grow up believing the Grankull's promises and become bitter and broken when it fails them. I've seen it all too often. But you're different. You were born knowing it was broken. You were born knowing the world isn't fair." She pursed her lips, jaw clenched, angry. "No matter how hard you try, how fierce you believe, or how true your dreams, the world is still cruel. You have to be cruel back."

Kai narrowed his eyes. "Cruelty is a choice. It is never an excuse."

"You only believe that because you've yet to have the power to wield over others. You've had no choice but to be small and weak and broken. That's what the Grankull wants you to believe. You and Rasia, outside of the Grankull's shadow, you could be hans of your own. I don't have to be your enemy."

"How the fuck do you think I'm going to ignore the fact that you want to kill my jih?"

"How the fuck do you retain loyalty for the place that bought the hit?"

Kai's jaw snapped shut. He didn't have a rebuttal to that.

"I'm just another player in this game. You'd do well to remember that."

CHAPTER FIFTY-SIX

10

"You tried to go *through* the Graveyard?" Nico interrupted.

"*Will you let me finish?*" As Rasia recounted her encounter with the scavengers and the ensuing chase, the others leaned ever forward, enthralled by her tale.

Rasia killed two facehunters? They were chased by a scavenger armada? Kai jumped a bone-link? It sounded like a legend straight out of the temple library.

"What do you mean Kai *magicked* you out of the ship?" Nico interrupted again.

"Exactly what I said."

"You're saying Kai transported you from the windship to a sand dune in the blink of an eye?"

"You turned into water not too long ago."

"I thought he didn't have magic?" Azan asked.

Rasia got that grin on her face. She leaned forward and spread her hands out in an explosion. "Kai cums magic."

"*What?*" Azan asked, startled. He swiveled his head toward Nico. "Is that a thing? Do *you* cum magic?"

Nico's face blushed when all eyes landed on her. Even Suri scooted a little closer to hear the answer. Nico knew it could happen, theoretically, but that was for magic-born barely in control of their magic. Ava-ta would be scandalized to hear of it.

"How would Nico know?" Rasia teased. "She's an untouched precious little flower saving herself for Naming night."

"*Enough*," Nico sputtered, desperate to get off the topic of both her and jih's sex lives. Nico established, "Kai has magic, but it's unreliable and usually acts on its own. Rasia, what happened after the scavengers captured you?"

"Right." Rasia shifted awkwardly around the bandages and pulled an iron collar out of her bag. Rasia waved it above her head, using it as a prop for the rest of her tale. Nico gazed at it in horror.

Rasia finished her story by declaring, "Every scavenger in the Desert is out hunting for Nico's head. Kai would have never been captured if it weren't for her. So. This is all Nico's fault."

"There's a bounty on Nico's head?! Why didn't you start with that?" Zephyr demanded.

"But why would anyone want to put a bounty on Nico's head?" Azan asked.

"Probably the same reason someone placed a hit on her in the Tents." Kelin shrugged.

"You admit to it, then?" Suri said, shooting to her feet. She pointed across the circle to Kelin. "Now everyone knows you're not to be trusted."

"Yeah, but Kelin doesn't want to kill her anymore," Azan defended.

"You know?" Nico asked Azan, shocked Kelin had told him. Zephyr had guessed Kelin's ulterior motives as she had, but Nico didn't think Kelin would outright reveal his intentions to anyone. She wondered if this flame between Azan and Kelin was more serious than she'd thought.

"*I* know that," Rasia scoffed. "Why else would a flock kid hang around you?"

"His name is Kelin," Azan corrected.

"Yeah, whatever."

Kelin muttered, "She *is* an asshole."

"Can we focus? Now that we know what happened with Kai, we need to make a plan."

"Let's circle back to why they want to kill you," Azan insisted, shoulders tensed, defensive on her behalf.

"I can only assume it's because I'm the deciding vote in the next Council meeting to determine a purge. Or it's because I'm the Ohan, and they want me dead. My opinions aren't exactly popular."

"Who wouldn't want her dead?"

"Shut up, Rasia."

"Back to the *plan*. Rasia, you said this Timar Han gave you three days? We don't have much time to save him. I propose that we—"

"This is the plan," Rasia declared, completely stampeding over Nico's words. "Nico and I go in with the collar on her neck. I secure Kai, win the collar key from Timar, then Nico floods the entire Graveyard. The dragon bones will float and topple everything over, killing every last one of them. The end."

"Would that actually work?" Azan asked slowly.

"Duh," Rasia answered. "Dragon bones are like bird bones. They're hollow. They float. That's why the Elder's bones are tied down. To keep them from shifting when it floods."

Nico was fundamentally opposed to this plan. "*No*. Why should we punish all the scavengers for the actions of one group? And what about the kids captured at the oasis? What about the no-faces? We need to save them too."

"Those kids at the oasis weren't going to survive the Forging anyway."

"Who are you to judge who lives and dies, Rasia?" Nico asked. "These kids are facing extraordinary circumstances because someone placed a hit on my head. Not everyone can power through like you. You have always had everything—either an abundance of resources, food, or the skill and talent to succeed in times of little. It is not these kids who have failed, but the Grankull that has failed them. I refuse to fail them too."

"This is ridiculous. Okay, maybe the Forging kids but the no-faces too? They were sold or captured by the scavengers for a reason. And what happens if we save them all? Where are they going to go? What are we going to do with them? They can't go back to the Grankull. *There is no food*. Why do you think the Council has turned a blind eye to the scavengers all this time? Because each person they take is one fewer mouth to feed. What is your solution, Nico?"

"I don't know. I don't have those answers, but I refuse to leave anyone behind. I *know* that I can't save everyone, but that doesn't mean I shouldn't try. You came to me for *my* help, to *my* kull. Therefore, we do this on *my* terms."

Rasia audibly slapped herself and dragged her hands down till the red of her eyes showed. "This is going to get us killed. This is going to get Kai killed. You know what? Fuck it. Walk in wearing the collar and get your head chopped off. At least then Kai goes free."

"That's not happening," Suri said. "Absolutely not," Zephyr snapped simultaneously.

"No one fucking asked the both of you."

"Enough!" Nico stood, resolute. "This is not your kull, Rasia. You can't bark orders at people and expect them to be followed. Everyone here is trying to help, and you should treat them with more respect."

"Whatever. We wouldn't be in this situation if it weren't for you. It's your head that they want."

"They took Kai because of *you*," Nico ground out. "If you hadn't swept him up on this dumb adventure of yours, we'd have killed a gonda and been home by now."

"Or this dumb adventure is the very reason the scavengers haven't been able to find you. You should be thanking me."

Nico opened her mouth and stopped herself. Arguing with Rasia wasn't going to move them forward. Nico forced herself to calm and took a step back. Tensions were running too hot. They needed a break.

"Everyone, drink some water. We'll regroup after high noon."

Everyone scattered. Rasia threw up her hands; she couldn't chase after them because of her leg, unable to get up as quickly.

"Rasia," Nico said, head hurting and tired. "I am trying, but you've got to meet me halfway."

"Ha! When the Elder breathes fire."

Nico reminded herself that Kai cared for this self-righteous monster of a brat. She barely stopped herself from summoning a deluge to sweep Rasia out over the rock shelf. *Barely.*

"Stupid skink," Rasia grumbled from where she lay curled around her injuries. Thoughts rampaged through her head. Nico was going to get herself killed trying to save every grubworm and dung beetle, and Kai was going to be all sad about it.

Rasia tensed at the sound of laughter. She glared over her shoulder at Nico's group. They sat eating lunch and laughing at some dumb joke. The flock kid leaned an elbow against the blacksmith's kid. Zephyr smiled . . . with dimples. *Who knew Zephyr had dimples?* The long-bow girl mixed a pot of tea, listening. And of course, Nico sat in the middle, an oasis at the center of bowing palm fronds, laughing and glistening and reflecting those around her.

Rasia didn't understand why people followed her. Nico barely knew anything, nor had she done anything of note or worthy of a name. Nico depended too much on her magic and was nothing without it. But as always, people buzzed around Nico and stuck to her like honey.

Rasia remembered her first day of school. Bright and optimistic and naive, Rasia had gone to every student and asked if they would be her friend. As the school season continued and the teachers grew more frustrated with Rasia's inability to sit still, all those kids she thought were her friends began treating her the same way the teachers did, as if something were wrong with her. Nico, on the other hand, got all the friends. Everyone always scrambled after the ohani's attention.

Rasia didn't go back to school after that first season. Who

needed false friends? Why should she have to change for their acceptance and approval? She had tah and Ysai, and they accepted her for who she was.

Until they were gone.

Now her only friend was captured by scavengers.

Rasia tensed at the encroachment of footsteps. She sat up and glared as Zephyr crouched next to her with a bowl of food. "What do you want? You're on the enemy's side."

"I'm on Kai's side," Zephyr said.

Rasia scoffed. "I see the way you look at her. So what, you've a kink for siblings?"

Zephyr rolled his eyes. In the Grankull, it wasn't odd for siblings to have had relations with the same person, rarer to be at the same time though. Still, Kai was Rasia's, and Zephyr was just being greedy.

"I like them both. I can't help the way I feel," Zephyr said. "Kai had broken things off with you, so I made my move. But he's committed to you. I respect that. And Nico and I . . . are complicated."

"Of course it's complicated," Rasia further scoffed. "Nico makes everything complicated."

Zephyr smiled at that and nodded in agreement. "That's who she is. She can't help it, but that's because she has a lot of considerations to make. Have you ever tried to comprehend her side of things? To try and understand the massive amount of responsibility she carries? She carries this kull, her family, the Grankull, the Tents, and as far as she is concerned, the entirety of the Graveyard as well. Would it be such a hardship to go a little easier on her?"

"That's not my fault. Nico chooses that shit. She doesn't have to."

"But she does. Every day she chooses it. One day she'll figure out the difference between those who need her, and those who don't. She'll figure out how to delegate, and how to prioritize, and then she'll do it. She'll carry the whole world. That's strength too, Rasia."

"Ugh. You've got it bad." Rasia shook her head.

"I hardly think you can criticize," Zephyr said, flatly. "The whole reason you are here is to go back for him. Do you really think Kai is going to be okay with leaving those kids behind? Kai stood up to you and exacted a blood price on my behalf. He broke up with you because he didn't want to dishonor his jih. It's ironic how you get along with him so well, considering he and Nico have a lot in common."

Rasia crossed her arms. She didn't see the similarities at all. They didn't even look that much alike.

"Get your head out of your ass, Rasia. Kai is more important than your pride." Zephyr sat down the bowl of soup. "That's from Nico."

Zephyr got up and left. Rasia grumpily pulled the bowl toward her.

As she ate, Rasia mentally ran through all her options and ended on the same brutal realization: She couldn't save Kai by herself.

"You only come back home when you're injured," Ysai's voice berated her, back when she wandered into the Grankull half-dead and starved atop the merchant kull she flagged down in the deadlands. She remembered tracking the windship trails and hoping someone would come along. She remembered the heat and talking to jih's blurred shadow till he swept away in a mirage of her own making and left her dying alone.

I was supposed to be invincible.

She remembered how Kai held her. She remembered how when she thought it was the end, he had refused to let her go. It was she who brought him out of the Lake of Yestermorrow and woke him back up. Kai whisked her off the deck of her windship before the collision, sensed enemies in the trees, and found the strength to tackle Timar while barely conscious. *Together*, they were invincible.

The lake tried to give me everything I could possibly want, but all I wanted was you. That's not fate, or bones thrown. I chose you. You and I, and our kull, that's forever.

Rasia was not alone anymore.

She was not a kull of one anymore.

She was a kull of two.

Kull of two.

Rasia pressed her hand to her chest in sudden realization. A laugh broke from her body, tinged with heat sickness and blood faintness. It hit like her thunder, tingling though her toes and traveling with excitement up her spine.

Rasia sprang to her feet with renewed strength and purpose. Nico could have all the followers and worshipers in the world. Nico could have all the friends and the jovial kull of found-family misfits. But Rasia only needed one.

Grow what makes you happy.

Rasia had asked Kai to trust her, and she didn't break her promises. Rasia would do anything to get him back. Even destroy the world. Even compromise. Even maybe, just maybe, get along with Nico.

Rasia strode toward Nico's group, and they looked at her like a jackal prowling too close to camp. Nico stood as Rasia planted her feet.

"Fine. We'll do things your way. Let's save everyone, but they are your responsibility and your consequences to deal with. I'm only concerned for Kai, but if those are your terms, I accept."

"I am glad to hear it," Nico said. "Maybe we disagree on the how but trust I will not rest until jih is rescued. We need each other. Kai is depending on us to figure out how to work together. I apologize, Rasia, for underestimating you, for lacking faith in you, and failing to see your vision. Perhaps I'll never understand, but I do see you better now. I can only hope you'll give me the chance to prove my aspirations are more than naivete and brittle bones. I fully accept the responsibility and consequences of my actions."

"I apologize for nothing," Rasia declared in turn. She had nothing to apologize for. "I suggest we approach this mission as the Hans of two kulls involved in a joint operation. I don't involve myself in the particulars of your kull business but matters and decisions regarding my windeka ultimately yield to me."

Nico gritted her teeth. Nico might plan to become her family's triarch, the head of Kai's household, but out in the field, the Han always took precedence. Either Nico would adhere to kull rules, or she'd assert her authority over Kai as both triarch and Ohan. *Let's see if Nico is truly willing to meet in the middle.* Actions were always far more important than words.

Nico visibly struggled with Rasia's terms. Rasia thought a strand of hair sprung out of the ponytail. Finally, Nico sucked in a breath and extended two fingers.

Rasia stared at the offer of truce with the realization they'd never in their entire lives touched each other in any way other than a physical blow. Rasia extended her hand and locked two fingers around Nico's own.

They shook on it.

"Let's get to work."

"This is what we know," Nico said once everyone regrouped. Rasia bit down on her tongue, annoyed Nico had automatically taken the lead. "The scavengers want me to wear the collar and trade myself for jih. The goal is to not only rescue Kai, but also rescue the kids caught at the oasis and the no-faces. Does anyone have any ideas?"

"The collar is crudely made," Azan said as he studied the collar's latch. "I can resize it, so you'll be able to use magic while wearing it."

"Perfect. That's great, Azan." Nico nodded. Azan grinned, and Rasia rolled her eyes at the pandering of it all.

Rasia watched the proceedings, but as promised, kept her thoughts regarding the management of Nico's kull to herself. Nico gave everyone a chance to voice their opinions and offer suggestions. The whole process was *sooo* slow.

"Rasia and I will go in with the broken collar, and I'll attack them with my magic. We'll rescue Kai and the others while the rest of you wait with both windships. Suri will be on standby for anyone wounded. Kelin will provide cover for our escape. Azan will steer our ship, and Zephyr will steer Rasia's ship . . ." Nico turned to Rasia. "If that's okay with you?"

Rasia huffed. "Your plan is stupid and it sucks."

"Then please tell me what's wrong with it." Nico invited the criticism, admittedly a far cry from the unmoving and know-it-all Nico from the beginning of the Forging.

"Gladly. First off, your plan lacks specificity and a back-up plan when everything inevitably goes to shit. For example, you're going to attack them with your magic? What move, exactly? At your best, your fighting style defends against what? An average of five people at a time? We will be surrounded by hundreds of scavengers. Even if you can turn into water, you'll have to take a breath sometime. Someone is going to get lucky and put an arrow through you."

Nico blinked, then conceded, "You're right. Perhaps a fog would be best to obscure their field of vision?"

"Can you contain it? If not, I can't think of a quicker way to signal to every scavenger in the Graveyard your location."

"I could practice containing it to a specific area. How large is the base? Perhaps you can draw a map, so we have a layout of where everything is?"

"Sure. I can do that. Second, you're leaving the majority of your kull behind because you are too concerned for their well-being. We are going up against hundreds of scavengers. Bring your two best fighters. I suggest Zephyr and the flock kid."

"Kelin."

"Right," Rasia said. "And have you considered what you're going to do if the no-faces don't want to come with you?"

"Why wouldn't they? We need to save them, Rasia."

Rasia rolled her eyes. Some people learned the hard way. She continued, "If we're going to save all those people, we'll need something big. Some sort of distraction . . ."

Possibilities and plans and schemes formed before Rasia's eyes. Her intake of air voiced a thousand clashing ideas and inspirations. Her lips coiled into a smile, and everyone around her leaned forward in anticipation. "I've got an idea, but only if you've got the bones for it."

"Let's hear your crazy, Rasia."

CHAPTER FIFTY-SEVEN

Ю

"Shit. There goes the plan."

"What's wrong?" Nico asked Rasia. As Rasia had predicted, the scavengers launched out to accost them the moment Rasia's ship came into view of the Graveyard.

"Those scavengers aren't Crimsons," Rasia said. "This should be interesting."

Nico frowned at that news. She adjusted the collar around her neck, modified with enough room for her to take a full breath. Azan had done a great job on it, and she hoped all his effort wasn't for naught.

Rasia stopped the windship, and Nico climbed down the stairs to meet with the scavengers. Zephyr and Kelin followed behind her. Suri and Azan were both absent, tasked with preparing the distraction with the other ship. Hopefully, things were going to plan on their end.

"Where is Timar, Han of the Crimson Scavengers?" Nico asked. It was Rasia's idea for Nico to take the lead. The more attention on Nico, the less attention on Rasia.

"We kicked that shroud out a day ago," the scavenger answered. "We represent the Serpentines. Timar might no longer be in control of this territory, but the Cobalt-Serpentine alliance is aware of Timar's deal and is willing to honor it."

"Fine. I offer to willingly exchange myself for Kai-ji. In addition, my kull will also come with me," Nico said, motioning to Rasia, Zephyr, and Kelin. "They will ensure that my jih leaves the Graveyard as promised."

The facehunters shared several glances with one another, trading silent words, before the leader nodded.

"Come, Ohan, and we will take you to your fate."

The facehunters led them to a small, covered path into the forest. Another facehunter jumped atop Rasia's ship and steered it through a wider road.

The biology of the fauna fascinated Nico. She spied plants she'd never seen before and flowers of colors the temple gardens would be envious of. She walked atop fertile soil that she wanted to pick up and carry to the more stubborn arid fields of the outer wings.

As they walked farther in, the lullaby of the Graveyard's bones grew ever more haunting. Unlike the Great Elder, which was alive and buzzing with energy, these bones slumbered. Nico caught snatches of mumbled words, brief yawns, and fragments of a dream.

As Rasia claimed, they had walked ten vibrations to reach the base camp. Hopefully, Azan and Suri were minding the time and keeping schedule. The scavenger base looked as Rasia described it, the only difference being a slender figure who sat atop the wooden throne. The figure wore a large elaborate green bark mask. Two familiar khopesh blades laid across their lap.

A larger figure wearing a black mask and holding a wicked bone axe over their shoulder leaned a leg on the throne's arm support. The tree of heads created a morbid chorus at each shift of the wind.

"Is this her?" the Serpentine Han asked in a thick scavenger accent. This scavenger was born here, and Nico tried to wrap her mind around the generations that had called this rough and beautiful place home.

"We believe so."

"They could be lying," the Cobalt Han said, pointedly eying

Nico. "Don't they have gold-eyes?"

"Not all are born with the eyes?" One of the facehunters said, rounding the sentence with a question, unsure.

"I could perform magic," Nico suggested, "but you would have to take off the collar."

The Serpentine Han curled a finger toward a pair of cages. Between the bars of those cages, Nico found faces she recognized from the oasis, including Faris, Loryn, Rianis, and Gysen. All their faces lifted in hope at the sight of her.

The facehunter retrieved Neema, hands bound, from the cage. Her braids had come undone, all her dragonglass beads lost, and her hair was now matted into clumped strips. Neema's curves had sharpened, and the pointed angles in her face could be replaced for knives. Immediately, Nico felt guilty for all the friction between them before.

The Serpentine Han asked, "I am told the Ohan was first placed on your kull. Is this her face?"

"It's a lie!" Neema yelled out. "They don't have him! Your jih is gone!"

A facehunter jerked Neema back. Another lifted their sword and plunged down the blade to behead Neema on the spot.

The facehunter's sword froze in mid-air. Every pump of their blood now in Nico's control. It was not the intended signal, but Rasia didn't hesitate.

Rasia raced forward with scimitar in hand and sliced off the facehunter's head, sending it flying into the massive tree trunk. Rasia immediately turned to attack the Serpentine Han, who flipped over the throne to land with Rasia's dual khopesh turned against their owner.

Zephyr scooped up Neema and cut through her restraints.

The scavengers recovered quickly, and the Cobalt Han shouted orders to attack.

Nico summoned a dense fog. Despite the cover, the Cobalt Han came charging through the mist, straight toward Nico.

Steel flashed across the Han's stomach, the shoulder, twice in the neck, in such quick succession Nico could barely follow.

The Cobalt Han dropped dead, and Kelin winked cheekily before sprinting for the cages.

A vibration trembled the ground.

At least Azan and Suri's part had gone according to plan—Nico heard a distant roar—or maybe not.

Kai thought he dreamed the first vibration, then jolted out of sleep when the second didn't stop. Timar ducked under a tooth decorated with a floss of vines and looked out over the Graveyard.

From this height, Kai could make out a dot—a windship?—breaking over the horizon, followed by massive sprawling shadows. The shadows formed into tentacles and rolling sand hills. They multiplied, and multiplied, until Kai counted at least twenty gonda bearing down on the Graveyard.

"It's Rasia."

"And the ohani. Another windship approached two kulls ago," Timar said. All this time, she had been scanning the skyline for Nico's windship, planning to swoop in after the inevitable fight weakened both Nico and the rival scavengers.

The windship baiting the gonda disappeared onto one of the wide ship roads of the Graveyard. Entire bones tilted and moved as the gonda cracked the border. Like ants, scavengers fled the bones from all sides. Thousands raced to get away.

"That kid is rutting brilliant," Timar spat as she watched the chaos, too far to touch them just yet. Entire bones were tossed to the side, ecosystems and trees disrupted as the gonda trampled through.

"Time to go," Timar said.

She collected her weapons and supplies. Kai spied the distant tail of Timar's previous encampment and wished he could make out what was going on.

A mighty roar rattled the bones.

A gold dragon burst out the sky, shattering clouds, and chased after the gonda feast. Aurum. Kai doesn't think *that* was part of the plan.

"Elderfuck," Timar cursed out and yanked on Kai's collar chain.

The dragon's attention shifted, and a zap went through Kai's spine when their eyes met. Kai recognized something familiar but distant, faint and hazy like déjà vu. The dragon's maw opened. Fire condensed on their tongue. Timar jerked Kai by the arm, into the dank neck, and a blaze consumed the mountainous skull.

"Are you crazy?" Timar asked.

Kai stumbled after her, slipping and stumbling as she led him through the neck to a windship she had hidden at the back of the skull. Despite the interspersed trees, ideally, it looked like you could drive the windship all the way down the spine, but it was going to be one elderfire of a ride.

Timar prepared the windship to sail, attention largely focused on periodically checking the dragon making circular sweeps overhead. Kai trailed after her on deck as much as the chain allowed. He glanced at a handful of rope at his feet. He'd waited for days, searching for that right moment.

Kai hit the deck with a thump.

Timar couldn't reach the steer at the back of the windship with Kai collapsed at the front. She whipped around, the chain rattled, and she cursed. Timar stomped over and reached down to grab him.

Kai snapped up and looped the rope around Timar's neck, tightened the knot, and held on for dear life. He pulled with all his strength, arms shaking, as Timar struggled against him.

They rolled across the windship. Kai's back slammed into the other side, but he refused to let go. If there were a moment Kai needed his body to not fail him, it was now. He held tight, straining. His shoulder burned as if on fire, but he refused to give up and fought for every arduous vibration until finally Timar sagged beneath him.

Kai dropped the ropes. Where he held on, the rough fibers

had scraped off his skin. His fingers ached at the stiffness. Timar lay unconscious across him while he blinked in disbelief. He did it. Kai might not be improving at the pace he wanted, but sometimes his body proved it was far stronger than he gave it credit for.

During the struggle, Timar's bone mask had tumbled off.

A large X crossed her face.

Kai reached into Timar's shirt, between her breasts, and pulled out the collar key. Kai unlocked the collar and chucked it overboard. He sucked in two great lungfuls. The best breaths he had ever taken.

Kai made sure to secure Timar with the rope, just in case. Then, he stripped Timar of her clothes. The pants were surprisingly big, so he used her breast wrap as a belt. Kai grabbed Ava-ta's sword, the one that had been passed down in his family for generations and tied it to his waist.

Kai grabbed ahold of the windship steer and stared down the length of the dragon's curved spine.

"You can do this," Kai said, and reminded himself, "You're a damn good windeka."

"You have something that belongs to me," Rasia said as she circled the Serpentine Han. The fog of Nico's magic swirled around them. The ground vibrated faster and faster. Nothing mattered but her opponent. She'd never killed a scavenger Han before. "Do you know who I am?"

The Han tilted the green bone mask. "Names and faces mean nothing here, kuller. Only strength."

Rasia brandished the scimitar straight with both hands, arms up, the gleam of the bright metal pressed to her face like a mirror. She lowered to attack. So did her opponent.

They charged.

Rasia blocked the double beat of her dual khopesh and slashed horizontally. The Han twisted around the scimitar with impressive flexibility. Rasia often found herself cutting at air. A smile crossed her face, and her hips dipped to the rhythm of countered blows.

A low kick aimed for Rasia's wounded thigh, but earlier that morning Rasia had wrapped the dirty bloody bandage around the wrong leg. Rasia took that hit with ease, bony foreleg against femur, and Rasia stabbed the scimitar with relish into the serpent's leg, straight through, staking the blade to the ground.

The Han slashed as they folded. Rasia jumped over the attack and, without mercy, landed both knees to the Han's chest. The Serpentine Han slackened, and their grip loosened. Rasia picked up her khopesh with triumph and kissed the flat of both blades. She sorely missed their balance.

Rasia kicked off the Serpentine's mask and found a child, a couple of years younger than her. Too bad. The kid had been better than Rasia at that age.

"I offer you to Death. You were a worthy hunt." Rasia said as she crossed her swords at the Han's neck. Rasia slashed her swords apart. "All hunters are hunted."

A gonda crashed through the scavenger base.

Some scavengers turned their attention to the giant monstrosity that invaded their camp. Some scavengers fled, others turned to fight, but a majority aimed for Nico in a last-ditch effort to collect the bounty. Nico tested the ground with her feet, determined her balance, and held her glaive against her forearm.

They all came at her at once.

Nico ducked under a swinging mace and swept the facehunter off their feet. She splashed an arrow out the air, then speared through the facehunter's chest. Her first kill. Nico barely had time to linger on it. She brought her glaive up and a sword screeched off the polearm. Nico dropped her shoulder, spinning with gravity, and kicked the facehunter's mask right off their face. Nico spun back around and slashed across the facehunter's neck.

Nico lashed a whip of water across a wave of attackers and flowed around her polearm, like rain-river flowing off the Elder's back, and slashed from one bone face to another.

Nico seethed when an arrow cut her arm. She reached for the archer, wrapped a stream around their throat, and splashed them from the tree branches.

Metal chimed behind her. Nico turned and found Rasia cutting down the attacker at Nico's back.

Nico fought because she had to. She fought to protect herself, and those who needed saving. Nico didn't know what she expected to find in Rasia's blood-speckled face, perhaps the wild bloodlust and feral battle rage of aged legends. It surprised Nico to discover that in the heat of battle, Rasia reminded her more of a musician.

Like Kenji-ta lost in music.

Kenji-ta's best songs were the pattern-breakers. The ones that acknowledged the Grankull's long tradition of musical tales, of chords people memorized, and melodies they hummed at work. He played with that framework, establishing patterns to upend expectations, playing with syncopation, twisting and swooping and turning notes into songs you'd never heard before. Rasia was a similar musician. She created her own beats, then upended them. Rasia twisted and swooped and turned, and everyone was stuck dancing to her tune. For Rasia, battle was a song composed on the fly and a thrilling dance all in one. It was rhythm.

Nico moved to Rasia's beat, in perfect understanding, and pressed together back-to-back.

Rasia's sword played notes behind her, chinking off metal and cutting slick through flesh. Nico added to Rasia's song with her own notes of breath, building a harmony, combining tones. They danced with each other. Water splashed. Blood dripped. Metal struck metal. Facehunters screamed and gurgled and choked.

Feet drummed as facehunters broke and ran.

Nico and Rasia breathed heavily against each other at the end, staring out at the piles of bodies that surrounded them. None who have killed as many as they have should feel as if they were having the greatest time of their lives. And yet, Rasia turned to Nico, eyes bright, grinning as if seeing Nico for the very first time. Nico couldn't stop her own smile. Rasia and Nico's forms were precise, their techniques things of envy, no strokes or breaths wasted. A beautiful awe-inspiring melody Nico could never have composed on her own.

Perfection.

Zephyr and Kelin protected the oasis kids' retreat. Kelin slashed with his curved dagger and reaped swathes of facehunters before they realized they'd been hit. Zephyr crushed them with his sword, often shattering bodies to the ground. The child of the Scorpion, and the child of the Crane, both from opposing Tent Hans, fought side by side.

A few other oasis kids had picked up weapons and assisted in covering the weaker ones' escape. Neema pursued every scavenger who crossed her path, and she was so focused on going after those who had imprisoned her that she paid no attention to the flailing tentacles.

"She's going to get herself killed," Rasia sneered. "I'm not saving her ass again."

"I'll take care of Neema," Nico said. "Distract the gonda."

Nico tackled Neema to the ground, right before a tentacle sailed over their heads.

The gonda's attention shifted toward Rasia, who raced in the opposite direction beating a stick to an amphora. But not even a gonda could deter Neema's war path. Neema rolled back up and threw a knife into the neck of a fleeing scavenger.

"Neema," Nico said, catching her by the arm. "I know you're angry, but you're making the situation worse. Go with the others."

"No. I want to help. We can kill these scavengers and slay the gonda. I know I can do it," Neema argued, despite not having the strength to wrestle out of Nico's grip. Nico feared Neema might faint.

"Neema," Nico said, more urgently. "You need to go. I owe you a gonda. I owe you that, I promise."

"Ohan!"

A body lunged in front of her. Nico caught the slackened body and stared aghast at an arrow pierced through the child's back. Blood spread quickly through the tattered linen shirt.

Neema swiped a pottery shard off the ground and hurled it at the sniper in the tree. The sniper crashed through the branches.

"Rianis," Nico exclaimed when she recognized the face, one of the kids from back at the oasis, the female who had told Nico the truth about what happened to Kai.

"You remembered my name," the child croaked.

Nico pressed her hands to the wound and tried suppressing the blood flow with her magic, but the arrow had pierced the heart. There was nothing she could do. Rianis's life drained a river out of Nico's hands.

Neema looked at the dead kid with a bitter expression. "*What about her gonda?*"

Zephyr and Kelin approached them at a run.

"All the Forging kids and no-faces have been freed," Zephyr reported, then glanced down at the bloody body in Nico's lap. "All the ones alive."

A roar, much louder and closer than the first time, rattled the bones, visibly bending and shaking the air. Any scavengers left dropped their weapons and ran. Nico looked toward the sky. With the Graveyard's thick density of brambles and bone, she couldn't see the dragon but felt every beat of its wings, like a drum, in her chest. Across the way, Rasia froze with a giddy grin plastered on her face.

"Did you hear that?" Kelin snapped, panicked. "*What was*

that?"

"Zephyr, take the body. I'll cover your retreat."

Zephyr hesitated, unwilling to leave Nico to face a dragon without him.

"*Go,*" Nico insisted.

Nico couldn't save Rianis, but she was determined to make sure her bones got home. Zephyr nodded reluctantly. He reached down and scooped the body over his shoulder. A powerful wing beat pressed against their heads sent Neema tumbling. Zephyr caught Neema's faint with the swoop of his free arm and threw her over his other shoulder.

"Kelin. Cover him."

Kelin didn't have to be told twice. He ran as fast as he could for the trees.

Nico turned back toward the still thrashing gonda. She had to make sure it didn't follow the others. The entire camp had emptied out and no one else remained to keep its attention but Rasia and Nico.

How fun.

Nico lunged out of the way when a tentacle came flying toward her. The gonda reared back, hissing, when a sudden arrow punctured the flailing limb. Suri and Azan emerged from the trees, arrow drawn and fan axe ready.

"We've got the windship positioned on the main road, and the Forging kids are on their way. They'll wait for us at the windship. We're here to cover your exit," Suri said.

"This gonda is too dangerous to be left alone. We need to take this thing down," Nico replied.

A loud clang struck the air. Rasia had thrown the amphora against a far-off tree trunk, briefly distracting the gonda. Rasia rolled over while the gonda chopped away at the poor tree.

Nico turned to Rasia. "We need a plan."

Rasia jolted back, surprised Nico had deferred the decision-making to her, but Nico tried to learn her lessons: Listen to the person who knew what they were doing. Besides, Nico had no doubt Rasia had come over to tell them what to do anyway.

"Exactly why I came over here," Rasia said. "There are too many trees for the gonda to navigate well above ground. Get it away from the clearing and into the trees. Use its limited mobility to our advantage. Suri, use your arrows to strike the tree trunks. The noise will confuse the gonda away from the rest of us. Nico and Azan, focus on the tentacles. I'll go for the hearts."

"Should I use my magic?"

"No. We might need the magic for the dragon."

Rasia concluded the plan by clanging her two swords together. She charged the gonda, shouting all the way.

"Come on, let's go. You heard her," Nico said.

Rasia led the gonda into the trees. Suri's arrows thudded and vibrated in the wood, throwing off the gonda's sense of sound. It thrashed and crashed into bones and vines. Nico found herself tripped up, unused to the territory, while Rasia boldly jumped from one land feature to another.

Nico slid under a fallen log and stabbed her glaive into a tentacle sliding by, pinning it. Azan jumped from the brush and cleaved his fan axe straight through it, cutting it clean in half.

The gonda twisted and roared in pain, creating the opening for Rasia to dart in. Suri's arrows shielded Rasia's charge. Rasia landed on the gonda's main body and dissected flesh to the hearts of it.

The gonda shuddered, then stilled.

The sky darkened drastically, sunshine to darkness in the blink of an eye.

"Get to cover!" Rasia shouted.

Nico looked up as the wingspan unfolded to block out the sun. Rasia leaped behind one of the tailbones. Azan pressed behind a tree trunk. Suri tripped. She wasn't going to make it.

Nico rushed in front of Suri and sucked in the largest breath her lungs could handle, and audibly, frighteningly, she could hear the dragon do the same.

Fire consumed the sky. Nico erected a wall of water, shielding her and Suri from the onslaught. Quickly, the heat grew unbearable. Her wall of water thinned and hissed with steam, burning the air and blurring the vision of the dragon into shadows.

"Go!" Nico commanded. Suri hesitated, but only for a moment before scrambling out of the path of the fire and into the trees. But Nico couldn't move, bearing the onslaught. The flames went on forever and ever.

Nico stood her ground.

Either Nico or the dragon was going to run out of breath first.

Nico wasn't going to hold. Rasia needed to do something before Kai's jih was burnt to ash.

Fire had erupted everywhere through the trees and brush, consuming the entire Graveyard in flames—everything but the bones. The aged bones of old dragons lay unfazed and unbothered. The tailbone Rasia hid behind didn't bend or distort under the heat. Rasia eyed her two dragonsteel khopesh, and a wisp of a plan formed in her head.

Rasia plucked up a broken, elongated shard from the ground, splintered off from a nearby tibia in the gonda's rampage. She tested the weight and found the aged yellow bone resilient enough to heft like a spear. She sheathed her dual blades and used one of her waist cloths to tie the large splinter over her shoulder.

Rasia hopped the tailbone. She ducked underneath a fallen tree, caught herself on an overhanging branch, and pulled herself up. She climbed the trunk, jumped to the next tree, the next bone, until she reached the highest crest she could reach: the topmost branch in the tree of severed heads.

Below her, Nico's impressive tidal wave shrank smaller and smaller. In the corner of her eye, Rasia noticed something unusual, something coming fast down the spine—a windship. It certainly wasn't Timar. That scavenger wouldn't be steering *toward* a dragon.

Rasia hefted the bone spear and aimed it at the dragon's eye.

She reevaluated. Then aimed at the dragon's throat.

Rasia pitched the makeshift spear to the wind. Like throwing bones.

Only a dragon can defeat a dragon.

The spear cracked through the scales and embedded deep within the dragon's throat. Aurum screeched in pain, shaking trees and vibrating air. The onslaught of fire ended. The dragon coughed out black ash, wheezing, then turned, infuriated, in Rasia's direction.

They came roaring toward her, talons wide and reaching. Rasia jumped, barely missing the talons as they ripped into the tree and yanked up deep roots. Severed heads rained from the sky. The dragon twisted with the tree, tossing it, before roaring and retreating into the clouds.

Rasia fell.

Suddenly, an updraft slowed her descent. The wind cradled her. Rasia floated gently, like a feather, into familiar arms. She smirked at the sight of Kai's wonderfully gorgeous face.

"I knew you'd catch me."

CHAPTER FIFTY-EIGHT

1

Ash scorched the ground in every direction, with the lone exception the resilient puddle at Nico's feet.

An unfamiliar windship whipped past. It rolled over dead bodies and came to a screeching stop.

Was that Kai?

Was that Kai's *magic*?

Kai dropped Rasia to the windship deck in one smooth motion, then kissed Rasia as if the world had not enough air and she had all he needed to fill his lungs. The sight was far from the hesitancy he'd displayed during the kiss Rasia had planted on him during the windship chase. This time, Kai kissed with every ounce of his being.

Soon, Nico realized, they might not stop.

Nico walked over and banged a fist on the windship hull. Rasia and Kai separated with shared smiles, and the happiness in Kai's face almost broke Nico into pieces. Nico hadn't seen Kai smile like that since they were children, since they were young enough to believe his magic was the power to turn invisible. It had been their secret world before hate and cruel understanding tore it down. Now he'd found another world, a truer world, of joy and light.

Nico climbed to the deck and noted the blood and bruising

around Kai's neck. Bloody bandages peeked out of the collar of his oversized shirt. Blue ringed his left eye.

For a moment, Nico was uncertain of her reception, but Kai's smile turned on her. He stepped forward and Nico rushed to meet him. They wrapped each other up tight. Nico sputtered, relieved to hold him whole and so, so sorry and hoping he could feel her remorse in every ounce of her strength.

"What a touching reunion," a female intruded, tied practically naked to the railing.

"Who are you?" Nico asked.

"That's Timar. The recently deposed Han of the Crimson scavengers," Rasia said, then asked Kai, "Why didn't you kill her?"

Kai shrugged. "I didn't have to."

"Nico," Zephyr called, stepping out of the trees. Kelin followed, then the no-faces they just rescued. Nico climbed down the windship to find out what was going on.

"You were supposed to wait with the windship on the main road," Nico said. "We're almost done here."

"The Forging kids stayed with the windship, but the no-faces wanted to come back," Zephyr explained.

A young no-face stepped before Nico. Nico almost didn't recognize the curly-haired female. Nico hadn't seen that face since a scavenger snatched the shroud off a child in the dark shadows of the Tents. Now, a large "x" was branded onto her face, an ugly reminder Nico had saved no one but her own conscience that day. Nico didn't know her name.

"My name is Yana, Ohan." Yana bowed in deference. She straightened, looking Nico in the eye. She was far from the trembling mess with the blond curls she had been when they first met. "We appreciate your help, but many do not wish to return to the Grankull. There is no place for us there. This tail is one of the most defensible places in all the Graveyard. If we can establish ourselves here, we should be able to take care of ourselves."

Nico frowned, uncertain. This place didn't look all that defensible anymore. Before, the scavenger base had been surrounded by the curved tail of a slumbering dragon, but now, the dragon woke in a state of war and unrest, half-turned over and clawing at the air.

"Ohan," Yana said, unwavering. "We can't go back. We have no faces."

Yes, but, realistically, how could a handful of no-faces on the edge of starvation survive out here by themselves? Nico wished she could have done something more for Yana. "I'm sorry. I failed to save you."

"That's not true. You have saved not only me, but all of us. Now, we can survive on our own terms."

A commotion broke out behind them.

Everyone had drifted toward the rip in the forest where the gonda had fallen. Nico shoved through the crowd to find her kull at the center of the disturbance, defending the dead gonda from the feverish expressions of the no-faces.

Kelin had both his knives out, turned on the people he had protected moments before. Azan used his axe to bar the no-faces from encroaching further. Even Suri stood on Kelin's side.

"What is going on?" Nico demanded, moving between the crowd and her kull.

"Tell them this is our gonda," Azan bit out. The no-faces tensed and wound tight at the words, and Suri aimed her bow in response. "We killed the gonda. We get to bring it back for our Forging."

"We should have left all the no-faces in their cages," Rasia muttered, butting in. She had an arm looped around Kai's shoulder and limped into the chaotic mess.

"Rasia," Kai said. "No."

Shockingly, Rasia only pouted in response.

"*Fine*, but I've got to say it." Rasia looked at Nico and raised her brows dramatically. "*I told you so.*"

Several no-faces swept forward, and Azan pushed them back with the sharp, wide curve of his fan axe. Many of the no-faces had picked up weapons from the ground, and Nico realized keenly that the no-faces far outnumbered them. If she didn't do something soon, this was going to erupt into violence. Against a trained kull with a tent assassin, magic, and Rasia on their side, Nico had no doubt the weak, starved no-faces would pay the highest price.

"This gonda belongs to the scavengers!" A voice bellowed out beyond the crowd.

The no-faces parted. A crimson mask with a bone leg came stomping through, freed from the windship she had been previously tied to. Yana walked loyally beside Timar, the Crimson Han.

"See? This is why you should have killed her," Rasia complained. She straightened off Kai's shoulder and unsheathed her khopesh, readying for a fight.

"You know you'd miss me." Timar winked at Rasia.

Timar looked out at the group, the very Han who had branded an X on all their faces. "This is our territory! This is our gonda! Do we choose weakness and allow these outsiders to take what is ours? Or do we choose our faces?!"

The group of no-faces looked at each other. All at once, they picked bone masks off the dead. They fitted those hard masks over their x's and became scavengers. In a sudden reversal, Timar confronted Nico with an army of scavengers at her back.

"Good," Rasia said, excited. "I was due a rematch."

"We *saved* you," Azan said, outraged. "This is our kill."

Timar laughed. "Whether yours by right, we are scavengers. We take what is ours."

Nico stood, undecided, uncertain. Nico found it hard not to sympathize with the scavengers' plight. Everyone's got to eat.

"Nico, don't," Suri pleaded.

"We saved your jih," Kelin hissed at her. "We rescued everyone. This gonda is our due. You owe this to us."

"He's right," Suri said, in support. "We don't have much time left. We need to get back. We need this gonda."

Nico turned to Zephyr, seeking his opinion on the matter. He looked conflicted, unsure what to do but gave a nod, a promise to back her play.

Kai placed a supportive hand on her shoulder. Nico turned to him for some sort of answer, but Kai looked at her like everyone else, waiting on her decision.

Growing up, people had always looked to Nico to tell them what to do, so Nico had developed the habit of giving out orders before they asked. Leadership was never anything Nico considered herself good at, but time and time again, especially in tough situations, everyone looked to her to make the tough decisions.

Nico took a breath and closed her eyes to center herself. She blocked out the rising voices. Rasia taunted Timar. Someone threw a rock, hitting Azan. Kelin surged forward, and Zephyr caught him by the shoulder.

Nico searched for the right . . . *rightest* thing. She considered their options. There had to be some sort of compromise, some sort of path between the two sides. Then Nico realized.

How could she forget? Nico couldn't believe how much desperation had clouded their logic. But Nico was clear of purpose now.

Nico faced Timar, decision made.

"We didn't rescue your people to leave them to starve," Nico said. "This gonda is yours."

"*What?!*"

Kelin moved in a flash. His dagger paused at Nico's neck, one motion away from ending her life.

Suri loosed an arrow, but Nico splashed it out of the sky. Kai tensed beside her, and Nico placed a hand on his chest to let him know she had this. Azan and Zephyr stilled, fearful any sudden movement might trigger Kelin's hand. Timar smiled, amused by the show.

Kelin clenched his teeth with anger shaking so strong he struggled to put words to it. Nico locked gazes with him, demanding all Kelin's attention, locking assassin to heir, tent kid to kuller, brown eyes to brown. Nico didn't say anything. She didn't have to.

"Fuck," Kelin cursed. He threw down his blades.

Azan rushed forward to drag Kelin away from doing something

more stupid.

"As I was *saying*," Nico said, looking at every member of her kull. "This gonda belongs to the scavengers. We did not save these people to abandon them to hunger. *But*, I still intend to keep my promise to you. This isn't the only gonda lured to the Graveyard this day. According to my senses, thirteen gonda have all met their end in various places of the Graveyard. Many of the scavengers have fled, which means it's a free-for-all as long as we get to them first."

Just like that, the tension popped.

Azan scratched the back of his neck in embarrassment. Kelin bowed his head, kicking at the ground. Suri lowered her bow. Relief billowed through both sides.

Rasia rolled her eyes. "Well, that was a whole lot of needless drama."

Then Timar had to add, ratcheting the tension right back up, "All thirteen of those gonda are ours *and* your head."

Nico raised a brow, hardly intimidated. "From what I understand, you like to make deals. Thirteen gonda are out there for the taking in a currently empty Graveyard. We can go collect the gonda and split the haul or continue to argue for the other scavengers to get there first. If my kull takes seven, and yours take seven, including this one here, that is no doubt far more food than the Grankull could have ever promised you."

Seven gonda should be enough to keep this small group of scavengers fed for a while, and more than enough to bring back for the Forging. The rules of the Forging explicitly required a hunt for every five participants. With the addition of the rescued oasis kids, the seven gonda should be enough for everyone.

"The Grankull promised us something far more important than food."

Nico blinked, surprised by this. She couldn't think of anything more important than food, other than water, but that was one resource the Graveyard didn't lack. "What could the Grankull have possibly promised you?"

"*Seeds*."

At that revelation, Nico saw the Graveyard with new eyes. The Graveyard had a hundred ancient dragons to the Grankull's one. Albeit asleep, these dragons imbued the ground with richness and fertility. What could this place become with the careful farming techniques and horticulture of the Grankull? It could be the solution to everyone's problems. Enough food for everyone.

"That is not something I can currently promise you," Nico said. "But when I become Ohan, I swear to you, I will give you more than seeds. I will grow you a garden."

The scavengers whispered. Timar scoffed. "An Ohan allied with scavengers?"

"I make this deal on one condition: no more no-faces."

Timar laughed at that, then looked at Nico cruelly and challenged, "Sure. When the Grankull stops giving them to us."

Fair.

"Can you at least tell me who in the Grankull bought the hit?"

"Done by proxy, nor did I ever care to ask."

Nico feared that might be the case.

"We will speak more regarding the particulars of an alliance at a later time," Nico said, "but for right now, gonda are out there waiting for us to retrieve them. In exchange for the help of your ships and people, I will identify where your gonda are located. Do we have a deal?"

Timar's lips quirked in an amused smirk.

"You have a deal, Ohan. Stay wary the Hunter."

CHAPTER FIFTY-NINE

⊢

Kai's shoulders slackened with relief. Once the deal was struck, the scavengers swept forward to begin butchering the gonda. Timar turned her attention to Kai once the initial tensions had calmed. She looked him up at down, and said, "You stole my clothes."

"You stole mine first."

"You stole my sword."

"The sword was never yours."

"You forgot something." Timar removed her bone mask, streaked in red dye, and handed it to him. "You defeated me. It's yours."

Beside Kai, Rasia's brows rose. "Is that how that works? Where is that fucker I killed?"

Rasia stormed off to search the dead bodies. Kai uncertainly accepted the mask, and Timar tapped her fingers atop the bone.

"Every scavenger in the Graveyard recognizes a Han mask. There will always be a place here for you, hani," Timar said, and then she left.

Kai traced his fingers over the whorls of the wooden mask. Rasia returned with a mask of her own, but hers was streaked in green.

"I wonder how we're going to sneak this into the Grankull

without it being confiscated? I can't necessarily get this easy up my vagina."

"Rasia," Kai said, amused, tired, breathless. He dropped his head down on her shoulder. They sort of just stood there. Everything and everyone rushed around them, unable to penetrate their bubble of peace in the chaos.

"Hey, Kai, you remember when you asked to court me?"

How could Kai forget one of the most embarrassing moments of his life? Right after a near-death experience probably wasn't the best time to spill his emotions all over a flame.

"Yeah . . ." Rasia drawled out. "Let's skip all that. Let's be together. Let's do the relationship thing."

Kai jerked back. "You changed your mind? What happened to wanting to experience different people?"

Rasia scratched her scalp, at the thin wisps of hair growing in. "The hardest thing I've learned traveling the Desert is that sometimes you can't take all roads, no matter how much you might wish to. Some will be gone by next season. Others lost and covered by sand, or time. Often, you can't come back and choose the other path. You've got to pick the one you think is right for you in the moment. Maybe it'll be a dead end, but maybe that's the one that goes on forever. Whichever the case, if you're too busy thinking about all the roads not taken, you can't enjoy the one you're on. So. I choose you. Let's see where we go."

"Oh," Kai said, covering his face. He laughed to keep himself from crying. His bruised throat ached either way. "I kind of sort of wanted to do the courting thing."

"You want to invite me to dinner with the parents and waste money on courting gifts?" Rasia snorted. "No, you don't. It took three years for Kiba-ta to commit to Shamai-ta. I'm not that cruel."

"I should at least have a namesake for you."

"We're not of age. What's the point if we can't wear them? We'll figure something out." Rasia pulled down Kai's shirt collar and inspected his throat. "Let's get you bandaged up."

"In a bit," Kai said, before pulling her forward by the hips and kissing her—his partner. No more friends with benefits. No more uncertainties and fears this ride could be over once the Forging ended. They were together.

Sometimes, Kai did achieve the impossible. He thinks he's getting the hang of it.

Nico ordered Zephyr and Azan to return to the Forging kids and draft their help with the gonda hunt. She ordered Suri to gather needed supplies from the scavengers. She turned to Kelin last, knowing he wanted to talk. Kelin approached her, head bowed.

"I should have trusted you," Kelin said, "but trust generally comes hard for me. The Flock is home, and I've been raised to see everyone outside of it as an enemy. Since the first day we've met, you've always been true and fair. I respect that. I'm sorry."

"You're forgiven. I understand; it was a tough situation. Everyone had their hackles up." Then Nico smiled, teasing. "You're a bad assassin though."

Kelin spluttered. "I would have you know I am a great assassin. Many of us generally have codes against assassinating our   friends . . ." Nico smiled at that, and Kelin said after a dramatic pause, ". . . depending on the price."

Nico rolled her eyes and nudged him. "Why don't you make use of all that espionage and see if you can find me some dirt on Timar?"

Information was always useful. Certainly, some of these scavengers joined Timar because they had to, not because they liked her. No doubt someone would be willing to talk.

Kelin raised his brows, intrigued. "I'll see what I can do."

That taken care of, Nico looked around for Kai and Rasia and found them missing. There was enough water in the Graveyard to easily locate Kai's whereabouts. The plants pointed the way.

Nico swept aside the linen curtain, which shaded the entrance of a conical dwelling to find Rasia naked and moaning in Kai's lap.

"*ARE YOU TWO HAVING SEX?!!!!!!*"

Shocked, Kai tossed Rasia off his lap, and Rasia landed on her back roaring in raucous laughter.

"*Nico*," Kai whined, scrambling for his discarded shirt to cover his lap. "*Get out, I wasn't . . . We weren't . . . I was using my fingers . . .*"

Rasia laughed harder, near tears.

Nico narrowed her eyes at him, then turned and stormed back outside. She crossed her arms, embarrassed, and stood waiting for them to make themselves presentable. She had been so focused on her way over here that Nico hadn't noticed how easily sound traveled from the cone. She very clearly heard Kai apologizing and his promises to make it up to Rasia later.

Rasia demanded the moment they exited the building, "*What do you want?*"

Nico gathered her composure. "We are going to leave soon to find those gonda. We could use your windship, and I'm hoping you could lead a team."

"Sounds fun and all, but no. I've got more important things to do."

"More important things . . ." Nico echoed the words, uncomprehending. "What do you mean you've got more important things to do? What could possibly be more important than—"

"I'll go," Kai volunteered. "If you need Rasia's windship, I'll steer."

"Sounds good to me. Good luck hunting!" Rasia called out, and then scrambled off to her "more important things."

"But-but-" Nico stammered after Rasia's retreating figure. Nico turned back to Kai. She glanced at his bandaged shoulder and the bruising around his throat. A few other wounds had been stitched and bandaged up. "You should stay. Your shoulder looks pretty serious."

"I can use my other arm, and besides, I thought you needed Rasia's windship. She's not going to let anyone else steer it."

Nico rubbed her temples. He had a point, and Rasia didn't leave Nico any other options.

"Fine," Nico bit out.

"Fine," Kai said in turn. Now that all the danger had passed, all the awkwardness and regrets came rushing back in to fill the holes between them. Kai turned his head, shoulders raised. "You *can* trust me."

"Can I?"

"I'm never going to put Rasia, and you, in that position ever again. I promise you that."

Nico clicked her tongue.

"Nico!" Someone shouted for her. Zephyr and Azan had returned with Neema and the other oasis kids. She glanced back at Kai, pulled in two directions.

"We're not done," Nico promised him.

"Is this going to work?" Suri asked, rowing the oars beside Nico. They rowed oars into the divots in the road, wheeling the windship through the Graveyard. "All these gonda died due to the actions of our kull. Technically, these kids didn't kill their own gonda. It violates the rules of the Forging."

Nico felt again the life of Rianis seeping out of her hands. Apparently, a whole ship had gone down on the Yestermorrow Lake after a mutiny. So many hadn't survived the trek to the Graveyard. And for what? The Council's secret agenda? No. Nico refused to let these kids pay for the Council's crimes.

"We lie," Nico said, steely. "Some of these kids don't have the strength to stand, much less the time to recover and hunt their own gonda before Forging's end."

Suri agreed. "It's not fair what these kids have been through. They never had a chance. Maybe when we get back, I can talk to my tah. Find out if she suspects anyone on the Council."

"What if it is your tah?"

Suri frowned, taken aback by the inquiry. "Tah paid for me to be on your Forging kull. How could it have been her?"

"If it was her, who would you choose?"

"*You*," Suri bit out. "How could you ask me that?"

"I don't know where we stand anymore, Suri." Before the Forging, Nico never would have thought Suri capable of betraying her and throwing a whole bunch of innocent kids under the hull, but Nico didn't know anything anymore.

"We might not agree about the Tents, and you might not consider me your friend anymore, but when the ground vibrates, I've got your back. *I'm* not the one who's put a dagger to your throat."

"No, just an arrow to my face."

Suri glanced at her. "I'm sorry about that."

From the tiller, Kai shouted to pull up on the oars. Their target was dawnward of the main road, into a thicket the ship could not follow.

Nico hacked into the thorny thicket with her spear to cut a path for them. Suri took up the rear, while Kai and one of the oasis kids, Gysen, walked between them. Nico glanced back at Kai. Ava-ta's sword tapped against his thigh in the sheath Timar had freely handed over as they stomped through.

"How is your shoulder?" Nico asked.

"It's fine, although I might not be able to help much with the heavy lifting once we get to the gonda. But I figure your magic will take care of most of it."

Speaking of . . .

"*Your* magic," Nico said slowly. "Do you have control of it? I remember, after our argument, for a brief moment I thought . . . and then you caught Rasia."

Kai went silent behind her, and Nico tried her best to nonchalantly keep moving. She felt his shrug even though she didn't see it. "It's more instinctive or emotional. I still don't have much control over it."

"Oh," Nico said, shoulders dropping, sort of hoping. It would have been nice to know at least Kai had his magic to protect him, but how useful was it if it wasn't reliable?

Nico glanced back at Kai and scanned her eyes over all his cuts and bruises, and for a brief flash, all Nico could see was that sickly jih whose hand she held during coughing fits. "I should have protected you better."

"This isn't your fault, Nico," Kai said. "The blame lies with the person who ordered the hit."

"You're right," Nico said, hacking away at the undergrowth. "I've been thinking about that too. After all, if they're willing to use scavengers to put a hit out on me, what's to keep them from targeting you or Rae? Once we find these gonda and return home, we will need to be extremely careful—"

"*Nico.*"

"We'll need to make sure Rae is in our sights at all times. We'll set up some sort of schedule. I'll make the time and we'll—"

"*Nico!*"

Nico stopped. Kai gave her a strange, unreadable expression. "I'm not coming back with you."

"What do you mean? There will be enough gonda for everyone."

"Rasia and I are still hunting our dragon."

That made no sense. "Kai, neither you nor Rasia are in the best of health. She can barely walk right now."

"Why do you think Rasia stayed behind? Rasia's 'more important things' is definitely about the dragon. During the fight, Rasia injured its throat. The dragon can't breathe fire anymore. Now is the time if any to take Aurum down."

"But Kai, you barely have enough time to make it back to the Grankull. It'll take twelve days to get back home, maybe better depending on the wind, but you essentially have *three* days to slay a dragon. What if you fail?"

"Then I fail and face the consequences."

Nico audibly sucked in air between her teeth. "Why don't you and Rasia return to the Grankull and report the dragon's injuries? Let the hunting kulls handle this. They are trained to fight dragons. They don't face the same risks that you do."

"We'll go on ahead," Suri said suddenly. Suri and Gysen walked between them and continued the work of hacking themselves a path. Nico grew embarrassed she had stalled things, but another part of her wanted to continue to argue. She didn't see why Kai had to be the one to risk himself by doing this.

If Kai was so determined, maybe Nico could send the gonda on with the others. "I could go with you."

"You're the *Ohan*. You need to go home. You need to protect Rae."

"But who'll protect you?"

"Nico! I know you think you've had to take up tah's mantle ever since she died, and I know you haven't always been able to protect me, and you think you're the only person I have in my corner, but I've got Rasia, and we do a good job of protecting each other."

"Didn't seem like all a good job to me when you seeded her," Nico bit out, then forcefully rubbed at her eyes. "I know Rasia cares for you. I see that. But what do you think is going to happen when we return home? Forging flames never last."

"Rasia and I are together. She's accepted my court. We're partners now."

Nico could have rolled her eyes out of her face. "You don't just accept the court of the first person who propositions you. You haven't even finished your Forging. Don't you think you two are moving recklessly fast?"

"I don't care what you think," Kai snapped. "You criticize her commitment to me when you were just complaining about her fickleness. No matter what Rasia does, you are always going to find something wrong with her."

"Ugh. How could you have let her come between us and tear our family apart!?"

"You can't tear apart what's already broken! We've been messed up since the day I was born. We've never been a real family. And I know that Ava-ta . . . that tah was my fault and maybe I don't deserve this and I'm being selfish and—"

"Stop. Her death was not your fault."

Kai didn't believe her. He never believed those words. No matter how many times Nico had said them, she couldn't get them to penetrate his thick, stubborn skull. Not once had he allowed himself to grieve their tah's death.

Kai's fists clenched, and he stared down at the sharp thorns hacked around them. "Tah never let go of me. She never let me leave her side, so afraid I would keel over and die at any moment. She never let me fall or run or play. She pulled me out of school because she feared the bullies would kill me."

"Those bullies broke your face, Kai."

"She never let me *grow*, Nico. She tried so hard to protect me from the world, that I could barely function once she was out of it. I don't want to be protected. I want to fall. I want to make mistakes. I want to know what I'm capable of. I want to *live*. On *my* terms. Tah hoped the bare minimum for me because she thought anything more was unattainable. I am more than the bare minimum, Nico, and yes, you're right in the fact that it's impossible for me to walk this world the same as everyone else. I will never be able to define a good life by everyone else's standards. I have to define it for myself. I have to live for myself, and I am done allowing tah or you to decide that for me!"

Kai shuddered, out of breath by the end of his spiel. Nico shook her head and croaked. "Why didn't you ever say these things before?"

Kai crossed his arms, tight, away from the prickly brambles. "I knew it would hurt you."

They turned away from each other, but these pained, uneven silences had always been half of their relationship. The two siblings stood in the middle of the scavenger Graveyard, surrounded by bones and thorns on all sides.

Nico sucked in a big, whole, mature breath. She'd say what she practiced, over and over and over again.

"Thank you," Nico said, "for helping me understand. If this is your choice, if this is what you want to do, I support you. I am not going to stop you. But for the record, I think you're being

451

stupid, brash, and reckless. I've always known you were capable of so much, and you don't need sex or a dragon to prove that. You have always been the strongest of us. But if that's what you need to believe in yourself, go chase your dragons. Rae and I will be waiting for when you get home." Nico sucked in another big, whole, mature breath. "*And* I—support—your—relationship—with—Rasia."

Nico felt like gagging a little at the end there. He was too young. After the Naming Ceremony, new faces were expected to spend years exploring bodies and preferences and pleasure. They spent years chasing flames and seeking courts. Even when they did find someone they wanted to commit to, it was a testing period, a time to be sure you'd chosen the right one. At this speed, Kai would be calling Rasia his kulani by tomorrow.

"Do you remember when Rasia snatched off my shroud in the middle of the market?"

"How could I forget? She violated you. I don't understand how you could forgive her for that. No one should ever have their shroud taken without their consent."

"You're right, Nico, but it happened to *me*, and I've forgiven her for it," Kai said. "I've forgiven her for it a long time ago. Back then when Rasia snatched off my shroud, she was looking for a monster. I've never forgotten the disappointment on her face to discover that I wasn't. Rasia has always *seen* me. Better than you, better than myself at times. She has always been the one. She *is* the one. She's my—"

Nico threw out her hands, alarmed. "*Don't say it.* You don't know. You. Don't. Know."

It wasn't a word you said to just anyone. You had to be certain. Because there was only the one. There would only ever be the one.

Kulani was the only name you ever get to choose.

Kai pressed his lips together, jaw tight. Knowing him, he probably never meant to say it out loud.

"And I'm sorry," Nico said. "I'm sorry for hitting you. And I'm sorry for the things I said. It wasn't fair of me. 'Never' was too harsh a word. I do believe you and Rasia can slay a dragon, that it's possible, but it'll be very hard and very difficult, even more so under these circumstances. The kull tryouts won't come easy. And tah hasn't been listening to anyone for two years and I don't know . . . I don't know. These things are going to be hard, Kai, and I wanted to make sure you understood that, and that despite the challenges, I'll be here to support you every step of the way. I promise, no matter what it is."

"Thank you, jih." Kai drummed his fingers against his thigh. For a moment, he looked like he was going to say something more but thought better of it. Nico wanted to fight for the words he kept to himself, but he's said so much already, and Nico didn't want to ruin this tentative understanding forming between them. Nico promised to be there when he was ready.

Nico said, "I just wished, for once, something came easy for you."

Kai raised his head and smiled. He said honestly, "Rasia came easy."

Nico's brows rose. "Oh yeah? Zephyr missed most of the gorge, so why don't you catch me up on how you fell for 'I don't need anyone' Rasia."

Nico lifted her arm, and Kai moved so Nico could wrap an arm about his good shoulder. He'd grown taller.

"Sure," Kai said. "After you catch me up on whatever is going on between you and Suri?"

Nico rolled her eyes. Of course, he'd notice that.

The siblings walked side by side, together, hacking their way through the brush.

CHAPTER SIXTY

1

Nico and her team towed two gonda behind their windship, approaching the rendezvous. They curved the outside edge of the Graveyard, rounding the bend to Zephyr and his team barreling toward them in the distance, also with two more gonda. Faris and his team, already at the meeting spot, had successfully retrieved one.

Five gonda. More than enough.

They all met the construction team in the middle.

Nico jumped decks and hurled out orders. They had a lot of work to get done. They needed to complete the final repairs on the additional Grankull ship Nico bartered from the scavengers, redistribute their cargo, determine what supplies they needed, and unhitch the gonda from Rasia's windship.

"Nico!" Someone shouted.

An immense shadow devoured the ship decks. Nico turned, and from out the widest road, the Graveyard birthed a massive warship. Nico's stomach dropped at the sight of it and hoped Timar wasn't reneging on their deal.

Nico grabbed the spyglass from her belt and peered through the citrine tint. The warship had gained several intimidating additions since Nico had seen it earlier in the shipyard. Someone had lined the railing with shields of bone plate, outfitted the ram with reinforced talons, and replaced the bowsprit with sharp barbed bone.

On the topmost mast of the warship, Timar's crimson standard had been cut down. Now, it waved a dirty grey, bloodstained linen.

"Kai, is that your *shroud*?" Nico asked.

"Seems like it." Kai shrugged.

Kai was right. Rasia was going after the dragon.

"Wait. Is she going to *stop*?"

The scavengers atop the warship strained at the oars. The wheels creaked. Nico covered her face at the dense spray of sand, and the windship lifted slightly on the rolling hill. The bowsprit stopped overhead and had come uncomfortably close to toppling them all over.

Up high, atop the bow, Rasia leaned over one knee with that infuriating smug smirk. Beside Nico, Kai smiled, enamored.

"Kai!" Rasia shouted down. "Wanna ride my warship?!"

Kai cupped his mouth and shouted up, "I'll ride your warship any day!"

Rasia tossed back her head and cackled with glee.

Rasia rocked against the warship's railing, waiting for Nico and Kai to make the climb up.

"Only five gonda?" Rasia asked the moment Nico reached to the warship deck. "That's it? I thought you said there were more than that?"

Nico bristled at Rasia's judgmental tone. Nico would have liked to have retrieved more gonda, but the sun had begun to set by the time they finished chopping up the second for transport. Nico heeded Timar's warning and did not want to get caught in the Graveyard at night.

Before Nico could argue the point, Kai placed a hand on Nico's shoulder and stepped forward. At once, Rasia brightened, and her attention fully swiveled in his direction.

"Kai, look at this," Rasia said, grabbing Kai's arm. She dragged him around the deck. "The warship has hooks to attach the windship, so we can bring the windship without worrying about steering them both. I stopped the warship close enough so the scavengers can throw down the chains to crank up the ship. They're going to show us how it works."

"My jihs would be so jealous."

Nico whipped around to find that Azan had climbed the stairs behind her. "What are you doing? You're supposed to be preparing for our departure."

"It's a warship," Azan said, with eyes lit up like a kid trailing their parents at the belly market. "When's the next chance we get to look around a scavenger warship?"

Following Azan came other curious Forging kids. Zephyr boarded last, with a shrug. "I couldn't stop them, so I called for a break."

Nico sighed and admitted, partially, that she was curious to get a closer look, too. The Grankull warships were unquestionably better constructed, but this one was so . . . big. Unreasonably so, in Nico's opinion.

Nico crossed the deck and joined Timar where she supervised the remaining scavengers throwing down the chains. Most of the scavengers had disembarked to return to the Graveyard on foot, going down while Nico and Kai climbed up.

"Good hunt, I presume?" Nico asked Timar.

"My group found four gonda. A fair good hunt, I'd say." Timar smiled cockily underneath a new bone mask. This one was even bigger and grander than the one before.

"I admit," Nico said. "I'm surprised you've given Rasia your warship."

"Your garden will take seasons to grow but killing that dragon will benefit us now. Rasia has proved she has a real shot at slaying the thing. Besides . . ." Timar said, shit-eating. "I have *three* warships now. Sacrificing one is a small price to pay to be rid of that beast."

Nico continually got the impression that she'd made Timar the strongest Han of the entire Graveyard. She hoped she didn't regret this decision.

With a sigh, Nico looked around the double-leveled deck, large enough to need three masts and three times as many sails. Nico asked, "*Can* two people steer a warship?"

"Rasia sure seems to think so. The sailing is the easy part. It'll pretty much plough over anything in its way. It's the starting and the stopping that need the bodies."

Nico was a little concerned.

Rasia had a warship, but would that be enough?

"I'm going with them," Zephyr said, once the ships were ready to set sail. Nico was woefully unsurprised. He'd been brooding since they returned from the warship.

"I figured." Behind Nico, the kids made final adjustments to the lines, and most were getting in their kull positions, bound for home. "You always are where you're needed most."

"Back home, I'm helpless," Zephyr admitted. "But Rasia and Kai need the hands and facing this dragon is something I can do."

Nico turned to face Zephyr fully. He carried his sword strapped to his back, his shroud about his neck, and his cloak and bags slung over his shoulder. He didn't look much different than the day he left with his father.

Yet another adventure without her, while again, Nico's responsibilities pulled her in a different direction. Secretly, Nico would rather face down a dragon than deal with the Council, the assassination attempts, and the bloodrites waiting for her back home. But . . . someone had to do it.

"I'll take care of your family," Nico promised. "I won't let anything happen to them."

"I know. I'll take care of yours."

Within Zephyr's verdant eyes, Nico saw all the emotions he held back, amplifying her own. He shifted forward. His lips soft, pliable like clay. Nico unconsciously tilted her head up and found herself both relieved and regretful when he pressed his forehead to hers.

"Come," Nico said, pulling away. "You need to catch Kai and Rasia before they leave. Looks like they're almost done."

Nico signaled to the others, then she and Zephyr climbed down the windship and traveled across the sands.

"Gentle!" Rasia shouted up, both hands planted on her hips as she watched from the bottom. Scavengers wound the last crank, then latched her windship firmly to the warship's side.

Kai, standing beside Rasia, turned to Nico as she approached. He opened his mouth to speak, but his attention shifted to Zephyr.

"You're coming with us?" Kai asked.

Rasia turned at that and raised a brow. She leaned an elbow on Kai's good shoulder.

Zephyr stopped before the two of them, but it was Kai whom he addressed. "I've made mistakes, but if you'd have me, I'd like to finish what we started."

"We've all made mistakes," Kai acknowledged. "There's always room in this kull for you."

"I guess." Rasia rolled her eyes. Zephyr snorted and moved toward the warship's steps.

Kai elbowed Rasia, and they exchanged a series of looks before Rasia rolled her body along with her eyes and spun on the heel of her foot.

She said, "*Zephyr.*"

Zephyr stopped on the second ladder rung. Rasia clasped her arms behind her back and said, "You're good bones. There's no one I'd rather have at my back when facing down a dragon than you."

Zephyr smiled. "Same."

Kai smirked, amused, after Zephyr had climbed up. "What

about me at your back?"

Rasia patted him on the shoulder consolingly. "That's nice."

"Wait! I'm coming! I'm joining too!"

All at once, everyone turned as Azan rushed toward them with all his bags ready to go. Kelin, Suri, and Neema followed after him. Azan flashed Rasia a grin before running straight past her to the giant warship. Rasia's head whipped at the speed.

"I'm coming too," Neema said, stepping forward with fists clenched so tightly they were shaking. She raised her chin. "I didn't come out here for a gonda to be handed to me. I came to earn it."

Rasia threw up her hands.

"You do understand there is a good chance we won't make it back in time to finish our Forging, right?" Rasia asked. "We've got two days to make it to the Dragon's Coast, a day to kill the thing, then twelve days to make it back home at full speed. There's no room for mistakes or for you not to pull your weight. And even giving it our all, it still might not be enough. At this point, we're throwing our bones."

"Then I choose to throw my bones on you," Neema countered.

"I'm not Nico," Rasia said. "If you freeze up like last time, I'm not saving your ass."

"Respectfully, Han, if I freeze up again my ass isn't worth saving."

"Fine." Rasia nodded.

Neema marched toward the warship, and Rasia turned to Kai, perplexed. "How come when I actually asked people if they wanted to join, they all said no?"

"We could use the hands," Kai said.

Rasia eyed Kelin and Suri. "Anyone else?"

Kelin returned Azan's wave, high on the deck of the warship, and said, "Nope, I'm good. I've had enough of this story."

"Same," Suri said, then turned to Nico to report. "We're ready. It's time to go."

Nico looked at the fleet of Grankull windships ready to launch, then she turned back to Kai. She ran forward and wrapped him up in one last hug. Kai squeezed her in turn, as if they were on the doorstep of their house and Nico were due to step out into the waspish morning air for school or for her apprenticeship. She'd left him on the veranda every morning, face covered in a shroud, and Rae in his arms. And never once did he ever ask for anything more until now.

For so long, she's the only one to have known him without a shroud, the only one to recognize Ava-ta in his eyes and Kenji-ta in his bones. Losing him felt like losing the both of them all over again. But she won't think about those fears. She had to let him go.

Rasia audibly groaned, pacing and huffing all throughout the embrace. It was hard to have an emotional moment with *someone* yowling like a jackal in the background. The hug might have lasted dramatically longer than Nico had first intended it to.

"All right, all right," Rasia said, finally breaking. "We don't have vibrations to waste. It's time to *go*."

Nico released Kai and wasn't able to wipe the gratification off her face fast enough. Kai shook his head. "I don't know what I'm going to do with the two of you."

Honestly, Nico didn't either. But that was a concern for another day. She hoped they returned in one piece for it to be a concern.

Kai lifted the dragonsteel sword at his belt. "I should give this back."

"No. It'll serve you better against the dragon, and I'm sure you'll take better care of it than me. Don't forget to take care of yourself. Eat, and drink water, and-" Nico knocked him hard on the forehead, "-keep it in your pants. *Fifteen days*, Kai. Surely, you can manage that."

Kai palmed his forehead with a pout, rubbing at the light tap, to hide his embarrassment. "I'll be careful, I promise."

"I'll hold you to that."

"*I know.*"

"Come on!" Rasia dragged her hands down her face.

"I should go before Rasia gets out the swords." Before Nico could catch another wind, Kai pressed his forehead to hers, and promised, "I'll be back."

Then he left, in the opposite direction. He walked away from her, on a path Nico couldn't follow, off on an adventure of his own.

This time, Nico would be the one waiting for him.

Rasia caught Kai's hand, swinging, as they walked toward the warship. Rasia cheekily grinned at him, with eyes lit aflame. "Guess what? Now we've got us a whole kull."

"And a warship, Han."

"And the greatest windeka this side of the bones."

They smiled at each other. Rasia orbited him, and Kai shone at her center. Whatever the ending, Nico knew she'd made the right choice. You couldn't protect them, but you could choose to protect their joy.

"Rasia," Nico called out. "It would be unfortunate if you didn't make it back on time and I earn more names than you."

"Ha!" Rasia spun, striding backward with a swagger, treading the world beneath her feet. "Watch for us on the horizon!"

Rasia's Map (revised)

TO BE CONTINUED

DRAGON YOUR BONES

Book II

A FORGING OF AGE

Duology

JOIN MY MAILING LIST FOR NEWS AND UPDATES.

www.tatianaobey.com

FOLLOW

@obeytheauthor

AUTHOR'S NOTE

I hope you have enjoyed the adventures of Rasia, Nico, and Kai. If so, please consider leaving a review on Amazon, Goodreads, your preferred review site, or on social media. Online reviews are critical to an indie book's success. In addition, please share with others. Tell everyone about it. Go purchase the book in a different format. I truly appreciate any and all support. This self-publishing thing is hard, ya'll.

ADDITIONAL NOTE

This book is meant to be read without a glossary. I have had the great fortune to live in countries other than my own, and I write to reflect those experiences. When you are a guest in someone else's world, it is your responsibility to engage. Most often, you aren't afforded all of the information. But every day is an opportunity to learn something new. Every day deepens your understanding. Life isn't an infodump. It's a journey.

ACKNOWLEDGEMENTS

Self-publishing is expensive. I pay for every word, and some persons are worth the recognition. I love you all: my way too many siblings, my mother, my stepparents, my grandparents, my friends, and my extended family: both lost and found. To Daddy, who passed last year to Covid, I hope the Cowboys win in heaven. Chill in peace.

I also want to give a special shout-out to my beta readers: Alegra Gaines, Agueda "Agatha" Lopez, Laura Montalvo, and Nohemi Romero. Thank you to the editors who wrangled my terrible grammar, Sydnee Thompson and Kristy Elam. Finally, thank you to Asur Misoa for that awesome cover illustration. I've had Rasia in my head for 15 years (terrifying, I know) and you have done her justice.

Thank you all so very much. I wouldn't be here without you.